Ginger's Heart

a modern fairytale

Katy Regnery

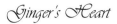

GINGER'S HEART

Cover by Marianne Nowicki
Developmental Editing by Tessa Shapcott
Copy and Line Editing by First Person Editing
Formatting by CookieLynn Publishing Services

Please visit my website at www.katyregnery.com
First Edition: March 2016
Katy Regnery
Ginger's Heart : a novel / by Katy Regnery – 1st ed.
ISBN: 978-1-944810-01-6

Ginger's Heart

a modern fairytale

Once upon a time there were two cousins:

one golden like the sun,

one dark like midnight,

one a protector,

one a predator,

one a Woodsman

and

one a Wolf...

both owning equal,

but different,

parts of a little girl's heart.

For George, Henry & Callie,
who share *my* heart.

Dear Everyone Else,

Please don't read the last page first.

Love,
Every Author Breathing
(#andnotbreathing)
xo

PART ONE

Chapter 1

~ Ginger ~

"Ginger, jump to me!" yelled fifteen-year-old Josiah Woodman, shoving a hand through his dirty-blond mop of hair. Gold as wheat in the late-afternoon sunlight, it was a perfect match to the pieces of straw that fell from the hayloft opening where she stood staring down at them.

Beside him, Cain Wolfram elbowed his cousin in the side as he grinned up at her. "Now, Miss Virginia, you ignore ole Woodman here and you jump to me, baby."

Bae-bee. The confident new twang in his voice made her twelve-year-old heart clutch and clamor. His black hair was almost blue, backlit by the sun, and his smile was as devilish as ever.

They were cousins, born to identical twin sisters not a week apart, and on account of their last names both starting with W, the whole town of Apple Valley, Kentucky, called them Double Dub or the Dub Twins. Well, the whole town except for Ginger. Because if anyone else knew Woodman and Cain as well as she did, they'd know that the cousins were nothing alike.

"Be smart, Gin," said Woodman, his voice low and earnest, his moss-green eyes beseeching her as he beckoned her to come with a twitch of his callused fingers.

"You think your scrawny arms gonna catch her?" asked Cain, snorting.

He shucked off his jean jacket and threw it on a pile of hay outside the barn door, revealing a Harley-Davidson T-shirt with the sleeves ripped off. His upper arms were well defined, thicker muscles as new as his twang, and Ginger eyed them greedily. He'd worked in her father's barn for as long as she could remember, but just this past fall she'd noticed what every other girl in Apple Valley had noticed too: Cain Wolfram was filling out.

His blue eyes sparkled. "Jump to me, sweet thing."

Only it sounded like "sweet thang," and she gasped lightly, drawing her bottom lip between her teeth. Her legs felt a little like jelly as his eyebrows jerked up a fraction of an inch flirtatiously.

"Gin," said Woodman, his familiar voice grounded and certain. Her eyes slid from Cain's dark beauty to Woodman's golden-boy handsomeness. "Come on, now."

Cain looked askance at Woodman, his dimples caving his cheeks in a smirk that Woodman didn't see. He was too focused on Ginger, never taking his eyes off her, not allowing anything to distract him from her.

But from two stories higher, Ginger could see them both perfectly, and when Cain fixed his eyes back on her, her belly swarmed with butterflies. He licked his lips and winked.

"Jump to the one you love the most, darlin'."

Cain, Cain, Cain.

He had *always* played dirty.

"Dang it, Cain!" she cried, stomping her foot on the wooden plank and frowning at him. "Now you went'n wrecked it!"

"What'd I do?" he asked, his arms open, his eyes wide, the very picture of surprised contrition.

"You know I can't choose between y'all. Not like that. That's not how it works!"

"Nice goin', jackass," said Woodman under his breath, exhaling a satisfied breath and chuckling at Ginger's sour puss.

They were supposed to catch her *together*. It was her annual birthday tradition, for heaven's sake!

When she was only six, she went missing when it was time to cut the cake, and her mother sent the cousins to look for her. They found her sitting in the hayloft door, two stories high, insisting that she was a princess trapped in a tower. Cain encouraged the birthday princess to jump into their arms so they could take her back to the party. That stunt led to the first of Ginger's many broken body parts wrought from Cain's brash suggestions, and gave her parents a convenient excuse to bar Cain from future parties unless he was giving pony rides.

Her mother also forbade Ginger to ever go into the hayloft again.

Of course she *did*.

Every year. And every year since her seventh birthday, the cousins had somehow managed to actually catch her, safe and sound.

Crossing her arms over her chest, she shook her head disapprovingly at Cain, then turned around and marched through the dusty, dimly lit hayloft, which smelled of old wood, hay, and horses. Turning at the ladder, she backed down the rungs quickly, jumping to the floor when she was a little more than three-quarters of the way down. Walking through the drive bay, her riding boots clicking on the concrete floor, she passed six stalls on each side before exiting out the side door where she found the handsome cousins waiting for her.

"Ain't jumpin' this year?" asked Cain, smirking at her, his roughened fists resting on lean, denim-covered hips.

"Ain't jumpin' to *you*," she said, turning up her nose.

"You're poutin', Gin," said Woodman, reaching for her folded arm to loosen it.

"And *y'all* are supposed to catch me together! Couldn't choose between the two of you if my life depended on it! That'd be like choosin' between my hands and my feet!"

Cain laughed, his eyes so blue she could barely force herself to look away.

"Well, darlin'," he drawled, "at least your momma won't come after us with a danged fryin' pan this year."

Ginger flicked her eyes to Woodman, whose shoulders trembled with laughter. Magnolia McHuid, dressed to the nines for her daughter's sixth birthday party, chasing after the Dub Twins with a frying pan was another of Ginger's favorite birthday memories. It had almost made the searing pain in her broken arm worthwhile.

Woodman's fingers slid down Ginger's arm to her hand, and he uncurled her fingers, clasping them in his.

"Shouldn't be jumpin' out of barn doors anymore anyway," he said gently. "You're twelve now. A young lady."

Ginger whipped her head to face him with a frown. Something about his words prickled and annoyed her, but she didn't linger on it. Cain made sure of that.

"A young lady!" he exclaimed, leaning down to grab his jean jacket and shrug it over his broad shoulders. "Whoo-ee!

What a joke! Woodman, you only see what you want to see, cuz!"

"She's *twelve*," muttered Woodman, straightening his back, his fingers tightening around Ginger's.

"'Zactly! *Twelve.* She's a kid." Cain chucked her under the chin. "And if you ain't jumpin', missy, I've got places to be."

Her heart lurched, and she tugged her hand from Woodman's to place it on Cain's arm. "But there's cake!"

"Got somethin' sweeter'n cake waitin' for me," said Cain, winking at her. "Not to mention, we all know I ain't invited to Miz Magnolia's festivities."

"We'll run up and git you some!" Distraught at the notion of Cain spending her birthday with another girl, she dug her fingers into his arm.

"No, thanks."

"You can't just *leave!*"

"Ouch! Am I missin' somethin' here?" asked Cain, jerking his arm away and rubbing over the spot she'd clawed. "Hell, yes, I'm leavin'. I got plans. But before I go, since you're such a *young lady* now, Miss Virginia, I guess I could give you a birthday kiss, huh?"

He took a step toward her, the steel toe of his work boot kicking up some dust between them. His blue eyes cut to hers, dancing and sparkling as he approached, looking down into her face. She gasped as she felt his palm land on her left cheek, his skin scratchy but warm. Her heart raced mercilessly, poundingpoundingpounding behind her budding breasts, making her breathless and dizzy. He leaned toward her, his face nearer and nearer, until she could smell him—the tang of his sweat, the spice of his deodorant, the scent of earth and horses and the BBQ ribs he must have had for lunch all mixed up together. Her eyes fluttered closed, and she held her breath, tilting her chin up so he could . . . so he could . . .

His lips—soft and warm—landed on her cheek, and the millions of butterflies already gathered in her chest spread their fluttering wings and beat them against her heart.

His voice, close to her ear, slow and thick as honey, whispered, "Happy birthday, lionhearted l'il gal."

When her eyes finally fluttered open, he was already swaggering away.

She watched him go—the confident forward motion of his long strides, his tight butt in faded Levi's, his too-long black hair curling over the collar of his beat-up jacket and glistening in the sun. He was going to someone "sweeter'n cake" and leaving her behind. And though Ginger couldn't possibly offer Cain what seventeen-year-old Mary-Louise "Big Tits" Walker could willingly provide in some nook or cranny down by the abandoned distillery, it sure did hurt her heart to watch him walk away.

"Oh," she murmured, the sound small and pathetic on the evening breeze.

Woodman's hand landed on her back.

"Don't fuss over him," he said, his tone annoyed as he watched his cousin go. "He's always been a jackass, Gin."

Ginger flashed her eyes up at her friend. "He isn't!"

Woodman pursed his lips and gave her a "quit bein' stupid" look, which made her cheeks flush. She dropped her gaze, kicking at the dirt under her boot.

"He's your cousin," she said softly.

"And don't I know it," muttered Woodman disdainfully.

She looked up to see Woodman brush a piece of hay off his blue gingham buttoned-down dress shirt. He'd dressed up for her party today—crisp khaki pants with an ironed crease down the middle and a fancy-pants new shirt. His hair was held in place with some kind of slick glop, making him look like a junior banker, which made a weird sort of sense since his daddy, Howard Woodman, was president of the Apple Valley Savings and Loan. She glanced forlornly down the lane at Cain. Josiah Woodman would never show up at a party in a torn-up T-shirt and beat-up jeans, even to catch a princess jumping from her tower. He knew better than that. But for some reason Woodman's Sunday clothes irritated Ginger now, like they felt somehow superior to Cain's simple duds, and she frowned at him, feeling unaccountably defensive.

"He's gonna catch somethin' nasty from Big Tits Walker," she said, hoping to shock him.

Woodman's eyes widened for just a moment before the edges of his mouth tilted up. He chuckled softly in surprise and nodded, tilting his head to the side as he stared at her. "I guess that's possible."

His smile quickly faded, and his gaze became uncomfortably searing, so Ginger looked away again, her eyes seeking one last glimpse of Cain. He was just a speck in the distance now, making his way down the long country road that followed the Glenn River and led to the distillery.

"You should go after him," she said, "and . . . and, I don't know, ask him to go for a joyride on Daddy's tractor or—"

"I'm *not* goin' after him," said Woodman gently. His voice was firm as he reached for her hand and pulled her away from the barn, back toward the party. "First off, wouldn't do any good. You know Cain as well as I do. He's goin' where he's goin', and nothin's goin' to get in his way but God or weather. Second? Pardon me, Gin, but I'm not cockblockin' my only cousin. He might be a jackass, but that don't mean I don't love him. And third? Your momma's fixin' to bring out the cake any minute, and there'll be hell to pay if you're not there to blow out twelve pretty candles."

Taking one final look down the road, she let loose a long sigh as she realized Cain was not coming back and Woodman was right. Her mother would have a fit if she missed the cake. But Ginger's heart ached to know that the same lips that had just brushed her cheek with such tenderness would be used for far less chaste activities for the rest of her birthday.

Her mother would say that she was too young to love Cain the way she did, with a full thumping heart and her preteen body going hot and cold whenever he came near. She knew this, and yet she couldn't seem to help herself. Her parents and Gran— and even Woodman—had fussed over her since her broken-heart episode when she was five, always telling her what she could and, more often, *couldn't* do. Cain was the only one who seemed to recognize that she was just as strong as anyone. He was the only one who challenged and dared her, who pushed her, who made her feel like she could do anything. He was an unlikely oasis from the smothering care of others who loved her, and she adored him for it. And most of the time, when Cain said "jump," Ginger jumped, without thought or regard for the safety of her arm . . . or her good-as-new heart.

"Christ! You're so quiet. Quit fussin' over Cain," said Woodman, an impatient edge to his usually gentle voice. "It's your birthday, and I still haven't given you your present yet."

Looking up at him, she relaxed her hand in his and matched his stride, walking around the barn and looking up to see McHuid Manor on top of the green, rolling hills of her childhood home. The arch over the driveway bore a sign that read "McHuid Farm" and, just under it, "Ranger Jefferson McHuid III, horse breeder." As her mother was quick to boast, her father was the "premier" horse breeder of Glenndale County, Kentucky, and for as long as Ginger could remember, McHuid Farm had hosted the wealthiest, most discerning horse buyers in the world.

In fact, her birthday party today included only five children—from Apple Valley's most important families, of course—and about fifty adults from Lord only knew where whom her mother and father had invited. Like most of her other birthdays, the party was much more about everyone else in the world than it was about Ginger, which made Woodman's thoughtfulness all the more precious to her.

"You got me somethin'?" she asked, the heaviness in her heart relaxing as she fell into step beside him.

"Course! You're twelve. Hell, next year you'll be a teenager, Gin, and then . . ."

"And then?"

He stopped halfway up the gravel road that led to the main house, the sound of glasses clinking and a fiddle playing bluegrass floating down to them on the breeze.

"And then you'll be . . . well . . ." He swallowed, dropping his eyes to his shoes.

"Woodman?" she prompted.

He looked up, his cheeks pinker than they'd been before. "Nothin'."

"You're actin' weird." She smacked his arm lightly and grinned up at him. "Now, 'bout this present . . ."

He smiled, his features relaxing as he dropped her hand and reached into his pocket, pulling out a small pink velvet pouch and offering it to her.

"What is it?" she demanded, reaching for it with an excited giggle.

"Open it and see."

She pulled the drawstring and opened her hand to catch whatever was inside, sighing "Ohhh!" as a silver charm bracelet caught the setting sun behind them and made the shiny metal sparkle in her palm. "It's just darlin'!"

"You like it, Gin?"

"I love it!" she said, throwing her arms around Woodman, the bracelet clutched carefully in her fisted hand around his neck.

His arms came around her, his chest pushing into hers like he was holding his breath. After a moment, he exhaled against her neck, and his warm, sweet breath kissed her skin like a promise. She felt her heart kick into a gallop, suddenly aware—all *too* aware—of Woodman's maleness. His body, pressed into hers, didn't have the flashy definition of his cousin's, but it was solid and strong pushed flush against her small breasts.

"I wanted you to have somethin' special," he whispered, his lips close to her ear as the picker on top of the hill switched from a bluegrass lullaby to "Sweet Virginia."

Her skin flushed with heat just as goose bumps popped up along her bare arms. She was cold and hot, and for the first time in her lifelong friendship with Woodman, she felt embarrassed, like a secret that he'd kept from her for years and years was suddenly out in the open. Confused and a little shaken, she stepped away from him, careful not to seek out his eyes and opening her fist to distract herself.

"What all's on it?" she asked, her voice trembling a little, her body aching for more of something she couldn't name.

His eyes, which seemed a darker green than ever before,

glanced down at the bracelet, as he cleared his throat. "Uh, um, well, a little barn there . . . to remind you of the annual jump. And, uh, an apple. For Apple Valley. That there's a little banjo, 'cause your pickin' sure is gettin' good. I thought that little silver horse looked like Heath. And then there's . . . a, um . . ."

She looked more closely and noticed a small silver heart behind the horse. "A heart."

Looking up at Woodman, she felt her own heart flutter with some indescribable emotion caught somewhere between hope and unease as she asked, "Yours or mine?"

He stared at her, his eyes as true and earnest as always, though his cheeks sported a deep pink now. Just this summer she'd noticed the blond hair on his face—the light mustache when he didn't shave, the stubbly beard along his square jaw at the end of the day, when he was covered in dust from working with Klaus. He was growing up just as fast as Cain, but it hadn't registered—she hadn't really *seen* it—until right now.

"Mine," he whispered, taking the bracelet from her palm and hooking it carefully around her wrist.

***

Two hours later, the party was winding down, and Ginger, who'd blown out her candles with Woodman beside her, stood alone at one of the many white-painted split rail fences on McHuid Farm, looking out over the bright green paddocks as she toyed with the bracelet around her wrist and remembered Woodman's declaration.

Mine.

She screwed up her face and sighed. She didn't like it that Woodman, who was her friend—her most beloved friend in all the world—had made her feel such confusing things this afternoon. She didn't like it that her cheeks had gotten so hot while they'd hugged. She didn't like it that she was suddenly so aware of the fact that he was growing into a man. Their mothers had practically planned a union between them since Ginger was born, but Ginger didn't see Woodman like that. He was the big brother she'd never had, her most treasured friend, a safe place when her feelings about Cain felt so confusing.

Turning away from the fence, she ambled slowly back up to the main house, relieved to see her grandmother sitting alone on the front porch swing of her tiny cottage, located a stone's throw from McHuid Manor.

"Gran!" she shouted, quickening her pace. She'd barely seen her grandmother—her father's mother—all day, and, after Woodman, Gran was her very closest friend.

Kelleyanne McHuid had moved into the in-law cottage after Ginger's parents were married, way before Ginger was born, which meant that she'd been a permanent fixture at McHuid's throughout Ginger's childhood. Though—she wrinkled her nose with worry—she didn't know for how much longer. Recently, Ginger had heard her mother and father discussing Gran in hushed tones behind closed doors. Gran suffered from Parkinson's, and Ginger's mother seemed to feel that she needed "more care" than they could provide at home, while Ginger's father refused to discuss putting his mother into a "damned home" yet. It worried Ginger near constantly to think of losing her Gran to the nursing home in town.

"Here's the birthday girl!" said Gran, patting the seat cushion beside her with a trembling hand. Gran's whole body trembled lately. More and more every day. Her eyes lowered to the bracelet around Ginger's wrist, and she grinned. "Whatcha got there, doll baby?"

"Gift from Woodman," said Ginger, feeling her cheeks

flush.

"Awful pretty," said Gran, reaching for the bracelet, her shaking fingers making it jingle as she looked at each one of the charms. "And awful thoughtful. Josiah's a good boy."

Just about everyone called Woodman Woodman except Gran and sometimes Cain. Gran insisted on calling him by his Christian name. Cain used Josiah and Woodman interchangeably, with no real rhyme or reason that Ginger could follow.

"Rumor is you're gonna marry him someday," said Kelleyanne to her granddaughter, her sixty-something blue eyes merry. "But what do *you* say?"

Ginger giggled self-consciously, thinking about her grandmother's question, something clenching in her twelve-year-old heart as she thought about marrying sensible Woodman and abandoning her wild feelings for Cain.

"I don't know," she said, feeling her forehead crease in confusion.

"Or maybe you're thinkin' you want to marry . . . Cain," said Gran softly.

Cain, with his jet-black hair and ice-blue eyes, appeared like a vision before her, and Ginger's heart thumped faster. The way he'd run off to see Mary-Louise Walker this afternoon made her brown eyes spitting green with jealousy. The way he swaggered made her breath catch. Woodman was so predictable, so safe in comparison.

Then again, Woodman hadn't exactly been predictable this afternoon, had he? He'd surprised her with the gift and even more with his words. His body had been hard and warm when he'd held her, the embrace awakening something new and foreign within her. Something she wasn't sure she wanted.

Something that didn't feel safe and even scared her a little bit. She pulled her fingers away from the charm bracelet and faced her Gran.

"What do I do if I love them both?"

Her grandmother's eyes, which had been mostly teasing, flinched, and her mouth tilted down in a sympathetic frown, which made her face seem so serious and sober.

"*Choose*, doll baby," said Gran. "Someday you'll have to choose."

The same feeling that she'd had in the barn, when Cain yelled, "Jump to the one you love the most, darlin'!" flared up within her—a fierce refusal to love one cousin more than the other, to give up one in lieu of the other.

Choose? Her memories skated back through a dozen years on McHuid Farm that had always included Cain and Woodman. When they were little children, they played together, swimming buck naked in the creek and racing over the green hills and pastures in impromptu games of tag. As the boys grew up, they started working with Cain's daddy, Klaus, who was her father's right-hand man, mucking out the stables and grooming the horses. She'd run down to the barn every day after her lessons to see them, working right along beside them until they were all covered in hay, dust, and barn grime.

Though the Wolframs weren't generally included in the McHuids' active social life, the Woodmans were, which meant that, in addition to seeing Cain and Woodman on the farm, she also saw Woodman at every holiday and birthday party . . . and they always managed to slip out unseen with some smuggled sweets for Cain.

They were the Three Musketeers of McHuid Farm, and Ginger knew both boys as well as she knew herself—Cain's smirking, hotheaded, impulsive ways, and Woodman's levelheaded patience, caution, and kindness. Regardless of their differences, she also knew that as the only children of twin sisters, Cain and Woodman were much closer than most cousins. Genetically speaking, they were half brothers, and while they surely liked to tease and torture each other, each boy wouldn't hesitate to jump in front of a train to save the other's skin either.

In Ginger's mind, she envisioned them like two halves of the same coin that she held carefully in the palm of her hand.

She loved them both desperately.

Choose?

No, her heart protested. *Impossible.*

"What if I can't?" she whispered, leaning back and resting her head on her grandmother's comforting shoulder.

"Then you'll lose them both," said her grandmother softly.

Ginger's shoulders fell, relaxing in surrender as she closed her eyes against the burn of tears.

"But don't let's think about that now, doll baby," said Gran, leaning her head upon her granddaughter's, the constant tremble of her unpredictable body almost soothing to Ginger as they rocked side by side in the twilight. "You're just twelve today. You've got your whole life ahead of you."

Chapter 2

~ Cain ~

"Ginger, jump to me!" yelled Woodman from beside him.

Cain glanced up at little Ginger, twelve years old today, standing two stories above him in the hayloft. Though his feet twitched to hightail it to the old abandoned Glenn River Distillery, he forced himself not to look at his watch. Whatever time it was, Mary-Louise would still be waiting for him when he got there. He was sure of it.

Last time they were together, she'd guided his fingers down to the slick nub of flesh between her legs, and he'd rubbed it until she'd screamed his name. To reward him, she'd gotten on her knees and sucked his cock into her pretty mouth, making him come in about three minutes flat and backhanding her mouth after swallowing every last bit. And damn if he hadn't gotten hard again right away because it was the sexiest fucking thing he'd ever seen.

And tonight? Well, if Cain had his way, tonight they were finally going to do the deed. Have sex. Fuck. Hell, he'd even *make love* if that's what Mary-Louise required of him. He'd been watching the breeding horses on McHuid Farm for as long as he could walk. Tonight, it was his turn, and he was about as jazzed up as a fifteen-year-old kid could be. It was *on*. It was fucking *happening*.

Cain shoved thoughts of Mary-Louise from his mind and grinned up at Princess Ginger in her tower. "Now, Miss Virginia, you ignore ole Woodman here and you jump to me, baby."

He and Woodman had engaged in this princess-in-the-tower tradition every year since they'd found the boss's daughter perched in the hayloft door on her sixth birthday. Cain willingly admitted that it was sort of a stupid ritual, but something had made him come here and hang out by the old barn all afternoon, waiting for Ginger and Woodman to break away from the party, even if it made him late for Mary-Louise. And damn if he hadn't had to work to keep his face from splitting into a grin when he saw them running down the hill toward the barn hand in hand. It wasn't like loafing around the McHuids' barn on a Sunday afternoon was a barrel of laughs so he'd kept his expression lazy, but inside he'd been rubbing his hands together with glee because the truth was, he loved this tradition just as much as he loved Woodman and Ginger. It made him happy, when not much else did.

Why should he be happy? His parents sure as shit weren't happy—they'd alternated between yelling at each other and giving each other the silent treatment for fifteen long, unhappy years. By the age of six, Cain knew that theirs hadn't been a love match—fuck, they barely tolerated each other. His father, Klaus, had come over from Austria in 1989 after working on the state stud farm of the Lipizzan stallions. He'd accompanied one of the

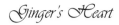

studs to Kentucky to be bred at McHuid's, seen Cain's pretty momma at the Apple Valley Diner, gotten her pregnant, unenthusiastically—if the wedding pictures buried in his mother's sweater drawer were any indication—married her, and stayed in Apple Valley to raise their son.

Meanwhile, Cain's Aunt Sophie, his mother's twin, had married the fucking president of the Apple Valley Savings and Loan a month before his parents, and the entire town acted like *their* wedding was the second coming. (How did he know this? Well, for one thing, *those* wedding pictures weren't hidden in a sweater drawer. About three hundred and eighty six gazillion of them were in ornate silver frames, jammed together on the grand piano at his aunt's house.) And actually, no, the wedding *wasn't* the second coming. *That* blessed event had come nine months later, when Josiah—fair-fucking-haired Josiah—was born. Josiah, who loved horses so much, he had slowly but surely become the son that Klaus had never had in Cain. While Cain was always running off to smoke cigarettes behind the Five and Dime Mart or meet girls at the abandoned distillery, goody-two-shoes Josiah—or Woodman, as everyone called him—was at McHuid's, becoming Klaus's right-hand man. And while Cain had no actual proof that his father loved Josiah more than him, he was pretty sure it was true. And while he didn't hate Josiah for it (his father was owed that honor), he couldn't deny that it hurt.

So his parents' marriage was doomed from the start, he was just short of a bastard, his aunt and uncle were local celebrities, and Woodman was worshipped almost as much as the baby Jesus.

Fuckin' fantastic.

Last but not least, *ring-a-ding-fuckin'-ding*, while Klaus's marriage was a bust, his partnership with Ranger McHuid was a horse-breeding match made in heaven. In fact, as the years passed, the McHuid horses had become such a passion for Cain's father that his wife and son became little more than an afterthought in his life. And it made Cain hate his father and hate horses. Add Ranger McHuid's ambivalence toward him and Miz Magnolia's refusal to include him and his family in her stupid parties since the year Ginger broke her arm, he pretty much hated everything about McHuid's.

Well, everything . . . except Ginger.

"Be smart, Gin," said Woodman.

Cain snorted, looking at his cousin in his fancy-pants party shirt. "You think your scrawny arms gonna catch her?"

Woodman frowned, his brows creasing, and Cain had it in him to feel bad. Even though Klaus appeared to prefer his nephew over his son, which had set up a natural rivalry between them, Cain couldn't bring himself to hate Josiah. Without the benefit of a brother or sister, Woodman was all he had, and deep down Cain loved his cousin as much as he could love anyone in the world. Woe to the fucker who messed with Josiah 'cause Cain would end him, but that didn't mean that he himself didn't love getting under Woodman's skin a little.

Cain pulled off his denim jacket and flexed his muscles, winking at Ginger. "Jump to me, sweet thing."

Woodman scowled at him before turning his eyes back to Ginger. "Come on, now."

Something in Woodman's voice—something *sappy*—distracted Cain, and he turned to his cousin, narrowing his eyes as he noted the earnest look in Woodman's eyes and the rigidity of his open palms as he stared up with devotion at the little girl in the hayloft door. Ginger had always been like a little sister to them, but something in Woodman's voice felt different. And it definitely *didn't* feel very brotherly.

Cain glanced up at Ginger, then back at his cousin's devoted expression.

Nah, he thought quickly. *She's just a kid. Woodman doesn't like her like that. He couldn't. She's just a kid. Just Princess Ginger.*

But he looked at his cousin's face yet again, and as the unavoidable truth sank in, he kept himself from rolling his eyes. How had Cain missed this? All those times Woodman had Heath saddled and ready for Ginger with an eager smile . . . or spent an extra hour combing the chocolate-colored mare . . . or hell, the way he always insisted on mucking out Heath's stall before Ginger came down to the barn . . . Well, Cain had just assumed that he was being his usual eager-beaver self. But, oh Lord, there was more to it. It was for Ginger. Woodman *liked* her. Liked a kid. Liked the little princess.

Smirking with amusement, Cain decided to test his theory, winking at Ginger before training his eyes on Woodman to gauge his cousin's reaction.

"Jump to the one you love the most, darlin'," he called.

Sure enough, Woodman's jaw clenched, and his cheek ticked anxiously, flinching as he waited for Ginger to choose between them.

Bingo.

"Dang it, Cain! Now you went'n wrecked it!"

Cain watched his cousin's shoulders relax, then turned to look up at Ginger, grinning at her frowny face.

"What'd I do?"

Aside from discovering that my cousin has a ginormous crush on you, little girl.

"You know I can't choose between y'all. Not like that. That's not how it works!" she yelled, then disappeared from sight, no doubt coming downstairs to give him what-for.

Woodman turned to face him. "Nice goin', jackass."

Cain grinned at Woodman, wondering how far he could take his teasing before getting decked. "Someone has a little crush."

"Shut up, Cain."

"She's practically still in nursery school."

"I said shut up."

"Touchy, touchy."

"About her? You bet your ass. And in case you hadn't noticed, she's not such a little kid anymore," said Woodman, thoroughly annoyed.

"And you're thinkin' . . . what? You want to be her boyfriend?"

His face was entirely serious as he answered, "Someday, yes."

"You stakin' a claim here, Josiah?" he drawled, trying not to laugh.

"Yes." His cousin's eyes were grave and serious, and his voice carried the tone of a man taking a vow. "I am." He paused for a moment, staring at Cain, then asked, "You got a problem with that?"

"Nope."

"Sure? Because I'm serious about this. About her."

"Serious about a little kid?" said Cain, a snicker escaping as he slapped Woodman on the back. "Hell, cuz, you ain't gonna get any honey from that little hive for a long, long time while I got a real woman waitin' for me. Frankly, I just feel sorry for you."

"I don't mind the wait," said Woodman softly. "I'm . . . well, I'm goin' to marry her someday. I'll wait for her forever if I have to." He shrugged Cain's hand away before snapping, "Don't you have somewhere else to be?"

Cain nodded, still chuckling at Woodman's ridiculous crush. "Yup."

"Were you even *invited* here today?"

"Nope."

They both knew he wasn't.

"Surprised *you* made the cut," said Cain, unable to keep a slight bite out of his tone, "with the amount of time you spend muckin' horse shit with my dad."

Woodman crossed his arms over his chest, looking imperious. "I'm here with my folks today, not as a stablehand."

"Of course you are," said Cain, feeling sour. He flicked a glance at the sparkling gold high school ring on Josiah's finger. Cain's parents hadn't been able to afford one for him, and since Cain was saving up for a pair of wheels, he'd gone without. "With the pretty hands to prove it."

"Hey, now." Woodman held up one callused palm. "My hands are just as--"

Princess Ginger suddenly appeared in the doorway of the barn with her hands on her hips and her face heaps of mad.

"Ain't jumpin' today?" asked Cain smoothly, cutting off his cousin.

He didn't want to hear about how Woodman worked just as hard as he did. Whereas working at McHuid's was bread and butter for Cain and Cain's family, Josiah saw his work at McHuid's more along the lines of a hobby. Cain and his father were there out of necessity. Woodman was there because he enjoyed it. There was a world of difference in their calluses, and

Cain didn't feel like comparing them.

"Y'all are supposed to catch me together!" Ginger pouted, folding her arms over her chest.

Her chest.

Wait a minute now.

Her . . . *chest.*

Little Ginger had a chest: two small mounds tented the front of her yellow and white sundress. When the hell had *that* happened?

Lifting his eyes quickly, he fixed a grin on his face. "Well, darlin', at least your momma won't come after us with a danged fryin' pan this year."

His cousin stepped toward her and wrested her arms apart, sliding his hand down Ginger's tan arm to clasp her fingers. But Ginger didn't seem to notice—her eyes were locked with Cain's.

Again, Cain felt a small, but certain, jolt of surprise as he looked deeply into her deep brown eyes, framed with long lashes, curled at the ends. Was that eyeliner she was wearing? And mascara? When had Princess Ginger started wearing makeup anyway? And when had her eyes gotten so mature lookin'?

"Shouldn't be jumpin' out of barn doors anymore anyway," said Woodman, his voice as tender as his gaze was cow-eyed. "You're twelve now. A young lady."

Ginger looked up at Woodman, her pretty eyes resting on his face for a moment, and something totally unexpected, incredibly ridiculous, and a lot like jealousy flared within Cain.

"A young lady!" he exclaimed, leaning down to grab his jean jacket and shrug it over his broad shoulders, uncomfortable with the way he was feeling. "Whoo-ee! What a joke! Woodman, you only see what you want to see, cuz!"

"She's *twelve*," said Woodman through grated teeth, a murderous glint in his eyes.

"'Zactly! *Twelve.* She's a kid." Whether he needed to prove the point to her or himself, he wasn't sure, but Cain chucked her under the chin as he would a baby. "And if you ain't jumpin', missy, I've got places to be."

Her brown eyes flashed. "But there's cake!"

"Got somethin' sweeter'n cake waitin' for me," said Cain, forcing his eyes not to drop to her small breasts again. *Mary-Louise. Mary-Louise and her big available titties are waitin'. The princess is just a slip of a kid. Just a kid.* "Not to mention, we all know I ain't invited to Miz Magnolia's festivities."

"We'll run up and git you some!"

"No, thanks," he said quickly, turning away.

"You can't just *leave*!"

Suddenly, Ginger's fingers were hot and tight on his skin, digging into the flesh of his arm, and Cain's mind flew to the gutter with such speed, it almost made him dizzy. Those same fingers clutching the back of his neck . . . clutching at his chest . . . clutching at his—

No.

No, no, no.

Not the princess.

Absolutely not.

Besides, his cousin had already staked a claim.

Cain yanked his arm away.

"Am I missin' somethin' here?" His heart beat like crazy as he stared down at her lovely face. "Hell, yes, I'm leavin'. I got plans."

Her eyes, fiery and wild and practically begging him to stay, had never affected him before today, but now they made his insides flare with heat. She looked at him like he mattered, like she needed him, like all the happiness in her world was somehow bound to him, and it made a fierce longing, like he'd never experienced before, spring up within him.

Barely aware of his cousin clearing his throat meaningfully behind her, Cain's eyes drifted to Ginger's pink lips before he locked his gaze with hers.

Just a taste. One little taste won't hurt anything.

"But before I go, since you're such a *young lady* now, Miss Virginia, I guess I could give you a birthday kiss, huh?"

Shutting out every objection, he took a step toward her, drowning in the warm bourbon color of her eyes. Reaching up, he placed his hand—his rough, unworthy hand—against the soft skin of her cheek to steady her face and leaned toward her. Her eyes fluttered closed, and she tilted her chin up. Her lips, full and lightly parted, beckoned him, but at the very last moment, common sense screamed *NO NO NO* so loudly, he changed course abruptly, letting his lips land safely on her other cheek instead.

He closed his eyes and rested there for a moment, his lips pressed against her sweet, sweet skin, his heart racing, his breath held painfully in his chest.

Finally he drew away, but his voice was hoarse in his ears as he whispered, "Happy birthday, lionhearted l'il gal."

Then, before he could think better of it, and because he had zero interest in resting his thoughts on the confusing things happening in his body, head, and heart, he dropped his hand and walked away.

***

"You're such a jerk, Cain Wolfram!" called Mary-Louise Walker, in a serious snit as Cain rounded the corner of the massive distillery and started across the high grass toward her.

Gesturing with her cigarette and wearing a frown, she sat on the low wall of an old stone gazebo in the Glenn River Distillery complex, which had been abandoned more than thirty years ago. It was against the law to trespass on the property, but every kid in Apple Valley knew a hundred ways to get in. Hell, Cain and Woodman had been exploring the bones of the old place since they were old enough to ride bikes.

"Why'm I a jerk, now, honey?" he asked, his cock stiffening as he got a closer look at her skin-tight jeans and even tighter white sweater.

She took a long drag on her cigarette and glared at him. "You said four. It's almost five now, and it's supercreepy here when the sun goes down. I shouldn't've waited for you!"

"But you did, darlin'," he drawled, giving her his sexiest grin as he made his way through the last of the overgrowth that separated them. Without asking her permission, he put his hands under her arms and pulled her up on her feet, jerking her against his chest.

She pouted prettily, arching her back so that her breasts pushed into him. "I'm a senior, you know."

"The hottest one at school."

She ignored this, taking another drag of her cigarette and exhaling over his shoulder. "And you're only a sophomore, Cain."

"Think of everythin' you're teachin' me, sugar. You're the best teacher I ever met, and I'm aimin' to get straight A's."

"Maybe I should just make you walk me home," she said as she dropped her cigarette to the ground and squished it with the toe of her dirty gray sneaker. "'Cause now I ain't sure if I want to continue our . . . lessons."

"Aw, c'mon, baby," he cajoled, pushing her sweater away to bare her shoulder and press his lips to her warm skin. "Educate me. I'm beggin' you."

"Tell me where you were first," she said, but her voice was gentler now, and she looped her arms around his neck, wanting more.

"Over at McHuid's," he murmured. He bit her gently, his teeth nabbing a pinch of her skin and holding for a moment before letting it go. She moaned softly, more and more like Jell-O in his arms.

"Didn't know you moved in such—" Cain released her waist with one hand and slid his palm under her sweater, under her thin cotton bra, resting his bare hand against the fullness of her naked breast. "Mm! Cain!—in, um, such distinguished circles."

Her nipple pebbled between his thumb and forefinger as he bit down on her shoulder again, then soothed her skin by licking and blowing, all the while rolling the stiff, hot nub between his digits. "Wasn't invited to the festivities. Only went to see . . ."

"See who?" she asked in a breathy, distracted voice, her head falling back as he continued to tease her.

"The Prin—uh, my cousin."

His second hand followed the first, burrowing under her sweater, under her bra, his palm covering the lush flesh of her other breast. Mary-Louise reached down for the hem of her sweater and flipped it over her head before reaching around to unlatch her bra in the front. She squared her shoulders and dropped her arms, and Cain watched the flimsy fabric slip down her arms, leaving her completely bare from the waist up.

He dropped his eyes to the hot fuckin' sight of his hands

on her breasts. In the dim light of the setting sun, the tall grass turned a golden lavender, and Mary-Louise moaned her approval as he plumped one breast in readiness for his mouth.

"Your cousin. W-Woodman," she sighed.

"Uh-huh," said Cain, bending his head to suck one bright pink bud between his lips. Mary-Louise arched against him, moaning with pleasure, and his cock, already as stiff as the stone of the gazebo, twitched eagerly behind his zipper.

"Ain't surprised . . . the banker's kid . . . was invited," said Mary-Louise between gasps of pleasure. "Wasn't it . . . wasn't it the, uh, the little girl's birthday today? Poor . . . little thing."

Cain flinched, and his teeth grazed her nipple a touch more roughly than he'd intended. Mary-Louise cried out in pleasure, digging her fingers into Cain's hair and raking his scalp with her sharp nails.

Part of the reason Magnolia McHuid had been so pissed about Ginger's broken arm on her sixth birthday was that Ginger had only just recovered from major surgery to fix her heart. Because the McHuids were as close to royalty as anyone could find in Glenndale County, everybody had known about Ginger's broken heart, and few, including Mary-Louise Walker, who had zero personal connection to the McHuids, had forgotten.

"That was a long time ago," he said.

"Ain't seen that l'il gal in an . . . age. They still . . . homeschool her, right?"

He wanted to yell at Mary-Louise to stop fucking talking about the princess because now a picture of Ginger's pretty face was firmly lodged in Cain's head. Thoughts of her fingers entwined with Woodman's made his eyes narrow. And thoughts of his own lips so recently pressed against Ginger's sweet skin made an unexpected flash of guilt steal his breath as he thought about where his lips were now: suckling at Mary-Louise's nicotine-scented tits.

He huffed in frustration, sliding his hands from Mary-Louise's breasts and panting raggedly as his palms skimmed her sides, finally resting on her waist.

"Aw, honey," said Mary-Louise, mistaking his abrupt halt for concern and reaching for his face. Her eyes were soft as she licked her lips. "You're sweet, worryin' about that kid."

"Ain't worried about her," he muttered, clenching his jaw, trying to resist the memory of Ginger's little breasts pushed up against her sweet yellow and white dress as Mary-Louise stepped closer to rub her naked tits against his T-shirt. "Her heart ain't broken no more. They fixed it. Probably stronger'n yours or mine now."

"Ain't no shame in carin' 'bout someone, Cain," said Mary-Louise in a meaningful tone as she reached for his belt buckle and dispatched it with practiced finesse. "In fact, I think it's awful sweet."

His button and zipper came next. Hooking her thumbs into his jeans and boxers, she yanked them down as she dropped to her knees before him. And not a moment later, all thoughts of Princess Ginger were banished from his dirty mind.

Chapter 3

~ Woodman ~

Two things fought for Woodman's attention as he watched his cousin swagger away toward the old distillery, leaving him and Ginger behind despite her pleas for him to stay.

The first? Mary-Louise Walker was only "sweeter'n cake" if that cake had been licked by every member of the Apple Valley High School football team. Multiple times.

The second? It bothered Woodman to hell and back that Ginger had chosen not to jump this year, but it bothered him even more to watch her face fall as Cain walked away.

Damn it, but it had *always* been like this.

Cain was like a twister, wreaking havoc everywhere he went, without a care in the world, while Woodman stayed behind to clean up the wreckage.

After fifteen years, he was getting sick of it.

Turning his glance from his dickhead cousin's retreating form, he looked at Ginger, placing his hand on the small of her back in a lame attempt to comfort her.

"Don't fuss over him," he said, his anger toward his cousin

mounting as Cain walked farther away. "He's always been a jackass, Gin."

"He isn't!" Ginger cried, flashing angry eyes at him.

And there was this, too. Every woman in the world—or at least at Apple Valley High School—was always so danged eager to defend him, like he was some wayward foundling angel who could do no wrong, even as he carelessly broke their hearts.

He saw the way women of all ages looked at his cousin, with a mixture of enchantment and hope, wondering if Cain would give them one of his megawatt smiles before swaggering away. Ginger was no different, and he hated it fiercely that she seemed so taken with Cain lately. He wanted her flashing eyes to look at him the way she looked at his cousin. To grab *his* arm and beg *him* to stay. To moan "oh" to his retreating form, like she wished she could keep him in her pocket and never let him go.

Patience, Woodman. Be patient, he reminded himself. *Slow and steady wins the race. And Cain ain't one to be kept in a pocket anyhow.*

Still, some part of him couldn't help being annoyed. Cain had just left despite her pleas. Woodman was still standing here beside her, and she didn't even seem to notice, didn't seem to care.

"He's your cousin," she said, her voice softer, her eyes filled with tears.

Damn Cain to hell and back for putting those tears there. And on her birthday, too.

"And don't I know it," he said, looking away at the speck in the distance that was his troublesome cousin.

As he watched Cain's retreat, he felt some of the anger leave his body. If he took Ginger's feelings out of the equation, he had to ask himself: what exactly was Cain supposed to do? Linger at the barn until he or Ginger could break away with a slice of cake like they used to, when he was little? Waste his whole afternoon on the outskirts of a party he wasn't invited to while Woodman and Ginger enjoyed the refreshments and music up at the main house?

It embarrassed Woodman that Miz Magnolia hadn't invited his Uncle Klaus, Aunt Sarah, and Cain to Ginger's party. Uncle Klaus and Ranger McHuid were about as chummy as two men could get, but when it came to rolling out the red carpet, the Wolframs had been left off the list for years now. It bothered Woodman's mother, Sophie, to see her twin sister slighted, though, he thought acidly, it didn't keep her from attending and enjoying the McHuids' many parties either.

And it bothered Woodman, who thought of his cousin as more like a brother despite his irritating behavior, that Cain was always left out.

But if Woodman was honest, he would admit that seeing *Ginger* upset dwarfed all other thoughts or concerns in his life. What Woodman wanted—more than anything else in the entire world—was to make Ginger McHuid happy.

He'd been there the day her heart had gone haywire, seven years ago. He'd been giving her a piggyback ride around her living room after an Easter egg hunt when she suddenly said she didn't feel good. Helping her slide down his back onto the couch, he turned to find her slumped against the cushions, her eyes rolled back, her body limp. He'd touched her cheek to find it cold despite a deep flush of red, and he could see the terrifyingly rapid flutter of her pulse in her neck.

"Miz Magnolia!" he'd screamed toward the dining room, cupping his trembling, clammy hands over his mouth.

"Somethin's wrong with Ginger!"

An ambulance was called, and later that evening five-year-old Ginger was airlifted from Central Baptist Hospital in Lexington, Kentucky, to the Vanderbilt Medical Center in Tennessee, where there was a doctor who specialized in pediatric heart surgery.

She was diagnosed with SVT and underwent a catheter ablation procedure to permanently eliminate the dangerous racing of her heart. After a week at Vandy, she was discharged, and Woodman was waiting on the front porch of McHuid Manor the day she came home.

As soon as she exited the car that day, Miz Magnolia pulled Woodman into her Chanel-scented embrace and kissed the top of his head over and over again, blessing him for being "my baby's very own guardian angel" and thanking him for saving Ginger's life. Exiting the car behind her mother, Ginger beamed up at him like he hung the moon and all the stars, and from that moment on, Woodman had made it his personal mission to protect, love, and serve Miss Virginia Laire McHuid.

Their parents were best friends, so Woodman checked up on her at every family dinner and party, celebrating Thanksgiving, Christmas, and Easter with the McHuids and spending lazy summer afternoons at barbecues together. Miz Magnolia heartily approved of his affection for her daughter, and throughout his childhood, Woodman had preened whenever he overheard her say to one of his parents, "God blessed this family when he gave our Ginger your Josiah." He was her protector, her watchdog, the big brother she'd never had.

But recently, so *very* recently, Woodman's feelings for Ginger had taken a turn. Not that he loved her any less than he always had, but he started loving her . . . differently. Not so much as a brother loves a sister, but more how a boy loves a girl.

And yes, he knew she was only twelve and he was barely fifteen, and no, of course he wouldn't do anything about his feelings until she was ready to return them, but he couldn't help the way he felt. He couldn't help it that he wished Ginger would stop seeing him as a big brother figure and look at him with the same yearning she reserved for Cain.

She frowned up at him now and said, "He's gonna catch somethin' nasty from Big Tits Walker."

Huh. He'd been careful, as a boy three years older than Ginger, not to use vulgar language around her, but apparently she'd picked up a few choice words from someone else. And he had to admit, hearing something so sexual and naughty escape from her sweet lips was a little bit of a turn-on.

He chuckled softly. "I guess that's possible."

She turned back to watch Cain go, and Woodman felt his fleeting smile fall.

"You should go after him and . . . and, I don't know, ask him to go for a joyride on Daddy's tractor or—"

God damn it! No! We don't need him, Gin! We got all we need right here, just bein' alone together!

"I'm *not* goin' after him," he said firmly, reaching for her hand with the practiced ease of someone who'd been reaching for her hand all his life, and led her back toward the party. "First off, wouldn't do any good. You know Cain as well as I do. He's goin' where he's goin', and nothin's goin' to get in his way but God or weather."

Now, she had just made a fairly sexual observation about Mary-Louise Walker's bosoms, hadn't she? What if he employed the same crude style of sexual observation? Would it be okay or make things awkward between them? "Second?

Pardon me, Gin, but I'm not cockblockin' my only cousin. He might be a jackass, but that don't mean I don't love him."

When she didn't flinch at the crassness of the word he'd chosen, he realized that they'd just a cleared a new level of communication in their relationship that now included observations of a sexual nature, and a tremor of sweet awareness made his heart thrum. "And third? Your momma's fixin' to bring out the cake any minute, and there'll be hell to pay if you're not there to blow out twelve pretty candles."

She walked beside him, but Woodman still felt her pull to the road, to follow Cain, wherever he was going.

"Christ! You're so quiet. Quit fussin' over Cain!" he said, feeling impatient. Instantly regretting the sharpness of his tone, he gentled his voice and added, "It's your birthday, and I still haven't given you your present yet."

"You got me somethin'?" she asked, finally turning to him, her voice considerably warmer for the first time since Cain had left them.

"Course!" he said, grinning down at her. "You're twelve. Hell, next year you'll be a teenager, Gin, and then . . ."

"And then?"

. . . and when you're a teenager like me, maybe you'll let me take you to the junior prom, or let me be your first kiss, and—please God—let me be your first everything else, too.

Carried away by the thoughts in his head, he abruptly stopped walking and cast his eyes down so she wouldn't see the longing there.

"And then you'll be . . . well . . ."

"Woodman?" she prompted, the edge of a held-back giggle in her voice.

He looked up at her, at her smiling brown eyes and wide

smile.

I love you, he thought, his fifteen-year-old heart threatening to beat out of his chest. *I love you so much, Gin.*

"Nothin'."

"You're actin' weird," she said with a light smile, smacking him on the arm. Her eyes twinkled with anticipation. "Now, 'bout this present . . ."

The little pink velvet pouch had been burning a hole in his pocket all afternoon. Fishing it out of his starched khakis, he offered it to her on his outspread palm.

"What is it?" she demanded, reaching for it with an excited giggle.

"Open it and see."

She pulled the drawstring and opened her hand to catch whatever was inside, sighing "Ohhh!" as a silver charm bracelet caught the setting sun behind them and made the shiny metal sparkle in her palm.

Woodman lifted his gaze quickly to her face, watching with undiluted pleasure as her lips turned up into a surprised smile. She flashed happy eyes at him. "It's just darlin'!"

His heart thrilled. "You like it, Gin?"

"I love it!" she said, surprising him by throwing her arms around his neck.

Woodman sucked in a surprised breath and held it while the world stood still.

While holding hands was run-of-the-mill for him and Ginger, full-body contact was not. He had noticed her breasts this summer—small and rounded beneath her T-shirts and Sunday dresses, but now, pressed flush against him, he couldn't help his body's reaction to her. It took all his self-control not to drop his lips to her bare shoulder and rest them there, as he silently prayed that his johnson wouldn't stiffen so much that it poked her in the tummy.

But even the prospect of that mortifying brand of humiliation wasn't enough for him to consider letting her go. Exhaling in a soft hiss, he wrapped his arms around her tightly and leaned his head down to whisper in her ear, "I wanted you to have somethin' special."

As if on cue, the banjo picker on top of the hill at the party finished a bluegrass lullaby and started playing "Sweet Virginia."

Woodman's eyes fluttered closed as he held her, this child–woman whom he had loved for as long as he could remember, on whom he'd staked a claim today, letting Cain know—in no uncertain terms—that Ginger was his. Their hearts pressed against each other's, and Woodman imagined them recognizing each other, silently communicating, agreeing to beat together. Reaching up, he smoothed his hand over her light blonde hair and sighed, trying to memorize how it felt to hold his girl in his arms.

Without warning, Ginger stepped away from him, and though he wished he could see her expression—to know if she was as affected by their embrace as he was—she kept her eyes down, staring at the bracelet in her hand.

"What all's on it?" she asked, her voice a little shaky.

Despite his prayers, his body hadn't entirely listened, and Woodman needed a moment to recover from having her so close. He hoped to God she wouldn't look at the slight bulge in his crotch as he cleared his throat.

"Uh, um, well, a little barn there . . . to remind you of the annual jump. And, uh, an apple. For Apple Valley. That there's a little banjo, 'cause your pickin' sure is gettin' good. I thought

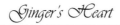

that little silver horse looked like Heath. And then there's . . . a, um..."

His face flushed with heat as he looked at the last charm.

He'd chosen the other four quickly—a barn, an apple, a banjo, and a horse—all important parts of Ginger's life. But was *he*? He knew he was a friend to her—a brother figure, too. But could he be important in her life in a different way than he'd always been before?

"A heart," she said, looking up at him, her brown eyes deep and searching. "Yours or mine?"

He stared at her, trying to decide what to say. He didn't sense that she was ready for a declaration of his eternal love, but Woodman wasn't ashamed of the feelings in his heart, so he kept his answer simple.

"Mine," he whispered, taking the bracelet from her palm and hooking it carefully around her wrist.

She showed no reaction to his simple admission, so he wasn't sure if she'd actually heard him or if he'd whispered too lightly. At any rate, it wouldn't make sense to repeat himself. As the bracelet latch clicked shut, he looked up at her, and she offered him a wobbly grin.

"Race you to the top?" she asked, then set off at a clip, running up the gravel hill in riding boots and a yellow sundress, heading back up to her birthday party.

Woodman didn't rush after her. He watched her go, shaking his head as he chuckled softly to himself, now certain in the knowledge that she'd heard him and just didn't know how to respond. That was his Ginger—marching headlong into a fight when she was angry or indignant, but running away when she felt bruised or uncertain. He didn't mind. Maybe she just needed a little time for the idea of owning his heart to settle and find purchase in her mind. That was just fine. If she needed time, she could have it. He wasn't going anywhere. That was for sure.

After all, the notion of Woodman and Ginger ending up together wasn't exactly a brand-new idea. For as long as Woodman could remember, he had taken for granted the knowledge that someday Ginger, and her family's farm, would belong to him.

A union between the Woodmans and McHuids was a favorite wish of both of their mothers, who spoke about a someday marriage in not-so-hushed tones (*"Won't your Ginger make Woodman a beautiful bride someday?" "Yes, and Woodman is just the sort of good boy Ranger and I would want by her side."*) and their fathers, who joked that their grandsons would be the best horsemen in Glenndale County one day. His feelings for Ginger, always strong, grew and deepened into something that felt more lasting and serious with every passing day. And Woodman loved McHuid Farm as much as Ranger McHuid or his Uncle Klaus, to whom Woodman had been apprenticed since he was a preteen able to properly muck out a stable.

Woodman had given Ginger his heart ages ago. The bracelet he'd given her today was just the first step toward securing hers, even though they had years ahead of them before they could finally be together.

As he continued his leisurely stroll up the gravel driveway, he thought about those years to come—about the carefully chosen plan for his life: currently a sophomore at Apple Valley High, he was in the top five percent of his class, but his goal was to be valedictorian by senior year. He also punted for the Apple Valley Appaloosas and had recently been elected treasurer of the student government. And he knew he'd need all these credentials

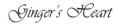

lined up to be accepted at the Naval Academy like his father and grandfather.

After being accepted at Annapolis and successfully completing four years of undergraduate work as a cadet, he would graduate as a second lieutenant and request to be stationed at Naval Support Activity Mid-South in Tennessee, where he could work with the Navy Recruiting Command. That way, he'd be closer to home and in a better geographical position to court Ginger. After five years of active service, he planned to enter the Reserves for three years, during which he'd return to Apple Valley, propose to Ginger, and take over a portion of the operations at McHuid's in conjunction with her father and Uncle Klaus.

And then? Woodman grinned. A gorgeous young wife in his bed whom he'd always loved. And someday? A little boy with her brown eyes and a little girl who shared her smile. He chuckled softly at the thought, holding it close to his heart.

"Basically, your average happily-ever-after," he said aloud, waving at his parents as they came into view and feeling like the path he was on was the perfect route to a sweet life.

PART TWO

Three years later

Chapter 4

~ Cain ~

"Ahh, baby," he groaned, grinding his head back into the pillow, "you're hotter'n a tin can in August."

Cain's flavor of the moment, Cherry something-or-other, giggled coyly, her bright red–dyed hair draped erotically across his cut abs as he leaned on his elbows to look down at her. Lips that matched her hair color were puckered around his cock, leaving garish red streaks as she pumped him in and out of her mouth, moaning like he was servicing her, instead of the other way around.

Reaching down, he grabbed a fistful of her hair tightly, letting out a low growl as her teeth razed his taut, tender flesh. Her ministrations became more vigorous, and Cain felt the inevitable tightening in his balls that told him the end was near.

"Don't finish me," he groaned.

Her fingers, clutching his ass like she was holding on for dear life, dug into his skin, and he sucked a hiss of breath through his teeth as his cock hit the back of her throat and his back arched off the mattress.

"In . . . your pussy," he managed to grind out, releasing

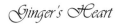

her hair and reaching for a condom from the pile on the floor beside them.

They were at Cain's little fuck pad in the old Glenn River Distillery, fully decked out with an old mattress, pillow, candles that had mostly burned down to nubs, and said stockpile of condoms. Cain wasn't exactly known for his discrimination when it came to giving and receiving pleasure, but he was fastidious about his safety. From the very first time he'd had sex with Mary-Louise Walker, not fifty yards from where he was right now, he'd never once engaged in unprotected sex. It had been a deal breaker for him many times, in fact, when a soft and willing woman offered herself to him and he found himself unprepared. But his carefully stocked love nest, tucked into a windowed corner on the second floor of the abandoned, castlelike distillery building, made such assignations a lot more convenient.

Cherry lifted her head and grinned at him, backhanding her messy scarlet lips as he jackknifed up and ripped open the condom, rolling it over his slick and straining erection before reaching for her hips and turning her around. With her facing away from him, he pushed her back forward and pulled her down onto his cock. She was hot and wet, quivering around his pole, and Cain clenched his eyes shut as his neck fell back in pleasure.

Keeping his hands firmly clasped on her hips, he pushed her away, then pulled her closer, sliding her back and forth on his slick cock until her gasps became moans and the moans became cries of pleasure. Pushing her forward to her knees and elbows, he rose up on his knees behind her and continued to thrust into her from behind, reaching forward to cup her swinging breasts and tease her tight, pierced nipples.

"Fuck, fuck, fuck, fuuuuuck!" she screamed as her inmost muscles spasmed around him.

Once she had found her pleasure, Cain slid his hands back to her hips, holding her tightly as he hammered into her twice more before biting down on his lip and growling into the climax of his own orgasm, which he rode out, pushing gently into Cherry's willing body until he was completely spent.

Reaching for the condom, he pinched it tightly before pulling out of her. Slipping it off his glistening cock, he tied a knot in the open end and threw it into the metal bucket near the foot of the mattress.

Candy fell onto her stomach, and Cain sat back, leaning against the wall beside her, watching her back rise and fall with her panting. His gaze wandered away, and he looked out the half-shattered, grimy window that remained in the once-grand sill to his left, then took a deep breath and exhaled loudly.

"Well, this was fun," he said, smacking her ass to signal that it was also over.

She raised her head, propping it on her elbow and looked up at him, eyes narrowed. "Wait a sec . . . That's it?"

No stranger to this particular conversation, Cain cocked his head to the side and opened his eyes wide, staring at her wordlessly.

She sat up, her gaudy lipstick smeared and cheeks still flushed from sex, looking at him like he'd just confessed to drowning puppies. "Are you fuckin' serious?"

"About what?"

"You want me to go? Just like that?"

He stared at her—at her angry face and bare breasts, bright pink from the bristles on his unshaven jaw. An hour ago, when he ran into her at the Gas & Sip, she'd seemed wild and edgy with her bright red hair and lipstick. Now she just looked . . . used.

He shrugged.

"You're an asshole," she said, grabbing her bra and panties off the dusty concrete floor and standing up to get dressed.

So I've heard.

He thought about saying *I didn't force you to come here. In fact, you practically insisted on followin' me. And from all that racket you just made while I was fuckin' you doggie style, I think you got as good as I gave. I don't remember either of us makin' promises. So what's the problem?*

But Cain knew from personal experience that that particular speech would, at a minimum, get him a slap across the face, so he didn't say anything—just looked up at her, his face void of emotion, because, well, he *didn't* feel anything. In fact, Cain had yet to feel anything significant when he flirted and fucked. He felt the same physical pleasure any normal, hot-blooded eighteen-year-old would feel, of course, but his heart remained unmoved, no matter how many women he bedded, and the list was long and ever growing.

Like my cock, he thought, smirking.

"Are you laughin' at me?" Cherry what's-her-name demanded, her voice screeching a little when she said "me."

He schooled his expression to bored and shook his head no.

"You are a total fuckin' asshole," she said, zipping up her jeans and swiping her T-shirt up from the floor. "You know what else? I hope they send you to Iraq. I hope you don't make it home."

He flinched, just barely, and she gave him a mean smile before grabbing her shoes from the floor and hurrying toward the stairs.

When the rickety stairwell door slammed behind her, Cain stood up and stretched leisurely, walking to the window to watch her stomp away from the building, through the opening in the fence they'd used to enter, and back to her car. She burned rubber pulling away, and Cain rubbed his jaw, thinking of the red marks on her breasts and thinking he should probably shower and shave before he headed to McHuid's to say good-bye to his father . . . and to Ginger.

***

An hour later, Cain pulled his motorcycle up the gravel driveway of McHuid Farm, turning right at the first pass, and headed straight to the barn, as he had thousands of times in his life. Today was his last chance to say good-bye to his father before shipping out to Navy boot camp bright and early tomorrow morning.

Since his parents had divorced, two years ago, Cain had been living with his mother in a small apartment on Main Street, while his father, who decided to sell their family home, had moved into the tack room at McHuid's. In a move completely sanctioned, if not encouraged, by Ranger McHuid, Klaus's work and life were seamless now, and Cain doubted his father left the farm more than once a week, and only then when he ran out for groceries or beer.

Pulling his fully restored 2001 Yamaha R6 into the gravel lot beside the barn, Cain cut the engine, pushed down the kickstand, and unhooked his helmet. Throwing his leg over the seat, he sauntered toward the barn.

Of all the things he would miss in Apple Valley, this barn was—in a perplexing contradiction—on the very bottom and at the very top of his list. He'd worked here with his father for almost ten years, a minimum of twenty hours a week, and he

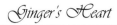

was grateful for the income it had provided. His parents hadn't ever been in a position to offer the sort of allowance that Josiah's parents could give. Working at McHuid's had made it possible for Cain to buy the parts to fix his motorcycle, for the gym membership that kept his body taut and toned, for the clothes on his back, and the help he gave his mother, who'd refused a cent of his father's money during the divorce.

But this barn had also been a prison of sorts. Because Cain had never enjoyed working with horses, his job at McHuid's had felt like aimless grunt work. A job for a check. Mucking stables. Shoveling manure. Birthing colts. It was hard, unglamorous work, and he wouldn't miss it. Not a moment of it.

Nor would he miss the way his father and Josiah enjoyed every moment of it with the same passion that Cain hated it. The way his father ruffled Josiah's hair or patted him on the back after a tough breech delivery. The way his father's face lit up when Woodman walked into the barn, anxious to tell him about the new mare's breeding lines or the stallion that Ranger was importing from England. It hurt Cain to see their natural, unforced camaraderie. Now that his parents were divorced, he didn't hate his father as much as he used to—he could see that both of his parents were happier, healthier people apart than they'd ever been together. And Cain loved Josiah as much as always. But seeing his father and cousin together still made Cain feel like shit, and he wouldn't miss it.

Then again, this barn was the place where Ginger had jumped into their arms year after year, her twelfth birthday notwithstanding. No matter what was going on in Cain's life, no matter what he was doing or whom he was fucking, he had caught Ginger McHuid in his arms almost every year of her life, and he'd miss it come October. Yes, he would.

Not that he spent much time around Ginger anymore. She'd started attending public high school as a sophomore this year, and she was around the barn a lot less, he'd noticed. He'd also noticed that she had grown into, *hand to God*, the prettiest, sexiest girl in Apple Valley. Golden blonde waves tumbled down her back, and those deep brown eyes that had so captured his attention on her twelfth birthday now caught the notice of every other guy under the age of thirty. Her legs went on forever, toned and muscular from riding, and her smile—Lord, her smile!—stopped his heart whenever she flashed it at him, which was every time he saw her.

But the very transparent reality of Cain Wolfram's life was that no matter what he felt for Ginger, there were three reasons he could never have her.

The first? She was way too good for him. She was as bright and shiny as silver in the sunshine, sweet, kind, smart, and rich. As for Cain? He was badly tarnished to a dull gray and cynical and selfish. He'd boned every girl worth having in a ten-mile radius. He'd been a poor student and a troublemaker, racing around Apple Valley on his motorcycle at all hours, and drinking down at the distillery with a rowdy crew of friends.

The second? Ginger loved Apple Valley. It was her home—a home he knew she loved to the marrow of her bones, when all Cain really wanted was to see Apple Valley get smaller and smaller in his rearview mirror. And if he had his way, he'd never return again.

But the third reason was the most implacable, the most nonnegotiable reason he could never have Ginger McHuid. Because she belonged to Woodman. Always had, always would. And Cain loved Woodman too much to lose his cousin's kinship over a girl. Even an angel–girl like Ginger.

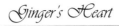

Will you miss her? whispered his heart.

That was like asking if he'd miss something he could never have. A better question would be, *Will you long for her?* And the answer, of course, was a sad and simple *Forever.* She would always be the sweetest something that the earth had to offer. And someday Cain would enter heaven or hell still wishing that he'd had a chance to love her.

Shaking off his thoughts and deciding against going up to the main house to find her and say good-bye (because, really, what was the point?), he walked into the barn and knocked on the tack room door. Looking around, he noted that the new stablehand, a sophomore from Apple Valley High who was probably a friend a Ginger's, was doing a good job. The concrete floor between the stalls was clean as a whistle, and the barn smelled like fresh hay. Cain inhaled deeply, grudgingly admitting that the smell wasn't totally unpleasant, and maybe even a little comforting.

"Papa?" he called, knocking on the door again, but there was no light shining through the crack under the door, and when he pressed his ear against the darkened window, all was silent on the other side.

Figures, he thought, tamping down feelings of anger and disappointment. He'd told his father he'd be by to say good-bye this afternoon, and his old man couldn't even bother to be around. *Bet he'd made time to say good-bye to Woodman.*

"Fuck it," he growled, turning on his heel and heading back out toward his motorcycle. He had better things to do. He had a few more hours of drinking and fucking before a 5 a.m. bus from Lexington to Chicago and a three-month hiatus from both. He had—

The sound of quiet weeping distracted him as he exited the

barn, and he looked up to see Ginger sitting in the hayloft opening, her legs hanging down and ankles crossed. She covered her face with her hands, and her shoulders trembled with sobs.

As though shot through the heart with adrenaline, Cain turned back into the barn, running through the stall bay and up the hayloft ladder, bending over at the waist to walk under the low-pitched roof as he made his way over to her.

"Gin?" he said softly from a few feet away, anxious not to startle her.

She gasped in surprise and turned at the waist to look at him, dropping her hands flat on the planks behind her.

"Cain," she sobbed, tears slipping down her cheeks as she looked up at him. "Thought I might've heard a m-motor below, but I wasn't sure."

"Aw, princess," he said gently, stepping over hay bales to make his way to her. He sat down carefully, letting his legs dangle beside hers and putting his arm around her shoulders. "What's got you so sad?"

She sniffled, her small body shuddering as she laid her head on his chest like a wilted flower. The scent of her shampoo—fresh lemons—surrounded him, and he flinched, closing his eyes and memorizing the smell so he could pull it out and remember her when he was far away from home.

Since the day of her twelfth birthday, when Cain had first started seeing her as a woman, Ginger had appeared regularly in his dreams. But even his fantasies were careful of her. Sometimes fully clothed, oftentimes not, she represented something lovely and untouchable, something clean and innocent that squeezed Cain's heart. Whether she was naked or not, her softness, her goodness, her undiluted, luminous beauty, beckoned him like an answered prayer, but Cain kept his distance. He never fucked Ginger in his dreams. He stared at her from afar. He silently worshipped her. He wished things were different.

She sniffled again and raised her head, looking up at him. Her deep brown eyes were filled with tears, but still huge and seeking, framed by dark lashes. Her lips, at which he'd stared a million times, were full pillows of soft pink, and her body had filled out into womanhood in the most distracting ways: full, high breasts, slim hips, and legs than went on for days. He rarely allowed himself to be alone with her, knowing how desperately he craved her and how unworthy he was to have her.

Cain *consumed* women. He ate them for lunch and licked them clean for dessert. He turned them from soft, pliant, smiling creatures to spitting, narrow-eyed harpies who hated him. But he'd rather die than to ever see Ginger's eyes flash at him with hurt, full of hatred.

Besides, Woodman loved her.

And he'd loved her longer.

And he'd love her better.

In every way that mattered, Woodman was the better man—smarter, richer, clean and honorable—and since Ginger deserved the best the world had to offer, Cain had no business going near her. And he hadn't. Fuck, how he'd tried to stay away.

Still, he couldn't see her so upset and just turn his back on her. Ginger had a right to the bit of softness in his tired, bitter heart, and if she needed him, he couldn't bring himself to turn away from her.

"Tell ole Cain what's got you so sad, baby."

She sniffled again, adjusting her head until her soft hair nestled into his neck, caressing his throat.

"Besides the f-fact that you and W-Woodman are leavin' tomorrow?"

"Aw, Gin. We'll be back before you know it."

"What if you get s-sent to w-war?" she sobbed.

"Well, we just might," he said soberly. "They need good men in Iraq."

"You could d-die."

"Is that what you're worried about, baby?" He hugged her closer. "Ain't no sense in fussin' over that. I'll look after Woodman, and he'll look after me."

"It scares me, C-Cain. I don't know what l-life looks like w-without you t-two." She hiccuped over her words, sniffling mightily and gasping for breath as she finished speaking.

"You listenin' to me, Miss Virginia?" he asked, his heart hurting from her tears, twisting to know that his decision to enlist was wringing such sadness from the princess.

"Uh-huh."

"Then fuckin' look at me," he demanded.

She slid her head off his chest and looked up at him, her wide eyes glassy and bloodshot. Her lips parted in surprise at his words, but she held her breath like it would keep her tears from falling.

"Ain't *nothin'* gonna happen to Woodman and me, baby. I *promise* you that."

"You c-can't—"

"Yes, I can." He reached for her chin and held it firmly, the soft skin making his fingers tingle. "I promise you. Ain't nothin' gonna happen to me, and you can bet your sweet ass ain't nothin' gonna happen to Josiah while I got breath in my body. We'll be back here to catch you on your eighteenth birthday, you hear?"

"I h-hear."

He nodded, offering her a little smile. "That's my girl."

She nodded back at him, but her eyes immediately filled with tears again, and she exhaled on a sob even louder than the ones before, letting her head hang down in sorrow.

He couldn't fucking bear it anymore.

"Don't make me spank you, Miss Virginia," he said severely, and she whipped her head to face him, snorting in such an unladylike way, it made him laugh. "Oh, you look a sight, princess."

But her surprised smile was fleeting, and her mouth trembled into a deep frown as she wailed, "Robby Hanson's got strep throat," before letting her head fall back onto Cain's chest.

Cain frowned. *Who the fuck is Robby Hanson, and why the fuck is he making Ginger cry?* The word *ass whuppin'* flashed in his mind as she continued.

"He was my d-date tonight. To h-homecomin'. My first f-formal. I think W-Woodman m-made him ask me, but I don't care. I w-was excited. I got a n-new d-dress and shoes, and now . . . now . . ."

"Now you don't have no one to take you."

She nodded against his chest, the hair on the top of her head rubbing against his throat, sending a bolt of heat from the pulse in his neck to the pulse in his cock and making it twitch. His eyes flared with panic, and he bit the side of his cheek until he tasted blood, willing his cock not to harden while he was sitting beside Ginger.

"It was h-hard enough startin' school this year after bein' h-homeschooled my whole life. They all t-treat me like I'm b-breakable or some sort of a w-weirdo, but . . . but I was goin' to f-fix that toni—"

"Gin," he said.

"What?" she asked, leaning back to look up at him.

"I'll take you," he said, shocked to hear the words leave his mouth. He didn't feel them coming, didn't know they were on their way from his brain to his lips until he heard them in his ears.

"You will?" she gasped, her face changing from mournful to joyful in the space of a second.

"If it'll make you stop cryin', then hell, yeah. I'll take you."

She gasped, a smile taking over her entire face as she threw her arms around his neck. And before, he'd barely noticed that their thighs were flush, but now—with her breasts pressed against his T-shirt—he tracked every place his body touched hers, and suddenly she was everywhere.

"Wanna know somethin' else?" she asked, her warm breath kissing his throat.

"Sure," he said, trying to stay calm, to ignore the way her body pressed against him.

"I was gonna kiss him. Robby. He was gonna be my first kiss."

His heart pounded as his arms wound around her, pulling her close to him, as close as he could, until her breasts were crushed against his chest. His cock sprang to life, hardening and thickening behind his jeans, wanting more from this beloved, forbidden girl.

"Never been kissed?"

"Not yet."

Blood pounded in his head as he reviewed what she was saying, and though he willed himself to ignore her thinly veiled suggestion, he found he couldn't. After three years of longing

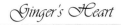

and a lifetime ahead, he just couldn't leave the moment alone.

"You still want that first kiss?" he asked close to her ear, his voice low and husky.

Her breath, which was hot and sweet on his neck, hitched. "You offerin'?"

"What if I say yes?" he whispered.

She drew away from him, still nestled within the circle of his arms, but her eyes, the gorgeous brown eyes that had haunted his dreams for a thousand nights or more, searched his face, caressing it, reading it, understanding it. He held his breath, his stomach in knots, his eyes flicking to her lips, before meeting her gaze again.

"I still want that first kiss," she murmured, raking her teeth across her bottom lip. She dropped her eyes to his mouth and let her hot gaze linger there.

Cain's tongue darted out, wetting his lips instinctively, his breathing shallow and ragged as he stared down at her.

"You're sure?"

Her eyes slid up slowly to meet his, certain and clear. "I'm sure."

Cain reached up for her cheek, placing his palm against the softness of her skin reverently as his fingers threaded into her golden hair. Her eyes fluttered and closed, and he touched her jaw with his other hand, cupping her face, drinking in the sight of Ginger in stunning submission as he leaned closer, lowering his lips to hers.

For all that this might have been Cain's millionth kiss, the most terrifying thing about kissing Ginger was that it felt like the very first. Like no one had ever come before. Like no one could ever come after. And as his heart thundered painfully behind his ribs, he knew—for the very first time, after years of hunting—

what it felt like to surrender.

Soft as rose petals, her lips were parted and still beneath his. She gasped as his mouth settled on hers, stealing his breath and making him dizzy. He closed his eyes, tightening his grip on her face as he nuzzled her nose, taking her top lip between his, then her bottom, then gently swiping the tip of his tongue along the loose seam of her lips. She opened to him like a flower to sunshine, her back arching as she touched his tongue with her own, trembling in his arms as he pulled her still closer.

He slid his tongue slowly along the length of hers, swallowing her moan as she arched against him instinctively. His fingers twined in the lush waves of her hair, holding her head in place as he tilted his face to the other side, resealing his lips over hers. Blood rushed furiously to his groin, and he growled, his hunger mounting as he claimed her mouth, as he memorized the taste of her, the way she felt in his arms, the way it sounded when she gasped, breathing him into her lungs.

His own breath was fast and shallow, and though he'd already stolen more than a moment from her, already betrayed the cousin he loved as a brother, he wanted so much more. He wanted her lying beneath him, her soft eyes encouraging him, the tight walls of her virgin sex pulsing around him. He wanted to watch her face as he made love to her and feel her wild heart pound against his as he held her in his arms for hours after. He wanted, he wanted, he wanted—

Without warning her, he jerked his head away from her, breaking off their kiss as his fingers, still threaded deeply into her hair, flexed and froze in horror.

This wasn't some girl with dyed hair that he'd picked up at the goddamned Gas & Sip! This was Ginger! The princess. Everything good and sweet and pure. And his lips . . . God, his lips had been in places he could hardly bear to think about right now, but he certainly had no business tarnishing her sweet lips with his.

And fuck. She was Woodman's Ginger, not his. She deserved someone like his cousin—someone upstanding and smart and clean who hadn't fucked half the county, who had a decent future mapped out for his life that he could offer to a girl like her. Hell, hell, hell, fuck. He panted raggedly, sliding his hands from her hair and wincing as he realized the full magnitude of what he'd just done.

"Cain?" she murmured, her eyes fluttering open, drunk and dark with lust.

His heart clenched, and he swallowed over the lump in his throat, and, God almighty, if he was wrecked one second ago, now he was ruined for life. She raised her hand to press her fingertips against her lips, and her eyes, so soft and sweet, were languid as her body leaned toward his and her chest heaved with breaths as labored as his own. Until he died, he'd have this vision in his head of Princess Ginger's blinding, angelic beauty.

"Sorry," he said harshly, edging away from her.

"No," she said quickly, dropping her fingers to reach for his arm. "It's okay. It's fine. I wanted—"

"You're a little girl. You don't know what you want," he said, his voice cold. He scooted away from her and stood up in retreat, leaving her hand suspended and lonely in midair.

"I *do* know!" she insisted, turning her whole body to look up at him. "God, Cain, I've *always* known! It's *always* been you."

I've always *known! It's* always *been you!*

The words cracked like a whip in his head, half heaven and half hell. Heaven because she wanted him and always had. Hell because it could never, ever be.

He put his hands on his hips, looking down at her, unable to process the feelings that were taking up all the space in his chest, barely leaving space for air, for his beating heart, for sane thought. He had to get out of here. Now.

"I'll, uh, I'll be seein' you, Gin."

"O-okay," she said softly, still staring up at him, fear edging out the lust that had made her eyes so soft and shiny. They were wary now. Worried. And he fucking hated it. "Cain, please don't be sorry."

But I am sorry. I'm sorry I know how kissin' you feels because I'm never goin' to be able to forget it. I'm sorry I betrayed my cousin's trust. I'm sorry I touched you when I had no right.

"Yeah," he said, swiping his thumb over his lips.

"I'll see you at seven?"

Seven? Oh Lord. Homecoming. No. He couldn't go. It was out of the question.

But her eyes looked up at him, exquisite and pleading, and he heard himself answer, "Uh, yeah. Seven."

Then he turned and hurried through the hayloft, down the ladder, by the stables, and out onto the gravel lot. He put on his helmet, straddled his bike, and kicked up the stand. Without looking up or looking back, he sped away, shame and guilt chasing him down the gravel driveway and onto the road that led to the distillery.

He was a thief who'd taken what wasn't his . . .

. . . and a fool who wanted what he could never have.

Chapter 5

~ Woodman ~

"She's a beauty, sir," said Woodman to Ginger's father before gazing back at the newborn foal.

"That she is," said Ranger, who always rolled up his sleeves to be present at the birth of a new McHuid horse, no matter what other business might be pressing. "With a sire like Rollin' Thunder, we knew she'd be gorgeous."

Woodman rubbed Bit-O-Honey's nose, and the mare groaned softly. "You did real good, mama."

"*Wie ist sein Name*?" asked Uncle Klaus, his ice-blue eyes flashing with rare excitement. "Her name?"

Ranger huffed, looking at the dark brown foal. "Magnolia started namin' all the mares after candy, and I shoulda stopped her at some point, but I never had the heart. With a daddy like Rollin' Thunder, guess we'll go with Rolo. Sound good?"

"Rolo," said Uncle Klaus, testing the name in his heavy German accent. "*Ja.* I like it."

Woodman stepped away from Bit-O-Honey as she sprang

to her feet, feeling grateful that her heavy breathing had started to normalize after the stress of an hour-long labor. His uncle pulled the placenta away from Rolo's soft hair, and the baby struggled a bit at first, but finally made it up onto all four legs.

The three men chuckled and clapped for the tiny mare, but oblivious to their praise, she made a small sound of discontent, sniffing the air for her mama's teats. She stumbled twice, but finally made her way over, latching quickly and drinking her fill.

"Congrats again, sir," said Woodman, picking up a wool blanket off the grass and slinging it over his arm. He'd drop it in the basket by the tack room to be washed before heading up to the main house to see Ginger.

Ranger McHuid, his brown eyes the same color as Ginger's, looked up at Woodman from where he knelt on the grass. "We're sure goin' to miss you, son."

Woodman nodded, "I'll miss you too, sir."

"McHuid's won't be the same without him, will it, Klaus?"

Uncle Klaus cleared his throat. "*Nein.* We'll miss you, boy."

"Sure you won't reconsider college instead of the military, son?"

Woodman shook his head. "No, sir. Besides, the decision's in stone now. My cousin and I ship off to boot camp in the mornin'."

"*Oh! Scheisse!*" exclaimed Klaus, snapping his fingers. "That remind me. Cain was comin' to say *Auf Wiedersehen.*" He flicked his eyes to his watch, grimacing. "Prolly missed him. Now I'll haveta head inta town tonight."

Ranger shrugged. "I guess Cain'll understand that you were needed here to help foal the new mare, huh?"

Woodman highly doubted it.

Without actually admitting it aloud, Cain had made it as clear as possible how much he hated working at McHuid's, his moods increasingly sour as the years went by, his attitude jockeying between gruff and sullen whenever he was at work. Woodman, who loved just about everything about McHuid's, wondered, from time to time, if it had anything to do with the way his Uncle Klaus sometimes seemed to favor him over Cain. But that wasn't likely, was it? Cain had to know that all Uncle Klaus ever talked about was horses, a topic that made Cain's eyes roll before glazing over. Woodman and Uncle Klaus had an interest in common, and that was it. It wasn't like they had deep discussions about the meaning of life that Cain was missing out on.

Woodman adjusted the blanket in his arms and stuck out his hand. "I'll be sure to write, sir."

"To Ginger, you mean," said Ranger, standing up and taking the younger man's hand.

"With your permission."

"Hell, Woodman, you're practically family. You don't need my damn permission."

Woodman grinned. "Just want to do everythin' right."

"Which is why Magnolia and I have such high hopes for you and our little gal."

Woodman squeezed his hand before dropping it, then turned to his uncle. "Think you can keep this place runnin' without me?"

"Oh, *ja*," said Uncle Klaus, looking up at Woodman and nodding with hooded eyes. "But I be waitin' for you boys t'get home."

Pulling his uncle into an awkward embrace, Woodman

whispered by his ear, "I'll keep an eye on Cain, Uncle Klaus."

"*Ja.* He need watchin'."

"He'll be okay. I promise."

His uncle cleared his throat and drew away, swiping at his eyes as he knelt down and started checking the filly's hooves without another word.

"Guess that's it, then," said Woodman, and Ranger clapped him on the back one more time.

Leaning closer to Woodman, Ranger said softly, "I 'spect ole Cain can watch out for himself well 'nough. Don't get pulled into any of that hellion's shenanigans. Just bring *your* bones home safe, Josiah Woodman."

"Yes, sir. Good-bye, now," he responded, nodding at Ginger's father before turning away and heading back down the hill toward the barn. He'd clean up in Klaus's tack room bathroom before heading up to the main house to say good-bye to Ginger, then home for dinner with his parents and a good night's sleep before the 5 a.m. bus tomorrow.

Even though Annapolis had been Woodman's plan, a slick late-summer football field last August had resulted in a torn ACL, arthroscopic surgery, and several missed weeks of school. Losing football as an extracurricular activity had been the first blow, but the second was the drastic dip in his first-semester senior-year grades because he was out of school for surgery and rehab for so many weeks. He still applied to Annapolis in December, but received a rejection letter in April—his grades simply weren't competitive enough. To be accepted, he'd have to redo his senior year and reapply next December.

Because his father and grandfather had served directly out of high school, and Woodman felt strongly about honoring the family tradition, he had decided to enlist in the Navy instead. At

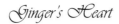

first, he was concerned that the September surgery would sideline him from enlisting, but after requesting his x-rays and full medical history right after graduation, MEPS had determined that Josiah's recovery was complete and ruled to allow his enlistment.

When Woodman had announced, at dinner with his parents, aunt, and cousin, that he had decided to join the Navy, Cain grinned at him and then promptly announced that he'd decided to do the same. Woodman wasn't sure when Cain had decided to enlist, though he strongly suspected it was at that same dinner table, the minute the words had left Woodman's mouth. He'd asked Cain several times if the Navy had been on his radar prior to his own announcement, but Cain never directly answered the question, just smirked and told Woodman that someone needed to look after him.

For as much as Cain had been, at times, the most infuriating part of Woodman's life, he couldn't deny the deep comfort he felt in knowing that they'd be tackling this hugely unknown new world together. In fact, they'd enrolled in the Navy's Buddy Program so they would be together for boot camp and their first couple of deployments. Without the pressures of home—of McHuid's, Cain's broken family, and Woodman's affluent one—Cain would surely show Woodman a different side. A less angry one. A more responsible one. Because he was fairly certain a more unhappy, less responsible Cain was impossible, and Woodman yearned for closeness with his only cousin.

Frankly Woodman didn't know what had stood between them over the past three years, but he felt strongly that an unspoken wedge separated them from true familial intimacy. It could have been a million things: the differences in their families' prosperity, Cain's parents' divorce, or the fact—as Woodman suspected—that Cain had some notions about Woodman being closer to his father, Klaus.

Or maybe it was the fact that they'd grown into vastly different men: Cain fucked everything in sight, loved his motorcycle the way Woodman loved horses, and got drunk down by the distillery every weekend, while Woodman spent his time studying, working at McHuid's, and spending his weekends in church.

They were as different as night from day, yes, but they were still cousins, and their increasing distance from each other bothered Woodman mightily. Whatever it was that had lodged so squarely between them, Woodman was ready, even anxious, for it to be eliminated. And he dearly hoped that embarking on this adventure together would give them a chance to renew the close bond they'd enjoyed as children.

Rounding the meadow, Woodman looked down at the barn at the bottom of the hill and was surprised to see two people sitting up in the doorway of the hayloft. He squinted from fifty yards away, and his heart lifted when he realized that it was Cain and Ginger. Maybe Cain had stopped by to catch her one more time before they shipped out tomorrow, since they'd be missing her birthday next week. Cupping his hands over his mouth to call to them, he stopped when he saw Cain reach for Ginger's face. She leaned toward him, closer and closer, tilting her head to the side until, until—

Woodman gasped, and the words of greeting got lodged in the terrible, instant lump in his throat, his hands falling listlessly by his side as he watched his cousin kiss Ginger, as he watched his indiscriminate lothario of a cousin pollute the pristine pink lips that Woodman had been planning to kiss for the very first time tonight when he bid her good-bye.

As he gasped, a soft, strangled sound of pain slipped from his lips, his eyes burning as he watched Cain wind his fingers through Ginger's blonde hair and pull her closer. There was no chasteness in this kiss, no brotherly farewell from an old friend. Their bodies were flush against each other, Ginger's breasts flattened against Cain's chest as she arched her back in a wanton way that made Woodman's fists curl in protest.

He didn't blame Ginger. Though he suspected she knew how he felt about her, his feelings were, as yet, undeclared. But Cain. Fucking Cain. Ginger was *his* girl, *his* love, *his* future, and Cain *knew* it. But per usual, Cain was thinking with his dick. He didn't give a shit that he was sliding a knife between his cousin's shoulder blades. He likely didn't give a fuck that a kiss like that was a sort of promise to a nice girl like Ginger (and Woodman was positive that Cain had zero honorable intentions toward her). He clenched his teeth together, his whole body rigid with fury and heartache because he was certain that all Cain thought of, as always, was his own pleasure, without a shred of regard for anyone else's feelings or anyone else's heart.

Between the bitter sting of his cousin's betrayal and the terrible ache of watching Ginger kiss his cousin, Woodman could barely breathe, and he bent over, bracing his hands on his knees and trying to catch his breath. When he looked up again a moment later, their positions had changed drastically. Now Cain was standing up with his hands on hips, his expression troubled, his body angled for retreat. Ginger, on the other hand, still sat with her legs dangling over the hayloft opening, and Woodman couldn't read her expression since she looked away from him, up at Cain, but she worried her hands in her lap.

They exchanged a couple of words that Woodman

couldn't hear from where he stood, then Cain disappeared into the darkness of the barn, only to reappear a moment later downstairs. Without looking back up at Ginger even once, he hurried to his bike, put on his helmet, and sped away, his face set in stone. Angry. Unhappy. Pissed. Cain was deeply shaken, and Woodman would be willing to place bets on where Cain was headed to make himself comfortably numb until he showed up hungover at the Greyhound station tomorrow.

As for Ginger? She looked forlorn as she watched Cain go, holding on to her bottom lip with her teeth, a slight frown troubling her usually sunny expression. Then suddenly, unexpectedly, her lips lifted into a brilliant smile, transforming her whole face to such beauty, Woodman sucked a hiss of breath through his teeth. She was happy about something, and it had everything to do with Cain. She looked down at her watch, then slipped back into the barn. Woodman watched as she came out of the barn on her cell phone.

"Gran? It's me. Cain's goin' to take me!" Her smile was so brilliant, even from this distance, it could have blinded him. Slowly, so as not to draw attention, Woodman crouched down behind a boulder and some tall grass to shield himself as she walked up the hill toward her grandmother's cottage.

"Yes, I'm serious! He's takin' me to homecomin', Gran." She giggled, the sound musical and happy as she walked by the place where Woodman hid. "Help me get ready? I'm headed up to the manor house now. He'll be back for me in two hours!"

As soon as she was far enough along the path, Woodman stood up and headed quickly down the hill to the parking area behind the barn, where his secondhand BMW waited.

He wasn't sure what the fuck was going on, because he'd arranged for Robby Hanson, one of the probies on last year's football team and a nice kid who'd been warned against making any untoward moves on her, to be Ginger's escort. Now, somehow, safe little Robby was out of the picture, and Cain, the big bad Wolfram, was in it.

But Woodman had seen the look on Cain's face as he zoomed away from McHuid's as fast as he could. Whatever Ginger *believed* had transpired between them, Woodman knew that Cain *wasn't* coming back tonight. And his heart lurched at the thought of Ginger spending hours waiting for Cain before she finally realized he wasn't coming. She thought she was going to a dance; instead, she'd end her evening with her heart in shreds. And the truth is, despite everything he'd just witnessed, Woodman loved her way too much to let that happen.

Which meant he needed to find Cain.

***

Although Woodman wasn't a stranger to the distillery grounds, he hadn't treated the crumbling, overgrown complex like a debauched combination of the local brothel and bar in which Cain had indulged over the past three years.

From time to time, his Aunt Sarah would call him and ask him to find Cain—generally after he'd skipped a night at home—and Woodman always ended up finding his cousin at Glenn River. He wasn't alone there, either. There was a whole crew of Apple Valley kids who frequented the distillery grounds, holding loud, raging parties on Saturday nights and hooking up in the shadows of the many outbuildings. Since Cain was a regular, it was never too tough to find him.

Woodman parked his car by the brush near the abandoned gates and walked purposefully along the chain-link fence to one of the many places where there was an opening. Slipping through it, he heard music on the breeze, likely coming from the old peristyle on the far left side of the property. Woodman circled the main building, built to resemble a castle back in the 1930s. He knew the way like the back of his hand, walking over crumbling concrete overgrown with weeds, through the well-trod dirt path into the high grass, taking a right at the rusted water tower, until he found a bunch of his former classmates gathered in one of the distillery outbuildings.

"Hey, Woodman!" cried Kim Nadel, one of his friends from senior trig. She slipped under a metal bar and ran the few steps to meet him, wrapping him in a big hug before he could even say hello.

"Hey, Kim," he said, patting her back.

They'd gone out a couple of times, but Woodman had never let himself get very serious about anyone. He'd given his heart to someone else a long time ago, and he didn't mind waiting for the girl of his dreams to grow up. Drawing away, he grinned at his friend. "Thought you were at Kentucky Wesleyan. What the heck you doin' here?"

"Just home for the weekend," she said, smiling back at him.

Kim, with her curly brown hair and bright blue eyes, was a pretty girl, and the way she checked him out told him she wouldn't mind spending a little time with him on his last night in Apple Valley. "Heard you're headed to boot camp tomorrow."

He nodded, placing his hands on his hips. "That's right."

"Chicago?" she asked.

"Town's called Great Lakes," he said. "Real near Chicago."

"Surprised everyone when Cain enlisted, too."

Woodman's eyes narrowed at the mention of his cousin, his anger rushing back quickly and crashing over him like a wave. He looked over Kim's shoulder but didn't see Cain's jet-black hair in the crowd of partying teens.

"You seen him around?"

"Cain?" she asked. "Uh, yeah. Sure. He just got here a little while ago. Saw him talkin' to Gina and Nicole over there by the lower pool."

She gestured to the rounded end of the peristyle, then turned back to face Woodman, placing a hand on his arm. "But don't go runnin' off. Knowin' Cain, he'll still be here an hour from now. Why don't you and me . . . catch up?"

The problem was, if Cain was still here an hour from now, he'd be standing up Ginger, a circumstance Woodman couldn't bear if there was any way for him to intercede on Ginger's behalf.

Woodman shrugged and gave her a sorry smile. "Got plans tonight. Sorry, honey."

"Always liked you, Woodman," she said, taking a step closer to him, her hand squeezing his arm.

Gently Woodman removed her hand, bringing it to his lips and kissing the back of it before letting it go. "You're a sweetheart, Kim. But I gotta go find Cain. Another time?"

Her eyes were cooler as she put her hands in her pockets and took a step back. "Sure, Woodman. Good luck. You know, with everythin'."

"You too, Kim."

Turning away from her, Woodman sidestepped into the crowd of bodies drinking, smoking, and dancing in the peristyle. The building was a thirty-foot-long rectangle with a large circle at the end, not unlike the shape of a white dandelion puff on top of a thin green stalk. The middle of the rectangle had a long pool of water, and it was flanked by large, once-white marble columns, like something out of ancient Greece or Rome. In the rounded area, there was a vaulted ceiling over a circular pool, and rusted railings where girls and boys leaned beside one another drinking and talking. Two sets of stairs on either side of the pool led to a lower walkway closer to the water, where more kids drank, smoked, and gyrated against each other to the beat of the music. And there, on the lower level, by the water, Woodman spotted Cain.

Leaning against the railing, he was talking to two girls, both of whom appeared utterly enraptured. Woodman set his jaw and made his way down the stairs, stopping alongside Cain with purpose.

"Cain."

"Cuz!" exclaimed Cain, his face denting from his goddamn dimples as he pulled Woodman into an enthusiastic embrace. "Hardly ever see your face here! What the fuck you up to, son?"

Cain smelled of cigarettes and beer, and his over-cheerful demeanor suggested he'd already had a few beers in the twenty minutes he'd been there.

Woodman, who'd remained stiff throughout Cain's warm greeting, pushed his cousin away, willing himself to control his rage. "We need to talk."

Cain leaned back slightly, his eyes scanning Woodman's face. "We do?"

"Yeah. Not here."

"Here'll do for me," said Cain slowly, crossing his arms over his chest. "Ain't you noticed I got company?"

Woodman shot a quick look at Gina and Nicole, whom he recognized as seniors at Apple Valley High. "Ladies, would you excuse me and Cain?"

"*Excuse* you?" asked Nicole flirtatiously. "Honey, we'd rather you *stay*. We'd like to show you *both* a good time the night before you head off to war."

"We're not going to war," said Woodman, working to keep the edge out of his voice.

"Boot camp. Whatever," said Gina, shrugging as she licked her red-painted lips. "It's so hot that y'all are headin' off to defend America. Hashtag DoubleDubHeroes."

Woodman rolled his eyes and turned back to Cain. "I need to talk to you. Now."

Cain scoffed, raising a brown beer bottle to his lips and chugging it slowly, his eyes on Woodman's the whole time. Woodman knew what his cousin was doing: he was trying to figure out why Woodman wanted to talk. He knew from experience that if his momma wanted him home, Woodman would have just said so by now. *Why does he need to talk to me?* Woodman could practically hear the question humming in the air between them.

Finally Cain lowered the bottle, his eyes widening as he nodded almost imperceptibly. "You saw. With the princess."

Woodman flinched, his nostrils flaring as he clenched his teeth and swallowed. He felt his fingers curl into fists by his sides, and he willed them to be still, though they longed to fly from his sides of their own accord.

"I did," he bit out.

"Didn't mean nothin'," said Cain, looking down at the ground, a hint of pink coloring his freshly shaven cheeks. "Forget it."

"Can't."

"Try, Josiah." He looked up at his cousin and shrugged. "It just . . . happened. Didn't mean a fuckin' thing." When his cousin didn't answer, his eyes narrowed in annoyance. "Get over it."

"What'd you promise her, Cain?" asked Woodman, his voice a low, focused growl.

They had attracted a small crowd. In addition to Gina and Nicole, who were still standing across from them, in fascinated silence, two or three other kids had quieted down to see what was going on between the Dub Twins.

Cain tilted his beer up again, finishing the last of it. "None of your fuckin' business, cuz."

Woodman moved fast as lightning, his reflexes faster on account of his sobriety. His fist slammed into his cousin's cheek, as good as a sucker punch and twice as hard. Cain's neck whipped back, the empty beer bottle falling from his hand and smashing onto the narrow concrete walkway under their feet. A few chips of glass slipped into the water, splashing before gurgling into the greenish murk.

It took Cain a few seconds to recover, but he swung at Woodman, missing him with one fist, but connecting to his ribs with the other, and Woodman groaned from the impact.

"Fuck *you*, Cain!" he yelled, wrangling the back of Cain's neck with his elbow, his other fist smashing into Cain's nose with a furious undercut. "What . . . did you . . . fuckin' . . . promise her?"

Cain reached forward and grabbed his cousin's legs in a giant bear hug, pulling Woodman off balance, and they both fell to the ground, Cain landing on top of his cousin and straddling him with strong thighs that had seen a decade of manual labor on McHuid Farm.

"Stop fuckin' hittin' me, Woodman!"

Woodman struggled under his cousin, but when Cain took him down, he'd pinned his cousin's arms against his sides and a piece of broken glass was gouging into his arm.

"Admit it!" yelled Woodman, fury making him writhe beneath Cain to no avail. "Admit that you promised to take her tonight!"

Cain swiped at his nose, which was bleeding, though it didn't appear to be broken. "If I let you up, don't you fuckin' hit me, Josiah. I fuckin' mean it. You hit me, I'll hit back. And harder. You hear?" Woodman nodded once. "I'll let you up, and we'll go talk."

Cain gave him one last meaningful look, then rolled off him, springing to his feet and offering his cousin a hand from a safe distance. Woodman ignored it, standing up and pushing through the assembled crowd like a bull, up the stairs and into the upper level of the peristyle. He stalked down the long rectangular alleyway flanked with mossy, once-elegant columns until he came to the end, then he took a few more steps into the tall grass and stood with his back to the building, silently fuming, waiting for Cain to join him.

A moment later, he felt a hand on his shoulder and shrugged it away, turning to face his cousin.

"You *knew*," he whispered, unable to keep the deep hurt out of his voice. "You fuckin' *knew* how I feel about her. How could you fuckin' make a move on her? On *her*?"

Cain flinched, hanging his head as he stared down at the ground. When he looked up again, his expression was sorry. "It didn't *mean* anythin'."

"You say that one more time, and I will break your fuckin' nose."

"You are too tightly wired, Josiah!" yelled Cain. "Fuck me! I'm *sorry* I kissed her. I shouldn't'a done that, but it's over and done, and I can't take it back."

Woodman took a deep breath, trying to calm down. "Why

are you takin' her to the fuckin' dance in the first place?"

"Her date got sick or somethin'."

Woodman tried desperately not to flinch. "So she asked *you* to take her?"

Hell, he'd only gotten her a date in the first place because he didn't think she'd want to be escorted by someone like him, who'd already graduated. He assumed she'd want to go with someone her own age. Fuck, if she'd been fine going with someone not still in high school, *he'd* have fucking offered to escort her. As it was, it hurt like hell that she hadn't come to him when things fell through with Robby.

Cain shrugged. "I offered. She was all sad and cryin' . . . and . . . Fuck, Josiah. What the fuck do you want from me?"

"*What the fuck do I want from you?*" Woodman repeated, his voice stuffed with incredulity and anger. "There is a girl who we have known all our fuckin' lives, and today you kissed her like the world is endin'. And fuck, that sucks, Cain. That sucks for me because I love her, but there's a bigger problem now. She is *expectin'* you to take her to a goddamned high school dance tonight, and I will be *damned* if I let you stand her up. So you tell me, Cain, are you plannin' to head back to McHuid's and fuckin' take her?"

Cain's face was stone as he stared back at his cousin. "No."

Josiah ran a hand through his hair, his face twisting up in frustration and anger. "Did you or did you not say you'd take her to the fuckin' dance?"

Cain ran his thumb over his lower lip and shook his head. "She was so fuckin' sad . . ."

"So you said you'd take her to a dance."

Cain nodded curtly.

"Then you better quit drinkin' because you've got a fuckin'

date tonight and you're goin' to fuckin' take her to homecomin', Cain, or I will beat you bloody until I can't stand up no more." Woodman trembled from the conflicting mess of feelings inside. Betrayal. Hurt. Anger. Sadness. But his love for Ginger trumped all other feelings. He concentrated on her lovely face in his head as he added, "You are *not* standin' her up while I got breath in my body."

Cain's eyes were wild and cold as he looked at his cousin. His expression was fierce but inscrutable, even for Woodman, who knew him so well. He read a mixture of frustration and sadness, anger and regret, but there was so much more—and for a moment, Woodman felt like he was seeing the root of the deep conflict between them. The distance that Woodman had felt for years now was simmering and seething just beneath the surface of all the commonplace emotions Woodman could identify. But before he could figure it out, Cain dropped Woodman's eyes and looked down at the ground, muttering, "You take her, Josiah."

"She's not fuckin' *expectin'* me, you monumental asshole. You fuckin' kissed her, Cain, Might have meant diddly-squat to you, but it fuckin' *meant* somethin' to her." Woodman put his hands on his hips, shaking his head in despair. "Jesus, brother. You can't keep treatin' people like this. Like shit on the bottom of your shoes."

"It was a mistake," said Cain softly, after sucking a breath through his teeth, the blood from his nose starting to dry a dull maroon on his upper lip. "She was sad about us leavin', sad that her date to the dance got sick and canceled. I was only aimin' to comfort her a little, and then . . . and then . . ."

"Your fuckin' tongue found its way down her throat."

Cain's head snapped up, and he searched Woodman's eyes. His voice was low and taunting when he murmured, "You know what, Josiah, you self-righteous fuckin' prick? She wasn't exactly complainin'."

Woodman's arms shot back, and his hands flattened on Cain's chest, pushing with all his might. Cain stumbled backward, ending up on his ass. He didn't get up, sitting in the grass and looking up at his cousin in defeat.

"Shut up already and take her to the goddamn dance, Josiah. Just fuckin' take her," said Cain, his voice resigned, the frustration and anger seeping from his eyes until only sorrow remained. "You know you want to."

Woodman nodded, staring down at his cousin in disgust. He spat on the ground right near Cain's hip, then swiped the back of his hand across his mouth. "Fine. I will. I will clean up your mess once again." He started to turn away, then paused and looked down at Cain, hands on his hips. The setting sun shone brightly in Woodman's eyes, which meant he was barely able to make out Cain's face. "But this is the last time. You hear me, Cain? The *last* time. You're on your own from now on."

Cain, who'd rested his elbows on his bent knees, looked up at Woodman, blocking the sun, and his icy blue eyes flashed white-hot in the dying light. "We're headed to boot camp tomorrow. Together. In the Buddy Program."

Woodman raised his chin, looking down his nose with wide, furious eyes. "Well, that is just a sorry fuckin' coincidence now because I am finished cleanin' up after you, *buddy*. Sink or swim startin' tomorrow, but you'll do it on your own. I ain't steppin' in for you ever again. You ain't my problem no more, Cain."

"Josiah—"

"No more," Woodman repeated firmly, then he turned and walked away.

***

As he pulled into the circular driveway in front of his parents' white plantation-style mansion, Belle Royale, Woodman looked at the clock on the dashboard. Six fifteen. He had but forty minutes to shower, shave, dress, and find some flowers in his momma's garden before driving back to McHuid's. And though, yes, he knew that some part of Ginger might be disappointed that he was taking her instead of Cain, Woodman's excitement grew with every passing minute because tonight was their first date. And though he wished it had happened a different way, he couldn't deny that there was no one on earth with whom he'd rather spend his final night at home.

But first, he had to break the news to his parents that he wouldn't be joining them for dinner. Walking into the house, he beelined through the breezeway to the back patio, where he found his parents sipping a chilled chardonnay and watching the sunset over the rolling pastures behind their estate.

"Josiah!" greeted his mother. "We expected you an hour ago! Go change, dear. Our reservation at the country club is for six thirty. You'll have just enough time for a cocktail with us before we go."

She tried to smile at him but sniffled a little, her eyes sad.

"Aw, Momma," said Woodman, walking through the open French doors and sitting gingerly on the arm of her wicker chair. "Don't, now."

Drawing a handkerchief out of her sleeve, she dabbed at her eyes. "I just don't understand why you'd go and enlist."

"We've been over this," he said, seeking his father's eyes for solidarity, but his father took a sip of his wine and looked away, ashing his cigar on the patio bricks. "I wanted to serve. I missed my shot at Annapolis, and I—"

"You could've gone to college and done ROTC," his mother half wailed. "You could've gone to Officer Candidate School after you got your bachelor's degree. But enlist? Like a common—"

"Now, Sophie," said his father, letting his rocking chair rock forward so he could pat his wife's knee gently. He looked up at his son. "What your mother's tryin' to say is that enlistin' is fine for someone like Cain, what with his low character and all those danged stunts he pulled in high school, gettin' suspended every other month and such, but you? You could've done your service another way."

"A *safer* way," put in Sophie.

Woodman scowled. "And here I thought you'd be proud of me for servin' my country."

"Dang it, Josiah, we are proud of you, boy! Just wanted better for you, that's all. We're worried about you."

Woodman nodded at his father, then put his arm around his mother's trembling shoulders. "I'll be home for a few days after boot camp, Momma. And it's not like I enlisted in the Army or the Marines—they're on the ground in Iraq. At the very worst, I'll be on a boat in the Gulf."

"Pastor Mitchell said a s-suicide bomber could c-crash a plane into a-a boat," answered his mother, sobbing into her handkerchief.

"Then Pastor Mitchell's a jackass," grumbled his father, huffing in annoyance. "What's he about, puttin' such ideas in your head? Ain't he supposed to comfort his danged flock?"

"I *know* you're not insultin' Pastor Mitchell!" said Sophie, clasping her hands together with indignation.

"Don't get your feathers all ruffled, Sophie," said his father. "Just sayin' it ain't no good puttin' maudlin thoughts in the boy's head with him leavin' tomorrow. Gotta think positive, now." He stood up and grabbed the bottle of wine out of the bucket where it chilled and refilled her drink before looking at his son. "Go on and change now, son. We'll head over to the club in a—"

"I'm sorry," said Woodman, dropping his arm from his mother's thin shoulders and standing up between them. "I'm not goin' to be able to join you for dinner."

"Why, Josiah!"

"But, son, we were expectin'—"

"It's homecomin' tonight, and Ginger's date canceled on her, so—"

His mother's face darkened. "So you're takin' Ginger to the dance. Instead of spendin' your final night home with your momma, who loves you."

"Momma, try to understand—she got stood up and has no one to take her. I'm sorry to miss dinner, but I can't let the young lady sit at home alone if I'm able to be her escort." His mother's brows furrowed deeply, but Woodman had made the perfect argument, and he knew it. She gave him a thin smile, and he turned to his father. "Can I borrow your tux, sir?"

"Course, son."

His mother sniffled delicately, reaching up to wipe away the last of the wetness on her cheeks. "I just hope that gal knows what a treasure you are, Josiah."

"Least I could do. Her date got strep throat." *And her other date is a bona fide asshole.*

"That's just fine." His father cleared his throat meaningfully. "A real reminder of what you got waitin' at home, son."

Woodman felt his cheeks flare with heat as he nodded at

his father. Though he appreciated the fact that his parents and the McHuids expected him and Ginger to end up together, sometimes it felt like there were a few too many cooks in that particular kitchen.

"Yes, sir."

"We'll drive you to the station tomorrow mornin'," said his mother. "*Just us three.* We can say our good-byes then."

"Yes, Momma. Wouldn't have it any other way."

Giving her son a somewhat happier smile, Sophie Woodman nodded, whisking her perfectly manicured fingers at him. "Well, scoot then! Go get ready for your dance, handsome."

He kissed his mother on the cheek and nodded to his father, leaving them alone in quiet elegance as the sun slipped below the horizon.

Chapter 6

~ Ginger ~

"Gran!" she exclaimed, bursting into her grandmother's kitchen, holding her homecoming dress in one hand and a large canvas bag in the other. "I'm here!"

She hung the dress on the coat hook by the door and placed the bag, which held hot rollers, makeup, three jewelry options, two shoe options, and four bottles of perfume, on one of two kitchen chairs. Scattered all around the small kitchen were taped-up moving boxes, which only multiplied as Ginger headed through the small dining room and into the screened porch.

"Doll baby," her grandmother greeted her, reaching for the cane that had become omnipresent. "Your parents . . . leave yet?"

Ginger's parents, who were on the board of the Apple Valley Country Club, had dinner plans tonight, which left Ginger to get ready at her grandmother's cottage. All things considered, it was for the best. They wouldn't have been pleased to hear that Ginger was being escorted to the dance by Cain and may have even forbidden her to go. Better to apologize later than ask permission now.

"No, Gran, don't get up," said Ginger, bending down to kiss her grandmother's cheek. "Daddy's still in the pasture with Bit-O-Honey—she had a girl!—but Momma left a while ago. She needed to check on the centerpieces."

"Magnolia does like . . . things . . . perfect."

Though her grandmother's mind was as sharp as ever, her body had become a minefield of tics and trembles over the past few months. The tremors had gotten worse, her physical movements had slowed to a tortoise pace, and she had trouble walking and balancing, resulting in several serious falls and finally necessitating a move to Silver Springs, the local retirement center/nursing home. Ginger's father had secured his mother their best-possible accommodations: a private suite with two bedrooms, a living room, a galley kitchen, and a bathroom. It was a lovely apartment, and Gran would be well cared for, with dining and activities available for all residents, plus twenty-four-hour nursing assistance and the adjacent nursing home for when that day came.

But, for the first time in Ginger's fifteen years, her gran wouldn't be living in the cottage one hundred feet from the manor house. She'd be living all the way across town, and the timing—Gran's move was scheduled for the same weekend that Cain and Woodman were leaving for boot camp—made it all the harder for Ginger, whose loneliness encroached at an almost unbearable speed.

Gran spoke slowly, struggling to keep her words clear. "You look . . . brighter'n . . . a new cop-per penny. Good to . . . see a smile . . . back on your . . . pretty face."

"Can you keep a secret?" asked Ginger, sitting down in the

chair beside her grandmother and grinning.

"You know . . . I can."

She tugged her grandmother's hand from her lap and embraced it between hers to keep it from shaking. "We kissed, Gran! Cain kissed me."

"Oh, my!" she gasped.

"My first kiss," sighed Ginger, beaming.

"And? How . . . was it?"

"Heaven," said Ginger, releasing her grandmother's hand gently and sitting back dramatically in her rocker. "Pure heaven."

"So it's Cain . . . is it?"

"Always, Gran. It was always Cain," said Ginger softly.

"Why?" asked her grandmother, a flicker of worry flaring in her eyes, "when Josiah . . . is so . . . good to . . . you?"

A pang of guilt made Ginger frown for a moment. "It's not that I don't love Woodman."

"So you . . . love them . . . both?"

"Of course," said Ginger. "Just in different ways."

"Cain sets . . . your blood . . . on fire."

Ginger blushed, looking up to meet her grandmother's eyes. "He does."

"And Woodman?"

Ginger covered her heart with one palm. "He's . . . he's . . ."

"Your heart?" asked Gran hopefully, flicking her blue eyes to Ginger's hand.

"My *friend*."

During the lonely years when Ginger was homeschooled, her grandmother had become her most trusted confidante, her most intimate friend. She didn't shy away from any conversation topic with Gran, but she also knew of Gran's strong preference for Woodman over Cain.

"Gran," she said evenly, "I can't make myself feel somethin' that just isn't there."

Her grandmother nodded, forcing a smile that looked lopsided. "Fair 'nough."

Again the flicker of worry in her grandmother's eyes.

Again Ginger ignored it, hopping up to plug in her rollers on the kitchen counter.

"Can you believe he's takin' me to the dance tonight?" called Ginger from the kitchen. "It's like a dream come true!"

She heard her grandmother grumble something unintelligible, but she didn't ask Gran to repeat herself, feeling defensive on Cain's behalf. It made her crazy that no one seemed to see the good in Cain—the sense of adventure, the humor, the sparkle, the swagger. Ginger loved these things about him, but everyone else—her parents, her gran, Woodman, his parents, even Cain's own father—*everyone* seemed to disapprove of Cain. And she hated it because she found so much to love.

"Always hoped . . ."

"Hoped . . . what?" asked Gran as Ginger reappeared in the porch doorway.

She shrugged. "That he'd *see* me. You know, not a little sister or a childhood friend or his boss's daughter. But *me*."

"And you . . . think he's . . . seein' you now?"

Ginger nodded. "Of course. We kissed."

Her grandmother's lips twitched, and Ginger couldn't tell if it was the Parkinson's or her grandmother's censure of Cain. Deciding it was the latter, she crossed her arms over her chest in resentment.

"Why can't you like him?" she burst out. "Why can't *anyone* like him?"

"Not 'bout . . . likin' him . . . doll baby. It's 'bout whe-ther . . . or not . . . he's good for you."

"He is! I want him. I've always wanted him. How could it be bad to finally have what I've always wanted? Why can't you be happy for me?"

Her grandmother nailed Ginger with her eyes, which were suddenly as sharp and focused as they'd been two years ago. Gran's body quieted as though on command, and her voice was clear and firm when she said, "I don't trust him."

"Why?" she demanded. "Why not? What's he ever done?"

"Aside from . . . the arrests and . . . suspensions? Nothin'," her grandmother answered evenly, the hand resting on the rocker arm, twitching. "Nothin'. That's the . . . problem."

"How? He's done nothin' *wrong*, but still you—"

"Doll baby . . . he ain't done . . . nothin' *right* . . . either." Her grandmother sighed, the worry she'd managed to control flooding her eyes. "You know as . . . well as anyone . . . he's a rascal . . . and he's angry. I don't know . . . that he's got . . . a loyal bone . . . in his body. And his . . . reputation is . . ." She raised an eyebrow. ". . . reckless . . . at best."

Ginger stared at her grandmother, the chill of her reproof seeping into Ginger's skin like ice and making her cold and lonesome. She searched for memories of Cain, for thoughts of him, for the heat of his lips recently slanted across hers, but the warmth she found was fleeting, unsubstantial.

"But Gran . . ."

"I ain't sayin' . . . he's *bad*. But . . . I am sayin' . . . if there's a . . . good man . . . hidin' in there, I've yet to . . . see him. And I'd surely . . . *like* to see him . . . before I tell my . . .

only granddaughter that . . . she's bettin' on . . . the right horse."

"I love him," Ginger murmured, feeling forlorn, turning back into the kitchen to see if the rollers were hot.

"I know you . . . think so. But do you . . . really *know* him? Are you . . . really seein' him . . . clearly, doll baby?" he grandmother called, her voice weaker, which made Ginger feel bad. She was tiring out Gran.

Taking out her cream velvet scrunchie, Ginger used her fingers to part her hair in the middle, then took a handful of the light strands at her crown and rolled them around the hot roller before securing it with a U pin. She rolled up two more, thinking about Gran's question.

Do you really know *him?*

Certainly, when she was a child, she knew Cain well.

Since she had been homeschooled until high school, with year-round tutoring every morning, Ginger had had every afternoon of her childhood free to spend with Cain, and she was an encyclopedia of knowledge about him. She knew his favorite baseball team (the Cincinnati Reds), his favorite food (ribs, lots of sauce), the girl he'd wanted to take to his freshman homecoming (Kim something-or-other, a rich and pretty girl who ended up going with Woodman), the motorcycle make and model he dreamed of rebuilding one day (a BMW R 60/2), and the fact that, although he often played dumb with his father, he was completely fluent in German and knew just as much about horses as Klaus.

But beyond mere facts, she also knew the nuances of his voice, the way emotions played across the sharp angles of his face, the innocent touch of his rough fingers against her skin, the vulnerable way his eyes softened and dimples deepened when he smiled at her. She knew it all. She *felt* it all. And even if she never saw Cain Holden Wolfram's face after today, on the day she died, Ginger felt certain she would still recognize Cain's soul in its purest form.

Are you really seein' him clearly?

The problem was that Cain's soul dwelled in the most profound depths of Cain's heart, where it was carefully obscured. And since their shared and happy childhood, he'd matured on the uneven ground of his family's modest means and his parents' deeply unhappy marriage. And little by little, the vulnerability in his light blue eyes had chilled to glacial ice, and the rough touch of his fingers had become decidedly less innocent.

And no discussion of Cain, internal or otherwise, would be complete without acknowledging that her grandmother was right: his name was mud. Well known as the county punk, he was known for sneaking around, raising hell at the old distillery, and he'd been arrested not once, but twice, for disturbing the peace. Luckily no charges had been pressed so his record had remained clean, but he'd also pulled the fire alarm at the Apple Valley High School several times (and been suspended for it), and everyone knew he tore around the county on his motorcycle at all hours of the day and night.

From eavesdropping on her father and Klaus, Ginger knew his grades were just above passing and his teachers wouldn't write him recommendations for college. Didn't matter. He didn't end up applying anyway.

More than once, some floozy or other had shown up at McHuid Farm looking for Cain, a fact that would have definitely gotten him fired had Ranger not relied heavily on Klaus's expertise and advice. And though Cain showed up surprisingly faithfully for work, he was surly and distant, even, on occasion, to Ginger.

A hellion and a troublemaker, Cain was not considered a nice or appropriate young man, which just made him ten times more fascinating and somehow Ginger's besotted heart clung to the notion that the Cain she'd known as a child was still alive, shrouded under the debris of disappointment and pain. He was just a troubled teenager who'd eventually straighten out. In her heart of hearts, she still believed that the Reds-hat-wearing, rib-loving, German-speaking kid who opened his arms and caught her every birthday could be recovered if she could just love him enough.

She took a mirror out of her canvas bag and checked out her reflection, staring at the porcupine quills of cooling rollers sticking out of her skull. They'd give her big, bouncy waves, and because Cain had called her princess for as long as she could remember, she'd borrowed her mother's Sun Queen 1985 tiara, and tonight she planned to be every bit of the princess he imagined. With her hair started, it was time to put on her face. But first she wanted to answer Gran's questions.

But do you really know *him? Are you really seein' him clearly?*

Placing the mirror back in her bag, she stepped back onto the porch.

"Gran? The answer is . . ."

Her grandmother's head rested on the back of the wicker sofa, soft snoring sounds filling the small porch. Pulling a blanket from an untaped box, Ginger draped it over Gran gently, careful not to wake her.

". . . I know his heart," she said softly.

And if he'd let me love him, I could help him *know it again, too.*

"And I *do* see him clearly," she whispered, her voice breaking with uncertainty as her own heart asked, *Do you? Or do you just see what you* want *to see?*

Biting her bottom lip in troubled thought, she headed back into her grandmother's kitchen to finish getting ready for the dance alone.

***

An hour later, Ginger sat on the front porch swing at the main house, having helped her grandmother to bed, with promises that she'd stop by in the morning and tell her all about the dance.

Trading worries for excitement, Ginger had relived the kiss a hundred times by now, giggling as she perfected her makeup and slipped her dress over her head. The way his tongue had slid against hers, making secret places in her body come alive, as though he'd flicked a switch and turned her on for the first time in her life. The memory of his hands on her face made her tremble, and the way he'd tenderly nuzzled her nose with his made her sigh. She wanted so much more from him tonight—a hundred more kisses to keep her company during the long, lonely months ahead, when he'd be far away. She would ask him to write to her, and he would, wouldn't he? Of course he would, she assured herself. She didn't know a lot about boys, but a kiss like that was real, was almost a promise—it told her she meant something to him, it told her that tonight was just the beginning of a million happy nights spent together.

Only the beginning . . .

She smoothed her hands over the homecoming gown she'd selected with her mother three weeks ago, happy she'd have a chance to wear it after all. It was royal blue, with a fitted, strapless bodice and a full, chiffon skirt. The bodice had silver and crystal beadwork that would sparkle as she and Cain danced

across the Apple Valley High School gymnasium. Her blonde
waves were held back by her mother's shimmering tiara, and
she'd borrowed a diamond and sapphire tennis bracelet from her
mother's jewelry box too. Grinning at herself in Gran's bedroom
mirror, she had to admit she looked every bit the princess
tonight—no jodhpurs or muddy riding boots in sight—and she
desperately hoped that Cain liked what he saw. He'd been with
so many girls over the past few years, from what she could
gather. She wanted to stand out. She wanted to be special. She
wanted him to want her as desperately as she wanted him.

Playing with the straps of her matching royal blue purse,
she looked up as she heard an engine turn from the road into the
driveway. But when she saw Woodman's BMW at the bottom of
the hill, her eyebrows knitted together in consternation. *Dang it.*
He was probably coming to say good-bye before he left
tomorrow, and while she was glad of that—because she *wanted*
a few minutes to say good-bye to him—the timing was terrible.
Cain would be here any minute, and she didn't want for
Woodman to be standing by the sidelines as she drove away
with Cain.

It's not that Woodman had ever declared his feelings for
her per se, but they were clear in the warmth in his voice when
he spoke to her, in the way his eyes lit on her and lingered. He
was smitten with her, and Ginger knew it, though she was
committed to ignoring it, lest her rejection create an
awkwardness between them.

The last thing she wanted was awkwardness with
Woodman. He was her escort to every country club dance, her
most frequent riding companion, her confidant and best friend
and big brother. She was closest to Woodman after Gran, and
she loved him deeply, but the reality was that, regardless of his

tender voice and loving looks, Woodman had only "set her blood on fire" once, a long time ago, for a fleeting moment on her twelfth birthday. He was handsome and kind, but most of the time Ginger wished he'd find a girlfriend and stop looking at her with those eager, longing eyes full of the kind of love she didn't feel and couldn't return.

Anxious to make their farewell as genuine yet brief as possible, she waved to him as he pulled into the circular driveway, coming to a stop in front of her and cutting the engine. She fixed a smile on her face that came easily and naturally. Though she craved some freedom from his watchful eyes, she also knew she would miss him desperately once he was gone, and she knew they both deserved an unrushed, heartfelt good-bye.

"Hey there!" she called as he opened his car door. "Stoppin' by on your way to the club for dinner?"

He stood up, and she grinned at his carefully groomed blond hair. But her smile faded as her eyes dropped lower. Woodman was wearing a tux. Why was Woodman wearing a tux?

"Awful dressed up," she murmured, her eyes slipping to the bouquet of flowers in his hand. "And are those your momma's prized dahlias?"

"They are," he said, raising his arm to offer them to her.

She didn't take them, because she was frozen, searching his face for the answers to unasked questions.

His smile was off. It was kind of hopeful, but kind of sad, and maybe a little bit worried too. It was the way he'd smiled at her the morning she found out that Bit-O-Honey's last foal had died during the night—a gentle smile that didn't reach his eyes, that tried to calm her before he said words that he knew would hurt her.

She raised her chin, cutting her eyes to his, and she saw it there too. Anger made his green eyes darker and deeper, but the color was brightened with a thick topcoat of compassion that made her fists ball by her sides, a growing realization flushing her skin to uncomfortable warmth.

She gathered her courage. "Say what you have to say, Woodman."

"First," said Woodman, that gentle, sorrowful smile still in place, "let me tell you how stunnin' you look tonight, Gin. You are a—"

"You're just makin' it worse. Say it."

His jaw tightened, twitching once, twice, and the smile faded completely, until Woodman's face wasn't gentle or sorry anymore, just angry.

"He's not comin'."

"Who?" she murmured, the sound of a baby barn owl waking alone in the darkness, calling for its momma while she was out hunting.

"Cain." Woodman took a step closer, letting the dahlias fall listlessly to his side. "Cain's not comin', darlin'."

Cain. Cain's not comin', darlin'.

She swayed in her dyed-blue, high-heeled shoes and heard the light rustle of Miz Sophie's dahlias hit the ground as Woodman's hand slid under her elbow to steady her. Her eyes filled with hot tears, and she dragged her bottom lip between her teeth, ruining her lip gloss, scraping off the imprint of Cain's lips brushing hers.

"Why not?" she managed to ask, staring down at the dahlias, which looked limp and forgotten on the gravel driveway.

"Because he's an . . ." Woodman made a tsking sound, then took a deep breath, and Ginger knew he was choosing his words. "Cain's Cain. You can't count on him, Gin. You know that, honey." Still holding her elbow, Woodman pulled her gently against his body. His arms came around her, and she closed her eyes, resting her cheek on his shoulder and biting her tongue to keep from crying. "I'm sorry."

She struggled to swallow over the lump in her throat, Gran's words coming home to roost in her head:

But do you really know *him? Are you really seein' him clearly?*

Dragging in a shaky breath, she understood the worry in Gran's eyes now. Somehow her grandmother must have known. And stupid, naive Ginger had still believed in Cain, had still hoped for the best.

A sob escaped her as she thought about the tenderness of his touch, the gentle pressure of his lips parting hers. *You still want that first kiss?*

It had meant everything to her but nothing to him.

Nothing at all.

Something very much like anger, sprinkled with a healthy dose of self-preservation, seeped into her heart, and she felt her tears dry. She wouldn't cry for Cain. No, goddamn it. She wouldn't cry for a boy who treated her like garbage.

"I'm so dumb," she sighed, her voice breaking a little as she tried to take another breath.

"No!" cried Woodman, holding her tighter, validating her instinctive demand for self-respect. "You're *not* dumb. You're— Gin, you're the most amazin' girl in the world. Don't let Cain make you feel bad. Cain is a, well, he's just a rat bastard, if you want to know the truth. I'm ashamed to be his cousin most days, but today? I'm furious. I'm so sorry he hurt you. I could just—"

Ginger leaned back, looking up at Woodman's face, and for the first time she noticed the reddish-purple bruise on his cheek. She reached up and brushed her fingers against it gently, and he flinched.

"Y'all fought?"

Woodman scanned her face, trying to figure out how she'd feel about that, but she kept her expression cool, wanting his honesty. Finally he nodded. "He deserved it."

Her lips twitched as she shook her head in disapproval. "How does the other guy look?"

"Split lip. Bleedin' nose."

A small, unladylike snort of laughter escaped through her lips. "Is it terrible that I'm glad?"

"If the image of Cain bleedin' makes you smile, darlin', I would have beat him up years ago."

"Woodman," she said softly, sliding her hand down his arm and weaving her fingers through his. "What am I goin' to do with you?"

"How about lettin' me take you to homecomin'?" He shrugged, looking down at his tux, then catching her eyes with a grin. "I'm a little overdressed for the club. And you are too beautiful to stay home alone tonight."

Part of her *did* want to stay home. Part of her wanted to throw her dress in the fireplace, change into pajamas, and cry herself to sleep. Besides the fact that her kiss with Cain—which had meant so much to her—meant absolutely nothing to him, it must have sucked, which made her feel embarrassed. What a foolish little girl, thinking an experienced man like Cain would be swept off his feet by her inexperienced kiss, content to take her to a stupid high school dance on his last night home. What a ridiculous, naive child to think that a kiss that had shaken the foundation of her world could mean anything to him.

She looked up at Woodman's sparkling eyes and managed a smile for him.

Here was Woodman, dressed to the nines. He'd beaten up Cain, picked his mother's sacred flowers into a bouquet, and raced over to her house to comfort her and take her to a dance. He was leaving for boot camp tomorrow, but he was choosing to spend his last night at home with her.

The sun slipped below the horizon, bathing the farm in a gold and lavender half-light, and Ginger looked closely at Woodman, at his burnished blond hair and handsome smile. He didn't have the dangerous flash and flare of Cain, but maybe she hadn't been looking closely enough all these years. Maybe Woodman, whom she'd friend-zoned for so long, deserved more of a chance.

"You *sure* you want to spend your last night at home with me?" she asked, cocking her head to the side.

"Baby," he drawled, sounding so much like Cain, she almost could have closed her eyes and tricked herself into believing he was here, after all, "ain't nothin' in the world I'd like more."

***

Two hours later, she was flushed and happy, holding Woodman's hands on the dance floor and hollering along with her classmates to a jazzed-up version of the Apple Valley fight song. Giggling with glee as she stumbled over the words, Ginger looked up as yet another popular high school senior approached them, politely interrupting their dance to have a short word with Woodman.

Here was something new she'd learned tonight: Woodman

was popular. And not just popular, but *stratospherically* popular, well liked, respected, and admired. Never having attended high school at the same time as the cousins, Ginger had not had a firsthand opportunity to see how the teens of Apple Valley regarded them. But she'd lost count of the number of people, students and teachers alike, who'd stopped by to wish Woodman good luck at boot camp.

He shook the senior's hand and clapped him on the shoulder, telling him to behave himself and "kick Canton's ass all over the field" next week. Ginger watched with a growing mix of fascination and pride. He was, by far, the highlight of the dance for everyone there, and he was her date. Hers.

He'd also saved her bacon tonight, showing up when he did. If he hadn't, she'd have sat on that old porch swing for hours, waiting for Cain, finally dissolving into pitiful tears when she realized she'd been stood up. She would have missed the dance, her new dress would be ashes, and she'd be huddled under the covers now, feeling beyond worthless. Instead she was at the dance with the uncrowned king—and instead of being Cain's princess, she was Woodman's queen.

She thought back to her twelfth birthday as he grinned at her, taking her hands for another rock-and-roll song. Although Woodman had held her hand and hugged her a million times since that afternoon on the driveway when he gave her the charm bracelet, that was the first and last time that her feelings for him had edged, just a touch, into the realm of more. Until now.

For years, she'd been pining for Cain, when right smack in front of her was the whole package: Woodman, in all his golden-boy goodness, was hers for the taking.

Placing her hands on his warm face, she pulled him to her

until her lips grazed his ear. "It's so hot in here. Can we go outside?"

When she drew back, his eyes were darker and less playful, his glance flicking to her lips before he nodded. "Sure."

Still holding her hand, he pulled her through the crowd of dancing students, stopping whenever a girl wanted to kiss his cheek or a boy wanted to shake his hand. She wondered if he'd taken her right hand by design so that he wouldn't have to drop it, and gradually she realized that his thumb was rubbing slow, soothing circles on her skin. She concentrated on his hypnotic touch, getting lost in it, even as the music thumped and Woodman's cheerful voice thanked every other student for his or her good wishes. Surrounded by a hundred or more moving bodies, she was aware only of him—the soft touch of callused skin, rubbing, lulling her into a simultaneous state of bonelessness and hyperawareness.

Finally he pulled her through the double doors at the back of the gym, and as they slammed solidly behind them, the cool air hit her damp skin, making her tremble. Tilting her head back, Ginger looked up at Woodman, her heart pounding, her breathing shallow and ragged.

His eyes were dark but soft—the same eyes that had annoyingly tracked her for years were now trained on her with total devotion, and she found she didn't mind at all.

"Gin."

"Yes," she murmured—an answer not a question.

"Yes . . . what?" he asked, his eyes both dazed and uncertain as his arms encircled her.

She flattened her hands against his chest, which jerked under her palms with the same breathlessness she felt.

"Yes . . . Woodman."

She heard his slight gasp of breath, saw the way his eyes slid down her cheeks to rest on her lips, felt the pressure of his arms flexing, and finally, as she closed her eyes, the featherlike touch of his lips brushing hers.

He groaned softly, pulling her closer and deepening the kiss, his lips moving insistently across hers. His tongue licked the seam of her lips, and she opened for him, letting his tongue tangle with hers as he hardened between them, his erection swelling against her belly.

And then . . .

It was over.

His lips broke away from hers, skimming her cheek as he held her tightly—almost *too* tightly—and buried his face in her hair. "Gin, Gin, Gin . . . oh God, baby, I *knew* it would be like this . . . I *knew* it would happen for us."

His voice was breathless with emotion, with wonder, low and drugged, full of manly emotion that made her shiver even as she opened her eyes wide and rested her cheek on his shoulder.

"You'll write to me while I'm gone?" he asked.

"Of course," she whispered.

He exhaled, kissing her temple and sighing with relief. She could *feel* his happiness. It was profound and alive—a living, breathing thing wrapped in gratitude that surrounded them.

"Can I hold you for a while?" he asked.

"Mm-hm" was all she could manage, grateful for the silence that descended between them as he pulled her close, leaning up against the brick wall of their high school gym, with his cheek resting against her hair, just behind her princess tiara.

Woodman was grateful for Ginger.

But Ginger was grateful for the external silence because inside, her heart was in chaos.

The kiss they'd just shared? It was a good kiss. A really, *really* good kiss. And if it had been her first kiss, she might have even believed that it was the best kiss that life had to offer.

But it wasn't.

She had kissed Cain.

She had kissed Cain and she knew—the way a little girl crosses the threshold to adulthood and truly begins to understand womanly things—that as much as her mind wanted to love one man, her heart would not be so easily swayed.

PART THREE

Three years later

Chapter 7

~ Cain ~

Cain sat beside a sleeping Woodman, his hands on the wheel as he drove their rental car closer and closer to home. It was a nine-hour drive from Bethesda, Maryland, to Apple Valley, Kentucky, not including stops for food, gas, and pissing, which had added another two hours to the drive. Thankfully, Woodman's pain meds had kicked in about an hour ago, and he'd been snoring ever since. Cain checked the dashboard clock: with a little under two hours to go, he was hoping he could pull into the circular drive of Belle Royale before nine o'clock tonight and surprise his aunt and uncle with an early arrival.

Woodman muttered in his sleep, a soft, low, guttural sound of pain, and instinctively Cain reached over and placed his hand over his cousin's, rubbing his thumb over the white, freckled skin until Woodman quieted down. It was over two months since the accident that had crushed and almost claimed Woodman's foot, and thus far the road to recovery had been long and painful.

On their way back to Norfolk, Virginia, after a port visit in Barcelona, Woodman was on deck, acting as a safety observer, when his right ankle had been accidentally crushed between an aircraft wheel and forklift. He'd been taken by helicopter to the Morón Air Base, then airlifted to the Landstuhl Regional Medical Center in Germany, where they'd set his broken fibula, but he'd had to wait several days for the swelling to go down on his ankle before the medical staff was able to reconstruct his ankle's crushed talus with cadaver bone, a plate, and five screws. After three weeks, his ankle bone had started to die from a lack of oxygenated blood, and he'd required follow-up surgery to reroute his veins to feed the remaining bones. Stable three weeks later, he'd been transferred to Walter Reed hospital in Maryland, and yesterday, nine weeks after the accident, Woodman had finally been given the okay to go home. His retirement was still under adjudication, but that was really just a formality since he'd been injured after three years of a four-year, active-duty contract.

For now he could get around okay on crutches since his upper-body strength was solid. He'd require at least a year of physical therapy (which could only do so much to improve the strength of his rebuilt ankle) when he got home, but the sad reality was that Woodman would probably walk with a limp and a cane for the rest of his life.

Cain, who'd taken several days of liberty at various ports of call over the past three years, hadn't actually taken an extended vacation since his enlistment. With seventy accrued days, he'd used ten of them to be with Woodman at Landstuhl and asked to use another thirty days to accompany his cousin home to Kentucky. It was unusual for a man of Cain's rank to be given a full month of liberty, but exceptions had been made based on his cousin's condition, which found them—here and now—speeding down Interstate 71 toward Cincinnati with the dying sun out Woodman's open window and the open highway up ahead.

Cain rolled down his window and leaned his elbow on the sill, his mind shifting to the moment he'd heard that Josiah was en route to Morón. Without a full account of his cousin's injuries, Cain had been almost paralyzed by the fear that Josiah's wounds were mortal, and had headed straightaway to his commanding officer, demanding, with all the composure he could muster, to be released from duty immediately so he could follow Josiah's transport. He'd be forever grateful for the compassionate calm that Lieutenant Carlson had shown, directing a distraught Cain into private quarters to explain the extent of Woodman's injuries and assure Cain that, while his foot was in grave danger, his life, most likely, was not.

After a full report on Woodman's condition later that day, Cain had formally requested leave and headed straight to Germany, where he spent a few hours every day keeping Woodman company. When Woodman wasn't totally out of it from the constant drip of pain meds, they'd play cards or swap stories about their shared childhood and their past three years in the service. The rest of the time, Cain's German came in handy as he caught up on a couple years' worth of sex with many a Rhineland Fräuleins.

Woodman's injuries notwithstanding, it was a strange and unexpected time of mending and healing for the cousins. Cain's priorities had shifted while they were away from home, his experiences in the Navy molding him from an unruly lump of clay, little by little, into the man he wanted to be. He'd learned loyalty and discipline, brotherhood and responsibility, and tied inexorably to this experience and growth had been Josiah—his cousin, practically his brother, and the best friend he'd ever known. He wanted and needed his cousin in his life, and he was determined not to act with the same selfishness he'd exercised as a teenager. Now that he felt the full measure of Josiah's camaraderie restored, he never, ever wanted to lose it again.

Prior to his transfer from Germany to Maryland, Woodman, who'd held out hope of making a full recovery, was advised that his career as a damage controlman was over and that his file had been remanded for retirement approval. Cain watched in horror as his cousin's indomitable spirit dipped dramatically, his eyes filling with uncharacteristic tears at the terrible finality of naval retirement at only twenty-one. In a sudden act of solidarity, Cain found himself promising that he'd meet Josiah at Walter Reed so they could drive home together. His cousin seemed encouraged by the idea that he'd have a wingman for the transition home, and Cain kept his promise, strolling into Woodman's hospital room three days ago and flashing the keys to a rental car.

"Hey, cuz! Ready to go home?" he asked with a grin.

Woodman lifted his eyes, and Cain worked hard not to register the surprise he felt at the changes in his cousin's appearance. Sitting in a wheelchair by a window, he looked like a caged animal who'd given up the hope of returning to the wild. He still had the muscle tone he'd built up over the past few years, so his chest was wide and strong under a thin blue hospital gown, but his face was bony and sallow, his eyes dull and discouraged, his beard shaggy.

"Cain," he said softly, mustering a small smile. "Good to see you, man."

"Josiah." Cain had sat down in the chair beside his cousin.

"You look . . . rough."

"Don't lie to me, huh?"

"I'm not a good bullshitter."

"Since when?"

Cain scoffed softly. "You workin' out?"

Josiah's eyes narrowed. "I'm crippled."

"One foot." Cain slid his eyes to his cousin's other foot, which was bare and in perfect condition. "Other one looks A-OK, sailor."

To Cain's horror, Josiah's lips trembled. "I'm not . . ." He cleared his throat and continued in a stronger voice. "I'm not a *sailor* anymore."

"Stop talkin' crazy. You'll be a sailor until you die."

Looking down at his lap, Josiah muttered, "Part of me sorta wishes that day would come sooner'n later."

The rest of Cain stiffened except for his left hand, which darted out and slapped his cousin's face hard enough to leave a red handprint. Staring at each other in shock, Cain mumbled, "You talk like that again, I'll break your neck."

Josiah's lip started trembling again, but to Cain's relief, his cousin was on the verge of laughter, not tears. "Well, that'd hurry things along!" he finally said between gasps of mirth.

Cain joined him, laughing along, but inside he was deeply troubled by Woodman's despondency and made a silent promise to do everything he possibly could to get his cousin back on his feet, proverbially and actually, before Cain had to return to his post.

Over the past three days at Walter Reed, slowly but surely, Woodman brooded less and laughed more in Cain's company. But in every quiet moment, Cain saw the profound change in his cousin—the frustration and anger brimming just beneath the surface, the fatigue and despair—and he hated it. Of the two of them, Woodman had always been the golden boy, kind and smart, decent and popular, destined for great things. Even in high school, when his torn ACL had sidelined him from Annapolis, Woodman had managed to pick up his spirits, rehab his leg, and find another path for his life. With gusto. But now? He just seemed so goddamned hopeless, and it worried Cain.

Added to his worries about Woodman, he wasn't that excited about going home after three years away. Things in his life had changed quite a lot since he'd left Apple Valley, and he wasn't sure of where he would fit in or—in light of his behavior in high school—what his welcome would be like.

Foremost in the changes at home was that the week after Cain left for boot camp, his mother had remarried and moved to Frankfort, almost an hour away from Apple Valley. The timing of her impromptu nuptials suggested that she'd known her new husband, Jim Johnson, for quite some time, and Cain couldn't help wondering if Jim Johnson had been partially responsible for his parents' divorce. Either way, he wasn't particularly eager to meet him.

Klaus, on the other hand, from whom Cain had felt such distance throughout his adolescence, had become Cain's most loyal correspondent, writing to him once or twice a month faithfully while Cain was serving. And it meant something to Cain. It meant a lot. Yes, his letters were filled with boring news from McHuid's—descriptions of new foals, favorite mares, and Ranger's exquisite taste in the latest farm equipment—but sometimes, occasionally, like a nugget of silver on a bed of sand, there was a brief mention of Ginger. And Cain just about lived for those blinding flashes of rare and unexpected beauty in his father's otherwise humdrum letters.

Glancing over at Woodman again, to assure himself that his cousin was asleep before giving himself permission to think about her, Cain took a deep breath and pictured her face. Having known Ginger all his life, he could flip through slides of her in his mind at will: little Ginger in pigtails following him around the farm . . . the day she came home to the manor house after her heart scare, looking as goddamned plucky as ever . . . her arms spread wide every October as she stood above them in the hayloft giggling . . . her body, softening into womanhood, as he checked her out covertly . . . her lips, parted and willing, waiting for him to claim them.

She was a constant, dull ache in his heart that throbbed like an open wound whenever he heard about her. And between his father's occasional mentions of her and the regular letters she sent to Woodman, from which he read aloud from time to time, that wound had never been able to close.

A thousand times it had occurred to Cain to write to her and apologize for standing her up the night of that homecoming dance three years ago. He had a million regrets in his life, but that cowardly fucking move was on the top of the list. He should have had the decency to cancel. Hell, he *should have* had the decency not to kiss his cousin's girl.

But in his dreams, he heard her sweet voice saying *I still want that first kiss.* God help him, the memory of her lips beneath his would be the last thought he grasped for on the day he died. The sweetness of her surrender to him, the trust, the fucking fireworks behind his eyes that had blown any other kiss out of his head and left hers glowing like magnesium in his heart.

He longed to apologize to Ginger with every fiber of his being. He longed to show her the man he was trying so desperately to become since leaving home. He longed to see the softness in her eyes, feel her body pressed against his, hear her voice near his ear whispering tenderly, *I've always known. It's always been you.*

He glanced at the lights of Cincinnati up ahead, then at Josiah sleeping peacefully beside him, hating himself for such weakness.

Cain set his jaw.

He needed to stay away from her.

Because no matter how much you longed for them, some things simply weren't meant to be. The one person—the one conversation topic—that brought a genuine smile to his cousin's dull, dejected eyes was Ginger, and Cain would sooner die than take that glimmer of hope away from him.

Ginger belonged to Woodman, not to Cain, and Cain intended to respect his cousin's claim.

Earlier today, he'd asked Woodman, who'd been slumped in his seat, his expression a mask of quiet anguish as he toughed through the pain of his foot, "Excited to see Ginger?"

Josiah's entire face had transformed at the mention of her name, softening, looking younger and more like his old self. But little by little it crumbled until he stared down at his lap despondently.

"Sure. Always," he said softly. "But I can't expect a girl like her to love a cripple."

"Then we ain't talkin' about the same girl," Cain said, his heart aching as he pushed all thoughts of her into Woodman's arms. "Girl I know wouldn't give two shits about your bad foot. In fact, with her in nursin' school? Bet she loves it. She'll have her own personal patient."

"I don't want to be her fuckin' *patient*, Cain. Don't want to be some half man who she feels sorry for, who can't do for her, who can't . . . can't . . ."

"Uh, did I miss somethin' here? Did your balls get crushed instead of your ankle?"

"Cain—"

"No, I'm serious, son. 'Cause it seems to me you still have a workin' pair."

"Shut the fuck up about my balls, huh?"

"I'm just sayin'," he continued, ignoring the cries of his own heart, "that you *can do* for her."

"Don't talk about her like that," said Josiah, but he wore a grudging smile, his cheeks turning pink, no doubt from thoughts of being intimate someday with Ginger.

And Cain's own knife twisted in his heart.

"Numbnuts," he muttered.

Woodman scoffed. "They ain't seen the action yours have, brother, but I promise you, they ain't numb."

This led them down the path to one of Cain's favorite conversations, and he gratefully left talk of Woodman and Ginger behind, the pressure in his chest easing.

"Tell me the truth: did you, or did you not, bang the redhead in Fort Lauderdale?"

"I plead the Fifth," said Woodman, reaching for a bottle of water and unscrewing the top.

"The blonde in Marseille?"

"Da Fifth," said Woodman in the same way the guys on *Saturday Night Live* used to say "da Bears."

"That hot piece of ass in Rome?"

"Which one?" asked Woodman with a snort.

"Oh, man, I love Italian pussy." Cain sighed, laughing along with his cousin until Woodman groaned in sudden pain.

"Hey, when can you take more meds?"

"Whenever I want."

"Then take one."

Josiah narrowed his eyes. "I can wait."

"Don't be stupid," said Cain. "Take it when you need to."

"You know how easy it is to get addicted to that stuff?"

Cain gave him a look. "You're not goin' to get addicted. You're in pain. C'mon, Josiah."

"Don't 'Josiah' me," said his cousin. "I'm toughin' it out. When I can't stand it anymore, I'll take one."

That conversation had happened at ten o'clock in the morning, and Woodman had lasted until six o'clock in the evening without even so much as an Advil. Finally the pain was so excruciating, he couldn't bear it anymore, and he took half a Vicodin that knocked him out.

As much as Cain didn't like his cousin wading through the pain when there was a more comfortable alternative, it was these little flashes of spirit that Cain clung to, that convinced him that Josiah would find his way out of the darkness of his injury. Cain looked over at Woodman—at the blond hair that had started growing back in, at the golden beard that he refused to shave, and the thousands of freckles he'd inherited from his mother. Woodman was his flesh and blood, his memory keeper and friend, and Cain loved Woodman as much as his heart could love anyone.

Which is why he pledged to stay away from her and hoped—even as the mere thought bled his heart—that Ginger would be there to guide Josiah back into the light.

***

"Cain! *Mein Sohn!*"

"*Servus, Papa!*"

Cain stepped forward into the tack room and allowed his father to wrap him in an impromptu hug. He still wore the jeans and T-shirt he'd been driving in all day, and his father wore the boxer shorts he slept in and nothing else. It didn't matter.

Cain couldn't remember the last time his father had embraced him, and he savored the moment, inhaling the smells of leather and horse, cut grass, and Head & Shoulders. He closed his eyes and breathed deeply. He was home, welcomed back into his father's arms like the prodigal son returned, and damn if it didn't make his eyes burn so much, he had to pull away.

"You got my postcards from Germany, Pop?"

"*Ja!*" said Klaus, releasing Cain reluctantly and patting him twice on the back as though needing to maintain contact or reassure himself that Cain was real. His face was older, more weathered, but his ice-blue eyes were as clear as ever. "I get them! But I ask myself, Why doesn't he go to *Österreich*? To visit my Lipizzaner?"

"Austria?" scoffed Cain with a wide grin, reaching back to close the tack room door. "It's landlocked, Pop. I been on a ship for three years."

"*Ja*, of course." Klaus looked around the small living room/kitchen, his eyes resting on the Keurig machine on the small kitchen counter. He clapped his hands together expectantly. "You want coffee? Or *heiße Schokolade*, like when you were little?"

Had his father always been like this? In those angry years of high school, had he missed his father's efforts to nurture and connect with him? One of his shipmates had pinned a father–son photo on a bulletin board over his berth, and beside the photo, he'd written a quote by Mark Twain: "When I was a boy of 14, my father was so ignorant I could hardly stand to have the old man around. But when I got to be 21, I was astonished at how much the old man had learned in seven years." At 21 himself, the quote suddenly had personal meaning for Cain, who grinned at his graying father. He wasn't in the mood for coffee *or* hot cocoa, but he nodded.

"Sure, Pop. Hot chocolate sounds great."

His father headed for the kitchen, and Cain looked around the sparsely furnished room, most of the items probably hand-me-downs from Miz Magnolia since they appeared to be of good quality. A leather reading chair and love seat by a potbellied stove, a modern kitchen with a flat-screen TV mounted under the cabinets and black granite countertops, and a small table with two chairs for dining. Adjacent to this common room were two bedrooms with a connecting bathroom. Warm and tidy, with wooden walls and barn smells surrounding them, Cain felt—for the first time—how good it was to be home and, in fact, how much he had missed it.

"Woodman is . . . at home?"

"*Ja, Papa*," answered Cain, setting down his bags by the love seat. "I dropped him off at Aunt Sophie's half an hour ago."

"How is he? *Der Fuß*?"

"Not good. His spirits are low, and he's got months of rehab ahead." Cain scrubbed his chin. "But he insisted on walkin' up the front steps of Belle Royale on his crutches, even though I was there to carry him."

"He will be okay. He's a strong boy. A good boy," said Klaus with soft conviction.

Cain grimaced as jealousy flared up inside him. But it was true, wasn't it? Woodman *was* strong and good—always had been, always would be—and it didn't take anything away from Cain to acknowledge it.

"The best," he agreed.

Crossing to his son, Klaus held out the steaming cup of hot cocoa and shook his head, smiling sadly at his only child. "*Nein, Sohn. Genauso gut. Nicht besser.*"

As good. Not better.

Cain clenched his jaw, staring at his father for a moment before dropping his gaze to the steaming mug in his hands.

"*Danke,*" he whispered. "*Danke, Papa.*"

It was a benediction to hear these simple words fall from his father's lips, and it filled him with a kind of hope with which he didn't have a lot of experience. He'd never had a strong vision for his future or the certainty that he deserved anything good. But for three years, with the exception of a few days leave here and there, Cain had been trapped on aircraft carriers with a thousand other men, and he'd had time to think. While Woodman mostly made his life happen, Cain had mostly gotten in his own way.

He'd been an asshole to his parents in high school. Yes, they'd always been unhappy. Yes, they'd gotten divorced when he was fifteen, arguably the worst-possible time in a kid's life. But for all that their interests didn't collide, his father had undoubtedly been the force behind Cain keeping his job at McHuid's throughout high school. And without that job—for all that he didn't love it or value it at the time—he would have felt even more worthless. The income from McHuid's had allowed him to buy and rebuild his bike and had given him whatever sense of freedom he'd found in those years. It had also given his father a chance to look after him and check in with him on a daily basis, even if Cain had barely grunted when spoken to. He'd never love horses as his father did, but he'd be forever grateful that working at McHuid's had given him a sense of stability and purpose that those years had otherwise lacked.

As for his mother, while it was possible that she had known Jim Johnson during her marriage to Klaus Wolfram, she'd stayed in Apple Valley throughout Cain's years in high school, just so he wouldn't have to deal with the upheaval of splitting his time between Frankfort and Apple Valley. She'd quietly made that decision *for* him. In return, he'd worried her sick half the time and humiliated her with his shenanigans the rest.

He knew it would take a little time, but the way he'd managed to mend his familial relationship with Woodman made Cain long to make things right with his parents too, and maybe even to prove to them that they could be proud of him now.

His father cleared his throat. "You are staying? A little while?"

"For a few weeks, if that's okay, Pop."

"And you'll help? On the farm?" His father's hopeful smile wasn't about relief in having help to cover the work—it was about spending time with Cain. He could see it. He knew it was true, and he felt another warm rush of affection for his dad.

"Course, Pop. Whatever you need."

His father smiled, nodding once, pleased. "I go make the extra bed." He patted Cain on the shoulder once more before heading back to the second bedroom.

Feeling unusually emotional and not altogether comfortable, he placed the mug on the table beside his father's reading chair and called, "I'm goin' for a short walk, Pop. Back soon. Don't wait up, okay?"

"*Ja, Sohn. Lauf herum.*"

Go wandering.

Cain left quietly as his father finished making up the spare room, closing the tack room door quietly behind him.

Ten minutes later, he stood with his elbows propped up on one of the many paddock fences, staring off into the night, picturing exactly what lay before him in the darkness, as he'd pictured it a million times from the hull of a ship: the brilliant green of the pastures, Heath and Bit-O-Honey grazing, blue skies, bright sun, and fresh air. He knew the valleys and vales of McHuid's like the back of his hand and realized how much this farm, which he thought he'd hated, had come to represent home.

Bright lights coming up the driveway disturbed the dark palette of his memories and made him turn. He saw a white SUV moving slowly toward him, and though he didn't recognize the car, he knew who it was, and every cell in his body braced itself to be in her presence once again.

Cain raised his hand in greeting, and she rumbled to a stop. Praying she wouldn't mow him down as he crossed in front of her car, he approached her window cautiously, peering inside, and making out her shadowed face.

She lowered the window, and suddenly, after three long years, her face was mere inches from his, and the subtle hint of lemons wafted from the warmth of her car as she raised her eyes to his.

"God," he hissed as the window finished its descent. He didn't know how he had expected to feel, but a sucker punch to the lungs about summed it up. He wanted to catch his breath, but he couldn't, and he wasn't accustomed to feeling so discomposed around a woman.

Her pink lips were plump and glossy, and her cheekbones high. Her blonde hair was pulled back in a ponytail, and she wore glasses. But behind them her eyes were as deep and dark as they'd ever been, trained, with wariness, on Cain.

"Welcome home," she said softly, pulling her bottom lip

between her teeth. Her voice trembled lightly, and it was slightly deeper than it had been three years ago, but otherwise familiar to his ears.

He placed his hands on the windowsill. "Hey, princess."

Her eyes widened, and her lips tilted up just a hair as she stared back at him, but he would have missed the small smile if he wasn't watching carefully. Her face adjusted into a scowl a moment later. "Ginger's good."

"Yes, she is," he agreed, smirking at her.

She shook her head, scoffing with annoyance as she broke eye contact with him. "Some things never change."

Her words bothered him because Cain felt that he'd changed materially in the years he'd been away. "How d'you mean?"

"Still the shallow flirt, huh?"

He winced, lifting his hands and stepping away from her car, though he still held her eyes. He swiped at his lower lip with his thumb before putting his hands on his hips.

"Still mad, huh?" he volleyed back.

She reached up and took out the rubber band holding her ponytail, running her hands through her hair. Her movements hypnotized him, and he watched her greedily as she turned her neck to face him again.

"Just saw Woodman." She blinked back tears, then lifted her chin. "Thanks for bringin' him home."

Cain shrugged. Here was common ground for them. Comfortable ground. "I'd do anythin' for him."

"Me too," she said evenly, her eyes finally softening.

His hand reached out from his hip, and he realized it was headed for her cheek—to touch it, clasp it, feel its warm sweetness beneath his palm once again. He forced it to change direction at the last minute and flipped her side-view mirror up so he could see himself. He ran his hands through his stubbly hair like primping had been his object all along, then winked at her.

"How do I look?"

"Like you're ready to raise Cain," she snapped.

He chuckled, righting her mirror. "I've changed. My troublemakin' days are behind me, darlin'. I protect and serve now."

"I'd sooner trust a fox with a chicken."

"Yup. Still mad as a wet hen," he said, grinning at her, wishing he wasn't enjoying himself quite so much.

She flinched just slightly at his teasing—just the barest narrowing of her eyes before taking a deep breath and turning away from him. "Welcome home, Cain," she said again without looking at him.

Then she raised the window and pulled her car forward, leaving him in quiet darkness once again.

Chapter 8

~ Ginger ~

"Trainee McHuid, you have a call on line one. Please make it quick."

Nurse Arklett, whom Ginger and all the other LPN student trainees called Nurse Ratched behind her back, gave Ginger a stern look before turning and walking away. Ginger patted Mr. Humphreys on the arm, placed the book of Roald Dahl stories she'd been reading on his bedside table, and made her way to the nurses' station on the fifth floor of the Silver Springs Care Center.

As a student at Apple Valley Community College and a practical trainee at SSCC, she wasn't permitted to have a phone on her person while she worked her shifts at the nursing home, lest it ring and wake or startle one of the residents, so she'd given her parents and friends the number at Silver Springs for emergencies only. Her mother, however, included picking up a bottle of milk on her list of emergencies. Nurse Ratched knew it and disapproved mightily of such misuse of privilege, though it was hard to say anything because, ever since Ginger's grandmother had become a resident of Silver Springs, her parents were its most generous patrons.

Tanya at the nurses' station gave Ginger a sympathetic look as she handed her the phone.

"This is Ginger."

"Honey, it's Momma."

Ginger lowered her voice. "Momma, you're not supposed to call me at work!"

"I know it. But I have such good news. I knew you'd want to know right away!"

She huffed softly. "What is it?"

"It's Woodman. He's home."

Her lips parted in surprise, and she turned her back to Tanya for a bit of privacy. "Wait, what?"

"Woodman. He's home, honey. Just got in half an hour ago. Sophie called to tell me."

"But he wasn't due home for another week."

"Well, he got a ride home ahead of schedule." Her mother's voice changed from excited to reproachful. "With Cain."

If the news that Woodman was home a week early had thrown Ginger for a loop, the notion that Cain was, after three long years, back in Apple Valley nearly fried her brain.

"C-Cain?" she whispered, her heart lurching at the same time her stomach flipped over. "Cain's home?"

"Well, I guess," said her mother dismissively. "But don't mind about him. What's important is *Woodman's* home!"

Ginger looked straight ahead at the small lounge across from the nurses' station, where several residents were watching *Jeopardy!* and four others were engaged in a game of bridge at the card table. A cheerful banner decorated with pumpkins and fall leaves was carefully hung over the four windows that looked out over the patio, and José from maintenance was replacing a bulb in the overhead light. It all seemed so *normal*, but how could *anything* be normal when Cain Holden Wolfram was finally home again? She swayed, then placed her palm on the column beside her to steady herself.

"Ginger? Ginger, are you still there?"

"I'm here, Momma."

"Well, you and Woodman bein' such old friends and all, I told Sophie you'd swing by on your way home from work tonight to see him. You get off at eight, right?"

"Eight. Right," she repeated dumbly, her mind still whirling, her eyes burning with tears as she recalled the last time she saw Cain. She blinked to keep the painful memories at bay, angry that the mere mention of his name could have such a profound effect on her after all this time.

"So . . . you will?"

"I will," she said. "Wait. Will what?"

"Land's sake, Virginia Laire! You're cotton-headed today." Her mother paused, lowering her voice to a sorority sister–style purr. "Or maybe just excited to see your beau."

"My . . ." Whatever trance she was in was quickly mitigated by her mother's suggestion. "Woodman *isn't* my beau, Momma. We're friends."

"He writes you once a week, and don't think I haven't noticed you mailin' your letters back to him. And every time he's home on leave, he's takin' you to the movies or for a bite at the club. You're heaven together, Ginger."

"*Friends*, Momma."

"Your daddy was my friend too," she said in a singsong,

all-knowing voice. "But I also knew a good thing when it walked into my life, and Ranger McHuid was every bit as good a thing as Josiah Asher Woodman. You mark my words, daughter."

Ugh. When her mother started calling her "daughter," her feathers were getting ruffled, and Ginger would just as soon keep the peace.

"I love Woodman," she said gently. "You know that, Momma, but I just don't—"

"Love is love is love," said her mother quickly. "You love him. That's all that matters. Don't forget to stop by after work and welcome him home, now."

"Momma? Momma! We're *not* . . . I don't see him like—"

But the dial tone humming in her ear told her that Miz Magnolia McHuid had already hung up the phone.

Ginger took a deep breath before turning around and handing the receiver to Tanya.

"Everythin' okay, honey?"

Ginger stared at Tanya's perky smile and nodded. Then she headed to the nearest ladies' room and promptly tossed her cookies.

***

An hour later Ginger pulled into the circular driveway at Belle Royale, cutting the engine of her white SUV and looking up at the grand old plantation house, second only to her parents' in Apple Valley. Flipping down the visor mirror, she freshened up her lip gloss and took a minute to compose herself before ringing the doorbell. If Cain was staying here tonight and she had to see him, she had decided, she'd be polite, but she refused to be warm.

"I'll shake his hand, and then I'll give all my attention to

Woodman," she whispered to her reflection, nodding her head with purpose.

But her heart wouldn't stop pounding, and her hands were all sweaty. And her reaction had nothing whatsoever to do with Woodman.

While she didn't regret kissing Woodman at the homecoming dance three years ago, the reality was that, as much as she *wanted* to have romantic feelings for Woodman, she didn't. She loved exchanging letters with him while he was away and spending time with him when he was home on leave, but the few kisses they'd shared in the past three years were . . . lackluster. And when she compared any of them—or all of them together, for that matter—with the one kiss she'd shared with Cain, they paled to almost nothing.

She did truly *love* Woodman, though. She looked forward to his visits home and loved being his date to the movies or out to dinner. Woodman was handsome and kind, and she felt like a queen on his arm. It wasn't a mystery how he felt about her—his eyes reaffirmed everything she'd always known. And while she felt an increasing pressure to return his feelings since she'd graduated from high school, last June, he didn't demand or force anything from her, which had allowed them to remain best friends who occasionally kissed. Mostly she just hoped it could remain that way indefinitely until they both found someone who set their souls on fire.

But who knows? thought Ginger, hopeful and doubtful at once. *Maybe someday your feelings for Woodman will change and grow into the sort of love he wants from you.*

After all, her feelings about Cain had certainly changed.

Once upon a time, he had been a god in her world, a bad boy she was sure she could reform with the power of her love for him. Now? He was a sharp and painful memory. The stupid little girl she'd been three years ago had actually believed that Cain couldn't have kissed her that passionately unless he felt for her what she felt for him: pure, unstoppable, undying, romantic love. And clearly he hadn't felt anything of the sort. After he'd kissed her, she'd never seen or heard from him again. Not an apology. Not a postcard. Not a visit. Not a word. For three years, nothing. And logic demanded she concede that his feelings for her had to be so inconsequential that she meant nothing to him. A little girl from back home. Not so much as a bean on his hill, while he'd been the sum and total of hers.

It had taken months to make her heart believe the truth. It had foolishly hung on for almost a year, hoping for a phone call or letter, praying that he'd show up with Woodman when his cousin came home for leave. But a year turned into two, turned into three, and no word from Cain meant that Cain had never cared for her and, by now, had probably forgotten her. So she buried her memories of him and did her utmost to forget about him too.

And now? Well, if he *was* back in Apple Valley, certainly she'd run into him sooner or later. God's sake, his mother had moved away, and his father *lived* at McHuid's. But she was no cow-eyed fifteen-year-old anymore. No, sir. She had graduated from high school, she attended college, and she lived, practically, on her own. Would she give him the time of day? Of course, she bristled. She was raised a lady, after all. But after kissing her and raising her hopes and standing her up and breaking her heart? Well, other than a polite hello, the most he could expect from her was exactly *nothing*. Screw Cain Wolfram to hell and back. She just hoped that he'd avoid her as absolutely as she planned to avoid him.

Getting out of the car, she walked purposefully up the wide steps of the mansion that had been in the Woodman family for two hundred years, and rang the doorbell. A moment later Miz Sophie appeared at the door.

"Why, Ginger!"

"Evenin', Miz Sophie," she said, her nose twitching from Sophie Woodman's strong gardenia scent. Miz Sophie reminded her of Pigpen from the *Peanuts* cartoons, only instead of being surrounded by dirt, she was surrounded by a cloud of strong flower smell.

"Well, don't you look simply precious in those work clothes," she said lightly, with a disapproving smile.

Ginger glanced down at her outfit—a lavender V-neck scrub smock over matching, loose-fitting, drawstring pants, and white Keds. Miz Sophie didn't approve of young ladies calling on young gentlemen, though she'd issued an invitation via Ginger's mother and overlooked that convention in this case because her son was incapacitated and their families were such old friends. That said, the delicate sniff of her nose made it clear that Ginger should have changed before stopping by.

"I came right from work," she explained, feeling her cheeks warm up.

"Of course you did. Always so busy. Not even a moment to . . . freshen up," said Miz Sophie, shutting the door behind Ginger. Finally she shrugged lightly, and her expression warmed the slightest bit. "No matter. Woodman's so tired, I bet he can't see straight. Don't stay long, now, lest you wear him out."

Leading the way through the elegant front hall, Ginger followed Miz Sophie by the twisting spiral staircase, through a solarium, and out to the back patio, where the Woodmans enjoyed cocktails every evening. And there, with his white plastered foot up on a cushion, sat Woodman.

She stopped in the doorway, waiting for him to look up, and when he did, she knew he didn't see her sneakers or scrubs, her hair in a ponytail, or her tired eyes. He looked at her face and beamed, and she couldn't help but answer his smile with one of her own, because he was one of her favorite people in all the world, and she would always—*always*—be happy to see him.

"Woodman," she sighed, her voice filled with warmth. "Woodman, it's so good to . . ."

Looking more closely at him, she concealed a flinch. He looked *awful*. His face was gaunt and his color was bad. A thin sheen of sweat covered his brow, and when he tried to take a deep breath, it hitched, she guessed, from the pain.

"Where are your meds?" she asked, worry sluicing through her veins.

"Hello to you too, Gin."

"Hello, Woodman. Where are your meds?"

He rolled his eyes. "Upstairs somewhere."

Ginger turned to his mother. "Miz Sophie, would you be an angel and bring Josiah his meds?"

Sophie darted nervous eyes to her son, who sighed heavily before nodding. "In the canvas rucksack. Outer pocket."

"You're not takin' them like you're supposed to," scolded Ginger as Miz Sophie hurried away.

"Gin, for the love of God, would you just come sit by me and let me kiss you hello? Take off the nursin' hat for one minute and welcome me home, dang it."

A slight smile made his eyes sparkle up at her as she leaned over him and kissed his forehead gently.

"Welcome home," she said softly, lingering for a moment. "I'm glad you're in one piece."

"Me too."

As she stepped back, she read his eyes clearly—the want, the longing, the bursting-at-the-seams love his heart held for her. She blushed and dropped his eyes, taking a seat in the chair across from him and leaving the one beside him empty.

"Did your retirement come through yet?"

The sparkle in his eyes dimmed as he picked up the mug of coffee on the table beside him and sighed. "Not yet."

"But it will."

He nodded. "That's what they tell me."

"Then what?"

"Then I'll be retired from the Navy at twenty-one."

"No," she said. "I mean, college? Work? What comes next for you?"

"Not college. I've had enough of takin' orders for a while." He shrugged, his expression agitated. "I don't know, Gin. Can I just get used to bein' at home first?"

His voice was terse, and, unaccustomed to his being short with her, Ginger sat back in her chair and stared at him in surprise.

"I'm sorry," he said softly.

"It's okay," she said, giving him a small smile. "I'm really, really glad you're home."

"Yeah?"

"Of course."

"Really, Gin?"

"You're my best friend, Woodman. Of course I'm—"

"Here we are!" said Miz Sophie, joining them on the porch and handing Woodman's rucksack to Ginger.

She nodded at Woodman's mother in thanks before glancing up at him and did a double take at his expression. It was hard and frustrated, annoyed and seeking. *What?* she wondered. *Why's he so—*

Of course.

You're my best friend.

That's what.

She couldn't seem to do anything right tonight. She wore the wrong clothes, made the wrong greeting, asked the wrong questions, and hurt his feelings by slapping him into the friend zone when he wanted more from her. Fine. Time to go. She'd head home in a minute, but not before she made sure he was taking his meds correctly. The nursing student in her couldn't leave without making certain.

She rifled through the outside pocket, taking out an amber vial of Vicodin and holding it up. "See this?"

Woodman nodded curtly.

"Says 'Take as needed every four to six hours for pain,' right?"

He nodded again.

"Are you in pain?"

His eyes were still narrow and hurt when he nodded yet again, but this time he added in a low, frustrated voice, "Yeah, Gin. I'm in pain."

She almost flinched at the double meaning in his words, but controlled her expression and ignored his innuendo. "Then you should be takin' one every four to six hours. When did you last have one?"

He shrugged, looking away from her. "I had half of one at four."

"It's eight thirty. Take another." She opened the vial and shook one into her hand, holding it out to him.

He took his time reaching for it, claiming and owning her

eyes as his fingers lingered far longer than necessary in her palm. "Fine."

She watched as he placed the pill on his tongue and chased it with coffee before opening wide to prove it was gone. "Happy now?"

She wasn't happy.

She wasn't happy that her friend was in pain, either because of his injury or because she couldn't give him what he wanted.

She wasn't happy that Cain was finally home, because it had taken a long time for her to bury the heartache he'd caused her, and his sudden presence in her life was likely to bring it all to the surface again.

No, she wasn't happy.

"Yes," she said, standing up to say her good-byes. "I'm happy now."

***

Ginger had chosen to become a nurse after her grandmother had been transferred to Silver Springs, three years ago—hell, she spent so much time visiting Gran and volunteering there, she already knew the facility inside out and most of the residents by name. When they had first moved Gran to Silver Springs, she seemed to improve. Seemingly cheered by the camaraderie of other seniors (she affectionately called Silver Springs the Old Folks Country Club), she still got around on her own and became very popular in many different social circles at the residence half of the facility. But just last month, Gran had taken two falls, the second worse than the first, and fractured a rib. And while the doctors had grudgingly decided that she didn't require a wheelchair *quite* yet, she was in significant to severe gait decline, which had affected her spirits. She had to start considering a move to the Silver Springs Care Center across the street, which was little more than a really lovely nursing home with proper hospital facilities.

Between Gran and Woodman, both frustrated by the limitations of their bodies and taking it out on those around them, it promised to be a *terrific* autumn, she thought sourly, then quickly chastised herself for such unkind thoughts. She was able-bodied, healthy and hearty—she had no right to judge Gran, whose traitorous body was giving up on her way too soon, or Woodman, who was retired from a job he loved at twenty-one and would likely be crippled for life.

"I'm just tired," she muttered, turning into her driveway. "I'll get into bed, and it'll all look better in the mornin'."

But her intentions were thwarted when she saw a lone figure, standing by one of the paddock fences, turn in the spotlight of her headlights and face her car. She couldn't really make out more than a tall silhouette, but she knew who it was. She knew exactly who it was, and her breath caught as her eyes burned with sudden and tiresome tears. As she braked without thinking, she clenched her fingers around the steering wheel and braced herself to come face to face with heartache after three years apart.

He raised his hand in greeting, crossing in front of her car to come say hello, and though it vaguely occurred to her to hit the gas and run him over, she decided that homicide would only make a bad night worse, so she pulled up the emergency brake and rolled down the window instead.

And—*Lord Jesus, Mother Mary, and all the saints in heaven*—he'd somehow gotten even better-looking while he was gone. Her lips parted, and a soft, whimpering sound escaped from her throat, but she prayed he didn't hear it. If anything, he looked a little unsettled himself to be in her presence again. As he strolled over to her car and rested his hands on the windowsill, she clamped her lips shut and tried desperately for a cool expression. She had no idea if she succeeded, because she was so distracted by the throbbing of her pulse in her ears.

She might have murmured "Welcome home," but she couldn't be sure.

"Hey, princess."

Princess.

Her heart, brimming with too much emotion to bear, thundered at the sound of his voice saying the beloved old nickname. She tried not to smile, working hard to scowl instead. Cutesy nicknames would only make her fall again, and falling for a pig like Cain was a recipe for more heartbreak. She'd already had her fill, thank you very much.

"Ginger's good."

"Yes, she is," he drawled, smirking at her.

Out of nowhere, fury erupted within her.

Unbelievable.

You stood me up for a dance three years ago without so much as an apology, and now you have the gall to flirt with me? She scoffed, looking down at the emergency brake, tempted to release it and speed away.

"Some things never change."

"How d'you mean?"

Looking up, she nailed him with a look that conveyed all the hurt still wallowing around in her heart. "Still the shallow flirt, huh?"

Wincing, he lifted his hands from her windowsill and stepped away from the car, having the audacity to look hurt. He swiped at his lower lip—*which only served to make her stare at*

it and remind her of how it felt moving on hers, damn him!—
with his thumb before putting his hands on his hips.

"Still mad, huh?"

Her lungs tightened, and the tears burning her eyes
doubled, but damn if she'd let him see how much his flippant
comment hurt. It was the first he'd ever acknowledged standing
her up, and apparently there was no apology forthcoming.

Yes! she wanted to cry. *Yes, I'm still mad. Yes, I'm still
hurt. Yes, you broke my heart. And yes, you made me insecure
about the way I kissed. And yes, if Woodman hadn't taken me to
the goddamned dance . . . Woodman . . . Woodman.*

"Just saw Woodman," she blurted out, looking up at Cain
and blinking back the tears. Woodman was mad at her, and Cain
was still a jackass, and all she wanted was to zoom away from
him, race into Gran's old cottage and hurl herself onto her bed
for a nice, long cry. But she had too much dignity to run away,
so she lifted her chin and opted for polite conversation instead.
"Thanks for bringin' him home."

Cain shrugged, his teasing expression sobering. "I'd do
anythin' for him."

"Me too," she said, the words coming easily.

Their eyes met, and for a moment—just for a split
second—she thought she saw more than smirky flippancy there.
She saw regret and wonder and longing and so many other soft
and wonderful things, she held her breath. His hand moved from
his hip, toward her face, and, holding his eyes, she tracked his
fingers in her peripheral vision, leaning just slightly toward him
so he could touch her face. Her whole body trembled as her eyes
fluttered closed, and she remembered how it felt for him to palm
her cheek, to kiss her, to—

The squeaking noise of the side-view mirror being

adjusted made her eyes whip open in time to see him rake his
fingers through his hair and grin at his reflection.

"How do I look?" he asked, winking at her.

*I'm officially the most pathetic person on the earth, and I
hate myself.*

She released her breath in a quiet hiss of disgust.

"Like you're ready to raise Cain," she snapped, relieved
when anger reared its head again, shoving hurt, and despicable
hope, aside. It wasn't hard to look pissed at him. She felt pissed
enough at herself to make it genuine.

He chuckled. "I've changed. My troublemakin' days are
behind me, darlin'. I protect and serve now."

"I'd sooner trust a fox with a chicken."

"Yup. Still mad as a wet hen," he said smoothly, grinning
at her.

It was a clever retort, and if she wasn't so hurt and turned-
on and angry and confused, she might have giggled and given
him credit for it. Instead she took a deep breath and turned away
from him. No doubt he was on the way to the distillery to chase
some tail, and she had a date with her bed.

But after two such disastrous reunions with two people
who'd meant so much to her once upon a time, she could barely
keep her tears at bay.

"Welcome home, Cain," she whispered. Then, before she
could embarrass herself, she raised the window and pulled her
car forward without looking back.

"You are an idiot," she mumbled, parking beside Gran's
vintage Ford pickup and slamming her door shut before
stomping into the cottage that still smelled comfortingly of Gran.

She was even more of an idiot if she thought she could
ignore Cain while he was home. They'd spoken for all of two

minutes, but it had proved several devastating truths that Ginger wasn't anxious to acknowledge:

One, she had never gotten over Cain.

And two, given the chance, he could break her heart into a million jagged splinters all over again.

Walking wearily upstairs to bed, she wiped the wetness from her cheeks and whispered into the darkness, "Be strong, Virginia Laire McHuid. *Don't you dare* give him that chance."

Chapter 9

~ Woodman ~

He hadn't seen the accident coming. That was the thing that haunted Woodman the most. One minute he was standing on the flight deck guiding a jet into position. The next, his ankle was being crushed from behind by a forklift. In his nightmares, he could feel the metal ripping his skin and splintering his bone, and he was trapped, and utterly fucking helpless to do anything to save himself.

Twenty seconds.

That's how long it took for Woodman's life to change forever.

He'd gone into shock fairly quickly, and he barely remembered the helicopter ride from Barcelona to Morón de la Frontera. By the time he was airlifted to Germany, he was so out of it on painkillers, he didn't wake up until his leg had already undergone surgery.

He had hated relying on the help of others. He hated that he couldn't take a piss in the hospital without calling a nurse to help him out of bed. He couldn't drive. He was in a wheelchair for weeks, and now he was dependent on crutches. It was the helplessness that bothered him the most. Around everyone, that is, but Cain.

Something about Cain made it feel okay—maybe it was that Cain was family, and family is allowed to see you at your worst, at your most vulnerable. Or maybe his brashness—the way he continued to treat Woodman like his injury was temporary and anything was still possible, made him feel like the world hadn't, actually, ended. But it was even more than that. After the abject horror of what had happened to his leg and foot, the trauma of the surgeries, and the slow but certain realization that his life would never, ever be the same again, he'd felt terrifyingly alone in the world. Until Cain walked into his room at the Landstuhl Medical Center.

The doctors and nurses had been clinically concerned about his treatment, of course. But Cain? The second he walked into Woodman's room was the second Woodman finally felt comfort. Because despite their emotional estrangement throughout their adolescence, when the shit hit the fan, Cain showed up. And seeing Cain's face felt like more than coming home. It felt like, well, it felt like undiluted comfort.

Lying in a hospital bed in terrible pain, Woodman had had some time to think about his relationship with his cousin, reframing it and making a conscious decision to be a better custodian of it. It was no wonder he'd often compared their relationship with that of brothers—as the sons of identical twin sisters, Woodman and Cain were, genetically speaking, half brothers. But the cruel reality of that comparison was that Sophie, Woodman's mother, had married a banker, whose chief pleasure in life, aside from making money, was to please her.

Sarah, on the other hand, had fallen for a dark-haired, blue-eyed foreigner who'd gotten her pregnant before they could decide if they even liked each other. Throw in the differences of culture, income, and language, and the marriages produced two very, very different children.

Life wasn't a challenge for Woodman. He knew he was good-looking, decent grades came easy, and the entire community of Apple Valley seemed to regard him as some godlike golden boy. But Cain? From a young age, Cain had acted out, likely to get attention from his unhappy parents, and had been labeled a troublemaker by the third grade. And like a self-fulfilling prophesy, that's exactly who Cain became for the good people of Apple Valley: their own little poisonous apple— beautiful on the outside but rotten to the core.

The Dub Twins. One light, one dark. One good, one bad.

Except that the good people of Apple Valley, who clearly loved the traditional fairy-tale roles of prince and villain, didn't actually know Cain at all outside of the inflated stories of his antics. They didn't know that there was nothing rotten, nothing poisonous at his core. They didn't know that he'd jump in front of a train for someone he loved. They didn't know that the risks he took were just a bid for the attention he'd missed from his folks. They didn't know that the endless succession of women he bedded was likely an attempt to feel connected to, or loved by, someone. And they definitely didn't know that the princess of their little kingdom had been in love with him since she was a little girl.

But Woodman knew all these things.

He knew them, and he mulled them over incessantly as he lay on his back for hours and hours on end, bleary from pain meds, unable to process the far-reaching, permanent consequences of his injuries and desperately missing home.

Was Cain the better man?

Woodman's brain insisted that he wasn't. He was uncouth, bad mannered, irreverent, impertinent, and irresponsible, with a mouth like a sailor before he'd *become* a sailor, and a dick that had seen so much indiscriminate action, it's a wonder it still worked. But Woodman's heart knew the truth: at his core, Cain's impulsiveness meant that he wouldn't consider his own safety before preserving that of someone he loved. And at *his* core, Woodman knew that he might make the same decision, but it wouldn't come from the same visceral, instinctive place from which Cain's actions were born. There would be a split second of thought, of weighing, of judgment. And it was that split second that gave Woodman his answer to the question. They were both good men, but Cain's nature—the very nature that led him to make such bad decisions born from emotion instead of reason—also made him the purer hearted of the cousins, the better raw material, however crude in his present form.

But Woodman wasn't accustomed to taking second place to Cain, so even though he acknowledged these thoughts, he guarded against them, far more comfortable in the traditional roles they'd come to embody throughout their lives: the golden boy and the blue-eyed devil. In fact, the only other person who seemed to recognize Cain's true worth was the princess. Ginger.

In the rose garden of Woodman's life, Ginger, of all people, was the unexpected thorn.

Because the golden boy, the fair-haired son, the prince, was supposed to win the princess. Not the villain. Not the devil. The prince, damn it. And yet, no matter how much he tried to be everything she wanted, it was Cain who owned her heart. Woodman was her second choice, though he longed, with every fiber of his being, to be her first.

Ginger had always been a part of his plan—the *best* part of his plan—especially because it was so easy to love her. She was beautiful, strong, and sassy—the perfect lady one minute, an unexpected minx the next. Woodman had adored her forever, and the most painful anguish of his life was that she loved him back, but not in the way he wanted.

He'd been hopeful on the night of her homecoming dance that they were turning a corner. She'd been so hurt by Cain. She was so angry with him. Woodman knew her long-held feelings for Cain were in turmoil, possibly even in jeopardy, and taking advantage of that elemental change, he'd kissed her. And for him, it had been a game changer, a life changer: that she would give him permission to kiss her meant that, whether he was first or second in her heart, he had a chance. And he'd live for that chance until he became her *only* choice.

And all things considered? His odds hadn't looked so bad before the accident. She wrote to him faithfully—funny, colorful anecdotes from home that kept him connected to Apple Valley and, more importantly, to her. And she always signed her letters *Love, Ginger*. He'd taken leave several times to go home, and though he was always glad to see his parents, his real purpose in visiting was to see her. Over time, she asked about Cain less and less, until she didn't ask about him at all anymore. Woodman knew how badly Cain had hurt her by kissing her and standing her up for the homecoming dance. Cain had broken her heart, and Woodman had been there to cushion the blow.

Instead of losing intimacy with Ginger during his three years in the military, between letters and visits home, he felt closer to her than ever. And that chance to win her, to be her choice, suddenly seemed stronger than ever. In his mind, he imagined he'd finish his four years and return home, seguing to the active Reserves and getting a job at the local fire department. She'd be finishing college at that point, which would give them just enough time to become reacquainted before he popped the question. And hopefully, by then, her childhood infatuation with Cain would be over, and Woodman would be—finally, finally, finally—Ginger McHuid's first and forever choice.

It was a good and solid plan . . . until a forklift crushed his foot, changing the course of his entire life.

Now, instead of returning home as a hearty and healthy choice for the rest of her life, he was returning as a twenty-one-year-old retiree, an invalid, a young man with an old man's gait, who would likely be plagued by pain and physical problems for the rest of his life. If he were a horse, he'd have already been shot.

"Almost home now," said Cain, who was sitting beside him, driving Woodman home to what felt like an uncertain fate—especially where Ginger was concerned. "You awake?"

He'd been awake for a while, musing about his life, trying to keep his fears at bay. "I'm awake."

"Well, cheer up, son!" said Cain. "Your momma's about to fuss all over you!"

Woodman tilted his neck to the side and gave Cain a dry look. "All things equal, I'd just as soon be back in barracks with you."

Cain matched Woodman's look, rolling his eyes. "With a bunch of smelly, sweaty squids? Bite your tongue, Woodman."

"I can't fuckin' walk, Cain. No better than a goddamn toddler."

Without warning, on a dark road about a mile outside of town, Cain pulled the car over abruptly, yanked up the emergency brake, and turned to face him.

"Shut. The Fuck. Up."

"You don't get it. You don't—"

"You're the best man I know, Josiah."

Woodman inhaled sharply. Cain was one of the only people in Woodman's life who used his given name, and when he did—in instances such as this—it lent a raw closeness to the exchange.

No, he thought. *You* are.

But he squelched the notion as quickly as he always did, turning to look at his cousin, desperately needing the pep talk he was about to get.

"And I do. I *do* fuckin' get it. Part of your life is over." Cain snapped his fingers. "In the blink of an eye, it was gone. But Josiah? You are the same man who tore his ACL and was *still* voted co-captain of the goddamn football team! I was never even voted captain of my own jerkin' off squad."

"Oh, really?" asked Woodman. "You lost that one?"

Cain's face shifted from serious to cocky. "Tied it up with Mary-Louise Walker."

In spite of himself, Woodman chuckled, but his laughter tapered off as he stared out the window at the cheerful lights of his hometown in the valley below.

"I was so close," he said softly, almost more to himself than to Cain. *I was so close to having her, and now . . .*

"What? To havin' it all?" asked Cain, slapping Woodman on the thigh of his good leg. "Believe me, Josiah. You're still goin' to have it all. You're the golden boy, son. The best man. If there is anyone on the face of the earth whose life I could safely predict would turn out a success, no matter what, it would be yours. So chin up, huh? You're goin' home. A whole new life is just beginnin'! And it's goin' to be great. I just know it!"

Woodman nodded gratefully at his cousin, and Cain released the emergency brake and pulled back onto the road.

The golden boy with a shattered leg.

The *second*-best man who still longed for the elusive hand of the princess.

The twenty-one-year-old cripple whose life had changed too swiftly to ever feel safe or predictable again.

Woodman's fingers curled into the seat on either side of his hips as they pulled into town. Whatever life was beginning, its success and greatness depended on one person and one person alone, and Woodman silently prayed that his destiny was woven into the beatings of her heart.

***

He didn't know that his mother had called Miz Magnolia until Ginger arrived, out of nowhere, standing in the patio doorway.

"Woodman," she said, her voice warm and lush, as welcome as summer rain and the sweetest music he'd ever heard. "Woodman, it's so good to . . ."

Her smile was huge, hurting him with longing just as much as it made his veins throb with pleasure. Sadly it only lasted a moment. Her eyes widened as she scanned his face and frowned.

"Where are your meds?"

"Hello to you too, Gin."

"Hello, Woodman. Where are your meds?"

Just as he'd feared, she saw him as a patient right out of the gate. He concealed his disappointment by rolling his eyes. "Upstairs somewhere."

Ginger turned to his mother. "Miz Sophie, would you be an angel and bring Josiah his meds?"

In addition to Cain, Ginger also used his given name from

time to time, but almost always when she was scolding him, which he absolutely loved.

"You're not takin' them like you're supposed to."

He was so glad to see her, he grinned at her, shaking his head back and forth.

"Gin, for the love of God, would you just come sit by me and let me kiss you hello? Take off the nursin' hat for one minute and welcome me home, dang it."

"Welcome home," she said softly, leaning over him. He caught a whiff of her lemon-scented shampoo and tilted up his face to meet her lips with his, but she disappointed him by kissing his forehead gently, like he was breakable. All things equal, he wished she hadn't kissed him at all. As she stepped back, taking the seat across from him instead of the one beside him, which would have let him hold her hand, he felt a chill pass through him. It was as though his worst fears were being confirmed. Did she see him as less of a man now?

"Did your retirement come through yet?" she asked.

"Not yet."

"But it will."

"That's what they tell me."

"Then what?"

Bitterness and disappointment made his tone caustic. "Then I'll be retired from the Navy at twenty-one."

"No," she said. "I mean, college? Work? What comes next for you?"

He shrugged, wishing she'd leave. He hadn't been ready to see her—he hadn't been prepared. He looked awful, felt awful. He wanted to look spit-and-polish for her, and instead he looked beaten and weak.

"Not college. I've had enough of takin' orders for a while.

I don't know, Gin. Can I just get used to bein' at home first?" he snapped.

Her eyes widened with hurt, and she sat back in her chair, staring at him.

"I'm sorry," he said softly.

"It's okay," she said, giving him a small smile that lit up her whole beautiful face and made his heart clench with the wanting of her. "I'm really, really glad you're home."

Well, that's something. "Yeah?"

"Of course."

Hope multiplied. "Really, Gin?"

"You're my best friend, Woodman. Of course I'm—"

Fuck, fuck, fuck, fuuuuuuck.

"Here we are!" interrupted his mother, handing his rucksack to Ginger.

Her timing was impeccable. If he'd already lashed out at Ginger for asking about his plans, he was about go to ballistic when she called him her best friend. But his mother's presence tempered his response, and he clenched his jaw, staring daggers at Ginger until she got the point and looked away. She busied herself looking for his meds, finally holding up a vial. "See this?"

All he saw was the girl of his dreams treating him like a patient, not a man. He nodded curtly.

"Says 'Take as needed every four to six hours for pain,' right?"

He nodded again.

"Are you in pain?"

He looked at her deep brown eyes, drowning in them, terrified that an injury he never saw coming would be the thing that ruined his chances with her for good.

"Yeah, Gin. I'm in pain."

She flinched slightly, fully aware of his double meaning, before lifting her chin and schooling her expression into Nurse McHuid's. "Then you should be takin' one every four to six hours. When did you last have one?"

He shrugged, looking away from her. *Go, go, please go. I can't bear this anymore.* "I had half of one at four."

"It's eight thirty. Take another." She opened the vial and shook one into her hand, holding it out to him.

He cut his eyes to hers, then, slamming into them, nailing them, owning them, hoping that she could see that there was still a strong, vital man sitting in this chair with his shattered foot up on a flowered cushion. He was a man and she was a woman, and they would fit together like lock and key if she would only give him the chance. She would never want for anything. He'd spend his whole life making her happy. If she could only see him— only *see* the wellspring of his love for her and deign to accept it.

He rested his fingers in her palm before taking the pill and swallowing it down. "Happy now?"

"Yes," she said, standing up and kissing his forehead again. "I'm happy now."

She didn't look happy one bit, but when her sweet lips brushed against his forehead in a chaste kiss that she'd give a brother or a baby, he closed his eyes and let himself bask in her touch. And to his surprise, his heart, which still clung to much higher hopes, despite everything, couldn't fathom giving up on her.

***

Even though things hadn't gone the way he wanted with Ginger last night, he still felt much better in the morning. He'd taken another Vicodin at three o'clock in the morning and slept until almost nine, when he took another. With the pain better managed, he still felt like shit, but not quite as bad as yesterday.

Not quite as bad physically, at least.

His heart, however, was feeling a little battered.

After Ginger's initial hello, she hadn't exactly welcomed him home with kisses and softness and excitement, and while he was champing at the bit to start officially dating, she was far more concerned about his pain meds. Maybe it was time, even long past time, to lay all his cards on the table. He was home. She was home. He wanted to be with her. It was time to say it.

When Cain arrived later that morning to check in on him, he was sitting on the porch, his mood still middling foul.

"How you doin'?" asked Cain, taking the free seat beside his cousin. "Good to be home?"

Woodman shrugged, reaching for a glass of the sweet tea his mother had brought them. "It's good to see my folks. But I hate the way they look at me."

"They're just worried, son. Give them some time to adjust."

"Yeah, I know," he muttered, setting his glass down. "Want to know the worst of it?"

"Tell me."

"I *liked* bein' a damage controlman, Cain. I *liked* puttin' out fires. I liked feelin' like a . . . a danged superhero. I would've done it forever. I would've stayed in for the four years like we promised, then come home and gotten a job workin' at the FD. No college, no need. Just a pension from Uncle Sam and a job right here, fightin' fires and savin' people. Maybe I would've even made assistant chief after a few years. With Ginger by my side, it would've been a good life. A real good life."

"You can still *have* that life."

"*How*?" Woodman lashed out, his frustration mounting. "How do I have that life when I can't even—fuck! I can't even walk around on my own goddamned *feet*? I can't *save people* from fires, Cain. I can't be a firefighter no more! I can't . . . I can't . . ."

"You can still contribute!" yelled Cain, looking furious. "Stop bein' so goddamned hopeless, Josiah! You can still go down to the fire department. You can, fuck, I don't know, answer the fuckin' phones! Share what you learned in the service! Have dinner waitin' when the guys come back from calls! Hell, you're still *useful*!"

"Everythin' okay out here?" asked his momma, sticking her head through the doorway and wringing her hands as she looked back and forth between the cousins, finally resting disapproving eyes on Cain. "Maybe your cousin's tirin' you out, honey?"

"Nah," said Woodman, shaking his head, his shoulders slumping. "It's not Cain. It's me, Momma."

"Why, you're just . . ." She stepped onto the patio, gesturing uselessly to his foot before looking at his face with glassy eyes.

"He's just recoverin'," said Cain smoothly.

"Recoverin'! That's all. Why, you'll be up on your . . ." Realizing what she was about to say, his mother gasped, pressing her hand to her chest.

"Up on your own two feet in no time," finished Cain with confidence. "Know why? 'Cause you're the toughest sumbitch I know."

"Oh my," said his mother, fanning her face at Cain's use of profanity.

"Don't cuss in front of my momma, Cain. Where were you born? In a barn?"

"Nah," he said, winking at his cousin "But I'm livin' in one!"

Woodman rolled his eyes, but his chest shook with laughter, and even his mother giggled softly before kissing the top of his head and returning to the house. Once she was safely out of earshot, Woodman leaned forward. "She fusses over me too goddamned much. Makes me feel like an invalid."

"She's your momma. Smile and say thank you."

"Yeah. I guess." He paused, changing gears and watching Cain carefully for a reaction. "Saw Ginger last night. She stopped by on her way home from work."

"Oh, yeah? Where's she workin'?"

"Silver Springs. You know, where they put her gran."

Cain nodded. "Sure."

"She's gorgeous, Cain," said Woodman, holding the rim of the glass between his lips, his gaze riveted on Cain's face. Surely, if he'd seen her by now, Woodman would see some spark of recognition in his cousin's eyes. "She's, well, she's everythin' a man could want."

"That right?"

"Just seein' her made me, well, it made me want to, I don't know . . . Maybe it made me want to stop feelin' sorry for myself and figure out what comes next."

Woodman felt relieved when Cain nodded, an encouraging smile on his face. "Glad to hear that, son."

But it wasn't enough. He needed to hear it. He needed to know that Cain had no designs on Ginger. He wouldn't rest easy until he was reassured.

"You wouldn't . . . I mean, I know you're stayin' there at

McHuid's for a few weeks, and you two had that incident a few years ago, but you'd never make a move on her . . ."

Leaning forward, Cain placed a hand on his cousin's knee. "You staked your claim years ago, son. She's yours."

A rush of powerful relief coursed through Woodman, and he felt his whole body relax just as a shot of adrenaline and hope sluiced through him. Cain had no interest in Ginger, and besides, he was leaving in two and a half weeks. And while Woodman would miss his cousin, he'd be the man left in Apple Valley, ready and willing to court Ginger. Lord willing, it would all work out as it was supposed to.

He grinned at Cain. "Hey, maybe you're right about the fire department. Maybe they could use someone to, I don't know, answer the phone, like you said, or I could share some of my trainin', or . . . What do you think?"

"I think you won't know until you ask."

"Give me a ride over there?"

Cain chuckled at Woodman's sudden gumption, raising his eyebrows and shaking his head. "I will. But give it a few days, huh? Rest up first, okay? For your momma's sake."

Sighing, Woodman sat back, knowing that Cain was right, but frustrated that a plan was forming in his head and he wasn't able to jump at it as he would have before the accident. "Friday, Cain."

Cain had agreed to come back on Friday to take him to the fire department, but in the meantime Woodman had taken out his laptop and set it up on the kitchen table, determined to familiarize himself with the department and maybe even to figure out where a man like him could be useful.

He wasn't expecting Ginger, but when the doorbell rang and she walked into the kitchen with his mother a moment later, he was glad to see her all the same.

"Gin!" he greeted her, looking up from his computer.

She looked like a picture, her hair all soft and golden, wearing fancy pants, a dark blue sweater, and pearls. It occurred to Woodman that she'd dressed up for him, and his heart just about exploded with gratitude and hope. Smiling broadly, she reached out a hand and he took it, squeezing it affectionately as he drank in the sight of her pretty face, letting his eyes dip lower, to her full breasts straining against her sweater as she sat down. She caught him, giving him a look of censure and pulling her hand away before sitting down.

"You sure look nice."

"Thank you," she said, sitting across from him. "Thought I'd stop by. Didn't like how we left things last night."

Nor did he, although seeing her had given him a bit of a kick in the ass. He was determined to get back on his feet faster than ever now.

"Woodman," said his mother, "I'm runnin' to the market. Anythin' you need?"

"No, thanks, Momma," said Woodman, his eyes totally focused on the gorgeous girl across from him. "I got everythin' I need right here."

His mother scurried out, and Ginger blushed a deep pink, which made Woodman grin like a crazy person. He affected her, and the knowledge was so welcome, he could have cried.

"Shouldn't say things like that," she said, getting up and walking across the kitchen to the refrigerator. "I think it makes your momma jealous."

He chuckled at her remark but composed himself when he realized she'd given him the perfect opportunity to share his feelings with her.

"But it's the truth, Gin. It's how I feel."

His conversation with Cain this morning had primed the pump, so to speak. She was eighteen and he was twenty-one, and Woodman had loved her ever since he was eight years old. It was high time to put his cards on the table.

"I'm home now," he continued. "Stable. Not runnin' off again." He paused, wishing she'd turn around and face him. "I'm ready for somethin' serious, Gin. With you."

"Woodman, we're not . . ."

He tensed. *Oh God, sweet girl, don't call me your friend again, when we both know I could be so much more.*

"Not what?"

"You've been gone for three years," she said, walking back to the table holding a carton of cream.

"That's right. And now I'm home, and I want to be with you, dar—"

She looked up at him, frowning. "Do we have to have this conversation right now? I have so much on my plate. I'm in school and workin', and Gran's sick, and I just don't . . . I mean, I don't have time to date *anyone*, Woodman. I don't need this kind of pressure on my life."

Her words weren't unreasonable, nor did they friend-zone him, nor did they outright reject his offer. Seen in a certain light, she was merely saying that his timing wasn't good, and he could buy that. In fact, he agreed that his timing wasn't good, but ever since the accident, he'd been anxious for control over his rapidly changed, out-of-his-control-feeling life.

Woodman could deal with bad timing—hell, he could even deal with being friend-zoned because he was sure he could wait her out and wear her down. But there was one reason for her not wanting him that he wouldn't be able to change or fix.

"Is it because I'm crippled?"

"Woodman!" she scolded him, her eyes widening in shock. "After *that* question? It's because you're *stupid*."

"*I'm* stupid," he repeated, trying to follow her and unsure of where she was going.

"Yes!" she said. "You're stupid if you think your injury would matter to me like that."

"So it *doesn't* matter to you . . . like that?" he asked, his lips tilting up just slightly, a rush of relief and happiness making him dizzy.

"It doesn't matter to me, other than I want you to be as whole as you can be. And that's goin' to take a little while. Woodman, you don't need a . . . a romantic distraction right now."

"And you don't *want* one," he said softly.

She took a deep breath, held it, and slowly let it go, looking up to meet his eyes. "It's not the right time."

"When will it be?"

"I don't know."

In fairness, she was right. His timing was total shit. Motivated by a need to control *something* in his life, he was pushing her to a place that was completely unfair, and he needed to back off. He'd been home for exactly twelve hours. He had no right to ask her to make a decision about dating him; they needed to spend some time together, get to know each other again on a daily basis, and see what happened. Besides, he was home for the long haul now, right? And he'd made his intentions and desires crystal clear. And, he reminded himself, feeling a strong sense of relief, she hadn't shot him down.

It was time to practice patience.

He nodded. "Okay, Gin. You know what I want, but I'll

leave the ball in your court. When you're ready, come find me. I'll be waitin' for you."

Her shoulders relaxed, and she grinned at him—a happy, more carefree smile. "And until then, we'll just be friends?"

Ugh. The dreaded word.

Patience. Patience. Patience.

He nodded in agreement. "Friends."

She rewarded him with a beautiful, beaming Ginger smile, picked up her coffee cup, and flicked a glance to his laptop. "What're you up to?"

"Oh, I'm just checkin' out the Apple Valley Fire Department website here."

"Huh. What for?"

"Might ask if I can help out there." He paused, looking up at her, searching her face for a reaction as he said his cousin's name. "Cain thought it would be a good idea."

"Cain," she practically spat, and again Woodman felt a deep sense of relief, which he immediately regretted. Cain had been good to him. Cain's support had made his injury and move home bearable. Despite the fact that he wanted to keep Cain and Ginger apart, he couldn't let her speak ill of him.

"I know you don't like him, but he's been real good to me, Gin. He took a lot of time off to see me in Germany, then more time off to drive me home. To tell you the truth, I don't know what I would've done without him."

"We're talkin' about *Cain Wolfram*?" she asked acidly. "Self-servin', self-centered, horse's ass Cain Wolfram, right?"

"Remind me to never get on your bad side, darlin'." Woodman chuckled softly, admiring the spark in her pretty eyes. "Listen, ole Cain's never goin' to be a perfect Southern gentleman, but he's changed, Gin. I swear it."

"Ha!" she snorted.

"I'm tellin' you, Cain's a better man than he ever was. Ain't drinkin' half so much."

"But whorin' double," she blurted out, then clapped her hand over her mouth.

Holy cow, she hates his guts, he thought.

"You always had a way with words, Miss Ginger!"

Her shoulders shook as she laughed with him, and Woodman felt a deep sense of contentment, sitting at his parents' kitchen table, drinking coffee, and laughing with the woman he loved.

We could have this forever. Life could be full of laughs and love and kids and . . . Patience. Quit getting ahead of yourself.

"I can't speak for his . . ." Woodman cleared his throat, still choking back laughter, "extracurricular activities, but I can tell you this: he's cleaned up his act. Never thought I'd say this, but when he leaves in two and a half weeks, I sure will miss him."

He meant the words, felt them suddenly in the pit of his stomach, how much he would miss Cain, how—when Cain left—his life in the military would truly be over. But he lifted his eyes to Ginger, hoping that she would be the anchor for him in civilian life that Cain had been in the Navy.

"Enough about Cain." She grinned at him sweetly. "Tell me more about your plans to work at the firehouse."

Chapter 10

~ Ginger ~

She stopped by to see Woodman before heading to work, and this time she wore cream silk slacks and a navy blue sweater set with pearls. She could change into scrubs in the ladies' room before her shift started.

Miz Sophie gave her a polite smile as she opened the door. "Ginger! You put a little extra effort into your visit today, I see."

Ginger bit back a smart remark and held out a loaf of zucchini bread she'd picked up from the farmers' market and smiled, as expected. "For your breakfast tomorrow."

"Why, thank you!" Sophie leaned forward conspiratorially. "I 'spose you're here to see Josiah? He's in much better spirits today."

As if they could get worse, she thought.

"Wonderful news," she said politely, following Miz Sophie to the kitchen, where she found Woodman sitting at the rustic kitchen table, a cup of coffee and a laptop on the table before him and his leg elevated on a chair under the table.

"Gin!" he greeted her, looking up from his computer. His hair and beard still looked unkempt, but his color was better, which meant he'd gotten a good night's sleep and was taking his meds as directed to keep the pain at bay.

She reached out a hand and he took it, squeezing it affectionately as his eyes wandered over her outfit. They rested on her breasts before sliding back up to her face. "You sure look nice."

"Thank you," she said, pulling her hand away and taking a seat across from him. "Thought I'd stop by. Didn't like how we left things last night."

"Coffee, honey?"

"Yes, please," she said, grinning at Miz Sophie, who placed a steaming mug before her.

"Woodman, I'm runnin' to the market. Anythin' you need?"

"No, thanks, Momma," said Woodman, sparing a quick look at his mother before focusing on Ginger again. "I got everythin' I need right here."

Miz Sophie's eyes narrowed for just a moment before telling them to behave and slipping out the door, leaving Ginger blushing and Woodman beaming at her discomposure.

"Shouldn't say things like that," she said. "I think it makes your momma jealous."

Woodman chuckled. "But it's the truth, Gin. It's how I feel."

Uncomfortable with this declaration, she stood up abruptly and crossed to the refrigerator, opening it in search of cream and grateful for the cool air on her cheeks.

"I'm home now," he said to her back. "Stable. Not runnin' off again." He paused. "I'm ready for somethin' serious, Gin.

With you."

"Woodman, we're not . . ."

"Not what?"

"You've been gone for three years," she said evenly, closing the refrigerator door and turning to face him.

"That's right. And now I'm home, and I want to be with you, dar—"

"Do we have to have this conversation right now?" she interrupted, feeling an edge of panic slip into her voice. "I have so much on my plate. I'm in school and workin', and Gran's sick, and I just don't . . . I mean, I don't have time to date *anyone*, Woodman. I don't need this kind of pressure on my life."

His face dropped, but he held her gaze. "Is it because I'm crippled?"

"Woodman!" she scolded him, her eyes widening in shock. "After *that* question? It's because you're *stupid*."

"*I'm* stupid," he said tersely.

"Yes!" she said. "You're stupid if you think your injury would matter to me like that."

"So it *doesn't* matter to you . . . like that?" he asked, his lips tilting up just slightly.

She sat back down at the table and poured a little cream into her coffee. "It doesn't matter to me, other than I want you to be as whole as you can be. And that's goin' to take a little while. Woodman, you don't need a . . . a romantic distraction right now."

"And you don't *want* one."

She took a deep breath, held it, and slowly let it go, stirring her coffee deliberately as she looked up and met his eyes. "It's not the right time."

"When will it be?"

"I don't know," she said simply, hating the fact that Cain's face slipped through her mind uninvited and unwanted.

Woodman stared at her for a long while before nodding. "Okay, Gin. You know what I want, but I'll leave the ball in your court. When you're ready, come find me. I'll be waitin' for you."

His words touched her heart, and she wished—for the millionth time—that she felt for Woodman half the attraction she felt for Cain.

"And until then," she asked, grinning at him with affection and relief, "we'll just be friends?"

He winced like he smelled something bad, then grudgingly nodded. "Friends."

Beaming at him as she picked up her coffee cup, she felt much better. She took a sip, then placed it back on the table, glancing at his laptop. "What're you up to?"

"Oh, I'm just checkin' out the Apple Valley Fire Department website here."

"Huh. What for?"

"Might ask if I can help out there." He paused, looking up at her. "Cain thought it would be a good idea."

"Cain," she said darkly, the name sour in her mouth.

"I know you don't like him," said Woodman, "but he's been real good to me, Gin. He took a lot of time off to see me in Germany, then more time off to drive me home. To tell you the truth, I don't know what I would've done without him."

"We're talkin' about *Cain Wolfram*?" she asked acidly. "Self-servin', self-centered, horse's ass Cain Wolfram, right?"

"Remind me to never get on your bad side, darlin'." Woodman chuckled softly. "Listen, ole Cain's never goin' to be a perfect Southern gentleman, but he's changed, Gin. I swear it."

I've changed. My troublemakin' days are behind me, darlin'.

"Ha!" she snorted.

But she couldn't help but wonder when he'd changed and how he'd changed, and if he deserved a second chance that she didn't feel like giving.

"I'm tellin' you, Cain's a better man than he ever was. Ain't drinkin' half so much."

"But whorin' double," she blurted out, then clapped her hand over her mouth.

Woodman's eyes widened to saucers, twinkling and merry. "You always had a way with words, Miss Ginger!" He cackled with mirth, and she knew they were both thinking of the time she'd called Mary-Louise Walker, Big Tits Walker.

Her shoulders shook as she laughed with him, relieved that their friendship appeared to be restored for now.

"I can't speak for his . . ." Woodman cleared his throat, still choking back laughter, "extracurricular activities, but I can tell you this: he's cleaned up his act. Never thought I'd say this, but when he leaves in two and a half weeks, I sure will miss him."

Leaves in two and a half weeks. Leaves. The words swam around in her head, making her dizzy, making her heart ache, making her long for peace with this supposedly new and improved version of Cain before he left again.

She picked up her coffee and took a long sip, wishing she could just shrug off her feelings and leave Cain in her wake once and for all, but Cain was in her blood, and she could already feel her clenched heart opening like a flower to the sun, hopeful, longing, wondering who Cain was now, and desperately wanting to know.

She caught Woodman staring at her thoughtfully and forced a cheerful grin. "Enough about Cain. Tell me more about your plans to work at the firehouse."

***

Three days later, she was watering the geraniums on Gran's front porch when Cain ambled up to the cottage, a distant look in his eyes and Klaus's toolbox hanging by his side. And, oh Lord, how her heart hammered. He was tall and muscular, his chest broad, his arms thick and corded, veins winding around the sinew. His jeans sat on his hips, slung low, and he walked with an unhurried grace, as though the world waited for Cain, never the other way around. He was comfortable and confident, at ease in his skin with a force field of masculine energy around him that fairly leveled her. And yet his face, lost in thought, had a sort of shocking ethereal beauty too—pale skin over cut angles and icy eyes under long, curled, jet-black lashes. He was a dark angel, a blue-eyed devil, the very embodiment of her fiercest desires and the apathetic object of her unrequited love. And for just a moment, she hated him. She hated his beauty and grace and potency. She hated it because she wanted it, longed for it, dreamed of it . . . and he had denied her of its having.

She straightened her spine and put her hands on her hips.

"What are *you* doin' here?" she snapped.

"Why are you *livin'* here?" asked Cain, casting his glance at the manor house before looking back at her. "Castle not to your likin', princess?"

She rolled her eyes, gesturing to his toolbox with a flick of her chin. "Klaus sent you to fix my sink?"

"Always wanted to get a look at your plumbin', Gin."

It was such an unexpected and teasing remark, her lips parted, and she felt an imminent smile. Unwilling to provide him

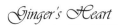

such approval, she turned around and huffed, heading back into the cottage to compose herself.

Don't fall for his wiles. Be stronger, Gin. Whether he's changed or not, doesn't matter, doesn't change how he left things between you. Be smart and keep your distance.

A rumble of light laughter filled the little kitchen as he followed her inside, and her longing to be closer to its source made her head to the farthest edge of the room and face him, crossing her arms over her chest as though annoyed. She gestured to her sink with an open palm. "It's clogged."

But Cain wasn't looking at the sink. He was looking at Ginger. Setting his toolbox down on the floor, he did nothing, in fact, but look at Ginger. Her breath caught as his eyes caressed her face, trailing from her hair to her eyes, sliding down her cheeks to her lips in leisurely perusal. Her pulse raced, throbbing in her throat, as he dropped his intense gaze to her breasts, holding there for an interminable moment before lowering his gaze to her hips and legs. She could hear the subtle increase in his breathing—the way it quickened, the way it grew more ragged as time stopped and Cain studied her.

As his eyes skated back up her body, they were hungry, and she was acutely aware of his size, so much bigger and stronger than she, in the small room they shared. But she wasn't frightened or intimidated—this was Cain, after all, whom she'd known forever, and she had a funny sense that he was trying to catch up, trying to figure her out the same way she was trying to get her bearings with him. He was logging the changes in her, and the shift in his breathing told her he liked what he saw, which made it the most erotic sixty seconds of Ginger's heretofore unerotic life. Her nipples tightened, her veins pulsed, and her private places flooded with a sudden rush of liquid heat.

Cain. Oh God, Cain, how do you do this to me with just a look?

She wanted to race across the room and leap into his arms. She wanted his lips on hers, his hands on her body. She wanted clothes littered across the kitchen floor. She wanted things she'd never experienced before—the weight of his body on top of hers, the heat of his skin branding hers, his breath in places that had never seen the light of day. She was on fire. She was . . .

Gaping.

And he was staring at her with wide eyes that seemed to know exactly what she was thinking.

"You done?" she sniped.

"Are *you*?"

"So full of yourself."

Cain took a deep breath and released it in a huff, stepping toward her. And she noted a change in him—his movements were still graceful, but they were tight and focused now, like a wolf stalking its prey. And his glance was less about exploration, focused with laserlike precision on her eyes.

"Princess," he drawled, moving still closer, "I know I was an ass to you once upon a time, but I swear I've changed."

"You seem the same," she murmured, but her voice lacked conviction because she wasn't telling the truth.

In some ways—*in the way he set a woman on fire with only his eyes*—he felt the same. He still teased her as he always had. His conversation was as loaded with innuendo as it had ever been. But there was something deeper and more earnest in his voice when he'd talked about Woodman a few nights ago, and now, when he said he'd changed, something about the way he said it felt less like a line and more like . . . honesty.

"I'm sorry, Gin," he said gently, taking another step

toward her, mercilessly holding her eyes and not allowing her to look away. He took a deep breath and let it go slowly before saying, "I'm so fuckin' sorry I stood you up that night."

These words. Oh God.

Her longing for these words—for *some* indication of Cain's remorse—had haunted her for three long years, taunting her with their unattainable sweetness. And now, out of nowhere, here they were, delivered by the devil of her dreams. Her eyes swam with grateful, relieved tears, and he blurred before her.

"You hurt me bad, Cain."

He nodded once, his eyes grieved. "I know. I'm sorry."

"Why didn't you say anythin' before now? Why didn't you ever write to me, Cain?" she asked, taking a step in his direction, closing the distance between them, wanting the warmth and strength of his arms around her, as much to comfort her as to satisfy her fierce desire to be touched by him.

"Because you weren't my girl."

"I *was*. I *wanted* to be."

And then, like he'd read her mind, he opened those arms that she'd missed like a second skin, and Ginger stepped forward, her forehead landing on the bare skin of his neck as he embraced her. She took a ragged breath and held it, savoring the familiar, reassuring smell of Cain. She closed her eyes and exhaled, letting her breath caress the skin of his throat and memorizing the way his hard muscles felt under her fingers.

Her hands were flat against his chest, and she could feel the furious pounding of his heart, the way it thundered under her palms, but she slid her hands to his sides and stepped forward so that her heart was pressed against his and she was holding him too. And in so doing, she offered him the forgiveness she'd withheld since that terrible night he'd hurt her. And as though accepting it, his arms tightened around her, and he pressed his lips to her head.

"I've missed you, princess," he muttered, his lips making kissing sounds against her hair, his voice low and strained. "I fuckin' missed you."

"Cain," she sobbed, forgiving three years of heartbreak as she accepted his apology and welcomed him back into her life. She felt hot tears pool in her eyes and fall onto his chest. "I missed you too."

"I dreamed of you, Gin."

Oh God, my heart.

She'd dreamed of him too.

"Every night," she murmured, kissing him, letting her lips touch down on the hot skin at the base of his throat and linger. She felt him shudder and reveled in his reaction, heady with this new power that she held over him. She lifted her lips, then dragged them over his skin again, her eyes closed, the muscles deep in her body tensing reflexively, instinctively, in preparation for something she hadn't yet experienced.

"Ginger, I . . ."

"Cain," she sighed, the words coming quickly and easily, and feeling as right as sunshine on a summer morning, "I'm yours."

But the words, which felt so right to her, weren't the right words at all.

He froze instantly, his hands lifting from her back as he took a sudden step away. Her body was jelly, and without the strength of his chest holding her up, she swayed. He reached out and put his hands on her shoulders to steady her as she opened her eyes, looking up at him in confusion.

"Ginger . . ." His face was stricken, torn, and confused. He searched her eyes, begging her to understand. *Understand what?* she wanted to ask, but he spoke again before her lips could form the words. "I just want us to be friends, Gin. Just friends, if that's okay."

Friends? After the warmth—*the heat*—of his words, *Ifuckinmissedyou*, this terrible, unexpected word, *friends*, bore a chill that smacked her face like a January wind. She didn't feel *friendship* for Cain. She hadn't felt friendship for Cain since she was twelve years old.

"Friends," she repeated dumbly, staring up at him in confusion, her mind trying to figure out what the heck had just happened.

Friends? Wait. No. No! Nothing about the way they'd just embraced felt friendly. His words, *I've missed you, I dreamed of you,* didn't feel friendly. The way he'd passionately kissed her hair and held her. None of it felt friendly. What the *hell* was going on?

He nodded, pulling his hands away from her. "Yeah. Friends. We . . . we grew up together, Gin. We should be friends, not enemies, don't you think?"

She looked up at his face. His jaw was tense, his eyes still dilated and dark, his cheeks flushed. His voice was offering her friendship, but it clearly wasn't what his body wanted.

"Cain, I—"

"I missed home," he said quickly, cutting her off and stepping away again. He looked away from her, as if meeting her eyes was painful. *You're lying*, she thought, letting her arms fall listlessly by her side as he continued trying to convince her that his impassioned words had somehow been impersonal. "Of course I missed you, but I also missed my pop and Apple Valley and even McHuid's. I missed *home*. I dreamed of it all the time."

She stared at him, unsure of what to say. She was positive she hadn't misinterpreted the way he'd touched her, the way he'd spoken to her, but it was also clear he wanted her to buy this song and dance about missing home.

I'm yours.

She'd said the words and meant them, but they'd made Cain push her away. Why? Was he frightened of being with her? Of belonging to someone? Of loving someone? His body had reacted to her nearness—his heart thundering under her hand, his breathing ragged and fast. But suddenly he'd frozen, and now he was building a little wall called friends to keep them at a distance from each other. Why? Why wouldn't he give the chemistry between them a chance?

His eyes searched hers, and as though he knew the questions she was about to ask, he shook his head, warning her not to.

"Friends," he said firmly. "That's all."

It hurt to hear him say it with such finality, but in the strangest way, there was solace in the fact that he was lying to her. She was positive he wanted her, even though he was denying them both. He wanted her, and she knew it, and she clung to it. It didn't matter if he called her his friend. His feelings for her ran deeper than friendship. She was certain of it.

He crossed the kitchen and stopped at the sink, bracing his hands on the basin. "Let me take a look at this, okay?"

"Okay, Cain," she said softly.

She didn't know why he wouldn't surrender to his feelings for her, but maybe it was because of their age difference, or because he was returning to the service, or because Woodman had always had a crush on her. Or maybe, as she suspected before, it was because Cain wasn't sure of how to love someone, how to belong to someone. And suddenly she realized that it didn't really matter why he needed space between them. He could call them friends all he wanted. He was home for two more weeks, and she planned to figure out why he wouldn't let her closer, why he was so determined to keep her at arm's length. And once she did, she'd untangle the riddle of how to love him the way he needed her to, and how to get him to admit he loved her back.

He looked so sorry, so frustrated and filled with yearning, she smiled at him. And into that smile, small though it was, she poured all her love, her desire, her profound hope that words were just semantics and the feelings they shared for each other were so strong, they wouldn't be denied.

He stared back at her, seemingly overcome.

"It's okay," she said gently.

He exhaled a breath on a low hiss.

"I'm glad," he said.

As much as she would have liked to ogle him for the rest of the afternoon, she needed to think. She needed to figure out what came next for her and Cain. She nodded, gesturing to the stairs. "I'll, uh . . . I'll be upstairs. Call if you need me, huh?"

Cain lay down on his back, sliding his head under her sink. "Will do."

Ginger turned and headed up the stairs, her hand flattened over her pounding heart.

Chapter 11

~ Cain ~

"Promised to take a look at the kitchen sink. At the cottage," said Klaus, who was sitting on a bench outside the barn on Thursday afternoon. "But I got to wait for Doc Keller to come. Ravenal's lungs is rumbling. So I thought you go up and take a look for me."

After running into Ginger in her car on Monday night, Cain had taken a long walk, thinking about nothing but her. In all the years he'd known her, he'd never experienced the sort of cold shoulder she'd given him as she drove up the driveway. Man, he must have hurt her. It was the one thing he'd never, ever wanted, and the reality of it—*written all over her face*— made him feel like total shit. And while he'd promised himself to stay away from her for Josiah's sake, he *needed* to make amends. He needed to find a way to let her know that he was sorry. And banking on the fact that he was living in the barn and she was living in the cottage, he assumed they'd eventually bump into each other. Just . . .

"Cain? The sink?"

. . . not yet.

"Uh, why don't I wait for the vet?" said Cain, sitting down on the bench beside his father.

Yes, he needed to apologize to her, and yes, this would be a good opportunity, but the thought of her ice-cold eyes made him pause. Waiting a few more days wouldn't hurt anything, would it?

"I'll wait for Doc Keller. You go check on Ginger's sink."

His father gave him a sidelong look. "*You* get the sink. *I* get the vet."

"Aw, plumbin' ain't my—"

"Cain," said Klaus, his light blue eyes suddenly all-knowing and all-seeing. "She live here. You can't avoid her *für immer*."

Für immer. Forever.

Cain swiped his thumb across his bottom lip. "What do you mean? I ain't avoidin' her. If anything—"

"You were friends. Now? You're not. But it's *gut* to be friends."

"Friends."

Klaus nodded. "Don't *ficke sie* like the others."

"Pop!"

"A father know his son. I know you're popular with the *Damen*."

"She's different," said Cain.

"*Ja.* She's special," said Klaus. "So go unclog the princess's sink and make everything *gut*. Take my advice. I'm old. I wish I had made things right when I had the chance."

As Cain walked up the driveway with his father's toolbox, he reflected that his father's words were the closest he'd probably ever come to admitting that McHuid's and his love of horses had gotten in the way of his marriage, but there was a peace to hearing his father confess it. And it allowed Cain to quietly forgive his father too.

He wasn't sure if it was because of a change in his attitude or the fact that Woodman wasn't around to steal his father's attention, but Cain found himself enjoying his father's company. Yes, Klaus talked about horses an absurd amount, but it was passionate, good-natured talk, and because Cain had practically grown up at McHuid's, he found he was able to contribute a great deal to the conversation. It made for pleasant evenings of slow-cooked chicken paprikash and boiled spätzle with cheese, full of unexpected camaraderie, and Cain felt grateful for the opportunity to get to know his father again, to see him through a new lens.

Since returning home, Cain hadn't been down to the Glenn River Distillery a hell of a lot either, though a couple of his old friends had stopped by to invite him to join them for a night of drinking. The contrast in their lives was startling. Cain had sailed the world, learned how to protect an aircraft carrier from all manner of fire, taken control of his life, and developed pride in his service, while most of them had lingered around Apple Valley for the past three years, mooching off their parents, getting fucked-up at the distillery, and holding down shit jobs. He just didn't feel like he had much in common with them anymore, and besides, he was anxious to show his father, and everyone else in Apple Valley, that Cain Wolfram could be more than troublemaking white trash.

A few of the girls he'd "dated" had stopped by, too, and Cain had to admit, they were still looking pretty fine. Point in fact, after he drove Woodman to the fire department tomorrow, he had a date with Mary-Louise Walker to get reacquainted at her place. And by *reacquainted*, he intended to fuck her five ways from Sunday and watch those epic tits rock and roll all over her apartment until dawn. His mouth watered just thinking about it.

"What are *you* doin' here?" demanded a saucy voice, interrupting his thoughts. He looked up to find Ginger, hands on her hips, standing on old Mrs. McHuid's little front porch.

"Why are you *livin'* here?" asked Cain, gesturing to the manor house with his chin before looking back at her. "Castle not to your likin', princess?"

She rolled her eyes, flicking a glance to his toolbox. "Klaus sent you to fix my sink?"

"Always wanted to get a look at your plumbin', Gin."

Her lips parted in surprise before she huffed in annoyance, turning her back to Cain as she stomped back into the cottage. But one, he could have sworn he saw her lips tilt up before her show of pique, and two, she left the door open.

Chuckling softly—because, Lord, the woman knew how to hold a grudge—he followed her inside, noting that she stood in the far, far corner of the tiny room—as far away from sink as possible. She gestured to it with an open palm. "It's clogged."

Setting his father's toolbox down on the floor, he took a moment—*stole* a short moment—to look at her.

She wasn't very tall, maybe five-foot-five inches, just tall enough for her head to nestle perfectly under his chin. Her blonde hair was up in a ponytail again, but she wasn't wearing her glasses from Monday night. She didn't wear makeup either, not that she needed any: naturally she was, hands down, the prettiest girl he'd ever seen, and he'd seen a lot of what the world had to offer. Her yellow T-shirt was scoop-necked and hugged her perfect size B tits like a fucking dream, and her jeans, standard Levi's, cupped her rounded ass like they'd been custom-made. Her waist was trim, hips narrow, and Cain knew her legs were probably even more toned now than they'd been three years ago. She was a fucking work of art, this woman. An *angry* work of art, he amended when his eyes skated back up her body.

"You done?" she sniped.

"Are *you*?" he countered, noticing the way she'd been ogling his chest before meeting his eyes.

"So full of yourself."

And that was it. He just couldn't bear her rancor anymore. He owed her an apology, and by God, she was going to get one.

"Princess," he drawled, taking a step toward her, "I know I was an ass to you once upon a time, but I swear I've changed."

"You seem the same," she murmured, though her face softened with uncertainty. She licked her lips unconsciously, and he knew—beyond any shadow of doubt—that she was suddenly remembering their kiss in as much detail as he was.

"I'm sorry, Gin," he said tenderly, taking another step toward her. "I'm so fuckin' sorry I stood you up that night."

She clenched her jaw, and though her eyes were severe, they flooded with tears as she stared back at him. "You hurt me bad, Cain."

He nodded. "I know. I'm sorry."

"Why didn't you say anythin' before now? Why didn't you ever write to me, Cain?" she asked, taking a step in his direction, closing the distance between them.

"Because you weren't my girl."

"I *was*. I *wanted* to be."

His arms, appendages he'd warned *not* to open to her

under any circumstances, spread wide, and Ginger stepped forward, her forehead landing on the bare skin of his neck as he embraced her, holding his breath and closing his eyes. The bony angles of her teenage body had rounded into womanhood, and as she clasped him to her body, her curves cradled his muscles.

And all thoughts of Mary-Louise Walker, and every other female creature, were banished from his mind. Cain had known a lot of women in his life—a *fuckload* of women—but *no* woman made his heart race, made his breath catch, made his insides a trembling mess of longing like Ginger McHuid. His chemistry with her, ever since her twelfth birthday, had been catastrophic and unmatched, and holding her now was no fucking different at all. If anything, they were both mature adults now, and Cain was hotter and needier than ever.

"I've missed you, princess," he muttered into her hair, pressing his lips to the citrus-scented golden strands. "I fuckin' missed you."

"Cain," she sobbed, and he felt the moisture of her tears against his skin, sliding between his pecs, baptizing him with her sorrow. "I missed you too."

"I dreamed of you, Gin."

"Every night," she murmured, her lips touching down on the exposed V of his chest and making him shudder. *Christ. More.*

"Ginger, I . . ."

"Cain, I'm yours."

You staked your claim years ago.

She's yours.

Woodman.

He froze, his hands lifting from her back as he took a sudden step away. She swayed slightly, unprepared for the loss of his body against hers. He reached out and put his hands on her shoulders to steady her and took a deep breath, willing his body not to react to her nearness.

"Ginger . . ." He swallowed over the lump in his throat and offered her a neutral smile as he uttered words he'd never before in his life said to a woman. "I just want us to be friends, Gin. Just friends, if that's okay."

"Friends," she repeated dumbly, staring up at him in confusion.

He nodded, pulling his hands away from her now that she was standing on her own. "Yeah. Friends. We . . . we grew up together, Gin. We should be friends, not enemies, don't you think?"

"Cain, I—"

"I missed home," he said, trying to explain away the passionate way he'd just held her. "Of course I missed you, but I also missed my pop and Apple Valley and even McHuid's. I missed *home*. I dreamed of it all the time."

Her eyes searched his, boring into his with the familiarity of someone who'd known him his whole life. She was confused and hurt, but talking about it wouldn't help, would only weaken his resolve. He wanted her so badly, he ached inside, but he wouldn't take away the girl who was Woodman's primary hope. Not when his cousin was still so goddamned hopeless.

"Friends," he said firmly. "That's all."

She looked so lost, so disappointed, he couldn't bear it, so he turned his back to her, clenching his eyes shut against the pain of keeping her at arm's length as he crossed the kitchen and stopped at the sink. He braced his hands on the basin, his fingers clawlike on the porcelain rim. "Let me take a look at this, okay?"

"Okay, Cain," she said softly, her voice hitching just a little.

Turning around to look at her, he saw the sadness on her face, but her sweet lips lifted up in a little smile—the first genuine one she'd offered him in three years—and his heart flooded with something big—no, *huge*—and warm, making it expand in his chest and thunder in his ears.

"It's okay," she said gently, and just like that, two little words that were common, everyday, ordinary words became his favorite because she wasn't pushing him for something he couldn't give, and accepting what he could.

He exhaled a breath he didn't know he'd been holding.

"I'm glad," he said.

And despite the disappointment in her eyes, and the unsatisfied longing in his heart, he *was* glad. A not insignificant part of him was glad that he'd had an opportunity to betray Woodman again, and this time, he hadn't taken it.

She nodded, her smile slipping. "I'll, uh . . . I'll be upstairs. Call if you need me, huh?"

Cain lay down on his back, staring up at pipes, grateful that his face was finally hidden from her. "Will do."

***

Never having had a close woman friend, it surprised Cain how easy and fun it was for him to have a friendship with Ginger over the next few days.

As she came home with groceries on Saturday afternoon, he helped her unload her car, joking about her choices as they stacked frozen dinners in the freezer. "Remind me not to come sniffin' around here for a home-cooked meal."

"Ha!" she retorted. "I can make biscuits and gravy with the best of 'em! But it's late when I come home from work, so forgive me for not whippin' up dinner from scratch."

He accompanied his father to Lutheran church on Sunday, running into Ginger and her parents at the Country Diner after services. While his father visited with Ranger and Miz Magnolia for a moment, exchanging pleasantries, Ginger had raised her eyes dramatically at Cain.

"Don't tell me you were at Sunday services! Did the roof cave in?"

He rolled his eyes. "I wasn't *that* bad."

"Yes," she said, her eyes twinkling and her voice even but not unkind, "you were."

"Well, I didn't see *you* there, Miss Virginia. People in glass houses—"

"I'm Presbyterian," she said, grinning at him.

"Welcome home, Cain," said Ranger McHuid, half standing to offer his hand. "Looks like the service is treatin' you well, son."

"Thanks, Mr. McHuid. It's been good for me, sir." He slid his eyes to Ginger's mother. "Nice to see you, Miz Magnolia."

"Why, Cain. You always were a handsome devil," she said, simpering as he shook her hand. "Sophie said you'd . . . improved."

Uncomfortable around Miz Magnolia, he dropped her hand quickly and shifted his eyes back to Ginger. She picked up her orange juice and sipped it to cover a giggle. When she set it down, she mouthed, "Most improved!" He felt the smile crack his face and damn near started snickering before the waitress interrupted to show him and his father to their table.

He found himself looking for her on Sunday, but they must have been running in different directions because he didn't see her. Nor on Monday, and by Monday afternoon he realized he was missing her sweet smiles and fun banter. Taking a walk up the driveway to see if she was home, he was disappointed to see her cottage dark and wondered where she was and with whom. Before his jealousy could get out of control, however, he remembered that she'd returned home late from work last Monday evening, too, when they'd said their first hellos on the darkened driveway.

She's at work.

She's just at work, not with . . .

Woodman.

Except she *could* be with Woodman.

His jaw tightened and his fists balled at his sides right before his eyes widened in horror. Fuck. Fuck, no. He wasn't *jealous* of Woodman, was he? Fuck. He *was*. He was jealous of *anyone* who got to spend time with her because he wanted her to himself.

"Aw," he groaned, "this is no fuckin' good."

He turned around and headed back down the driveway muttering, *Just friends, just friends, just friends* in his head like a mantra until he was safely back at the barn.

Lying in his bed, staring up at the dark ceiling, he knew it wasn't okay to be jealous of Woodman. First of all, it was stupid since Woodman was the better man in almost every way, and second, Woodman *needed* Ginger. Cain just . . . aw, fuck it. Cain just *wanted* her.

For the rest of the week, he'd studiously avoided her, even hiding in the bathroom of the tack room apartment once when he saw her approaching the barn through the window of his father's little kitchen. She wasn't his, he was leaving in a week, and he had no business developing the sort of feelings that led to jealousy. No, sir. He'd avoid her until it was time for him to leave, and that was that.

***

On Thursday he rode his bike over to Belle Royale to check on Woodman. As he pulled up, he noticed an oil leak on the driveway and asked to borrow his uncle's tools. Woodman used his crutches to get to the porch and sat on the steps in the sunshine, keeping Cain company as he tinkered on his motorcycle.

"So," asked Cain, seated on the ground beside his bike, back to Woodman, a wrench in his hand. "You got a job? At the firehouse?"

"Sure did. Remember Gloria Kennedy?"

"Cute redhead with huge ta-tas?"

Woodman chuckled. "That's the one. She's havin' a baby next month, which leaves them short a dispatcher, so she's trainin' me for the job."

"That's great," said Cain, genuinely pleased. Woodman looked way better since last Friday. His color was better, his beard had been shaved, and he'd moved with more purpose and confidence from the back patio to the front porch. "Perfect fit for you, son. By the way, you look a hell of a lot better'n you did. How's the physical therapy goin'?"

"It sucks," said Woodman, "but after PT, I head to the fire department every day, and you know? It feels good, Cain. Real good. Sort of balances out the bad, you know?"

Cain's heart, which had been in knots, expecting Woodman to say that time spent with Ginger was responsible for his improvement, relaxed, and he let go of a breath he didn't know he'd been holding.

"I'm glad for you, cuz."

"I've almost got the switchboard figured out now." He

shrugged. "It ain't exactly fightin' fires, but it feels good to be pitchin' in."

"Don't tire yourself out."

"Quit bein' a nursemaid," he said. "Though, speakin' of nurses, know what else?"

Cain's head whipped around to look at Woodman, and the sparkle in his cousin's eye made Cain brace himself as he turned back around, his fingers curling over a hot metal pipe. "Tell me."

"I been seein' some of Ginger."

Putting the metal wrench on a bolt and twisting hard, he managed an "Oh?"

"Sure have. She comes to see me every other night after work."

Cain winced and his eyes fluttered closed. So she *was* coming here after work. "That right?"

"Yeah." Woodman cleared his throat from the porch. "You, uh, you see her at all over at McHuid's?"

Cain opened his eyes and shrugged, determined to keep his voice casual. "Here and there. But I'm workin', she's workin'."

"Mmm," said Woodman. "So you've seen her."

"Sure."

"She's prettier than every girl we ever met in Europe combined," said Woodman softly.

Yes, she is.

"Ha!" he exclaimed, his chest compressing as he heard the tenderness in Woodman's voice. He stood up and wiped his grease-stained hands on his jeans. He needed to get out of here before Woodman saw the truth, that Cain's feelings for Ginger were just as real, just as big, just as deep, as his.

"You don't agree? You need glasses, brother."

"Probably," he said, reaching down for the wrench and turning to his cousin. "Well, I guess that does it."

"You headed out already?" asked Woodman, shielding his eyes from the sun as he looked up at Cain.

"Uh, yeah. Got a date with, uh, Mary-Louise Walker," he said. "Almost forgot."

Woodman's shoulders relaxed, and his expression flicked neatly from relieved to impressed. "You hittin' that again?"

"Every other night," said Cain.

It was true. He was fucking Mary-Louise every chance he got, which was actually fairly despicable since every time he buried his cock inside her, he closed his eyes and pretended she was someone else.

"Lucky dog," said Woodman, winking at Cain before leaning back so his face was flooded with sunshine. "Well, I guess you should . . ."

"Yeah," said Cain, throwing the wrench in his uncle's toolbox, latching it shut, and placing it on the front steps beside his cousin.

"Cain!"

"Uh-huh?" asked Cain, pivoting to face Woodman, who had one eye cracked open.

"It's all workin' out," he said, measuring Cain's expression carefully as he reminded him of his words from their car ride home. "Me and Gin. Just like you said it would."

Cain's smile wasn't forced as he looked back at his cousin. He was happy for Woodman. He *was*.

Fuck it, he *wanted* to be.

"You deserve everythin' you want, Josiah," he said, meaning every word.

"Thanks, Cain," he said, closing his eyes again. "I don't

care how busy you get with Mary-Louise, you come and see me before you head back to Virginia next Friday, you hear?"

Cain's eyes widened and he blinked at his cousin. Head back. Holy smokes, he'd lost track of time. He was leaving in eight days. Just eight more days.

He straddled his bike and buckled his helmet. "You bet."

As he sped down the driveway, Woodman's words trailed through his head: *It's all workin' out. Me and Gin. Just like you said it would.*

Of course it is, he thought, clenching his jaw until it ached, his throbbing heart drowned out only by the raging motor between his thighs.

The girl he loved was making the right choice.

The cousin he loved was getting the girl of his dreams.

And Cain?

He was going back to a job he loved, in a world he understood, where Ginger and Woodman and Apple Valley would eventually lose their sharpness and color, and he'd figure out a way to bear their loss.

It was enough, right? It would be enough?

"It's all you get! It *has* to be enough!" he shouted, his eyes burning, his voice lost in the roar of his bike rounding a hairpin curve like it was on rails.

Wincing as he sped away from the McHuid's driveway, Cain tucked his head down and kept right on going till he reached the old distillery.

Chapter 12

~ Ginger ~

On Saturday Cain had helped her bring some groceries inside the little cottage, and she'd run into Cain and Klaus at the Country Diner after church on Sunday, but the few times she'd stopped by the barn to see him that week, he was either off-site getting a horse shoed, or his bike was gone. No matter what time she showed up, he wasn't around, and by Thursday she got the distinct feeling that he was actively avoiding her.

Just like insisting they be friends had been a way of keeping her at arm's length, he was doing the same by lying low and staying busy. But after a week, Ginger had had enough. They'd left things badly enough three years ago. She wasn't about to let their awkward conversation in her kitchen be her last glimpse of Cain for another handful of years.

So on Friday she skipped her morning classes, called in sick to work, and headed down to the barn at six o'clock in the morning, determined to sit on the goddamned bench across from the tack room and wait until Cain showed his face. Which, unfortunately for her, didn't happen until almost nine.

When the tack room door finally opened, her eyes widened in pleasure as Cain stepped out into the barn in a pair of jeans and nothing else, rubbing a hand through his black stubbly hair, his eyes still half closed. He stumbled to the open barn doors and faced the sunshine, stretching his arms over his head and giving Ginger an excellent opportunity to check out his bare torso.

A soft mewling sound escaped her throat, and Cain whirled around, opening one eye wide, then the other, surprised to see her.

She stood up and put her hands on her hips. "Are you avoidin' me?"

"Maybe," he said with a sweet, sleepy smile, his voice scratchy like it had always been in high school after a night of hard drinking.

"Out partyin' last night?" she asked.

He shrugged. "Wasn't much of a party, princess."

"Distillery?"

He took a deep breath and sighed, cocking his head to the side. "What do *you* know about the distillery? Nice girl like you shouldn't hang out down there."

"Maybe I'm not as nice as you think," she said, feeling sassy. "Besides, I'm eighteen, Cain. Everyone in Apple Valley has hung out at the distillery at some point or other."

He shook his head, grinning at her. "As long as you ain't a regular."

"I ain't a regular," she conceded, grinning back.

"Aren't you supposed to be at work?"

"Shift got canceled," she lied.

He took a step closer to her, and she could smell the stale

booze and cigarette smoke on his skin. "What you want, Miss Virginia Laire McHuid?"

She wrinkled her nose. "First? I need you to take a shower, Mr. Cain Holden Wolfram."

His smile just about set her panties on fire. "Yes, ma'am. And then?"

"Why, I need a *friend* to go ridin' with me," she said, putting on a thick Old South accent.

"And I 'spose you're thinkin' that friend should be me."

"Why not?" She shrugged playfully. "You shower. I'll saddle up Heath and Thunder. Deal?"

"I can't turn down a proper Southern lady wantin' to go for a ride," he said, turning back toward the tack room and giving her a glorious view of his denim-clad ass in retreat. "Gimme ten minutes."

"I'll give you nine," she said, marching toward the stalls with a lift in her step.

***

An hour later, they stopped by the Glenn River, eight miles downriver from her house and two from the distillery where Cain had partied last night.

"We should water them," he said, reining in Thunder and dismounting with the ease of a lifelong horseman.

She reined in Heath, who nickered in protest, and grinned down at Cain who reached up for her. His hands lingered for an extra moment on her hips as she slid down the front of his body. Leaning her head back, she stared up at him, daring him to pull her closer, to kiss her, to admit that this whole friends thing was bullshit on fire. But he clenched his jaw, cleared his throat, and dropped his hands.

"Thanks," she murmured, her voice husky in her ears as he

stared down at her, his eyes flinty and dark.

Taking Heath's reins with a grunt, he turned away from her, leading the horses to the river's edge and leaving her to follow. She leaned down to pick up a flat stone and skipped it across the slow-moving water.

"Not bad," said Cain.

"*You* were always the best."

"Nah," he said. "Woodman was better."

"Nope," she countered, picking up another stone. "Woodman was good, but you were better. Remember that Fourth of July when you skipped eleven times? *Eleven* times. It was a record."

Satisfied that the horses were calm and drinking their fill, Cain leaned down and grabbed a rock of his own, skipping it over the dark water.

One, two, three, four, five, six, seven . . .

"Wow!" she said, clapping lightly. "You've still got the touch!"

He turned to her, grinning. "You always get excited about the littlest things. What's it like gettin' a kick out of everythin', Gin?"

"What's it like gettin' a kick out of nothin', Cain?" she asked, her voice full of sass.

"I'm gettin' a kick out of *you* right now, princess."

A charge zapped between them as the words left his mouth, and her breath hitched and held for just a moment, but she looked down and picked up another rock. She was enjoying today too much to go back to Awkwardland.

She skipped her rock, which sank after three measly hops.

"Remember when you saved my American Girl doll from certain doom in this river?" she asked him.

He screwed up his face. "Wasn't me. Must have been Woodman."

"It was *you*!" she insisted. "Not Woodman!"

"Savin' a dolly? Please. That has Woodman written all over it. I couldn't have cared less if it drowned."

"But *I* cared," she said softly. "Which is why you saved it."

"Fine. Have it your way," he said, sitting down on a large rock near the water's edge.

She sighed, squatting down to wash her hands in the clear water before looking back at him. "Why do you do that?"

"Do what?"

"Let Woodman take credit for all the good things?"

He shrugged, looking away from her, out at the water. "I don't."

"You just did. Twice."

He sighed, giving her a long-suffering look. "If somethin' good happened, chances are it *was* Woodman's doin'."

"How do you figure?"

"He's the better man, Gin," said Cain, his eyes severe, his words deliberate.

She stood up slowly, turning her body completely to face him. "Do you really believe that?"

He looked away. "It's the truth."

"Cain. Cain, look at me." Her words didn't feel like enough so she beseeched him with her eyes too. "You're just as good a man as he is."

"Ha!" scoffed Cain, standing up. "Not in this life, princess."

Ginger had been witness to the differences between the cousins her whole life. Woodman came from happy parents and wealth, and his life had followed a natural course toward popularity and success, while Cain had come from unhappy parents and just-enough, and his life had followed a natural course toward rebellion and apathy. Except that Cain had somehow figured out a life for himself and pursued it, and from all outward appearances, his time in the military was a good and solid choice that was making him a better man. She couldn't bear it that he should be so hard on himself.

"You're wrong," she said. "Y'all are very different, you and Woodman, but I . . . I wish you could see yourself through *my* eyes."

He looked up at her then, and the tenderness, the *gratitude*, in his eyes made a lump rise in her throat, and it occurred to her, for the first time, that while her parents were telling her how much they loved her and Woodman's parents were telling him how much they loved him, no one was telling Cain he was loved. Klaus was too busy at McHuid's to be bothered with his small son, and Sarah had been a deeply unhappy, distracted mother. She thought back to nine-year-old Cain, hanging out by the barn during parties he wasn't invited to, hoping his friends might slip away with a piece of cake. Just an unwanted little boy looking in, finding his worth in everything left unsaid.

"Lionhearted l'il gal," he said softly.

Tears filled her eyes, but she smiled tenderly at him. "*You* skipped the most stones. *You* saved my doll. *You* are good, Cain."

"Princess," he said, his voice reverent and low, but softly pleading. "You're goin' to break me if you don't stop."

Then he stood up and crossed to the horses. He grabbed the reins and held out Heath's lead to her without meeting her eyes. Before she could mount up and turn Heath away from the stream, Cain and Thunder were already gone.

***

Ginger was afraid that their heart-to-heart by the river would create another awkward fallout with Cain and he would start avoiding her again, but the next morning she awoke to the sounds of whistling and water outside her upstairs window. When she slipped out of bed and looked down, she found Cain below in the driveway washing Gran's old Ford pickup.

"Hey!" she called.

He looked up at her from under the brim of his black cowboy hat, his lips widening into a breathtaking smile as he switched the water off. "Hey, yourself, sleepyhead!"

She grinned down at him, resting her elbow on the sill and her cheek on her palm. "What're you doin'?"

"Washin' your gran's truck. If you're goin' to use this old lady as a lawn ornament, it should always be shiny."

"Is that right?"

"That's right, princess," he said, putting his hands on his hips and taking a deep breath, which swelled his chest under his damp white T-shirt.

"You hungry after all that hard work?" she asked.

"What'cha offerin'? I already seen your freezer full of frozen pizzas."

"I'll have you know that I make a very decent sunny-side-up egg."

He chuckled, flashing a grin to the high autumn sun and adjusting the brim of his hat. "I don't doubt it."

"Then finish up and come on in."

Before he could answer, she lowered the window and stepped back into her bedroom, clasping her hands and giggling softly at this new wonder of wonders. They'd actually managed to have a deep conversation yesterday and he hadn't run away today.

"Cain," she whispered, her breath hitching as her heart swelled with an old love that suddenly felt new, that felt exciting—and finally finally finally—*possible*.

She pulled her nightgown over her head and tossed it onto the hardwood floor, pulling open her bureau drawer and selecting a white lacy bra and matching panties. She'd bought them on a whim before her senior prom, but hadn't ended up wearing them because her date—Silas Varner—had arrived drunk as a skunk to pick her up two hours early. Daddy had escorted him off the grounds of McHuid's holding a shotgun, and that had been the unceremonious end of Ginger's prom. Not that she'd really minded, she thought, pulling on her skinny jeans and rummaging through her closet for a soft pink V-neck T-shirt. Silas was nobody special to her.

Pulling her hair into a ponytail, she grinned at herself in the mirror before hurrying downstairs barefoot, glad to still hear the sound of the hose splashing across Gran's windshield.

She took a frying pan from the cabinet beside the stove and set it atop the burner, then pulled a carton of eggs from her refrigerator. As she set them on the counter, she cocked her head to the side, looking out the window over the sink to steal a glimpse of Cain. Between their quick "Good morning" and now, he'd taken off his T-shirt, probably to keep it dry as he rinsed off the truck he'd lovingly scrubbed.

His collarbone winged out from the base of his throat, strong and solid. As she followed the void between the bones down the black-haired valley from his neck to the V of muscle that disappeared into his jeans, she felt her face flush with heat. Slipping her gaze higher, she tracked the ripples of his abdomen, which led to his firm pecs, and—

God damn it!

That was precisely the moment Cain looked up and caught her staring. She felt her eyes go wide as dinner plates and took a step to the side, away from the window, her heart pounding uncomfortably as she heard his bellow of laughter.

"Someone's a peeping princess!" he yelled, spraying her kitchen window with the hose, and she reached up to place her palms against her cheeks, a soft giggle escaping as she shook her head in embarrassment.

After a moment, she remembered what she was supposed to be doing and whirled around to grab the comp'ny butter from the cupboard, slicing off a soft glop and shaking it into the hot frying pan. Four eggs followed, and when she put the carton back in the fridge, she pulled out the bread, putting two slices in the toaster and pressing the lever.

About two minutes later, the eggs were ready, and she was buttering Cain's toast as he stepped inside, his T-shirt back on.

"Didn't want to distract you from your breakfast," he teased, taking off his hat and placing it on a peg beside the door.

Her cheeks, which had just gone back to normal, flushed again, but she didn't care. Cain was here in her kitchen having breakfast, which made her so happy, it should have scared her. But all she saw was Cain, finally home again, *in* her home, back in her life, where her heart was sure he belonged.

"Still a cocky so-and-so," she observed, pouring them each a mug of coffee.

"Says the gal oglin' me from her kitchen window."

"You know what, Cain?" she said, pivoting around with the coffee in her hands.

"No. Tell me what, Gin," he volleyed back, sitting down at her small table and looking up at her with a twinkle in his eyes.

She giggled, shaking her head at him as she would at a naughty boy who was incorrigible and adorable. "I'm glad you're home."

"Is that right?" he asked.

"That's right," she whispered, holding his eyes until his smile faded and his eyes grew dark and hot.

Finally he swallowed, looking down at the eggs she'd prepared. "No frozen pizza, I see."

She placed the coffee in front of him and sat down at the other chair across from him. "I make good on my promises, Cain."

He picked up his fork, about to dig in, when he suddenly stopped, looking up at her, seizing her eyes with a sort of desperate, grateful gaze. His lips tilted up as he speared some egg on his fork. "I'm glad to be home too."

***

After breakfast, they went for another ride, dismounting again by the river and walking the horses side by side. As they meandered over the woods and meadows of Glenndale County, Cain told her about his last three years in the service—little anecdotes that made her smile, and even a few that made her eyes tear up. And what it all added up to was a man who was vastly more contented than the boy he'd been when he left, the sum of which made Ginger's heart burst with happiness because a happy Cain might be a Cain who had room in his life for her.

"It's like I was always meant to be a damage controlman," he said, threading and rethreading Thunder's reins through his fingers as they ambled at a steady pace. "I never loved horses, you know?"

"I *did* know," she said. "I could tell."

"I liked machinery."

"Like your motorcycle."

"Uh-huh. Like my bike. I never . . . I mean, don't take this the wrong way, Gin, but I never really felt like I fit in here. In Apple Valley." He scuffed the tip of his work boot on some pebbles dotting the path through Conrad's Meadow. "Only thing that made it bearable was you and Woodman."

"And the girls at the distillery," she said, giving him a sidelong glance.

He chuckled softly. "Yeah, I guess. And them. But you know they didn't *mean* nothin' to me. Not like you and Woodman."

They walked in silence for a few moments while Ginger savored the welcome warmth of his words. When she looked up at him, his angular face seemed almost soft in its own way—like for once he wasn't fighting where he was or whom he was with, like he might actually be content.

"I'm glad that you and Woodman patched things up."

Cain flicked a glance at her before nodding slowly. "Yeah. Me too. Almost fucked things up between us for good when I . . . when you and me, well, you know."

"Woodman didn't have a claim on me, Cain. I *wanted* you to kiss me."

He kept his head down, his boots crunching over pebbles and fallen leaves as they ambled along the well-trod path that crossed the meadow. "You were young."

"I knew what I wanted," she said simply.

"Let's not talk about it," he said tightly.

Ginger bit her tongue and forced herself to be silent because she *wanted* to talk about it. She wanted to get it all out in the open. Why did he run from her every time it seemed like their relationship might veer from platonic to more? Why did he shut down their conversations when they approached the topic of their attraction to each other? Why wouldn't he succumb to the feelings she sensed he had for her? It was maddening, especially since today was Saturday. Time was running down. A week from today, he'd be gone, and she didn't have any idea when he'd be home again. She had this overwhelming, fierce need to make the most of the time they had left together.

"How'd you decide on nursin'?" he asked her.

"Huh. Well, my folks moved Gran to Silver Springs three years ago, and I would go to see her whenever I could. Guess I got used to bein' there."

"You like it."

"I do," she said, listening to the sound of their boots on the path. "I even *love* it."

"That's real good, Gin," said Cain, elbowing her lightly in the hip. "How come you say it like it's a secret?"

"My folks hate it. They would have preferred I go to college in Lexington or Frankfort, or somewhere like Vanderbilt."

Cain scoffed. "Who gives a sh—*snit* what they want? It's your life, not theirs."

Warmth spread in her chest, and she turned to look up at him. Cain had always encouraged her to jump when everyone else wanted her to stay still, stay quiet, stay safe. How she longed for his swagger and strength as a constant in her life. How tiring it was to fight her little battles alone. Melancholy enveloped her as she thought about him leaving her again.

"You lookin' forward to goin' back on Friday?" she asked in a small voice.

He shrugged. "Half yes, half no."

"Tell me about the halves."

"Half yes because I'm good at what I do, and I feel, I don't know, in charge of my life when I'm servin'. Responsible. Useful. Like I fit in in a way I never did while I was livin' here." He scrubbed his free hand over the jet-black bristles of hair on his head. "It's a good match—me and the military. I *found* myself there, Gin. Jeez, that sounds so stupid, but—"

"No, it doesn't," she said, but her heart ached a little, imagining that if he loved the military life so much, coming home and settling down in Apple Valley, which Ginger loved so desperately, wouldn't be a very appealing prospect to him. "You goin' to make a career out of it?"

"Maybe," he said. "I don't know yet. I've got another year on my contract, then I can take a few months off and figure it out."

"Figure out whether or not you'll reenlist?"

"Yeah," he said, nodding. "Lately I've been sort of thinkin' that I'd like to get on my bike and ride it across the country. Or across Canada. Or across Europe. Or hell, all three. I've seen all these amazin' places from the sea. I'd like to see them from the ground too."

"Wanderlust," said Ginger softly.

"Wanderlust," he repeated, and she could tell he was trying out the word for the first time. "Hey, I like that. I think I might have found a new name for my bike, Gin."

"So you finish your year, you ride across the U.S., Canada, and Europe, and then you figure out whether you reenlist or . . ."

"Or," he said with finality, as though "or" could be a choice, and probably—in Cain's world—"or" *was* a choice, which was maddening for Ginger, who wanted plans and promises, who wanted to know he'd be back on such-and-such a date so that she could circle it in red on her calendar and look at the circle whenever she had a bad day.

Suddenly he stopped walking and pressed Thunder's reins into Ginger's hand. She looked up and watched him sprint across the meadow a little ways to an apple tree at the edge of an orchard. He reached up, his long body stretching skyward as he picked four apples, cradling them in his arms as he ran back to her.

"Think old Mr. Pinkney will notice four missin' apples?"

"Bet not," she said, handing him Thunder's reins and taking two of the apples. One she gave to Heath, and the other she bit into, letting the tangy sweetness slip down her throat. "You never talked about the other half."

"The other half?" he asked, apple juice pooling at the corner of his mouth. For just a moment, she imagined herself being bold enough to lick it off.

"When I asked if you were looking forward to gettin' back, you said, 'Half yes, half no.' What's the 'half no'?"

"Oh," he said, raising his eyebrows and taking another bite of his apple as he gazed down at her, and she wished she knew what he was thinking because he winced just slightly before turning away from her and pulling on Thunder's reins to start walking again.

She followed him, good at knowing when Cain had talked himself into a corner, but also certain that if she stayed silent, he'd talk himself out of it.

After a while, he said, "There's this quote I like, about how teenage boys see their fathers as stupid, but by the time they turn twenty-one, they're shocked by how much their fathers have learned."

Ginger chuckled softly, taking another bite of apple before offering the rest to Heath.

"It's a little like that with my dad," said Cain. "We never .

. . I don't know . . . we never really got along. He was so into the farm and the horses. Always seemed like he had way more in common with Woodman than me."

"And now?"

"Either he grew up . . . or I did . . . or we both did," said Cain thoughtfully. "Thing is, he still talks about horses all the danged time, it's just that—"

"You don't hate it so much?"

Cain shook his head. "I don't hate it at all. Kind of like it, actually. There's somethin' . . . familiar about it."

"Comfortin'."

"Yeah, I guess."

"And the farm?"

"Same thing," he said. "I was so fuckin' anxious to leave here, but it's been a surprise comin' back, you know? Comin' home? Like seein' it all through different eyes and realizin' that everythin' you thought you hated really wasn't so bad."

"That's 'cause you're different," she said.

"You think so?"

"Oh, yeah," she said, looking up as a flock of geese honked above them, heading south in a V formation. "I *know* so. You're not half as mad or hotheaded. I mean, you're still a flirt," she said, elbowing him in the side. "But you grew up a lot while you were away, Cain."

"That's because I found a purpose," he said. "Same way you have, Gin."

But my purpose keeps me here, while yours will take you so very far away from me, she thought mournfully, imagining him leaving for Virginia on Friday and not coming home for a long, long time as he finished his commitment, toured the world on his motorcycle, then reenlisted for another four years. It was so depressing, a lump formed in her throat, and she stared down at the ground wishing it away.

"So, yeah, I think I'll miss my dad. And I'll be sorry to leave my cousin. Ain't never been a sailor without him around."

"I'll look after him," she said, chancing a glance at Cain's face as she said this. He clenched his jaw, reaching up to swipe at his bottom lip with his thumb.

"I'm sure you will," he said, an edge to his voice.

When you're ready, come find me. I'll be waitin' for you.

Woodman's words knocked around in her head, and she thought about them . . . thought about Cain being away for the past three years . . . thought about him going away again and never really coming back. Even if he didn't reenlist, he wanted to see the world, and her world was here, in Apple Valley. If she was smart, she'd forget the way her heart fluttered around Cain, the way her fingers longed to touch him and her ear inclined to the low, sweet sound of his voice. If she was smart, she'd get on her horse right now and ride away, over to Woodman's house, and tell him that she'd decided to give them a try. If she was smart, she'd put every ounce of effort she had into loving Woodman, in dating him with her whole heart, with every good intention, and see if there was a good life for them to share, just waiting to be discovered.

"And I'll miss you too, princess," Cain whispered, slowing down until he stopped walking. "I'll miss you somethin' awful."

She stopped just in front of him, processing his words for a moment before turning around to look at him. He met her eyes with such open tenderness in his gaze, she was helpless to look away.

"You'll be missin' me from Timbuktu," she said, trying to keep her voice light, but failing.

"Wherever I am," he said in a tone of such heartbreaking longing, her breath caught and held in her chest, "I will *always* be missin' you."

As she stared into his blue eyes, thunder rumbled over the meadow, and Ginger looked up in time to see a dark cloud roll over the sun.

"Storm's comin'," said Cain, staring up at the sky in concern. "We'd best get back."

He braided his hands together, and though she hated to leave their conversation where it was, she stepped into his hands and he helped her onto her horse, then leaped up on Thunder's back, settling easily into the saddle.

Glancing back at her, he said, "Ride hard. You're fast and strong. We can outrun it. I'll be right behind you."

Fast and strong. The last two things she felt like right now.

Her eyes were so full of unshed tears, she couldn't see him clearly, but she nodded, then kicked Heath into a gallop. Tears slipped from her eyes as the wind whipped into her face, and she closed them, grateful that Heath knew the way home.

***

The next morning was Sunday, and more gray skies made the world feel cold and uncertain, and Ginger awoke feeling unsettled and confused after her talk with Cain yesterday. Her dreams had been wild and restless, leaving her tired. Instead of leaping out of bed and dressing for church, she burrowed under the covers seeking a peace that she couldn't find.

On one hand, he seemed determined to keep her at arm's length. On the other, she couldn't have misunderstood his meaning about missing her. Unlike that time in her kitchen, he hadn't tried to cover up his words with some song and dance about missing his dad and Woodman. When he said he'd miss her, he'd been speaking to *her*. And she'd heard him, loud and clear.

But at twenty-one, Cain really didn't seem to have a plan for his life. He seemed much younger than her and Woodman in many ways, talking about touring Europe on his motorcycle, without any idea if he'd reenlist or do something else with his life. Before leaving for boot camp, Woodman had had such a clear plan for his life: five years in the service, three years in active Reserves, then working on her father's farm and volunteering at the fire department until he saved up enough to buy a house in Apple Valley. And yes, his plan would have to be rearranged a little bit in light of his injury, but at least she'd known his plan, and she liked the comfort and security of it. The predictability of it appealed to her and felt safe. But Cain? Cain was footloose and fancy-free—no solid plan for his life. Just a young man with a twinkle in his eye who saw the world as a playground just waiting to be explored.

For all her parents' wealth, which could have easily funded a wanderlust of her own, Ginger had no real interest in travel. She was a small-town girl who liked her small-town life. She was content to live in the cottage on her parents' property until she got married and settled down, content to take nursing classes at a community college and intern at the retirement home where her gran lived. Ginger didn't have big dreams about leaving Apple Valley and traveling the world. Her dreams were small and local. Which meant that here and now—at eighteen and twenty-one—she and Cain were all but incompatible when it came down to their visions for the future. They wanted different things from life. They wanted very different things.

And yet.

She closed her eyes and allowed herself free rein,

fantasizing about what she *really* wanted.

In her wildest dreams—in her perfect world—she would give her virginity to Cain over the next few days, and he would take it tenderly, declaring his eternal and undying love for her. When he left, he'd promise to write, and they would exchange passionate letters sharing their deep and growing love and counting down the days when they could be together again. She'd meet him in Virginia, and they'd spend a long weekend in a hotel together. He'd surprise her by coming home for a weekend in the spring, unable to stay away, and they'd hole up in her cottage until it was time for him to go. And then, well, when his year was up, he'd race home to her, all wild fantasies of biking through Europe thrust to the side because being with her was all the adventure he really wanted. He'd decide not to reenlist and go into the active Reserves instead, because choosing to be away from her was unthinkable. Over time he'd come to truly love Apple Valley for the first time in his life— she'd *help* him love it, help make a home for him, help him be happy. He'd work at the fire department, and one day she'd come home from work and he'd pop the question—*Will you marry me, princess?* And she'd say *Yes, yes, yes!* And they'd live happily ever after.

"Happily ever after," she whispered. "Ginger and Cain Wolfram."

But saying the names aloud sounded so unlikely that the beautiful, impossible dream in her head blurred as her eyes filled with tears that pooled in the corners until they slipped into her hair. The problem with this plan?

It wasn't Cain's plan.

It was Woodman's.

And the great dilemma of her life—loving two different

parts of two different men—came into stark focus as she realized, yet again, that while one man could offer her the sweetness and stability she craved, it was the other who challenged her and set her heart on fire. She could have security with Woodman or electricity with Cain, but she couldn't have both with one. Neither cousin could offer her both.

Flipping onto her side, she nestled her cheek into her pillow, staring out the window at the meadows and fields of the farm. She was frustrated and sad, and time wasn't on her side where Cain was concerned.

"Stop thinking about forever," she pleaded with herself. "What do you want *now*?"

The answer came swiftly: *I want Cain. For however long I can have him.*

The thoughts were perfectly formed, and if she hadn't yet seen them in her head or heard them in her ears, it didn't matter, because she recognized their absolute truth now. Cain had been her first kiss. She wanted him to be her first lover too.

Her inexperienced body came alive when Cain was near— secret, hidden places clenching and releasing in want and readiness, her nipples beading, and shivers of pleasure sluicing down her back. She didn't feel this sort of desire for anyone else—she never had. And at eighteen, she was long past ready to experience lovemaking, but she'd saved herself . . . for Cain.

And yes, she knew that dozens had come before her, but she also knew he hadn't loved any of them.

And yes, she knew that he would leave her to go back to the service, but part of her hoped that if they slept together, he'd have something to come home to.

And yes, she knew that he had a yearning to wander, but another part of her hoped that if they loved each other—if they shared their bodies and said the words and knew they were true—that he'd consider a future in Apple Valley because *she* was in Apple Valley, and his longing to be with her, to choose her, would be so great, he'd have no choice but to obey it.

And in the end, yes, it was possible she'd give Cain her virginity and she'd never see him again, but . . . but . . .

She rolled onto her back, staring up at the shadows on her ceiling. Could she handle that? Could she bear having Cain for a handful of days and then losing him forever?

The answer came swiftly yet again.

Yes, I could bear it.

The only thing she couldn't bear was never having him at all.

She had five days left with Cain, and regardless of when and if she ever saw him again, she wanted all of him now. She wanted to know, even for a few short days, what it felt like to love and be loved by him. If she had to, she'd live on that bliss, that certain heaven, those passionate memories, for the rest of her life.

And, yes, she'd make a good life for herself in Apple Valley with a good man. She'd have a home and children—a decent, respectable, stable life that she would guard and treasure. But, like Cain's lust for wandering, Ginger lusted for Cain, and she wanted the memory of fleeting hours spent in his arms, of his body moving against hers, of her heart in his hands, of her soul tangled up inexorably with his before he left her indefinitely again.

***

"*Servus, Klaus*," she said, swinging by the barn on a search for Cain after church and finding his father mucking out one of the many stables.

She'd put her increasingly impure thoughts out of her mind for an hour of services, but all her lusty feelings had returned in a rush when she'd gone home to change into her white lace underwear, tight jeans, and a form-fitting scoop-neck black sweater. Her hair was down, curlier than usual because rain was imminent again, and she'd darkened her eyes and lips with makeup. She didn't want Cain to hesitate. She wanted this to happen.

"Ginger! *Guten Tag.*" He leaned on a shovel handle and grinned at her. "I sent him over to the old barn to pile wood."

Ginger nodded, turning to leave. "Thanks. I'll go find him there."

Klaus dropped the shovel and rushed ahead of her, grabbing a yellow raincoat from a peg outside the tack room and holding it out for her. "Rain comin'."

"*Danke,* Klaus," she said, grinning at the old man she'd known her whole life.

His ice-blue eyes, replicas of Cain's, searched hers before he nodded, swallowing whatever words he was about to say.

She waved good-bye and headed out to find Cain.

The old barn was a structure that had originally housed the McHuid horses a hundred years ago, when Ginger's great-grandfather had first bought the land of McHuid Farm and settled in Apple Valley. When Ginger's grandfather had taken over the farm, in the 1950s, he'd built the present manor house and in-law cottage on a bluff about a mile south of the original farmhouse and barn. The small farmhouse had been razed to discourage squatters and unsanctioned teen parties, but the old barn had been kept in working condition for visiting stock. Ginger's father, however, had renovated the modern barn at the foot of the hill and hadn't had any use for the old barn in a decade or more. The last time she'd visited the place, a year or two ago, it had been dilapidated, the roof caving in and boards missing from the walls. Klaus was determined to dismantle the barn piece by piece and sell the wood, much of which was still in excellent condition. And Ginger's father had told him he could keep whatever profits were to be made if he handled the work and sales on his own.

As Ginger hiked through one empty paddock and then another, a light rain started to fall, and she was grateful for Klaus's foresight, regardless of the fact that the buttoned slicker ruined her sexy outfit. No matter. She was a woman on a mission, ignoring the fluttering in her stomach and the condom in her pocket. If she overthought her plan to seduce Cain, she might lose her nerve, and she couldn't miss out on this chance. She had to act quickly if she wanted to be with him before he left again.

After fifteen minutes of trudging, she arrived at the ridge that looked down into one of the many McHuid valleys to see the old barn down below. And there, working in the rain, carrying boards to a neat pile a few yards from the barn, was Cain.

Standing unobserved on the hill, she watched him for several long moments, her heart throbbing and bursting with love for him. He was bare chested again, his jeans low on his hips, haphazardly tucked into beat-up, tan work boots. His chest was shiny—either from sweat or the rain, she didn't know—but she was mesmerized by the toned, sculpted beauty of him.

"Cain!" she called, raising her hand in greeting.

He turned around, and as always, his smile was quick and wide, taking over his face the moment he laid eyes on her. It gave her confidence and hope. It propelled her forward, down the hill, and hopefully into his arms.

"Hi," she panted, offering him a smile of her own as she drew closer. She took a deep breath to quell the butterflies in her stomach. The old barn looked ethereal with the dark clouds overhead, and she ducked inside, hoping he'd follow.

"What're you doin' here, princess?" he asked, leaning down to pick up a water bottle he'd left on one of the abandoned stall doors to take a long sip.

Ginger stared at his lips, watching the way they puckered and drank, the way his tongue slipped between them to lick the excess droplets, the way he backhanded his mouth and grinned at her with curiosity.

"Cat got your tongue?"

She searched his face. Now that she was here, her courage was failing, and she couldn't seem to find the words she needed.

"I wanted . . . I wanted to see you. I have somethin' I need to say." Her voice sounded thready and high, and she cleared her throat, gesturing to the bottle in his hands. "Can I have some?"

He reached out slowly, handing her the bottle, and she took it, her fingers brushing his and sending a jolt of electricity up her arm. She held his eyes as she raised the bottle and placed her lips around the spout where his had just sucked.

Cain stared at her with interest, in growing realization, his eyes increasingly hot, his half-naked body primed and sleek before her.

When she lowered the bottle, she licked her lips slowly, deliberately, her breath hitching as his eyes lowered to her mouth and lingered there.

"What do you want, Gin?" he asked, still staring at her mouth, his voice low and gravelly.

She stepped forward, closing the distance between them.

Her raincoat pressed against his chest, her breasts straining through two layers of clothes. "Cain, there isn't much time until you go, and I want . . . I mean, I feel like . . ."

He didn't move away from her, and when he took a deep breath, his chest pushed into hers insistently, making her tender breasts ache for his touch. She gasped softly, and he cut his eyes to hers, reaching out to put his hands on her upper arms and kneading them gently. "You feel like what, princess?"

"I'm in love with you," she blurted out, gasping again as soon as the words left her mouth, then holding her breath as she stared at him in wide-eyed panic. Adrenaline pumped uncomfortably through her body, and out of nowhere she heard herself add, "I want to *be* with you, Cain."

"Ginger," he ground out, the sound shocked and stilted.

"You're the one I want. I have *always* wanted you. You were my first kiss, and I want you to be my first . . ." Her words trailed off as her cheeks flamed with heat. "Cain," she half gasped, half whispered, "I want you to make love to me."

His eyes searched her face, shocked and wild, and she licked her lips, her breath coming in fast, short spurts as his hands tightened around her arms. As he stared at her lips, she arched her back, pressing her body against his and whispering, "Please."

Like a match to a fuse, he yanked her against his chest, wrapping his arms around her as his lips crashed down on hers. Groaning into her mouth, he kissed her madly, backing her against the old barn wall and slamming his groin into hers, his tongue parting her lips and sweeping into her mouth.

Ginger's hands were trapped between them but she flattened her hands on his chest, her fingers curling into the wall of muscle, and her back arching so that her breasts rubbed against him through their clothes. His hands slipped back around her waist to her front, pulling at the buttons of her coat, and she worked to help him release them, their fingers meeting in the middle. He opened the coat and dropped his hands to the hem of her sweater, skating underneath until the flesh of his rough hands landed on her soft belly. His tongue tangled with hers as his hands stroked her skin, higher and higher. He pushed his pelvis forward, and she felt his erection, hard and straining against the zipper of his jeans.

His hands found her breasts, cupping them through her bra, and she whimpered, fighting to release her hands from between them and wind them around his neck, pulling his head down to hers and sliding her tongue along the smooth hot velvet of his.

He groaned, dropping his lips to her throat, kissing, licking, sucking, as his thumbs rubbed her nipples, the friction of the lace over her taut skin sweet and sharp at the same time. Sweet and sharp. Like Cain. Like her and Cain together.

Letting her head fall back against the wall, she moaned his name—like a prayer, a litany, a plea: "Cain, Cain, Cain . . . I love you. God, I love you so much."

His lips paused against her neck, and his hands stilled over her breasts.

"Gin," he groaned. "Oh, fuck, no. What're we doin'?"

Her eyes fluttered open. "Cain, wait . . ."

"No," he panted, though his body still pressed into hers, and she could feel the heat of his breath on her throat. "No, this is wrong. This is . . . no."

"Stop sayin' no," she said in a voice that broke into a sob.

He slipped his hands out from under her shirt and rested his forehead on hers, his breath coming in light pants against her cheek.

"Princess, we can't do this."

"Why not?" she sobbed, tears of rejection and humiliation streaming from her eyes.

"'Cause I'm no good for you."

"You *are*. You *are* good. And I'm in love with you."

"No, you're not."

"Don't tell me how I feel, Cain. I love you. I want you." She leaned forward, trying to kiss him again, but he pinned her shoulders to the wall, holding her away from him. "I'm offerin' myself to you. Please don't turn me away."

He winced like her words hurt him, *really* hurt him, then suddenly his eyes grew cold.

"You want the *truth*?"

"I want *you*," she mewled, her voice small and broken.

He continued as though she hadn't spoken. "Do you know where I go every night, Ginger? I go fuck Mary-Louise Walker. Every night. Three, four, five times a night. At her apartment. On my bike. At the distillery. Against the bathroom wall at O'Halloran's between shots of Jack Daniel's."

Ginger gasped, whimpering her disbelief and fury, and struggling to slap him, as if hitting him would somehow negate the words. But he reached out and held her upper arms in his iron grip, his erection still swollen against her belly, his eyes icy cold.

"More truth? You might be playin' the role of junior tramp today, offerin' your flower to a man who's seen more pussy than a porn star, but this is not *you*, princess. You are the sort of girl a man settles down with and marries, and I *ain't* the settlin' *or* the marryin' kind."

Her body slumped against the wall as his words lashed out at her, whipping and stinging, embarrassing her and making her feel foolish. She mustered whatever small reserves of courage she had left. "I'm not *askin'* for you to marry me. I just want us to give this . . . this *thing* between us a chance. You're leavin' on Friday, for God's sake! I'm only askin' for a handful of days. Why can't you do that, Cain? Why can't you *be* with me? Why can't you give us a *chance*?"

"You *know* why," he growled.

"I don't!" she screamed.

"Because my cousin's in love with you, Ginger," he bellowed. "Woodman is *in love* with you!"

"But I'm in love with *you*," she sobbed.

He clenched his eyes shut for a moment, his face in pain, his lips tight and grim as he breathed forcefully through his nose. When he opened his eyes, they were mean. When he spoke, his voice was dirty.

"You know, Gin," he said, grinding against her, "you do a pretty fair imitation of bein' his goddamned girlfriend, you know that? Writin' him letters. Kissin' him when he's home. Spendin' every night over there with him when you get off work. You didn't think I knew about all that? Well, I do. He talks about you every goddamn minute of the fuckin' day. And here you are comin' on to *me*—eyes all dark, lips bright red—like some sort of slut from the distillery. I don't think you have any idea what the hell you want, princess."

"I *do*. I want *you*. Woodman and I are . . . complicated. But we're just friends—"

"No, you're *not*," said Cain, finally releasing her roughly and stepping back. He shook his head as he placed his hands on his hips and gave her a dirty look. "Even *I* can see that you two are more than friends. And if you can't, you're blind . . . or a cock-teasin' bitch."

"Cain!" She gasped at his vulgarity, grappling for control in a conversation that had long jumped the rails and turned out nothing like she'd hoped when she was lying in her bed this morning. "I'll talk to him. I'll make it clear we're not—"

"Are you fuckin' crazy?" demanded Cain, taking a furious step toward her, his eyes glacial. "Don't you *dare* do that! Do you know how depressed he was? Do you know how badly that injury fucked with his head? You didn't see him. You weren't there. He wanted to *die*, Ginger. He wanted to fuckin' *die*! The thought of you—*of comin' home to you*—was the only thing that kept him hangin' on most days. You think I'd take that away from him? You think there's any way in hell I'd hurt him like that? You think I'd let *you* hurt him like that? Don't you get it? It *doesn't matter* if you love me. Fuck, it wouldn't even matter if I loved you, Ginger, because I sure as fuck don't hate *him* enough to destroy him!"

His words were furious and final, a sucker punch to her gut, that forced the breath from her body in one exhausted, painful whoosh. She sagged against the barn wall in defeat as tears streamed down her face. Cain made a small grunting sound as he stared at her, then swiped at his eyes before dropping his gaze to the floor.

He had rejected her advances completely, and something in her heart—something naive and childish that probably should have died a long time ago—splintered into a million jagged pieces.

"This conversation is over," he said without looking up at her. "Go home."

She blinked her eyes so that the last of her tears for him would roll down her cheeks and slip away. Then she lifted her chin and waited until he looked up and met her eyes.

"I know you love me, Cain. I can see it. I can feel it. I know it's true," she said, her voice broken and small as the words poured from the shattered place inside her. "But it doesn't matter anymore. This is the last time you will *ever* reject and humiliate me. I promise you. The last time."

Then, with all the dignity she could muster, she pushed away from the wall and walked past him, out of the barn, out of his life.

For good.

Chapter 13

~ Woodman ~

Sunday supper at the McHuids' was not a new occurrence in Woodman's life—he and his parents had been invited about once a month since he was a child, and he'd always put up with his mother's and Miz Magnolia's good-natured teasing, and shared uncomfortable looks with Ginger as their parents pretended to plan their wedding and name their imaginary grandchildren. But this time, he had to admit, their mothers were taking it a little far.

"Woodman," said Miz Magnolia, waving away the server who paused beside her with a platter filled with sliced ham, "what are your plans now that you're home? Steady employment? Lovely home? Blushin' bride?"

"Momma, please," said Ginger softly, her voice small and tired.

"Well, I'm just thinkin' how stunnin' it is here at McHuid Farm in June. Perfect place for a weddin'."

She giggled, and Woodman's mother swatted at her

playfully. "Magnolia Lee, you are so baaaaad!"

But Miz Magnolia preened, winking at Sophie before fixing her eyes on Ginger. "You've been waitin' for Woodman to come on home now, haven't you, Virginia? Well, here he is. What're you goin' to do about it?"

Ginger's cheeks flushed as she stared down at her full plate. She'd barely eaten a bite, and she seemed especially fragile tonight. It made him feel worried, and he was anxious for dinner to be over so he could speak to her alone.

"You are lookin' just fine, Woodman, bum foot notwithstandin'," boomed Ranger McHuid from the opposite side of the table.

"Thank you, sir."

"Damn proud of you for servin' like you did," Ranger continued, helping himself to a third and fourth scoop of mashed potatoes.

"It was my honor to serve, sir."

"Chip off the old block, eh, Howard?"

Woodman's father nodded, taking a serving of ham and reaching for the saucer of honey on the table. "That's right. Woodmans are naval men. Josiah carried on a fine tradition."

Sophie smiled at her son indulgently, then flicked her eyes to a despondent Ginger. "Magnolia, your Ginger here arrived at my house last Monday in the sweetest little violet outfit."

Ginger's mother cut her eyes to her daughter with disapproval. "You did not wear your scruffs to Miz Sophie's house!"

"*Scrubs*, Momma," said Ginger quietly, by rote.

"Tsk! My God, I don't understand this fascination with bedpans and old people. It's just so unpleasant, daughter."

"*It's your life, not theirs*," Ginger said in a broken,

faraway voice.

Woodman kicked her lightly under the table with his good foot, warning her not to engage. It would only make it worse.

"You say somethin', miss?" asked Miz Magnolia, finishing her third glass of Chablis and nailing her daughter with narrowed eyes. "You say somethin' to the momma who pays for your SUV, let you lives in her cottage rent free, pays for your schoolin', and doles out your generous allowance?"

"No, ma'am."

She turned to her friend. "Sophie, you think our grandbabies will look more Woodman or McHuid?"

Woodman gave his mother a pleading look, which she ignored.

"A fair mix of both, I hope."

"Don't you hog my grandbabies, Sophie, you hear?"

"Why, Magnolia, I believe you're worried I'll be more popular."

When neither Woodman nor Ginger engaged in their deeply embarrassing silliness, it lost its fun, and Miz Magnolia asked his mother if she'd heard about the latest scandal involving the Methodist pastor and Mrs. McGaskell from the choir.

"Let's get out of here," said Woodman softly, and Ginger, whose face had been set in misery since the meal started, looked up at him with tears in her eyes and nodded gratefully.

"Gin and I are goin' for a walk," he said, clutching the table to stand up on his good leg as Ginger retrieved his crutches from the corner of the room and brought them to him.

"What a fine idea," said Miz Magnolia. "But just neckin', you hear?"

"Jesus, Momma!" yelled Ginger in the first show of spirit

Woodman had seen all night.

"Don't you *dare* cuss at me, daughter!"

Ginger huffed loudly, biting back whatever smart-ass comment was on the tip of her tongue, then turned and beelined out of the room, leaving Woodman to hobble behind. He found her sitting outside on the porch swing, arms crossed over her chest, eyes brimming with tears, looking a combination of dismal and furious.

"You'd think it wouldn't be so much fun for them after ten years," she said.

Woodman chuckled at her pique. "They were worse'n usual today."

"They treat us like Daddy's horses. *Go breed us some grandbabies, daughter!* It's disgustin'."

"Aw, come on, now. They've always been a little silly about us."

"It's just a big game for them—who we love, who we want."

Who do *you love, Gin? Who* do *you want?*

Maneuvering himself as best he could, he plopped down beside her on the swing, and she moved a little to the left to give him some room.

Before their mothers had made tonight's supper the most embarrassing on record, he'd noticed how quiet and distracted Ginger seemed. She barely said a word during dinner, and Woodman's mind had segued easily to the awkward ending of his conversation with Cain on Thursday afternoon, when he'd left on his motorcycle in such a hurry after Woodman brought up Ginger.

He remembered the way Ginger used to look at Cain when they were kids, like he turned on the stars every night, and suddenly Woodman had a strong suspicion that something had happened between them this week. Something complicated. Something that was pulling them both away from him and hurtling them toward each other.

"Ginger," he started.

"I'm nobody's puppet, Woodman," she said, turning to look at him.

"I know that," he said gently. "You've always had a mind of your own, darlin'."

She took a deep breath and sighed. "Even if you want to control people, you can't. Our hearts make decisions that our heads don't even approve. We can barely control ourselves. And nothin'—*nothin' on earth*—ever works out the exact way you want it to."

Her words, said passionately with the hint of a sob, reverberated in his head. *Even if you want to control people, you can't. We can barely control ourselves.* And suddenly Woodman had an epiphany that took his breath away.

I can't control Ginger.

I can't control Cain.

He'd always been pretty good about loving Ginger quietly and giving her the time and space to decide what she wanted, but something about his accident, about the loss of control he felt in the wake of his injury, had made him push her for answers from the moment he'd arrived home. And even though she'd stopped by faithfully and they'd had some good talks, he'd strained their relationship because he was putting expectations on her that she'd never promised to meet. And suddenly he realized with startling and blinding clarity:

It does no good to stake a claim on someone's heart. Unless they give it to you, it isn't yours to take. All you can do is share your heart and hope she wants it. All you can do is offer it and hope she takes it. All you can do is love her and hope to God she finds a way to love you back.

"I'm sorry," he whispered.

"For what?" she asked.

"For tryin' to force you to love me."

"Oh, Woodman," she said, her voice thick with emotion. "I *do* love you."

"I know you do. Like a best friend. Like a brother."

She shrugged helplessly. "And at times . . ."

He waited for her to continue.

"There have been times," she said softly, "when I thought I felt somethin' more."

With his good foot, he pushed off and the swing rocked gently as he processed her words; those times—those precious moments—when she'd felt possible for him, he'd felt possible for her too. It gave him hope. It restored his patience.

"I love you," he said gently, staring straight ahead at an old oak tree that was blocking the setting sun. It created a sunburst of orange-gold that made the tree look like it was on fire. "I've been in love with you for as long as I can remember."

"Woodman," she sobbed.

He didn't look at her. He stared at the tree as the orange-gold sun set the grass on fire and watched as the old oak was slowly bathed in a calming lavender.

"If you told me 'no,' Gin, if you told me 'never,' I'd leave you be. You know that, don't you? It would damn near kill me, but I'd . . . I promise you, I'd walk away. But until you say those words, Ginger, I will keep hopin' and keep waitin' for you."

She took a deep, sobbing breath beside him, and he knew if he looked at her, he'd see tears spilling over the rims of her eyes, but he didn't look. He watched the grass turn lavender, then purple. He focused on the dying light.

"Gin," he whispered, hating the question but needing the answer, "are you in love with Cain?"

Peripherally, he saw her shake her head back and forth, letting her neck fall forward until her chin rested on her chest and her shoulders shook the swing with silent sobs. And then he knew for sure. It had happened. Somehow in the space of just a few days she'd fallen for Cain again.

"Gin," he said gently, putting his finger under her chin and tilting her face up to look at him. Her blonde hair shone in the porch light over their heads as the rest of the world darkened into purple dusk little by little. "Cain is my cousin and I love him, but I just . . . I just don't think he's right for you."

"*Why*?" she demanded, her voice breaking on the simple, pleading word, as though she truly wanted an answer, as though she'd already posed the question to herself and come up with nothing.

Because he's cock deep in Mary-Louise Walker right now while you're weeping over him. The words sat perched on the tip of his tongue, but he couldn't bring himself to say them—he couldn't bear to hurt her like that, and frankly he didn't want to villainize Cain like that, not even if meant winning Ginger.

"I see you with *me*, not *him*," he said simply. "Darlin', I'd be so good to you. Don't you know that?"

She nodded, tears streaming down her lovely face, limp with sadness.

Reaching down, he took her hand gently, lifting it, bringing it to his chest and placing it directly over his heart.

"You can have this heart to break," he said softly, devoutly, surrendering everything to her—his dignity, his control, his very soul—"if there's even the smallest chance you might want it someday. Because here is what I know: even if you can't ever give me yours, mine already belongs to you."

Tears coursed down her cheeks and fell to her chin, dripping onto her lap as she stared at her hand, flattened against his shirt. When she raised her eyes, she tried to smile at him, but more tears spilled from her eyes instead. "God *damn* it, Josiah. Why're you s-so good to me?"

"Why's the sky blue, Ginger?" he asked, raising her hand to his lips and kissing the translucent skin on the underside of her wrist before entwining his fingers through hers. "Because it don't know no other way to be."

"I'm so tired," she said, letting her head fall to his shoulder. She took a deep, ragged breath that shook her whole body, and he put his arm around her, pulling her into his side and using his good foot to push off the ground again and set them in a gentle motion. Back and forth. Back and forth. Woodman sighed and let his head lean over to rest on top of hers.

"Then you go ahead and rest," he said. "I'm not goin' anywhere, Gin. My heart belongs to you. If you're ever ready to give me yours, well, you come find me, darlin'. I'll be waitin'."

She tried to catch her breath but ended up sobbing and sniffling before continuing. "You d-deserve the best, W-Woodman."

"Which is why I'm waitin' for her to come to her senses," he said, chuckling lightly.

"You love me that much?"

"That much and more," he said, the words coming easily and feeling right. "Close your eyes and rock awhile beside ole Woodman. I love you, Gin. I've got you covered. You just take your time, darlin'."

The next breath she drew was finally clean and deep, and he felt her relax against him, her fingers still braided through his, her head heavy against his shoulder. And Woodman closed his eyes too, his heart strangely content in its surrender, in giving up any remaining control to the woman he loved, and placing his destiny completely in her hands.

Chapter 14

~ Ginger ~

Dinner with the Woodmans was an exercise in torture after what had happened with Cain, and it didn't help that her mother drank too much Chablis and started in on her and Woodman getting married someday. After her charged exchange with Cain, it was the very last conversation she cared to have or listen to. All she really wanted to do was curl up in her bed and cry herself to sleep, so she stayed quiet and pushed her food around her plate as she tried not to burst into tears at her mother's dinner table.

Woodman, who seemed to sense her despondency, suggested they take a walk, and finally they excused themselves to sit on the porch swing. Though she couldn't tell him what had transpired with his cousin—not that she wanted to, it was almost too humiliating to bear—at least she wasn't subject to her mother's unbearable teasing anymore.

"You'd think it wouldn't be so much fun for them after ten years," she said.

Woodman chuckled softly. "They were worse'n usual

today."

"They treat us like Daddy's horses. *Go breed us some grandbabies, daughter!* It's disgustin'."

"Aw, come on, now. They've always been a little silly about us."

She'd cried all the way from the old barn back to her cottage this afternoon, and then for an hour or more on her bed, until the Woodmans arrived for supper. And now her tears threatened to return again so she summoned anger to try to negate her deep sorrow. "It's just a big game for them—who we love, who we want."

"Ginger—"

"I'm nobody's puppet, Woodman," she said, turning to look at him as he sat down beside her on the swing.

"I know that," he said gently, his face grieved. "You've always had a mind of your own, darlin'."

"Even if you want to control people, you can't. Our hearts make decisions that our heads don't even approve. We can barely control ourselves. And nothin'—*nothin' on earth*—ever works out the exact way you want it to."

She was talking about Cain, of course—about how she'd stupidly thrown herself at him, believing that he'd draw her into his arms, make love to her for days, and declare his undying devotion. And he had soundly rejected her, trouncing her heart, humiliating her, and closing the door on whatever future she'd dreamed they could have.

So Woodman's next words surprised her because he must have assumed that she was talking about *him*.

"I'm sorry," he said.

"For what?"

"For tryin' to force you to love me."

"Oh, Woodman," she said, her voice thick with emotion. "I *do* love you."

"I know you do. Like a best friend. Like a brother."

She shrugged helplessly, a sudden memory of him taking her to the homecoming dance flashing through her mind. "And at times . . ."

She looked over at Woodman—at his blond hair and clean-shaven face. He was handsome and kind, and he'd do just about anything for her. Ending up with him would be a good life, a fine life, a life that would suit her far better than a life with Cain, and maybe, just maybe, if she let her dreams of Cain die, she could open her heart completely to Woodman.

Suddenly she remembered him giving her the charm bracelet for her twelfth birthday, how she'd felt a strange surge of attraction to Woodman, and again at the homecoming dance, when he'd saved her bacon and kissed her for the first time.

"There have been times," she said softly, "when I thought I felt somethin' more."

"I love you," he said, as though her words had given him the courage to say what he felt. "I've been in love with you for as long as I can remember."

As the very words she'd wanted so desperately from Cain spilled from his cousin's lips with such tenderness, such constant earnestness, a dam broke inside her, and tears of hurt and frustration streamed down her face.

"Woodman," she sobbed.

"If you told me 'no,' Gin, if you told me 'never,' I'd leave you be. You know that, don't you? It would damn near kill me, but I'd . . . I promise you, I'd walk away. But until you say those words, Ginger, I will keep hopin' and keep waitin' for you."

She took a deep, sobbing breath beside him, grieving her

lost chance with Cain today and feeling the strong pull to surrender to Woodman. How easy it would be to choose him, to build something with him. No more frustration and heartbreak. No one challenging her or asking her to jump. No more arms pushing her away, just pulling her into a warm and safe embrace.

"Gin," he whispered, "are you in love with Cain?"

And just like that, her heart broke all over again, but this time, for Woodman.

Because she knew how painful it was for him to ask the question, and yet he asked it and he asked it kindly, his voice filled with love and understanding. Her shoulders trembled, and her chin fell forward to rest on her chest as she wept.

I love the wrong cousin. Oh God, help.

"Gin," said Woodman, putting his finger under her chin and tilting her face up to look at him. His eyes were sad but kind as he looked down at her. "Cain is my cousin and I love him, but I just . . . I just don't think he's right for you."

"*Why?*" she asked, finding that she was desperate for an answer. *What's so wrong with me that he can't choose me?*

"I see you with *me*, not *him*," Woodman continued. "Darlin', I'd be so good to you. Don't you know that?"

She nodded, tears streaming down her face because of course she knew it was true. It had *always* been true. He reached down and took her hand, placing it directly over his heart.

"You can have this heart to break," he said softly, his voice gravelly with emotion, "if there's even the smallest chance you might want it someday. Because here is what I know: even if you can't ever give me yours, mine already belongs to you."

And inside Ginger's heart, something gave way. Something happened that she hadn't expected or seen coming: a tectonic shift of broken, shattered plates. It wasn't that she suddenly loved Woodman in the wild, passionate way she'd always loved Cain, but for just a moment, her heart recognized him as more than he'd ever been before. And after the beating her heart had borne earlier in the day, it felt like a blessed relief.

When she raised her eyes, she tried to smile at him, but more tears spilled over. "God *damn* it, Josiah. Why're you s-so good to me?"

"Why's the sky blue, Ginger?" he asked, raising her hand to his lips and kissing the underside of her wrist before entwining his fingers through hers. "Because it don't know no other way to be."

"I'm so tired," she said honestly, letting her head fall to his shoulder. She took a deep, ragged breath that shook her whole body, and he put his strong arm around her, pulling her into his side and resting his head on top of hers.

And in Woodman's arms, she found a profound and unexpected peace at the end of a long and emotionally exhausting day. In Woodman's arms, there was unconditional love, support, admiration, and acceptance. In Woodman's arms, she was safe and wanted. And right now? Right this minute, in the wake of Cain's devastating rejection? Safe and wanted felt good, felt right, felt like the right path for her future, for her whole life.

"Then you go ahead and rest," he said. "I'm not goin' anywhere, Gin. My heart belongs to you. If you're ever ready to give me yours, well, you come find me, darlin'. I'll be waitin'."

She tried to catch her breath but ended up sobbing and sniffling before continuing. "You d-deserve the best, W-Woodman."

"Which is why I'm waitin' for her to come to her senses,"

he said, chuckling lightly.

She'd woken up this morning certain that she wanted to give herself to Cain, yet here she was, ending her day in Woodman's arms, tucked against his side, and feeling more peace and comfort than she had a right to.

And suddenly it occurred to her that it was within her control—right here, right now—to leave Cain behind, to banish him from her aching heart, to forget she ever wanted him . . . and give all her love to Woodman.

Don't think about it so hard. Just do it. Make a good choice. Make the right choice.

"You love me that much?"

"That much and more," he said tenderly, and she knew—beyond even a shadow of doubt, that the words were true. "Close your eyes and rock awhile beside ole Woodman. I love you, Gin. I've got you covered. You just take your time, darlin'."

Again, the perfect words, said just exactly when she needed them. She took a deep, clean breath and relaxed against him, closing her eyes as he'd instructed. She squeezed his fingers for reassurance and let her head rest heavy against his shoulder, but restfulness didn't come. A vision of Cain, pushing her away, appeared front and center in her mind as his cruel words echoed in her head, making her beaten heart constrict with pain.

Do you know where I go every night, Ginger? I go fuck Mary-Louise Walker . . . I don't think you have any idea what the hell you want . . . cock-teasin' bitch . . . This conversation is over. Go home.

She winced from an onslaught of fresh anguish, opening her eyes. She couldn't bear it. She had to do something—

anything—to erase Cain from her mind once and for all. And suddenly the answer revealed itself to her like a light in the darkness, like warmth after cold—a choice that would soothe the broken rawness of her shattered heart.

"I don't need any more time," she said, lifting her head and nailing Woodman with the hottest look her virgin eyes could muster. "I want to be with you."

Chapter 15

~ Cain ~

I know you love me, Cain. I can see it. I can feel it. I know it's true. This is the last time you will ever *reject and humiliate me. I promise you. The last time.*

He'd relived their fight for the rest of the day, hearing her words in his head over and over again until the sun set and a sort of panic took hold of him.

There was such a cold finality to her words, and frankly it frightened him. Why? Because he'd known since her twelfth birthday that there was a chemistry, a once-in-a-lifetime electricity, between them. He'd ignored it and denied it and tried to put it aside for Woodman's sake, but the idea of losing her for good?

No, it wasn't just frightening. It was terrifying. It was too final. In its own way, it felt like death.

I just want us to give this . . . this thing *between us a chance. You're leavin' on Friday, for God's sake! I'm only askin' for a handful of days. Why can't you do that, Cain? Why can't you* be *with me? Why can't you give us a* chance?

Those questions circled around and around in his head as he pulled boards off the old barn and threw them into the pile. Her words plagued him mercilessly as he worked his fingers to the bone, splinters burying under his skin, nails digging into his flesh. He didn't care. All he could see was her shattered eyes. All he could hear was her voice—her broken voice, begging him to see what was between them and give it permission, give it legs, give it life.

Why can't you give us a chance?

Because of Josiah.

Because she was Josiah's girl.

Because Josiah had been in love with her for almost as long as Cain could remember.

The problem, Cain realized as he left the old barn at dusk to walk home, was that he wouldn't feel fear like this—*anguish like this*—unless he was in love with her too. And the recognition of the feelings he'd had since he was a kid—the realization that he was every bit as much in love with Ginger as Woodman—just about made him want to die. Because this was a no-win, terrible, awful situation.

Two cousins.

One girl.

Someone wins.

And someone loses.

And Ginger had all but guaranteed his win today, which meant Josiah— his best friend, his cousin, his brother, his flesh and blood—would lose. His breath caught. He wasn't sure he could bear that.

But *fuck!* Was it fair that Woodman, who'd claimed her when they were only kids, was the ice wedged between the fire that Cain and Ginger shared? Just because Woodman wanted her and loved her didn't mean that Cain didn't love and want her too. He did. He always had. He'd just realized it a little later than Woodman had.

Reaching the barn, he opened the tack room door and called, "Papa? Pop? You here?"

When his father didn't answer, he felt grateful. He needed the time alone to think.

Crossing the dark, quiet room, Cain took a Kölsch from the refrigerator and popped the bottle cap off, placing his lips on the icy glass and relishing the cold bubbles on the back of his throat as he leaned against the kitchen counter.

Finally lowering the bottle, he pulled his bottom lip into his mouth and clenched his eyes shut.

"Fuuuuuck!" he yelled into the silence, desperation and frustration ramping up until his heart pounded like he'd run a mile.

She was furious and hurt when she left.

And he was leaving in a few days.

Whatever window he had to fix this was swiftly closing, and if he didn't go and talk to her now, it would be too late by the time he came home again. He'd practically pushed her into Woodman's waiting arms, and with the two of them in Apple Valley together, proximity would assure that Cain lost any chance with her . . . forever.

"No!" he growled, taking another long sip from the bottle, then slamming it down on the counter.

He tore off his dirty T-shirt and threw it on the floor, unbuttoned his jeans, and headed for the bathroom. He turned on the shower and shucked off his boxers as he waited for the water to warm up, then he stepped inside, sighing as the hot water hit his weary muscles.

He had only four full days left at home before he was due back in Virginia, and he couldn't bear the thought of spending those days avoiding Ginger when all he wanted was to reach for her, touch her, kiss her, love her, make enough memories with her to get him through the years ahead without her.

He soaped his chest, his fingers playing over the contour of muscle, wondering what it would feel like for Ginger's soapy hands to slide over his skin. His cock twitched and swelled, remembering her eyes this afternoon. God, the strength it had taken for him to refuse her after that kiss—that scorching-hot fucking kiss. If he'd just taken when she was offering, by now, she would have been his. She would belong to him in every possible sense of the word. Leaning his forehead against the shower wall, he let the hot water sluice over his back, down his legs, until it ran clear of soapy bubbles and he was clean.

He wanted her. Fuck, how he wanted her.

"You can't fuckin' have her," he muttered, shutting off the water and pushing the curtain aside. He plucked a clean towel from the pile on the back of the toilet, and as he dried his body he considered the changes in his cousin over the past few weeks.

Woodman was doing better now, wasn't he? Sure, his full recovery would take some time, but he was working at the firehouse and his spirits had improved. He was shaving, taking care of himself. No more talk about life not being worth living.

Cain huffed as he pulled on some fresh boxers. No, the fucking timing was not fucking ideal, but if Ginger wanted him and he wanted Ginger, there had to be a way to make that happen, right? He could lay his cards on the table, get Ginger to forgive him for the hurtful things he'd said today, and then they could talk to Woodman about everything together. They could explain everything, couldn't they? Put it in a way that would soften the blow, but still help him understand?

Pulling on some jeans, he tried the words.

"Josiah, we need to . . . um, no." He tried again. "Josiah, here's the thing: I know how you feel about Ginger, but I feel the same. No. I feel . . . fuck, I feel like I . . . fuuuuck!" he yelled, zipping and buttoning his pants. He ran a hand through his wet hair. "Okay. Woodman, we need to talk to you . . . No. Fuck. Okay . . . Woodman, we need to be honest with you about something." He looked at himself in the mirror, nodding. "That's good. That's good. Um, we need to be honest with you about something, and we know you're not going to like it, but we . . . we, uh, *what?* We need you to hear us out . . . Yeah. Okay . . . We need to be honest with you, and we know you're not going to like it, but we need you to hear us out."

He nodded at his reflection again, practicing a small speech as the words came to him one by one. *I can't help it . . . I wish I could . . . I love her too . . .* And finally, when he had all the words he needed, he threw on a clean, white buttoned-down shirt, slipped his feet into sneakers and hurried out the door.

First he had to make things right with Ginger.

***

Walking up the driveway to the McHuids' manor, he noticed his aunt and uncle's car parked in front of the house and wondered if Woodman had come with them. For a moment he rethought his decision to speak to Ginger, especially since he wasn't exactly welcome at Miz Magnolia's supper table, but he cast his eyes at Ginger's cottage and decided it couldn't hurt to check and see if she was home.

Bypassing the main house, he took the path that wound around the side of the porch and led to the cottage, and was relieved to note that the lights were on. He knocked on the door lightly, then stepped back, looking through the window, hoping to see her face as she approached to let him in. As he stood waiting, he thought about what he was going to say to her. Yeah, she'd still be hurt and probably spitting mad so it would sure take a lot of sweetness, but—he grinned to himself as he remembered the feeling of her lips beneath his earlier today— Cain was good at making up. And they still had Monday, Tuesday, Wednesday, and Thursday to make up for lost time. Anxious to see her, he stepped forward and knocked a little harder, but the door must have been shut hastily, because it wasn't latched and swung open.

He took a step into her kitchen, listening for signs of life. "Ginger?"

There was no answer, but just as he turned to leave, he heard something. A clunk, like a small piece of furniture falling over above his head, and he turned back around.

"Ginger?" he called again, but still no answer.

Damn it, he didn't want to intrude on her, but he didn't want to waste any more time either. He needed a chance to make things right with her and convince her to go with him to break the news to Woodman. Surely, if they all sat down together they could figure this out, right? Right.

Heading quietly up the stairs, he walked down the upstairs hall, his sneakers muted by the plush carpet Ginger's gran must have chosen. He stopped and listened for a moment, then, hearing a noise from the room to the left at the top of the stairs, he turned and paused before the door.

I know you love me, Cain. I can see it. I can feel it. I know it's true.

It *was* true.

It was true, and no amount of pretending it wasn't would make it go away. And he deserved the chance to love her if that's what she wanted. Because Lord knew he wanted it too.

Raising his hand to push her bedroom door open, he froze as he heard a man's voice—his cousin's voice on the very brink of sleep—groan, "Gin, I love you."

What? What the fuck was Woodman doing in Ginger's bedroom?

He leaned closer to the door and listened for her voice, but didn't hear it—didn't hear anything.

Without knocking, he pushed the door open soundlessly.

It took his eyes a minute to adjust to the half-light of dusk, of dreams and nightmares, of everything he wished he could unsee and unknow.

They were both naked, tangled together in her bed, their bodies pale and relaxed. Woodman was on his back, and she was on her side, next to him, nestled in his arms. Her hair lay across his chest in a softly curled mess of gold. One of her arms was buried beneath her, but the other lay flat on his chest, covered by his, their fingers intertwined like lovers.

Cain's lungs slowly drained of oxygen until his head swam, and he backed up into the hallway, grasping at the chair-rail molding with clawlike fingers, trying to stay upright.

"Fuck," he whispered with the last breath in his body, his eyes burning, his head dizzy. *I have to get out of here.* He made his way to the stairs and half slid, half stumbled down the carpeted stairs, lurching through the small kitchen and toward the open door.

This is the last time you will ever *reject and humiliate me. I promise you. The last time.*

Had she known? Had she known, even then, that when she

walked away from Cain, she'd walk directly into his cousin's arms and offer herself to him instead?

He walked through the darkness like a drunkard, his feet slow and uncertain at first, then picking up momentum and balance until he was running down the driveway like the devil was at his heels. When he got to the barn, he walked into the tack room, grabbed his keys, then pulled the door shut behind him. His dog tags were around his neck. Anything else could be sent or replaced.

Heading out into the night, he straddled his bike, threw on his helmet, and turned the key, clenching his jaw and eyes shut for a moment as the engine thundered to life. The Ginger of his dreams, the sweetest, loveliest girl who ever lived—*the princess of his broken heart*—was just another fickle, fucking bitch.

Opening his cold, flinty eyes, he turned his bike toward the road and squeezed the throttle. He roared down the driveway, down the road, out of Apple Valley, out of Kentucky.

All that mattered was distance.

All that mattered was getting as far away from both of them as fucking possible.

PART FOUR

Three years later

Chapter 16

~ Ginger ~

"What do you think, Gran?" asked Ginger, holding the paint chips closer to the light. "Sandy Beach or Ray of Sun?"

"D-doll b-baby," Gran said slowly, shifting her troubled eyes from the almost-identical colors to her granddaughter's face, "D-does it . . . m-matter?"

A nurse peeked her head into the room and smiled kindly at Ginger. "Afternoon visitin' hours are over in ten minutes, Miss McHuid. You can come back this evenin' after supper if you like."

Ginger's shoulders slumped. "Anna, please stop callin' me Miss McHuid!"

"Nurse Ratch—I mean, Nurse Arklett prefers for us to address visitors properly." Anna shrugged an apology and gave Ginger a polite smile before turning and leaving the room.

Ginger sighed deeply, pulling the pile of paint chips back into her hands and squaring them neatly like a deck of cards.

Nine months ago, after Woodman proposed, and under

oppressive pressure from *her* parents, *his* parents, and *him*, she finally agreed to take a "leave of absence" from her job at SSCC in order to concentrate on wedding planning and festivities. Except she didn't really feel needed—it seemed that every detail had been taken over by her mother, future mother-in-law, and their very expensive, very exclusive wedding planner, Charm Simpkins. Which basically left Ginger choosing paint colors for the little house that Woodman had purchased in town last year. Though she still kept all her clothes and personal things at her cottage, to maintain an expected propriety, and wouldn't start decorating the house until they were officially married, on New Year's Eve, sometimes it all felt like a silly charade since she slept over there two or three nights a week.

"I guess I better be goin', Gran," said Ginger, looking at her grandmother, who had been transferred to a private hospital-style room about a year ago, when her health had taken another bad turn. Since then, however, she'd leveled off again, and while she couldn't get around without a wheelchair, her speech had somewhat stabilized, and her thoughts were still clear when she was able to express them. She tired easily, though, and after half an hour spent looking at paint chips, she was probably ready for her afternoon nap.

Gran's trembling hand reached out to cover Ginger's. "We s-still have . . . eight m-minutes."

Her grandmother had been the only person in her life who didn't support her decision to stop nursing. In fact, for a month or two it had actually created a divide between Ginger and her grandmother, which Ginger had mourned deeply. She also mourned the loss of a career she loved so much, but she kept telling Woodman that she planned to go back to work as soon as they were married, and he said, though she suspected he was humoring her, that he'd support her whatever she decided to do.

"How's . . . J-Josiah?"

She looked away. "How is he? He's real good, Gran. I told you he made lieutenant last month, right? Amazin' because he doesn't actually go to the calls, but he's become indispensable down there at the firehouse. He's basically in charge of all internal operations and—"

"*Y-you* . . . and J-Josiah," her Gran clarified with slightly narrowed eyes.

Ginger raised her chin. "We're real good."

Without saying a word, Gran let her disapproval seep into the room, and Ginger blinked before looking away from her again.

"I never should have told you that, Gran. Never should have talked about it. Never."

Her grandmother's hand, which had been limp and trembling over Ginger's, squeezed lightly, and Ginger looked up.

"T-tell . . . m-me how . . . you're d-doin'. F-for real."

Ginger had never made very close friends during her three years of high school—most of the girls had been friends since preschool, and besides, Ginger was sort of an oddity. Everyone knew who she was—the girl who'd had the heart trouble, the little princess from McHuid Farm—but no one seemed to want to get to know her for *real*, on a personal level. There'd been no slumber party invitations or midnight phone calls from girlfriends wanting to talk about boys. Just Ginger, quiet and shy, friendly to everyone but friends with no one.

She *had* made a couple of friends while in nursing school, but since she'd taken her leave of absence from SSCC, she felt an ever-widening social divide between them. And while she was making some friends in the ladies auxiliary group at the firehouse, she wasn't on intimate terms with any of those women yet, which meant that Ginger didn't really have anyone besides Woodman to talk to. Anyone, that is, except Gran.

A few weeks ago, after the first of her four bridal showers, during which she'd received a cache of sexy lingerie from her mother's friends, she had visited Gran after two or three cups of spiked punch. Unfortunately, she'd been a touch too honest about things in the bedroom, and essentially Gran had gotten a drunken earful about Ginger's mediocre sex life.

"Gran, *please* leave it alone and forget I said anything. It's *fine*," she said in a hushed voice, feeling her cheeks flush with heat.

"N-no . . . it . . . isn't."

Ginger pulled her hand away, feeling defensive, even protective, of her relationship with Woodman and wishing to God she'd never gotten drunk and mentioned anything to Gran. She cleared her throat, sitting primly in her sundress as she sorted and resorted the stacked paint chips in her hands, refusing to speak.

She'd known, of course, since the first time she slept with Woodman, that either the romance books she'd read were lying, or she and Woodman didn't have the sort of special chemistry that made sparks fly. While he grunted his pleasure above her, his face a mask of rapture, she had, more or less, *endured* the act of lovemaking.

The mechanics hadn't shocked her, nor had her lack of orgasm. She'd grown up on a horse farm, and she'd never yet seen a mare throw back her head in ecstasy as she was bred. What *did* surprise her was that it hadn't hurt very much, but that was probably because riding horses had torn any thin wall of resistance long ago.

Woodman had been gentle with her, reverent and careful, and frankly there wasn't much to like or dislike. In the end, the entire thing had lasted about five minutes.

Some women—maybe even *most* women—might have felt intense disappointment from such an inauspicious entrée into the world of sex. But brokenhearted from Cain's rejection and confused out of her mind, what Ginger remembered now more than anything else was the comfort of Woodman's arms around her after it was over. She liked the warmth of his bare skin pressed against hers, the sound of his strong heartbeat under her ear, the way he petted her hair and whispered tender things about the happy life ahead. She'd fallen asleep in her bed, in his arms, waking up hours later able to bear the pain of Cain's rejection. Woodman's love—his faith and tenderness and unfailing devotion—had made it possible for her to bear it.

She often reminded herself that she hadn't been trapped into anything. She wasn't a victim. She'd *chosen* Woodman, and in return for his kindness to her she would—no matter what—honor her choice.

Finally the strained silence between her and Gran became too much to bear and Ginger broke.

"There are all different kinds of marriages, Gran. Yes, there's the passionate kind, but there's also the kind where two friends decide to make a life together. That's a marriage built on kindness and respect. On history and . . . and, yes, love. Real love. Just not the sort of true love that they maybe write about in fairy tales or those books at the grocery st—"

"Gin-ger . . .," whispered her grandmother.

Ginger looked up.

"I w-wanted . . . that k-kind of . . . l-love for . . . you. *T-*

true . . . l-love."

Sudden tears pricked the back of her eyes.

In the weeks following her disastrous conversation with Cain and her sudden decision to sleep with Woodman, she'd been in a sort of daze. A haze, really, that Woodman must have believed was a mirror image of his own joy manifested like awe in Ginger. But really she'd felt like a character in a movie. Or like she was watching a movie of her life, her own part almost unrecognizable. Her heart had been broken beyond repair, and no airlift to Vanderbilt Children's Hospital could fix it this time. And Woodman's love was the only oasis from her heartbreak.

They hadn't actually slept together again for a while after that first night, choosing to backtrack in their relationship and start dating properly in the months leading up to Christmas. And during those long, lonesome nights after Woodman dropped her off at home, when the shards of her broken heart dug into the softest places inside her, she read poetry and songs and stories about lost love, and felt the almost unbearable cruelty of Cain's rejection.

Unbearable because she knew—beyond any shadow of doubt—that the kind of true love Gran spoke of was the kind of love she could only find with Cain. On this earth, in this lifetime, Cain, and no one else, was the split-apart half of her soul. It was clear in the way her heart leaped in recognition of his whenever he had been near. In the way she longed for him like a ceaseless ache, dreamed of him nightly, desperately fought to forget him in her waking hours. Her body, her heart, her very soul would always yearn for Cain. But deprived of that soul-based, forever sort of love, she gratefully accepted what she had: Woodman.

Her tears receded, and she sniffled softly, mustering a

smile for her grandmother.

"What I have is exactly what I need. I *want* Woodman, Gran. I *choose* him."

"B-but you . . . l-love . . . Ca—"

"Woodman," she said firmly, forbidding her grandmother to say *his* name. "I *love* Woodman."

Her grandmother took a shaky breath and sighed, looking grieved but defeated. Unable to fight her fatigue any longer, her eyes drifted closed while Ginger stood up and kissed her grandmother on the forehead before leaving.

***

As she hurried down the sidewalk, with the early October sun beating down on her back, Ginger reviewed the rest of this week's appointments in her head: today's cake tasting at Southern Belle Confections, check. This evening's dance lesson at the Winston Schultz School of Dance, check. Tomorrow she and her mother were meeting with the caterer again, and on Friday she was meeting Woodman and his groomsmen at Tanner's Tuxedos to finalize their rentals before the monthly firehouse dinner, at which she and Woodman always lent a helping hand.

They were a pair now, she and Woodman—the de facto prince and princess of Apple Valley: junior members at the country club, volunteers at every firehouse social function, and regulars at the Valley View Presbyterian Church every Wednesday for bingo and every Sunday for services. It was the life that Ginger had always imagined for herself, and yet, inexplicably, Apple Valley had started to feel increasingly small to her since her engagement, and as her wedding approached rapidly, the town she'd always loved felt downright confining.

"Cold feet," she muttered, checking her watch and

scrunching up her nose when she realized she was running late.

After her heart surgery, her mother had hired a tutor who'd taught Ginger at home for the ensuing ten years, but from the time she was twelve, she'd begged and pleaded to attend public school. Her mother had always refused her wishes, reminding her that she was safest at home. Finally, a few weeks before her sixteenth birthday, Ginger had walked from the farm to Apple Valley High School, gotten the forms for enrollment, filled them out, and presented them to her parents. Only then had they relented, and she'd enrolled in tenth grade. Sadly it was too late. Cliques had been cast, relationships formed, and Ginger was an oddball whom no one really knew.

After high school, she had to fight tooth and nail to get her parents to agree to pay for her LPN and RN degrees. Her mother wanted her to go Asbury University in nearby Lexington, where she could have studied youth ministry or French, but Ginger had stayed firm in her desire to nurse, and her parents had finally acquiesced, under the condition that Ginger continue to live at McHuid Farm under their watchful eye. She, in turn, had moved out to her Gran's empty cottage, which had made her mother fuming angry, though technically, Ginger reminded her, she was still living on the farm.

These would have been small victories in someone else's life, but in Ginger's, which had been under the oppressive eyes of her parents since her early childhood, they felt huge. They felt like proof that she was growing up and looking for a life of her own.

But now? Stopping work and getting married to her parents' chosen mate at twenty-one? Suddenly she felt like the six-year-old girl with a broken heart all over again. Small and helpless, at the mercy of her parents' decisions and control.

Something about her life right now felt like giving up, felt aimless, and it scared her that when she got married, she'd just disappear a little more.

Of course, Woodman had an answer for that. He didn't want her to disappear. Aside from being his wife, he had another job all laid out for her, and just last night they'd had another little tiff about it.

Rolling away from her, he'd sighed, pulling off the condom and tying a knot in the end before throwing it in the trash. With his back still to her, he said, "Any idea when we might stop usin' these, darlin'?"

It wasn't the first time he'd asked, but she had noticed that as their wedding approached, he asked with increasing frequency.

"What? Condoms?"

He turned to her, putting his hands on his naked hips and raising his eyebrows.

She averted her eyes from his naked body. Turning onto her back, she reached under the covers for her pajama bottoms and pulled them back up to her waist. "I'm not ready to start a family."

"Gin, you're twenty-one. I'm twenty-four. We're gettin' married in two months, and between my pension and paycheck, we're more'n comfortable." He reached down for his boxers and pulled them on, sitting on the edge of the bed and twisting to face her. His voice was gentle. "We've got this sweet little house. You're not workin' anymore. You want kids, don't you?"

Sure she did. In a roundabout, someday sort of way she wanted kids, but not yet. She wanted to go back to work, maybe even travel a little—have a little fun together before they were tied down forever.

"Not yet."

Woodman sighed, lying down on the bed and pillowing his hands under his head. "Everyone expects us to start a family right away."

She clenched her eyes shut. Everyone expected them to date. Everyone expected them to get engaged. Everyone expected her to quit her job. Everyone expected her to marry Woodman. Now kids?

Who gives a sh—snit *what they want? It's your life, not theirs.*

Her heart clutched from the sound of Cain's voice in her head, but she ignored it as she always did and opened her eyes. "And we will. Someday."

"You happy, baby?" Woodman asked, turning his head to look at her. His eyes dropped to her pajama top, which had remained on while they'd had sex, and he frowned before looking back up at her. "Tell me the truth, you happy to be marryin' me?"

"Course," she said.

"'Cause sometimes you don't seem . . ."

She took a deep breath and held it, knowing what was coming.

He shrugged. "You don't seem . . . *into* it."

"The weddin'?" she asked.

His cheeks flushed. For all that he'd spent his childhood watching horses breed, when it came to talking about sex with her, he was clumsy. "No, baby. Us."

She hated this conversation. She hated it because the wall of cloudy glass that she'd erected was very thin, and tapping on it too much could break it, bring it down, force them to face the truth that Gran was right and they were wrong—there was a place in human life for a marriage based on friendship, but it wasn't when you were twenty-one years old.

Her stomach turned over. "Wouldn't have said yes if I didn't want to marry you."

"But are you *happy*?" he'd asked again.

"Yes. God," she'd said softly, turning away from him to stare at the ceiling. Her voice was annoyed, but she was too tired to make it warmer. "I'm happy, okay?"

Thinking back on their conversation now made her sad, and she didn't want to feel sad. She was a bride headed to a cake shop to taste cakes and choose one for her wedding. She'd made her choice. She'd chosen Woodman. End of story.

As for children? Well, mostly she was too tired to fight the expectations of her parents and fiancé; it was easier to acquiesce than push back. But if she didn't hold the line, that meant she'd wake up in five years married to Woodman, with at least two kids, trapped living a good, decent life in Apple Valley. And maybe it was wedding jitters getting the best of her, but there were moments—small flashes of time—when she just wasn't sure that's what she wanted. Yes, it's what she'd wanted at eighteen, when she was a girl barely out of high school. But it just didn't feel as . . . *right* anymore.

As a rule, she didn't allow herself to think about Cain, and when she did, she preferred to think of him as dead. But she knew, through the very occasional news Woodman received from his cousin, that Cain had taken six months off after his first contract and ridden around Europe on his motorcycle. Many, many nights she'd dreamed of his jet-black hair blown back, his bike curving around mountain passes in the Alps and through valleys of olive trees in Italy. She could almost feel the wind through her hair too, the way her arms would wind around his torso and her hands would clasp over his heart. The word *wanderlust* would stick on her tongue, bittersweet as anything, and she could almost taste the way she wanted a little adventure of her own—something to look back on when she had a bunch of kids yelling "Momma" years and years from now.

But there was always morning. And in the light of every new day, with Woodman snoring softly beside her, she reminded herself of what she couldn't have and what she could have. And gratitude reigned. She would be loved and cared for all the days of her life by a man who thought the sun rose and set in her eyes. It would be enough, wouldn't it?

"It's all you get. It *has* to be enough," she whispered.

She turned from Main Street onto General Lee Lane, stopping in front of the adorable storefront that looked like something out of Candy Land. She straightened her pearls, ran a hand through her blonde waves, and opened the door.

The tinkling bell overhead announced her arrival, and four sets of eyes—her mother's, Miz Sophie's, Charm Simpkins's, and the baker's—looked up from a fancy photo album with pictures of wedding cakes, each a mile high.

"Why, Ginger!" said Miz Simpkins. "You're barely late at all!"

"Hello, Miz Simpkins," she said softly, pausing just inside the bakery door, a trifle apprehensive, uncertain of her place with so many other ladies in charge of her wedding.

"Afternoon, Ginger," said Earline Ford, the premier baker of Apple Valley, looking up from the album and offering her a warm smile. "Almost ready to be a blushin' bride? Just three more months!"

She felt her lips twitch into a small smile for the baker who'd been sneaking her mini cupcakes under the counter since she was four. "Yes, ma'am."

"Come take my seat, honey. I'll get another chair."

With no other choice but to sit down between her mother and Miz Sophie, she took Miz Ford's erstwhile seat. "Hi, Momma. Miz Sophie."

"You look a picture today, Ginger. My grandmother's pearls do complement your lovely complexion," said her future mother-in-law, narrowing her eyes at the family heirloom that had been an engagement gift from the Woodmans. "Magnolia, I can't keep it a secret!" She turned to Ginger. "Did Woodman tell you about the gift we're thinkin' about givin' you two?"

"No, ma'am," she said.

Miz Sophie swapped a gleeful grin with Ginger's mother. "We've had Woodman's cradle and rockin' horse sanded down and completely repainted! They're gleamin' white for now, but we can add a little powder pink or robin's-egg blue once you find out what you're havin'! We were thinkin' of how darlin' they would look in the spare room at Woodman's place. What do you think? I can have Howard bring them by tonight!"

Ginger looked down, twisting her ring uneasily as anger boiled up within her. There were so many things about this announcement that bothered her, she barely knew where to begin.

One, she didn't like how Miz Sophie didn't recognize that the house Woodman had purchased belonged to both of them; she always called it Woodman's place like Ginger wasn't his future wife.

Two, she didn't especially like the notion of her mother-in-law decorating said house, especially when she and Woodman might like to use that extra bedroom for something else.

Three, the assumption that she and Woodman were ready

to have children right away made her grind her teeth in frustration.

And four, Miz Sophie had *clearly* brought this up to Woodman who'd kept it to himself. Likely because he hoped the gift would be a nudge in the right direction. Still, she resented him for not warning her and letting her be blindsided.

"Ginger," her mother prompted, kicking her lightly under the table. "what do you say?"

"I'm not expectin'."

"Well, I should hope not," said Miz Sophie. "Not *yet*, at least."

"Umm . . .," she stalled, looking up at Miz Sophie and hoping that her face didn't register the anger she felt. "I'm sure we'll need those things . . . someday."

Miz Sophie's excited grin faded until her lips were a grim slash of hot pink.

"I see. Well, I don't know about you, Magnolia," said Sophie, glancing away from Ginger with an annoyed sniff, "but I always said, the younger the mother, the happier the baby. I certainly hope your daughter's not plannin' to make my boy wait forever for little ones."

Magnolia pursed her lips in shared disapproval. "Well, daughter?"

It was on the tip of her tongue to say, *I guess that's between me and Woodman*, but there were still three months before the wedding, and she wasn't interested in Miz Sophie playing the martyr for the duration.

"It's a lovely gift, Miz Sophie. And you'll be the first to know if Woodman and I have any . . . news."

Mollified, Sophie nodded at Ginger and turned to Magnolia. "It'll all work out like we always planned."

Without warning, Ginger bolted up, knocking her chair back. It clattered to the floor, and the ladies gasped in surprise, looking up at her.

"I . . .," she started, her chest so tight, she could barely breathe.

"Virginia!" her mother exclaimed, her face a strange mix of irritated and worried.

"Excuse me," she murmured, hurrying to the powder room across the room and closing the door behind her.

Bracing her hands on the sink basin, she took a deep breath that filled her lungs and diaphragm, then exhaled slowly, opening her eyes.

Looking back at her in the mirror was such a pretty girl: blonde hair, brown eyes made up carefully with eyeliner and mascara, a little gloss on her lips and pink in the apples of her cheeks. She wore a sundress and a cardigan sweater with a double strand of pearls around her neck and large pearl studs in her ears. She looked perfect. The perfect Southern bride-to-be.

She also looked sad. So very alone. So very, very lost.

Turning on the water, she held her hands under the cold stream until they were almost numb, then she turned off the water, dried her hands, and returned to the table to apologize and help choose her wedding cake.

***

Ginger didn't know what had come over her at the cake shop, but ironically, when she was feeling like this—freaked-out about the wedding and the future and forever—there was only one person who could truly make her feel better, so Ginger half walked, half ran to the Apple Valley Fire Department, a few blocks away, anxious to see Woodman.

"Hey, Gin!" yelled one of the guys, standing outside the

firehouse with a cup of coffee, checking his phone.

"Hey, Logan. Woodman here?"

"Woodman's always here!" he said, hooking a thumb inside.

"Lookin' good, Ginger," said Fred Atkins, the assistant chief, as she opened the door to the lobby.

"Thanks, Fred."

Miss Melody Grace, the receptionist for the department, waved hello and buzzed her in, and Ginger beelined to the communications room, where she knew she would find her fiancé.

As she swung open the door, a Nerf football nailed her in the forehead, and she stumbled back a little as she heard Woodman's voice say, "What the hell, Austin?"

Rubbing her forehead, she opened her eyes to find a sheepish Austin Wyatt to her left and Woodman crossing the room at a clip. It had been several months since Woodman stopped using his cane, and though he'd always have a pronounced limp, he moved around better than anyone had expected. His physical therapist said he'd never seen anyone work as hard as Woodman to be whole again, and Woodman laid all that progress and all that improvement at Ginger's feet. He credited her—the way she'd welcomed him home, into her arms, into her bed, into her heart—with giving him the strength and reason to push harder, be stronger, get well, be whole.

When he'd proposed, last New Year's Eve, he said, "You gave your heart to me. I want to give my whole life to you."

Tears tumbled from her eyes as he said the words. He didn't know that her heart had been shattered two years before, in an old barn, splintered into a million jagged pieces. He didn't know that when she said her heart was his, he was accepting something broken beyond repair.

But if he wanted it, he could have it. Whatever was left of it belonged to him.

"It's yours," she'd whispered tearfully, and he'd slipped his grandmother's ring on her finger.

"Austin should've caught that," he said, cupping her face with his hands and looking at her forehead with concern. "You okay, darlin'?"

She took a deep breath and stepped forward, into him, letting herself be enveloped in his scent and strength. She wrapped her arms around him and closed her eyes, resting her cheek against his chest.

"Mm-hm," she hummed. "I'm fine."

"You sure, baby?" He tipped her chin up and brushed his lips against hers.

They were warm and soft. Comforting. But when he tried to deepen the kiss, she pulled away to answer him. "I'm sure."

"How'd it go at the cake place?"

She sighed. "Our mommas and Miz Simpkins run the whole show."

"Aw, baby," he said, his hands making soothing strokes up and down her back. "They're just excited, is all."

Quietly she bristled. Though she knew, or believed, that when push came to shove, Woodman was on her side, he was so conciliatory, so easygoing. She wanted him to slay dragons for her, but instead he became friends with the dragons and made excuses for their fire-breathing ways.

She leaned back in his arms and gave him a peeved look. "Your momma mentioned somethin' 'bout a weddin' gift?"

Woodman cringed. "Too much?"

"*Way* too much."

"I just thought . . . well, honey, she was so excited about havin' those things refinished. How about we take them and put them up in the attic for now?"

Another step closer to a destiny that isn't mine.

"Fine," she said, leaning her forehead on his shoulder and feeling beyond weary.

"Besides," he said, "it's just a weddin' gift. What matters is that we're gettin' married. You and me forever, right?"

She nodded against him, an unrelenting heaviness that even Woodman couldn't lighten, making it hard for her to speak.

"Right," she managed to whisper.

"Happily ever after, Gin," he said, pressing his lips to her temple.

"Happily ever after," she repeated, closing her eyes and trying to remember how to breathe.

Chapter 17

~ Woodman ~

"Austin should've caught that," said Woodman, cupping her face with his hands and looking at her forehead. Her skin was soft and smooth, and she was so beautiful, most days he couldn't believe she was his. "You okay, darlin'?"

Instead of answering, she did something he loved almost more than anything else in the world: she stepped into him, flush against his chest, and let him hold her. She wrapped her arms around his waist, and his heart exploded with tenderness for her.

"Mm-hm," she hummed. "I'm fine."

Woodman pressed his lips to her hair, clenching his jaw with worry. The problem was that, despite her reassurances, he just didn't feel like she *was* totally fine. She hadn't been fine for a while. Though she always assured him that she was happy when he asked, since he had proposed, she had been unusually emotional. She cried more. She seemed more anxious and withdrawn. And Woodman couldn't totally figure out what was going on.

Was it just wedding jitters? Dear God, he hoped that was all it was. He hoped that once they said "I do," she'd start being herself again.

Though, if Woodman was truly honest, the person Ginger used to be had changed even before he asked her to marry him. He couldn't quite pinpoint when the change had started—for a year or so after he came back, it just felt like they were adjusting to each other, getting used to being boyfriend and girlfriend after so many years of being friends and the sudden shock of sleeping together. Little by little, they'd become a couple with all the trimmings—him staying over at Ginger's cottage and her staying at his place once he'd bought the house. They spent every weekend together, every holiday, celebrated every important milestone together, and shared their challenges at work and annoyances with family. But sometimes Woodman got the feeling that Ginger was going through the motions—like maybe her whole heart wasn't invested in their relationship in the same way that his was.

The biggest problem of all, as far as Woodman could tell, was that even after three years together as a couple, their relationship had never quite segued completely from friendship to romance. Well, for him it had, but not for her. When he was her friend—when they were having dinner together or talking about their days at work or he was comforting her as he was now—she seemed relaxed and comfortable. But when he wanted to be her lover—to tease her, caress her, make love to her—she became standoffish.

Right now, with her breasts pressed against his chest and her soft hair brushing his throat, his body came alive with hunger. But he knew her well enough to know that she was holding on to him because she was in a snit and a hug from him comforted her because he was still, as he had ever been, her best friend first and foremost.

"You sure, baby?"

"I'm sure," she said.

He tipped her chin up and brushed his lips against hers, unable to keep himself from trying—hoping that this time she'd wind her fingers through his hair or arch her body closer to his. He longed for the sound of a sweet moan from the back of her throat, or to feel her shiver in his arms, so that he'd know that she wanted him just as much as he wanted her.

Her lips were warm and soft beneath his, allowing his kiss, puckering to kiss him back, even, but turning away before it had even started. His disappointment was all too familiar, but he reminded himself that he'd gotten exactly what he'd asked for.

Three years ago, when he'd sat on that porch swing with her, right before she'd given him her virginity, he'd told her that his heart belonged to her. He'd offered it to her without demanding any promises in return. He'd wanted her that badly. And now she was his, marrying him in just a few more weeks. So what did it matter if they were still best friends and a little short on the heat? He'd gotten what he wanted, hadn't he? *Don't beg for rain when you just got the sun. One thing at a time. It'll come. Eventually.* And Woodman had every hope and expectation that it would.

"How'd it go at the cake place?"

She sighed. "Our mommas and Miz Simpkins run the whole show."

"Aw, baby," he said, his hands making soothing strokes up and down her back. "They're just excited, is all."

They're more excited'n you. Everyone's *more excited'n you.*

He had asked her last night, after a lackluster few minutes of lovemaking, if she was happy, but she'd brushed him off, insisting that she was.

And he hadn't pressed it, because her words relieved him even if he questioned them. The fact of the matter was that he loved her so much, he'd take her any way she offered herself to him. Sure, it bothered him that they didn't reach for each other passionately, that she'd never—in the two years they'd been sleeping together—initiated lovemaking after the first time or cried out in ecstasy ever. But she also didn't pull away from him. She didn't deprive him of her warmth and her body. And when he'd asked her to marry him, she'd said yes.

Most of the time Woodman concentrated on the good and trusted that he had enough love for her to last them both a lifetime. Really, everything had worked out exactly the way it was supposed to for them. And hey, maybe things would get better with time. He looked forward to a long life with her, and he'd make every possible effort to keep her happy.

Apparently, however, Ginger's happiness wasn't on the agenda *today*. When she leaned back and looked up at him, her pretty face was sour.

"Your momma mentioned somethin' 'bout a weddin' gift?" she asked, her eyes wide and accusing.

Oh, shit. The cradle and rocker.

He cringed. "Too much?"

"*Way* too much," she said without a fleck of humor.

He gave her a sheepish smile. "I just thought . . . well, honey, she was so excited about havin' those things refinished. How about we take them and put them up in the attic for now?"

A brief rebellion flashed across her face—a little bit of the old Ginger spirit, and Woodman almost goaded her further because he missed that part of her. He wanted it back. But before he could say anything, she leaned her forehead against his shoulder.

"Fine."

Damn it! Fine *again.*

"Besides," he said, "it's just a weddin' gift. What matters is that we're gettin' married. You and me forever, right?"

"Right," she murmured.

"Happily ever after, Gin," he said, pressing his lips to her temple.

"Happily ever after," she said softly.

He clenched his jaw, thinking about the postcard in his pocket, thinking that now wasn't the time to share that particular bit of news with her. He'd make some time later to have a talk with her.

It certainly wouldn't help her present mood to know that Cain was coming home tomorrow.

***

As a freshly minted lieutenant in the Apple Valley Fire Department, Woodman could think only about—aside from Ginger and their upcoming wedding—being given permission by his doctor to suit up and start actually fighting fires again. But after six reconstructive surgeries at the Lexington VA Medical Center, which included a vascularized bone graft, an osteotomy, total joint replacement, core decompression, and two years of physical therapy, his injury still hadn't healed completely. In fact, Doc Collins hadn't even given Woodman the official okay to give up his cane yet.

It was a source of ongoing frustration for Woodman to watch the rest of the guys suit up and know that he couldn't do his part. Sometimes he'd throw on a coat and go to the fire just to watch and be on hand, but he could feel it in his gut—the longing to be in the action, to be a hero again. He wanted it for himself, of course, but he also wanted it for Ginger. He couldn't chase away the nagging thought that the reason she was unenthusiastic about their sex life *might* stem from the fact that she didn't see him as a whole man.

When she'd first offered herself to him, that amazing night three years ago on her parents' porch, he'd been so overcome with lust and devotion, he hadn't really thought twice about taking her virginity and sharing his own. He'd been waiting forever to sleep with the girl he loved—he wasn't going to say no when she suggested it. And while it had been quick the first time, she'd nestled into his arms right after, falling asleep against his chest, her warm soft skin touching his everywhere. Woodman had believed himself in love with her before that moment, but that's when everything changed for him. After knowing the heaven of sleeping beside her, he could never give her up.

She was uptight and jittery about the wedding? That was okay. As long as they met at the altar and said "I do," the wedding would come and go.

She still saw him as her best friend? That was okay too. They had a lifetime to find the romantic rhythm that all married couples eventually discovered.

She didn't love sex? Well, Woodman figured that could be remedied too. The minute she saw him as a whole, fully functioning superhero of a man, she'd feel different about being intimate with him. He just had to get there.

"Woodman!" greeted Doc Collins, stepping into the exam room. "How we doin', son?"

"Very well, sir," he said, shifting his thoughts from Ginger to his ankle and praying that this time he'd be given a clean bill of health.

Doc Collins thumbed through some papers in a manila file folder. "How's the ankle?"

"Real good, sir."

"Any pain?" asked the doctor, locking his eyes with Woodman's.

"Nothin' I can't handle."

"But there *is* pain?"

Woodman shrugged. "Tells me when it's gonna rain, that's all."

It was a lie. The pain was chronic and much more than an occasional twinge. Still, he wasn't lying when he said he could handle it. He could. He *did*. Every day, without complaining.

Doc Collins cleared his throat, glancing at a chair in the corner of the room where Wodoman's cane lap atop his jacket. "Still usin' that cane like I told you?"

"Yes, sir."

"No skippin' days, now?"

"No, sir."

Another lie. He wasn't using the cane and hadn't for several months. He hated it and felt like an old man hobbling around. Ginger was young and gorgeous; he didn't want to be escorting her to dinner or to the movies walking with a goddamned cane. Most days—unless the pain was truly outrageous—he left it at home.

His doctor took out an x-ray and held it up to the light. "Everythin' looks good, I have to say. Bones seem to be healed and settled. Pulse ox in your toes tells me the circulation is fine. You're tellin' me there's no pain. We're surely gettin' there, Woodman." He placed the file on the counter behind him. "Why don't you lie back and let me take a look."

Woodman lay back on the crackly tissue paper and held his breath. This was the closest he'd ever come to getting the okay to go back to work.

"Sure would like to be able to help out at the fires," he said.

"I know that. I know. But I wouldn't be a very good doctor if I let you take a barely-healed foot into an unsafe situation, now, would I?"

The doctor handled his foot gently, feeling the plates and screws, the grafts and nails that held it all together. He made a face and tsked softly. "Got a little swellin' here. Not a lot. Just a bit."

Fuck. Fuck, fuck, fuck.

Woodman held another breath as Doc Collins poked around and forced himself not to wince from the friction of the nails being rubbed against his flesh.

The doctor sighed. "Well, you're surely gettin' there."

But . . .

"But I don't think you're ready for firefightin' just yet. Let's give it a bit more time, huh?"

"Doc, if I'm that close, maybe I could just suit up?"

"You can *sit* up." The doctor pulled the file from the counter, opened it, and wrote some notes on the top page before looking up at Woodman. "Not yet, son. I'm sorry. But I can't risk givin' you the okay and somethin' bad happenin' to you or someone else. You understand. Keep usin' that cane. Keeps the weight off it while the bones continue to heal. Human body's a funny thing—that injury may have taken one man a year to recover from, the next man a lifetime. You're doin' just fine. You'll be on that fire truck before you know it."

"Thank you, sir," said Woodman, his disappointment crushing.

Doc Collins took an Rx pad out of his breast pocket. "Swellin' tells me there's pain. I want to prescribe somethin'."

"No, sir," said Woodman.

The doctor placed the pad on the counter. "Bein' in pain's not goin' to help anythin', son."

"I said I'm fine."

The doctor sighed but shrugged before finishing his notes in Woodman's file. When he looked up, his smile was professional but compassionate. "Soon, Woodman. I promise."

Doc Collins offered his hand, Woodman shook it, and he left.

Finally letting out his breath in a long, annoyed huff, Woodman reached for his socks and pulled them on his feet. As he slid down the table, he looked across the small room and noticed the Rx pad that Doc Collins had left behind. He stared at it, then forced himself to look away, picking up his shoes and pulling them on. Once he was ready to go, he stepped over to the sink and looked down at the pad, swallowing uncomfortably. Woodman didn't break the rules—never did, never had—but this was a special situation, wasn't it? Certainly he knew his body better than Doc Collins, didn't he? All he needed to do was take a slip of paper and write "Cleared for all duties" on it. He bit his lower lip.

"You can't," he muttered, turning away.

But as his fingers curled around the doorknob, Ginger's face flitted through his mind. Before he could give it another thought, he tore off the top sheet from the pad, stuffed it in his pocket, and headed out the door.

***

Dance class with Mr. Schultz hadn't exactly felt terrific on his ankle, and afterward it throbbed like a bitch, but Woodman insisted on taking his fiancée out to dinner. They headed over to the Danvers Grille, waving hello to the many friends who greeted them.

"Dum, dum, dum *dum*!" sang Sallie Rialto, a waitress Woodman and Ginger had both known since childhood. "How many days till 'I do'?"

Ginger blushed, grinning up at Miz Rialto. "I've still got time, Sallie! Don't rush me."

Her words were goodnatured as Sallie handed them menus, and Woodman relaxed, looking over the top of his menu at his future wife's breathtakingly pretty face. *Wedding jitters and adjusting. That's all it is when she seems different. Once we're married, it'll all be perfect.*

"Was it me, or was ole Mr. Schultz deafer'n usual tonight?"

She giggled. "Remember when we took that ballroom dancin' class together when I was eleven? I think he was nigh on deaf then."

He nodded, chuckling. "He made you wear white gloves."

"And you wore a suit."

"That's right. I loved those Thursday nights, Gin. Fairly lived for 'em."

She smiled sweetly but shook her head like he was lying. "For dancin' with your little sister?"

He hated it when she said shit like that. He sucked his lip into his mouth and released it. "For the record, you were never my little sister."

Her cheeks flushed. "Oh, I know. I only meant you had to take some little girl dancin' instead of playin' baseball or runnin' around with . . ."

Her voice broke off, and she blinked before sandwiching her lips between her teeth and looking down at her menu quickly.

"With Cain? Hell, I never ran in the same circles he did. You know that."

But she didn't answer him. In fact, it was almost like she hadn't heard a word Woodman said. Ever since Cain had left Apple Valley that night three years ago, she'd all but refused to say his name. Mostly she just didn't bring him up at all, but when she did, it was like she hit a wall before she could say his name or remember him fondly.

He didn't know what had happened between them. He'd never asked, and Ginger had never offered the information. Whatever it was, however, it had made Cain leave and thrust Ginger into Woodman's arms. He wasn't going to go poking around in it. Whatever it was, it could be her secret. After all, she'd chosen *him*, not Cain. He didn't much care why, only that it was so.

But the unfortunate reality was that Cain would be back in Apple Valley this time tomorrow night, and Woodman needed to tell her before he showed up out of the blue. He sighed because he dreaded it. Hated bringing up anything that made her upset or mad, and since she refused to even *talk* about Cain, Woodman could only imagine that his cousin's visit would send his already off-kilter bride over the edge.

"I'm thinkin' chipped beef on toast. How 'bout you?" she asked, her face serene and composed once again, but the playful sparkle she'd had when discussing Mr. Schultz was gone.

"Yeah. Sounds good." He placed his menu on the table, and after she'd done the same, he took her hands in his. "I gotta talk to you 'bout somethin'."

Her eyebrows furrowed. "Did somethin' happen with Doc Collins today?"

Huh. That wasn't where he was headed, but yes, he needed to discuss that with her too.

He nodded. "Yep. Got permission to start firefightin' again."

She gasped, her whole face transformed by surprise and happiness. "Woodman! That's huge news!"

He nodded, the lie pricking at him, even as he returned her smile. *It was worth it. It was worth it for this reaction.*

"Yeah? Yeah. I know!"

"Honey, I'm so happy for you!" she exclaimed, picking up his hands and kissing them with tenderness and excitement.

It was such an unexpected thing for her to do—to make a physical move like that—it made his heart clench and heat uncoil in his stomach.

"I just knew you'd be okay! Oh, I could sing a song! At least we need Champagne. You think Miz Rialto might have some?"

Woodman stared at her from across the table—the way her brown eyes sparkled and shone—and hope burst in his chest. Maybe, just maybe, she'd start seeing him as a whole man, as her *mate*, not just her friend. The thought made his breath catch with longing, with optimism and faith.

And frankly he refused to ruin such a moment by telling her about Cain's visit.

She was grinning at him like a fool. "I'm going to go ask Sallie if she's got any bubbly!" She leaned across the table and gave him a quick peck on the lips, then slid out of the booth and skipped over to the counter.

He'd figure out a way to tell her about Cain tomorrow.

Chapter 18

~ Cain ~

With his BMW R 1200 RT—customized with a Saab 900 engine he'd acquired in Sweden and installed with a moto-nut mechanic in Iceland—between his thighs, Cain Wolfram roared through Huntington, West Virginia, headed west. The red, orange, and gold trees on either side of Highway 64 were pretty fucking beautiful, and he had to admit that, despite every amazing place he'd seen in his six years of travel, nothing quite compared to the good ol' United States in October.

Flicking a glance at the dash clock, he wasn't surprised to see that it was almost two. He'd been riding since six o'clock in the morning, with only a couple of stops for snacks and gas since he left Norfolk, Virginia. With any luck, he'd make it to Versailles by four.

Versailles, Kentucky.

Cain's new home.

He hadn't been back to Apple Valley since that October day three years ago when Ginger had declared her love for him, offered herself to him, then turned around and fucked his cousin instead.

He ground his jaw as he revved the motor and ducked his head down lower.

It still hurt.

After three fucking years—which included six months of fucking his way through Europe with every señorita and mademoiselle who'd spread her legs—it *still* fucking hurt.

A million times he'd reviewed in his head the details of their meeting out at the old barn: her passionate declarations and heavenly fucking body flush against his. The way her tits had felt under his palms, beaded and greedy, the way her mouth—which was the eighth wonder of the fucking world—had opened and sucked his tongue inside. But even though her body had been *made* for the sort of sin Cain loved best, it was her words that haunted him, taunting him as visions of her naked body snuggled next to Woodman blazed through his head night after night.

Cain . . . I love you. God, I love you so much.

You are. *You* are *good. And I'm in love with you.*

I know you love me, Cain. I can see it. I can feel it. I know it's true.

And when he thought the ache of remembering her sweet words—her sweet, sweet *lies*—would break him, he'd torture himself just a little more and remember her eyes when she left him that afternoon—the broken fucking way they'd looked, and how it had practically ripped his heart out of his chest to watch her walk away.

. . . it doesn't matter anymore. This is the last time you will ever *reject and humiliate me. I promise you. The last time.*

And boy, had she made good on her word.

The last one to get rejected hadn't been her. Between the two of them, it had been *him*.

She'd never know how hard he had to fight himself from reaching for her again that afternoon, how much his body ached and heart throbbed for her, how fucking much he wanted to run after her after she'd left him. She'd never know that he showed up hours later at her fucking cottage to try to work things out, to try to give them the chance she'd begged for. And she'd never, ever know how much he'd loved her—and that the loss of that love felt like a massive earthquake in the foundation of his being, with tremors that had rocked his world for years after. The fault had left a crack zigzagging down his broken heart like a gaping void in the earth, too jagged and deep to ever be filled, too shattered to ever be solid again.

There were so many Gingers who lived in his mind: the little girl he'd known as a child, the twelve-year-old sass-mouth who'd refused to jump on her birthday, the gorgeous fifteen-year-old to whom he'd given a first kiss, and the stunning eighteen-year-old woman who had made him feel more whole, more welcome in her presence than he'd ever felt in his entire life. It hurt to think about her playfulness when he'd been washing her gran's old truck. It was like a knife to his heart to remember their rides and walks, talking about everything and nothing as they wandered through meadows and munched on freshly picked apples. And the old barn? Well. If he had his way, he'd burn it to the ground and incinerate all the memories it held. Because it hurt too fucking much to remember, and sometimes Cain feared that it always would.

It had taken a sizable amount of courage to decide to return to Kentucky, but Cain prided himself that he wasn't a hotheaded teenager anymore, he was a grown man. And he finally realized that coming home to Kentucky was a choice he could make independently of his memories of Ginger. Furthermore, *fuck her*.

Coming home was about *him*—about seeing his mom and dad, and cousin, who'd asked Cain to be his best man. And most importantly, it was about Cain taking control of his future and finally putting down some roots. It pissed him off that bitter thoughts of Ginger had poisoned the well of his better memories. After three long years away, he was sick of her being the thing that stood in the way of his return home—it gave her control over his life that she didn't fucking deserve.

So he'd eventually decided to take it back.

Woodman had written to him two months ago, asking Cain to come home and be his best man when Cain's contract was up in October. His initial reaction was "Hell, no!" But despite Cain's painful personal history with Woodman's two-faced bride-to-be, every time he sat down to write back to his cousin, he found he couldn't say no. And he finally realized it was because, although Cain liked travel and had enjoyed seeing much of the world, as his final days in the Navy came to an end, he found himself—almost shockingly—longing for home.

After six years in the military and very little in the way of expenses, Cain had managed to save almost $30,000 in a U.S. bank account, and during a few days of liberty over the summer he'd flown into Lexington without alerting his family and spent two days with a commercial real estate broker. Looking in Lexington, Frankfort, and every little town in between, he'd finally found what he was seeking in Versailles, located about fifty minutes away from Apple Valley, just south of the I-64 corridor that connected Lexington and Frankfort.

It was a four-thousand-square-foot brick structure that included a large carport, a double-bayed garage, a drive-through showroom with finished, but stylishly rustic wood paneling, and a small office with a full bath. The lease was $1,800 per month, locked in for a full year, and Cain's small collection of three additional motorcycles would be arriving on a transport next week to populate the showroom. He planned to modernize the building to his liking, then open the garage to service and sell motorcycles starting in January.

He'd gotten the idea of opening his own business when he stayed for a month and a half with his friend Sven in Iceland. He'd learned how Sven did his books, serviced bikes, took on pet projects like restorations, and moved a small number of new models. Though there would certainly be hiccups to being a new business owner, Cain had been reading up on small business ownership in Kentucky, and he felt ready to tackle a new future.

It felt strange to think of leaving the service after six such life-changing years, but Cain had enrolled in the active Reserves with a December 1 start date, which kept his leg in and meant he could still enjoy some of the perks of military life: medical insurance, training at a GI Bill–approved learning institution should he decide to seek out some technical courses, local commissary use, and a modest ancillary income relative to his retirement rank of seaman first class.

And sure, he'd still travel when the wanderlust bug bit him. He was dying to see the Pacific Ocean, a place he hadn't been able to visit during his active service in the U.S. Sixth Fleet. Cain had seen a lot of the Eastern seaboard of the United States and the coasts of Africa and Europe, not to mention the harbor lights of the Mediterranean from the vantage point of a flight deck. But he'd never gotten to the Pacific. Being his own boss meant that, after Woodman's wedding, Cain could close his garage for a few weeks, jump on his bike, and spend some time riding from Washington State to Baja.

For the first time in his life, he had a plan for himself that felt grounded in his interests but would still give him the freedom he needed when he craved it.

Fast approaching Lexington, he stepped on the gas, bypassing the exit that would take him north of the city to Apple Valley and continuing west toward the exit that would take him home. But of course his eyes tracked the exit, and his mind shifted seamlessly back to Ginger like a homing pigeon whose cage is gone but who can't seem to find a new home.

Would it be awkward to see Ginger?

"I don't know and I don't care," he snarled, looking back at the highway ahead.

As far as he was concerned, she was dead. She didn't exist. And he certainly didn't plan to spend any time near her. He'd never crush Woodman by relating the events of that terrible day three years ago, and if he couldn't stand there with a cheerful fucking smile plastered on his face while Woodman said "I do," he should have just said no to his cousin's letter.

A promise is a promise, he thought ruefully, so he would show up at the Valley View Presbyterian Church and stand up next to his cousin as Woodman made the biggest mistake of his life. *Mistake* because Cain knew one thing for certain in his gut, and it burned like acid: Woodman, who'd been in love with her since childhood, deserved *much* better than fickle, faithless Ginger McHuid.

***

As he pulled his bike into the drive bay, Cain's phone buzzed. He plucked it from his back pocket as he pulled off his helmet and swung his leg over the saddle.

JAW: What's your ETA, cuz?

Cain grinned. Damn it, but he was looking forward to seeing Woodman again.

CW: Can be there tonight. You got plans?

No one, not even his cousin, knew that Cain had signed a lease in Versailles, and for the time being Cain wasn't interested in sharing the news. He could just imagine his aunt Sophie's disapproval when she discovered he was doing something as menial as opening a garage to service motorcycles. He wasn't in the mood for anyone to piss on his dreams.

JAW: Firehouse dinner. BBQ. You still like ribs?
CW: Fuck yeah. What time?

Not only did Cain like ribs, but a firehouse dinner seemed like a safe bet for pulling off his reunion with Woodman while still managing to avoid Ginger. Besides, hanging out with a bunch of firemen sounded like a solid way to spend an evening—he was accustomed to the company of men, and he'd enjoyed enough pussy in Virginia that he didn't feel the need to track down Mary-Louise Walker on his first night home.

JAW: Six o'clock.
CW: Aye, aye, shipmate.

Shoving his phone back into the hip pocket of his jeans, he pushed his sunglasses on top of his head, unzipped the pocket of his Kevlar jacket, and pulled a pair of keys from their depths. There was still a key fob that read "Versailles Realty," but he'd get a new one soon enough that read "BMW" or "Harley-Davidson." He shoved the key through the lock and twisted, a feeling of anticipation making his heart beat a little faster.

This place is mine. All mine. I'm not a worker here, like my dad was on McHuid Farm. I'm the owner. The boss.

He pushed the door open and stepped into the empty space, taking a deep breath that smelled of motor oil and fresh paint. The Realtor had arranged to have the floors painted a gleaming battleship gray for him, but Cain looked forward to doing any additional work himself. And hell, maybe he could even get his dad and Woodman to leave McHuid's for a few hours and give him a hand . . . help him make Wolfram's Motorcycles a success.

Leaving the door ajar, he stepped back out onto the carport and opened the left saddlebag, removing a backpack filled with clothes and toiletries. Moving around to the other side, he took out another bag that contained a sleeping bag, a pillow, and a towel. He'd sleep in the office until he could find a little place to rent somewhere in Versailles.

Checking his watch, he noted the time, 4:20, which left him forty minutes to shower, shave, change, and head up to Apple Valley. Shutting and locking the door of his place behind him, he walked across the showroom and into the office and threw his bags on the floor. And then he took a moment to appreciate everything that belonged to him . . . and ignore his despised longing for the girl who never would.

Chapter 19

~ Ginger ~

"Hey, Gin," said Woodman, kissing her cheek as he joined her behind the serving table at the BBQ. "I have to talk to you about somethin'."

The oversize aluminum container of Leigh Ann Chumsky's potato salad that she'd just picked up was just about ripping her arms from their sockets. She offered him the tray and sighed with relief when he took it.

"I swear she uses rocks instead of potatoes. I have to put that in the fridge," she said. "How'd it go with the tuxes?"

"Good, but Gin—"

She led the way back into the firehouse with Woodman at her heels. "Y'all liked the simple white shirts? I liked them better without the pleatin'. You too?"

"Yeah, they're fine."

"You're goin' to have to choose a best man from one of

these guys sooner or later," she said.

Of course, her choice of attendants had been commandeered by her mother, who'd nixed the idea of Ginger's nursing friends standing up with her and had recruited five cousins from Charleston instead. It hadn't mattered a bit to Magnolia that Ginger barely knew them. They were all Tri Deltas and would look "gorgeous" in the pictures.

"Yeah, about that . . . "

She opened the lobby door for him and held it. "Oh, shoot! I forgot to get the tray of coleslaw. That's got to be refrigerated too. How about you take that to the basement fridge, and I'll—"

"Cain Wolfram!"

Ginger's neck snapped around so fast, it's a wonder it didn't break. Her hand dropped from the door handle, and her entire body froze except for her eyes, which scanned the crowd with a mixture of greed and panic.

"Cain Wolfram, as I live and breathe!"

Her mouth went dry and her hands started to shake as she heard a woman's voice say hello. He was here? Oh God, was Cain somehow here? It couldn't be. It *couldn't* be. Why would he come back *now*? Out of the blue?

"You come over here and give me a hug!"

Ginger blinked, watching as a tall, dark-haired man threw one leg over the motorcycle he'd just parked in the lot, took off his helmet, and placed it on the saddle. She gasped, deafened by the thundering of her heartbeat in her ears, transfixed by the sight of him.

"Cain," she murmured, the sound a hiss of breath.

"I tried to tell you," said Woodman.

She didn't acknowledge Woodman's words, didn't look at him, couldn't look away from the sight of Mary-Louise Hayes sprinting over from setting up the dessert buffet to welcome Cain Wolfram back to Apple Valley. Ginger stiffened as she watched Cain's ex-girlfriend wrap him in a tight embrace, fleetingly thinking that it was pretty damn inappropriate, considering the fact that Scott Hayes was looking on.

Firehouse BBQs were busy. There were several picnic tables set up, a huge serving table with the big smoking grills in the back, country music playing, and about a hundred people milling around, eating and visiting. It was busy enough that Cain hadn't noticed her yet, though she was only a few yards away.

Ginger watched his lips intently as he greeted Mary-Louise.

"Hey, darlin'," he said, grinning as he hugged her back. "What're *you* doin' here? You a firefighter now?"

She leaned back in his arms, smiling flirtatiously. "Ha! As if! It's the monthly dinner. All the wives and girlfriends come."

Cain raised his eyebrows, still grinning but releasing her and taking a step back. "And which are you, Mary-Louise Walker?"

With a huge smile, she raised her left hand, waggling her fingers to flash her wedding ring in his face. "That's Mary-Louise *Hayes* to you, Cain Wolfram. Couldn't wait for you forever."

Ginger rolled her eyes at Mary-Louise's easy flirting, even though her stomach flipped over. *Neither could I.*

"You married ole Scotty Hayes?"

"Sure did. Two years ago. My momma's watchin' our l'il 'un tonight."

Scott Hayes had finally stood up from his spot at a long picnic table, and now he offered his hand to Cain as his other arm slipped around his wife's waist, pulling her against his side.

"Thanks for stayin' away so long."

"No problem." Cain chuckled good-naturedly. "You're a lucky man."

"Don't I know it," said Scott, kissing his wife's temple. "Get you a beer, sailor?"

"Sounds good to me," said Cain, following Scott to the keg over by the dessert table.

Ginger's lungs started to burn, and she realized she'd been holding her breath. Letting the air out in a dramatic wheeze, she took another breath quickly, trying not to out-and-out panic.

Cain's back. Cain's back. Cain's *here*.

"Baby, let's get this salad inside and talk a spell," said Woodman.

"No," she whispered, a sound so small and broken that even Ginger winced. "I have to . . . I have to get the coleslaw."

"It'll keep."

"No, Woodman," she said, turning to face him, her anger toward him mounting.

He'd obviously known that Cain was coming, but he'd taken no steps to tell her? To warn her? It didn't matter that her fiancé didn't know the full extent of her history with Cain; he knew there was bad blood between them.

"You should have told me."

He looked down at the foil-covered tray in his arms, then back up at her face. "I didn't want to upset you."

She blinked, her eyes burning with sudden tears that she absolutely refused to allow to fall. "Well, you failed."

Woodman raised his eyebrows, taken aback. "He's my *cousin*. He grew up here. His father lives at your parents' farm, Ginger. It never crossed your mind he'd come home someday?"

"You should have told me," she repeated, grit in her tone.

"Why?" he asked softly. "Why does it matter so much if Cain comes home for a visit? You knew he'd come back for our wedding, Gin, right?"

She was clenching her teeth together so hard, she felt her nostrils flare. He'd never asked what had happened between her and Cain in the days leading up to his sudden departure. Never asked. Is that what he was doing now?

Well, it was too late.

She'd been a broken, confused, profoundly heartsick girl that evening on the porch when she'd offered her body to Woodman. He hadn't asked any questions then. He didn't deserve any answers now.

Grabbing the tray of potato salad from his arms, she lifted her chin and walked past him into the firehouse without looking back.

***

The following hour was an exercise in appearing normal and cheerful while her insides were in chaos and turmoil.

Woodman was giving her space, and Cain still hadn't noticed her, though she watched him like a hawk as he moved around the picnic tables, shaking hands with former classmates and accepting pats on the back in thanks for his years of service. If he'd been handsome at twenty-one, he was devastating at twenty-four, a fact that made Ginger's heart leap and her lips frown.

After leaving Woodman, she'd stood alone in the basement, tears pouring from her eyes in waves and sobs of shock and anger. Shock at suddenly seeing Cain and anger at Woodman for not warning her topped her maelstrom of emotions, but there were too many others to count: embarrassment over the last time she'd seen Cain—the way she'd poured out her heart to him and been soundly and viciously rejected, regret that she'd ever believed he could want her, guilt that she'd kept the facts of that day from Woodman, shame that she'd slept with Woodman when she'd been in love with his cousin at the time.

Something inside her had died that day at the old barn. Her childhood. Her wishfulness. Her sass. All gone. She became a woman that fateful day not just because she gave her virginity away but because she gave up on the dearest dreams of her heart. And now? With Cain swaggering around the BBQ without a care in the world like a returning war hero? All that old pain had surfaced.

Ginger globbed a spoonful of mashed potatoes on another plate, backhanding her brow. She'd chosen not to make herself a plate and sit down. Instead, she was working in the food area, making up plates with potatoes and corn on the cob that other auxiliary members took over to the BBQ grills and pit before serving the members and guests. She preferred to work. And to stay hidden.

"Hey, Ginger," said Jenny Whitley, the girlfriend of a young fireman, "I'm grabbin' drinks for all y'all workin' back here. You want anything'?"

Ginger looked up at Jenny and saw Cain's profile just beyond her. He was talking to Woodman and two other firefighters, and whatever he said was making them laugh like crazy.

"Yeah," she said. "I'll take a beer." Woodman slapped his cousin on the back, and Ginger's eyes narrowed. "In fact, make it two."

***

Thirty minutes later those two beers had shot through Ginger's system like white lightning and she needed to go to the bathroom. Because she wasn't a regular drinker, she noticed that she was, ahem, *tipsy* as soon as she started moving. Aware of every step she took, she walked carefully toward the firehouse to use the ladies' room, turning back to the festivities just in time to see Cain throw his head back with laughter at something Mary-Louise Hayes had shared with a group of men that included Scott and Woodman.

Nobody seemed to recall that Cain had been a hellion and troublemaker. Nobody seemed to care. He was the highlight of the BBQ, and part of Ginger was really pissed about that. He'd made her suffer. Part of her wanted him to be as unwelcome to everyone else as he was to her.

"Ugh!" she muttered. "I *hate* him!"

Swinging open the door, she stepped into the lobby and beelined for the ladies' room. After relieving herself, she took a moment to wash her hands and blot her sweaty face.

"Lord, I'm hungry," she said to her reflection as her stomach growled loudly.

In the mirror her eyes were dark and deep, fizzing with an energy that she could feel in her fingertips, buzzing in her lips, rolling in her gut, and making her heart race. *Beer*, she thought, suddenly remembering the time she'd stopped off at Gran's after drinking the bridal shower punch. Was she drunk? Shoot.

"Get a plate of food and a bottle of water. And when you're finished eating, go home. That's the plan."

It would have been a good plan, too, if Cain hadn't been standing just outside the ladies' room door waiting for her.

As it was, she didn't expect anyone to be standing just outside the restroom, so she plowed into his chest when she exited. Suddenly engulfed in his familiar smell, an ache started in her heart that hurt so much, her breath caught.

"Cain," she sighed, her voice almost a purr.

"Ginger," he said in a much less besotted tone, steadying her by putting his hands on her upper arms.

She finally exhaled and took another breath, bracing herself before lifting her eyes. His ice-blue eyes, which she'd known since her earliest days, which she still saw every night in her dreams, seized hers, searching them, unblinking. She heard the small gasp he made, felt the pressure of his fingers around her arms increase. But then he jerked his hands away from her like they were on fire and narrowed those cold eyes to slits.

"What do you want?" she asked, stepping away from him, back against the bathroom door.

"I thought we should get this over with."

"Get *what* over with?"

"Let's just say hello and agree to be civil," he said, crossing his arms over his broad chest. "For Woodman's sake."

There were a million insults and put-downs winging through her fuzzy head, but the reality was that his words were well chosen, and they resonated. As far back as she could recall, Cain had never set out to purposely hurt Woodman. And Ginger knew, from the look in Cain's eyes, that whatever affection he bore his cousin was as strong and solid as ever.

Civility for Woodman's sake.

"Fine," she said, putting her hands on her hips.

"Fine," he answered with an edge in his voice, still standing before her with his arms crossed.

It was the very definition of a standoff, she thought— neither of them looking away, neither making a move to leave.

She reached for her arm and rubbed it meaningfully. "Don't *ever* touch me again."

"No problem," he sneered, his mouth a thin slash of disgust.

The last time she'd seen him, he'd called her a "cock-teasin' bitch," and apparently his opinion of her hadn't changed since. Still, his words felt like a slap and hurt just as much, but she lifted her chin and remained impassive, refusing to let him know he affected her at all.

"Great," she said. "Hello, Cain. Goodbye, Cain. Civil enough for you?"

She edged around him and walked away, ignoring the trembling of her fingers and raging thunder of her heart.

"Ginger," he said in a voice so low and lethal, it made the hair on the back of her neck stand up. She stopped. But she didn't turn around. "He deserves better than you."

She flinched, cringing at the hateful tone he used. But her anger at him—seething and raw—rose up within her and she whipped around to face him.

"How *dare* you! What gives you the right to judge me? To . . . to even *speak* to me! Who do you think you are, coming back here and—"

"Who am *I*?" He covered the distance between them in two long strides, his eyes almost white with fury. "Last time I checked, you were pourin' out your heart to me, offerin' your pussy to me like a little slut, and then . . . then you—"

"You *rejected* me, Cain! You told me to fuck off!"

He pointed his finger at her. "I *never* used those words. And I had my reaso—"

"I don't care about your goddamned reasons! You made me feel like trash for bein' honest, and I hate you for it, Ca—"

"Woman, are you pure crazy? You hate *me*? *You* were the one who left that barn and marched straight—"

Suddenly the lobby door opened, and they both turned to find Woodman just inside the firehouse, staring back and forth between them. Ginger had her hands on her hips, and Cain still had his index finger jabbed in her face.

"What the *hell* is goin' on here?"

Ginger blinked rapidly, stepping away from Cain and staring down at the floor.

"Cain?" Woodman said.

He exhaled shakily but somehow managed to keep his voice level. "Nothin', cuz. Just . . . catchin' up."

Ginger flicked a glance up at Cain, annoyed to find him mostly composed but for two bright spots of red in his cheeks.

"By *yellin'* at each other?"

Ginger cleared her throat, her stomach rolling and head swimming. She needed to get out of here. Oh God, she needed some fresh air or water or . . . or . . .

Nope. It was too late. It was all just a little too much for her to handle.

Her stomach heaved, her mouth opened wide, and two partially digested, shotgunned beers ended up on the floor at their feet.

Chapter 20

~ Woodman ~

Woodman watched in shock as Ginger doubled over and threw up on the lobby floor. When she'd heaved three or four times, she righted herself, looked back and forth between the cousins with horror in her eyes, then ran through the double doors of the firehouse.

"Jesus!" cried Cain, staring at the enormous puddle of puke on the floor. "What the *fuck*?"

Woodman turned on his cousin, shocked as fuck inside but also feeling defensive on Ginger's behalf. "She got sick. People *do* get sick, Cain."

Cain scrunched up his nose at the smell. "Did she drink a whole fuckin' keg of beer? Since when does Princess Ginger drink so much?"

Woodman could smell it too and was wondering the same thing. "She was workin' here all afternoon. Probably had a beer and forgot to eat."

Looking down at the floor, Cain shook his head. "Sorry,

cuz, but that's more than one."

"You know what?" Woodman started, about to lay into Cain, then shook his head and took a deep breath. "I gotta go after her. But what the hell were y'all fightin' about? She just *vomited* on the floor, Cain."

Cain gave him a look. "God forbid anyone upset the princess."

"Can you just call her Ginger?"

"*Ginger* and I aren't exactly besties," answered Cain.

Woodman was losing his patience. "What just happened between y'all?"

Cain paused for a moment, pulling his bottom lip between his teeth before looking down at the floor in disgust. "Nothin'. Just dredgin' up old stuff from a million years ago."

"Homecomin'?"

Cain shrugged. "Sure. Shit like that." He looked around the lobby. "You, uh, you got a mop? I'll clean up this fuckin' mess, and you can go after her."

"Thanks. Over there." Woodman pointed to the supply closet in the corner of the room. He started for the doors then turned back around. "Cain . . . "

Cain looked up, his eyes troubled, his voice stern. "Just stop. Don't go diggin' around, Josiah. Ain't no treasure to be found."

Woodman furrowed his brows, taking in Cain's defensive stance and squared-off jaw.

"I was just goin' to say it's good to have you back."

"Oh," said Cain, looking sheepish. "Yeah. Thanks. It's good to be, uh, good to be home."

***

Whatever had happened between Ginger and Cain, thought

Woodman as he walked quickly down the sidewalk, toward his house, it seemed like a little more than a simple dredging up of high school grievances.

First of all, Ginger hadn't raised her voice above a polite "yes, ma'am," "no, ma'am," and "that's fine" in months, but when he approached the lobby, he could see them clearly through the glass doors, toe to toe and spitting mad. And again, it didn't seem like their conversation was about something from a million years ago. It seemed current. It felt alive. The air fairly crackled with immediacy, with fury and frustration, when he interrupted them.

Second of all, Ginger McHuid, who'd been the perfect picture of a young Southern lady since their engagement, had just tossed her cookies on the lobby floor of the Apply Valley Fire Department. Good God, he'd never seen anything like it. And he had to believe that something fiercely upsetting was the genesis of such a reaction.

And third of all, as Cain had pointed out, the vomit was primarily beer. No, *all* beer. And more than one.

He saw her up ahead, walking fast, head down, and he sped up as much as his ankle would allow to catch up with her. His foot, already compromised by yesterday's dancing lesson, throbbed in his orthopedic sneakers, but he needed to talk to her. He needed to understand what was going on, so he pushed himself to move faster.

As he caught up, he grabbed her arm. "Slow down."

"Let go," she growled, shaking him off, continuing her breakneck pace.

"I can't keep up. Slow down, Gin. Now!"

She stopped midstep, turned, and looked up at him. Her eyes were full of tears, her cheeks slick, and she had a wet stain on the front of her melon-colored T-shirt.

"What the heck's gotten into you?" Woodman asked. "You barely ever drink."

"I can drink if I want," she said, glancing down at the stain of puke, then crossing her arms over it.

"Never said you couldn't, but I'm goin' to notice it when it's somethin' you don't normally do, baby."

Her eyes welled a little more, and she swiped at her cheeks. "Can we please not talk about it? I'm dyin' from humiliation as it is."

He took her hand gently, weaving his fingers through hers.

"No, Gin," he said. "I think we need to talk about it."

"Woodman," she sighed, looking down at the sidewalk. "*Please.*"

"You two were *screamin'* at each other when I walked in. What the heck were y'all so worked up about?"

A small sobbing sound escaped from her throat so her voice was thin when she answered, "Like Cain said . . . we were just catchin' up."

Woodman started walking again, this time at a slower pace, though his ankle protested with each step.

"That wasn't catchin' up. Don't lie to me."

"I *don't* want to talk about it," she sobbed, walking beside him.

"Baby," said Woodman as his heart clenched with a huge and growing worry, "we talk to each other. That's what we do. We don't lie to each other. We may not have the most romantic relationship in the world, but I know how much our friendship means to both of us. It's solid. It's true. I can't think of anythin'—not one thing—in my life that I couldn't talk about with you. Why can't you—"

She stopped walking and squeezed his hand, and he paused midsentence, looking back at her curiously. "Gin?"

"We *could* be more romantic," she whispered. They were stopped in front of the white picket fence that surrounded Woodman's house. Ginger looked at it, then back at him. "Make love to me? Right now?"

He'd imagined her saying these words to him a million times. Every morning. Every night. Every time he saw her. And he'd always imagined that when she did, they'd finally be in a place in their relationship where their love for each other—their *romantic* love—had been fully realized.

Never in a thousand years did he anticipate the stark, cold, knife-through-the-heart anguish it would cause him. The air wheezed from his lungs as he stared at her, as the plates of his world shifted, and he was forced to acknowledge what he'd always known but tried so desperately to ignore.

"Gin," he said, holding her hand firmly as his heart splintered down the middle and broke in half. "In the entire time I've known you, there've been two times you ever asked me to make love to you. The first was the day Cain left Apple Valley, and the second was the day he came home."

He watched her face—her beautiful face that he loved like no other—crumble. Her eyes widened to a heartbreaking deep brown before fluttering closed, her lips trembled into a terrible frown, and her neck fell forward, as though whatever was happening in her brain was too heavy for her to hold it up anymore.

She drew in a long, sobbing breath. "This has nothin' to do with—"

"Cain," he said. "Say his name."

"C-Cain," she murmured for the first time in three years.

"And you're lyin', darlin'," he said gently. "It has *everythin'* to do with Cain."

When she didn't answer, didn't deny this, he closed his eyes and squeezed them shut, feeling an ache in his chest that surpassed anything he'd ever endured during his accident and rehab. She didn't deny it, because she couldn't.

Something in Ginger *fed* off something in Cain—it was palpable and overwhelming, and he'd known it the second he'd walked into that lobby and saw them together: there was more chemistry, more passion, in Cain and Ginger's hate than there would ever be in Woodman and Ginger's love. There was something in Ginger that cried out for Cain and something in Cain that answered that cry. Something about being with Cain turned her on like a light being plugged into a socket—he made her vibrant and alive, made her stop saying "fine," made her *feel*, even if the feeling was fury. That was the way it was. That was the way it had always been. And that was the way it would always, always be.

And Woodman couldn't deny it any longer either. Nor could he compete with it. Lord knows he'd tried.

At one point in time, he'd believed that *having* Ginger was worth the fact that she might not love *him* as much as he loved *her*. But the agonizing reality, he now understood, was that he'd been wrong. She didn't belong with him. She belonged with someone who made her come alive. She belonged with Cain, and keeping her from Cain was wrong, no matter how much it would hurt him to give her up. He loved her way too much to stand in her way anymore.

"Please, Woodman," she sobbed softly, looking up at him with pleading, desperate eyes. "I love you. So much."

"And I love you," he said, his voice breaking. "I will

always love you, but I—"

Suddenly the alarm on his phone sounded, and, echoing it, the alarm from the tower of the fire department down the street, blaring out over the town, calling all members to the firehouse.

Woodman looked away from Ginger, fishing his phone out of his back pocket and staring at the message: *10-23 All hands 10-25 Laurel Ridge Farm Barn.*

He looked up at her, part of him grateful for the reprieve from the terrible, painful conversation they were about to have. "I gotta go."

"Where?"

"Laurel Ridge. I'm active again, remember?"

She took a ragged breath. "Woodman . . . "

"Stay tonight, Gin. We need to talk when I get home."

"Of course I'll stay over. Where else would I stay?" she asked, the last words almost inaudible as her voice broke into sobs. "Woodman . . . you're s-scarin' me."

He leaned forward and cupped her face, the pain in his chest so tight and terrible, he could barely breathe, but he managed to press his lips to her forehead, his eyes burning as he touched her sweet skin.

"I love you," he whispered. *I love you so much that I'll let you go because I can't make you happy, baby.* "And I'm sorry."

And then, before she could say another word, he turned and—for the first time in his life—Josiah Woodman walked away from Ginger McHuid.

***

When he got back to the firehouse, every bay was open, and there was organized chaos in the ready gear room, where every man who hadn't been hitting the keg hard, including Cain, was suiting up.

"You comin'?" Woodman asked, taking a seat on the bench where Cain was pulling on some spare bunker pants.

"Hell, yes. First night back and I get to go to a big one! Chief said he could use an experienced pipeman."

Cain waggled his eyebrows as he said this, but Woodman wasn't in the mood to joke around with Cain. Frankly he didn't know how the hell to feel about Cain. With the exception of that one time, when Ginger was fifteen and he kissed her, Woodman didn't believe that Cain had ever betrayed him. In fact, looking at things in a certain light, he had to wonder if Cain had stayed away all these years out of respect for Woodman's claim on Ginger. As the thought passed through his mind, he felt the truth in it, the yes of it, like a light bulb going off in his head. Cain had stayed away on purpose. It made it hard for Woodman to hate him.

"Why don't you ask me 'bout Ginger?" asked Woodman, fastening his bunker pants and looking at Cain dead in the eyes.

"She ain't my problem," said Cain, his face losing its teasing and excitement.

"Huh," said Woodman, stepping into his boots, then pulling the pants down over them.

"This is a bad 'un!" yelled Scott Hayes, the Battalion Two captain. "Double-time it, men! Suit up!"

Cain and Woodman pulled their Nomex hoods over their heads at the same time, grabbed for their bunker coats, and shrugged them on.

"How's the foot?" asked Cain as he reached for a helmet.

Woodman grabbed a radio from a charger and attached it to the strap near his shoulder. "Fine. Cleared for duty."

Cain nodded. "But I heard all that was recent. How long has it been since you were inside a live one?"

"Don't worry 'bout it," said Woodman, placing his helmet on his head and hustling toward Scott. "I had the same trainin' you did. Cleared is cleared."

Cain looked dubious. "Whatever you say."

"Where you need me, sir?" Woodman asked Scott.

Scott pointed to Engine Two. "Stay back for tonight, Woodman."

"I'm good to go, sir."

"Stay back," said Scott again.

"Yes, sir," he said.

"I'll follow Woodman?" asked Cain from behind him, and Woodman bristled. He didn't need a fucking babysitter. Not tonight. Not when he already felt like half a fucking man.

To his relief, Scott said, "With me. Engine Three. Lineman. Got it?"

They both hurried into the bay, side by side, but Woodman grabbed Cain's arm before he headed for Three.

"When we get back, we need to talk."

"About what?"

"Ginger."

"Christ, Josiah. Stop beatin' a dead horse. I got nothin' to say."

"I do," said Woodman grimly, just as the sirens started to wail.

"Fine," said Cain, turning toward his assigned truck. But a moment later he turned back. "Hey, are you okay?"

"Always, brother," said Woodman.

Cain saluted him with a grin and Woodman watched him go.

Watched him go.

***

"You heard about it?" yelled Logan McKinney over the scream of the sirens.

"Not much. Tell me," said Woodman, holding on to the bar in front of him as the truck lurched out of the garage and raced down Main Street.

"Barn fire at Laurel Ridge. Heard it's bad. They got, like, fifty, sixty horses there. No hydrants on the property. Fred Atkins called twelve more stations to assist. Overheard him say it might take twenty to get it done."

"Shit."

"Yeah. Bad, right?"

"Don't sound good," said Woodman.

"You been through shit like this, Woodman?"

"Barn fire?" He shook his head. "Ship fire was more my style."

"I'ma say a prayer until we get there, okay?"

Woodman nodded grimly, watching as Logan, who'd only joined the department last year, clasped his gloved hands together and bowed his head, his lips moving in prayer.

It vaguely occurred to Woodman that maybe he should say a prayer too, but his prefire prayers had always started with "Everyone goes home," which was every firehouse's mantra. *Everyone home.* Except that Ginger had always been his home, and after he broke off their engagement later tonight, he wouldn't have a home anymore. He'd have a cold and empty place inside, where Ginger had always lived, where he'd loved her, where she'd let him love her. Even if everyone else came home tonight, he wouldn't. His home was all but gone.

"Amen," said Logan. "I said a few words for you too, Woodman."

"Thanks for that," he said, though he felt deeply the words

were in vain. Without her, he'd be entering a dark valley without hope, without meaning, without a future. He'd be poor ole Woodman, whose cousin took up with his ex-fiancée. He'd be pitied, when for the better part of three years he'd fought for respect and equality, pushing away pity with all his might.

Logan interrupted his thoughts. "Fred's got me settin' up an unmanned monitor in sector Charlie. Most of the flames is in sector Alpha, I guess. How 'bout you?"

"I'm s'posed to help you," said Woodman, cupping his hands over his mouth so that Logan could hear him.

Logan's face, which had looked a hair shy of frightened, relaxed a little, and he grinned at Woodman. "Oh yeah? Hey, that's a relief. Thought I'd have to go in alone."

"No, sir," said Woodman, looking ahead, where fifty-foot flames licked the clouds and a mass of brownish-gray smoke, acrid and heavy, made the sky dark as eternal night. "Everyone goes home."

Chapter 21

~ Cain ~

Twenty minutes into the blaze, the water in Engine One was gone, and Cain was holding a foam pipe that was running low too. A tanker from Lexington was about to be pulled into their space to take over.

Cain had seen electrical fires, aircraft engine fires, and even a couple of mess fires during his time in the Navy, but he'd never seen anything that felt as huge and as bad as this. So far eight departments had shown up with their engines and tankers, trying to bring enough water to quell the flames, with little luck. The horses had been removed from the inferno, thank God, but the wind had just changed, and the flames were licking through the center of the barn now.

Scott Hayes hit him on the shoulder. "Done here. Let's move her out."

The hose was wound, the truck was moved back, and a moment later the Lexington truck had taken its place, her men willing and ready to jump into the fray.

Cain headed back to Scott. "You seen my cousin?"

Scott shook his head. "Put him on Engine Two, which was headed for the back of the barn. Heard it was quieter there."

"You sure?"

Scott nodded, looking up at the flames that still jumped and spat. "How long till you think this roof—" Just as Scott said the words, Cain watched as the structure appeared to cave in, the front half of the roof collapsing into the middle of the burning structure as flames started eating their way quickly to the back.

"Fuck," said Cain as he watched it fall.

A loud scream crackled over Scott's radio. "Fuuuuuuck!"

Scott ripped the radio from his shoulder. "Uh, Fred? What's happenin' back there?"

"Fuckin' roof just caved! 10-88, Code 1! Must have traveled from the second floor. We need trucks back here! Now!"

Cain's eyes widened. "You said it was quieter back there!"

"Thought it was!" yelled Scott. "10-75 on sector Charlie. I need water on sector Charlie!"

Scott hurried off to coordinate trucks to the backside of the building as the hairs on the back of Cain's neck stood up on high alert.

I liked *puttin' out fires. I liked feelin' like a . . . a danged superhero. I would've done it forever.* Woodman's words from three years ago came screeching back into Cain's head, and suddenly Cain knew where his apprehension was coming from: there's no way that Woodman would stand down. No way.

With his heart in his throat, he raced around the barn in the growing darkness, jumping over apparatus and forcefully pushing other firefighters out of his way until he'd rounded the massive structure to find the back of the barn was in just as bad shape as the front. What he hadn't been able to see from his vantage point at the front was that the barn peaked in the middle. The middle of the roof hadn't quite fallen in yet, but both lower sides, in sectors Alpha and Charlie, had.

"Where's Woodman?" he asked a probie he recognized from Apple Valley who stared up at the blaze with his mouth open.

"I don't—"

The probie's buddy stood beside him, and Cain grabbed his shoulders, forcing him to focus. "Where's Woodman? Where the fuck is Woodman?"

"He was, uh, he was with Logan McKinney."

"Then where the fuck is Logan McKinney?" he demanded, yelling over the licking flames and sounds of structural collapse inside the barn.

"I don't know," said the kid, shrugging helplessly.

Cain pushed him out of his way and continued through the crowd of firefighters until he finally found Fred Atkins. "Where's Woodman?"

"Woodman? He's 'round somewheres. Scott and I both told him to stand down."

"Where's Logan McKinney?"

"Logan? I sent Logan in fifteen minutes ago to set a monitor. He's 'round here . . . " Fred looked around, his brow creasing as he counted his men and didn't see Logan among them. He nudged the guy next to him. "John, you seen Logan?"

"Logan? Nah."

Fred pulled his radio into his hand. "I got a 10-66 on Logan McKinney."

"And Josiah Woodman!" yelled Cain.

Cain laced his fingers behind his neck, shutting his eyes

and trying to tune out the cacophony that surrounded him. Radio chatter, sirens, the fire itself, the structure collapsing.

"Speak to me, Woodman. Jesus, *please* speak to me!"

"Caaaaaain!"

He wasn't sure if he'd imagined the sound of his name or not, but his eyes opened wide, and he ran from Fred Atkins toward the burning building. His boots crunched and skidded over the gravel just outside the mouth of the barn.

"Woodman?" he screamed, taking a look inside. It was a death trap, a full-on blaze of orange and blue, with beams strewn across the floor, at odd angles, slowly charring as the flames licked them into submission.

"Caaaaaain!"

This time there was no question. It was coming from inside, and it was Woodman.

Turning to the fireman closest to him, he grabbed the man's lapels and said, "My name is Cain Wolfram. I'm goin' in there for my cousin, Josiah Woodman."

Then he placed his oxygen mask over his nose and mouth and ran inside.

***

Being inside a fire was something he wouldn't wish on anyone, but there was a sort of beauty to it too—the orange-colored smoke, the pattern of the flames, the crisscrosses of black beams collapsed in triangles, backlit by orange and blue. The whirls of smoke. The ravenous flames eating, consuming, destroying.

With his mask over his mouth, he couldn't yell very loud, but he didn't need to. He found Logan McKinney almost immediately. He was facedown on the floor between what used to be stall bays. He looked unconscious, not wearing a mask. Cain didn't stop to think. He reached down and hefted Logan onto his back, the dead weight forcing Cain's muscles to work overtime, and ran back out of the barn as fast as he dared, stopping at the mouth of the barn and screaming, "Help him!" to the crowd of firefighters that had amassed there, waiting as Engine Three's pipes were socked and opened. They rushed forward to take Logan's body, and as soon as he was free of the other man's weight, Cain turned and ran back inside.

Taking off his mask for a moment, he screamed, "JOSIAH!" at the top of his lungs, then replaced the mask.

More debris fell from the center of the barn—parts of the roof that hadn't collapsed yet, but were fixing to at any moment. He was at the exact spot where he'd found Logan, and he could go left, right, or forward. He opted for left, then heard Woodman scream his name again from the opposite direction.

"Caaaain!" he heard, weaker than before.

He whipped off his oxygen mask and screamed, "Josiah! I'm comin'!"

Reminding himself to step carefully, lest he upset any more of the unstable structure, he made his way toward the sound of his cousin's voice, his body on autopilot, only one goal in mind: to find and save Woodman.

Finding him proved to be simple. He was also facedown on the floor without a mask, but across his back was a support beam that must have fallen when the roof caved in.

Cain tore his mask from his mouth and knelt down, placing it over Josiah's mouth and nose.

"I'm here, but you're pinned. I'ma push it off."

Standing back up, he leaned down and took hold of the beam with his gloved hands, grunting with the effort it took to move it an inch or two off of Woodman's spine.

"Crawl, Woodman!" he screamed, but Woodman remained

immobile, and Cain watched in horror as another beam fell, not ten feet from them.

He was breathing in soot and smoke now, and his eyes were burning so bad, he could feel the tears trailing down his face. As gently as he could, he replaced the beam on his cousin's back and leaned down close to Woodman's ear.

"Can you hear me?" he yelled, coughing over the last two words. "If you can hear me, listen, Josiah. I will lift, but you have to crawl out. You are one tough sumbitch. When I tell you to, you fuckin' move your ass!"

Josiah's eyes opened and closed, and he made a sick gurgling sound that Cain took for a yes.

Leaning down again, Cain gripped the beam on either side of Woodman and used every drop of strength in his body to lift up, his arms shaking, his muscles burning. Josiah's fingers curled into the concrete floor, and he pulled himself, inch by fucking inch, out from under the beam.

As soon as his cousin was clear, Cain dropped the beam and reached down for his cousin, turning him onto his back first, then putting his hands under Woodman's shoulders to drag him out.

Another beam cracked overhead and fell, flames and sparks spitting above them. Cain stumbled as he walked backward, trying to look back at where he was going, but the smoke was thicker than before and the heat felt hotter. And fuck but his lungs burned like the devil had set up shop, and fuck, maybe he had.

"Cain!" He turned with relief to see Scott Hayes coming toward him. "I'll take him!"

Scott put his hands under Woodman's arms, and Cain staggered back, his energy reserves almost depleted.

"Get out of here!" yelled Scott.

Cain turned toward the entrance and directed Scott where to step as he made his way out. Until finally, finally, gravel crunched beneath his feet, and he knew they'd made it to safety.

Scott pulled Woodman over to a grassy patch to the left of the burning barn and laid him gently on the ground. Cain unbuttoned and unzipped his jacket, shrugged off his O_2 tank, and balled up his coat as best he could to squeeze it under Woodman's head. His cousin's face was covered in soot and ash, there was a bad burn over his left eye, and his left glove was charred to a crisp. His oxygen mask was askew, and Cain knelt down beside his cousin to straighten it.

"We made it," he told Woodman, coughing up black mucus and spitting it onto the grass.

He felt Scott's hand on his shoulder. "I'll get an ambulance."

He vaguely heard Scott's voice on his radio behind him saying, "10-45. 10-45, Code two. I need a fuckin' ambulance. Now. Back of the fuckin' barn. Sector C. Now."

"Cain . . . ," Woodman rasped, his green eyes wide and wild. They weren't focused on anything or anyone, just searching and blinking. And then Cain realized: Woodman had been blinded by the smoke and heat. He couldn't see.

"I'm . . . oh Jesus . . . I'm here, Josiah." He reached for his right hand and pulled off his cousin's glove so he could hold his hand.

"Cain . . . listen . . . " His voice was so soft, Cain could barely hear him, so he shifted his position on the grass, dropping Woodman's hand and gently lifting his cousin's head from the bunker coat onto his lap. Woodman had lost his helmet at some point, and as Cain looked down more closely, he realized that

Woodman's mask was partially melted onto the left side of his face.

Cain gasped at the terrible sight of melted skin, fear rolling inside him, gathering, growing stronger and bigger with every passing moment. "St-stop talkin', okay? I . . . I need you to save your strength. They're gonna bring you some oxygen. Scott's got the ambulance comin' and—"

"She loves . . . *you*," Woodman said softly, his green eyes searching desperately for Cain's blue.

She. Ginger. Because in Josiah's entire life, there had only ever been one *she*.

Cain's eyes burned with tears as he tenderly stroked Josiah's hair off the right side of his face. "No. No, she don't. She loves *you*. Stop talkin' crazy. Just hold on. They're gonna . . . you're gonna be just . . ."

A paramedic slid to the ground beside them and opened his field kit. He tried to put a new mask on Woodman, but Woodman groaned, "No," and tilted his head away.

"Josiah," sobbed Cain. "Please." Then, "*Where's the fuckin' ambulance at?*"

The paramedic pressed his stethoscope to Woodman's neck. He winced at whatever he heard there and slowly pulled the instrument from his ears.

"Cain . . . be . . . good . . . t'her."

Cain caressed the skin by the burned part of Woodman's face tenderly, but his cousin didn't even flinch. There was no physical reaction. No pain.

"Care . . . for her." His lungs were barely moving up and down now, and every word sounded thinner. "Love . . . her." His voice was thready and weak, each breath wheezing and ragged. "Promise."

Tears ran down Cain's face in streams as the wail of an ambulance got closer. The paramedic was on one knee beside Cain, motionless, and when Cain looked up at him, the other man blinked back tears before mouthing, "I'm sorry."

"*Aw, fuck.*" Cain sobbed softly, using the back of his hand to wipe his tears away.

"I don't need to promise," he said, leaning down to press his lips to Woodman's forehead, his tears plopping onto his cousin's face. He knew Woodman couldn't see them, didn't feel them. "You . . . you're gonna be fine, Woodman."

Woodman's green eyes searched the darkness for a face he couldn't see. A strangled sound crawled up from his throat, and black soot mixed with blood streamed out of the corner of his mouth.

"Pl-l-lease," he murmured through the wetness.

"No!" Cain cried, clutching his cousin closer, leaning down to press his forehead to Woodman's and willing every ounce of strength in his body into his cousin's. *Stay with me. Stay with me. Oh God, stay with me.* "No! I ain't promisin' nothin'! Don't you fuckin' leave me, Josiah! You're goin' home to Ginger. You're gonna be—"

"P-promise," said Woodman, his voice less than a whisper, his lungs failing as his deep green eyes swam with tears.

"Yes!" he wailed, pressing his cheek to Woodman's, their tears mixing where their skin touched. "I fuckin' promise! Josiah, I promise." He sobbed, clenching his eyes shut, his voice breaking. "I promise."

And then, as if given permission to finally let go, whatever breath was left in Josiah Asher Woodman's lungs escaped in a peaceful sigh, and he lay, limp and lost, in his cousin's arms, sightless staring up at the sky.

Cain lurched up to a sitting position, and a gurgled scream rose from the depths of his being as he put his hands on Woodman's shoulders and shook his cousin. "NO! FUCK, JOSIAH! No! No! Don't you go. Don't you leave me alone! No! You hang on. You fuckin' hang on. Josiah! Josiiiiiiiiah . . . "

His cousin's name became a wail, a sobbed lullaby, a lament, and a terrible plea for something—for some*one*—who was already gone.

***

Woodman's body was placed in the back of the ambulance, and Cain stood in his bunker coat and pants, blinking in shock as he watched it drive away into the night. He watched until the red headlights were pinpoints in the darkness, until they finally disappeared.

Fred Atkins had called Aunt Sophie and Uncle Howard to meet Woodman at the hospital. He hadn't told them that their son was dead. That was news, apparently, that they'd receive upon arrival at All Saints. Cain ran a hand through his hair as he fully recognized the nightmare they were about to walk into.

Fred and Scott had encouraged Cain to head to the hospital in the ambulance with Woodman to be with his grieving aunt and uncle, but there was someone else who needed to be told about what had happened, and she deserved to hear it directly from him, not from some well-meaning firefighter she'd known for the past couple of years. Whatever choices she'd made that Cain disdained, she had made Woodman happy. Telling Ginger fell to him.

He heard footsteps behind him and turned to see Scott Hayes approaching.

"Cain," he said softly, his face a mask of sorrow, "I'm so goddamned sorry." Cain clenched his jaw to keep his tears at bay and nodded. "Fred asked if I'd stop by Ginger's place and—"

"No," said Cain. "I'll tell her."

"You sure?"

He nodded again. "Yeah. I, uh, I've known her forever. It should come from me."

Scott's eyes were heavy, and his face was covered in soot, a reminder that the last moments Cain had had with Woodman he owed, in part, to Scott's bravery.

"You were the only one who followed me in," said Cain. "Thanks for that. I owe you."

"Maybe this ain't the right time but . . . " Scott shrugged. "I love my wife. I don't kid myself that I was her first, but I love that woman. I know which ones treated her like shit and which ones didn't. You never bragged about her, never talked dirty about her behind her back, never made her feel like trash. That meant a lot to her. And she means a lot to me. So you're welcome, but you don't owe me nothin'." He paused, swiping at his eyes. "Huge fuckin' loss, your cousin. Wish I'd gotten there sooner."

"Me too," said Cain, choking back tears.

Scott reached in his pocket and held out the keys to his official AVFD SUV. "I'll get a ride with one of the guys. You go set with Ginger a spell. Won't be easy."

"I don't . . . I don't know how to tell her . . . "

Cain swallowed over the lump in his throat. He had no idea what to say, no idea what to tell her, how to look into the eyes of someone he'd known his entire life and say the words, *Woodman's gone*. He could barely *think* them, let alone *say* them.

He cleared his throat, using his thumb and forefinger to

rub his burning eyes, feeling helpless and horrified and sick with grief.

Scott put his hand on Cain's shoulder. "The words'll come."

"Yeah," he murmured, staring down at the ground. "Thanks, Scott."

Without looking back, he strode away, toward Scott's truck, and let the tears fall freely as he drove from Laurel Ridge Farm to Woodman's house, where he assumed he'd find Ginger. As he was driving, his mother called, her own voice thick with tears.

"Cain, it can't be true!"

"Momma," he sobbed. "I didn't get there in time."

"Oh, baby. I'm so sorry. I'm so sorry, Cain. The doctor at the hospital had to give Sophie a sedative. Howard just called. I'll be there tonight. Jim's drivin' me down. We'll be at Sophie's. Come and meet me over there in an hour or so."

He nodded. "Yeah. I got somethin' to do first."

"Cain . . . don't go drinkin'."

"No, Momma," he said. "Nothin' like that. I'll, uh, I'll see you over at Aunt Sophie's later." Before she could say anything else, he hung up the phone, wiping his eyes and concentrating on the road.

His body ached, but his heart, oh God, his heart felt like someone had taken a club and smashed the shit out of it. It felt battered and raw, bloody and broken. His lungs were still congested too, but he had no interest in seeing a doctor. He'd be okay in a few days.

Turning down Main Street, he held the steering wheel with an iron grip at a red light.

What the fuck are you goin' to say? How are you goin' to

tell her this?

"Fuck!" he yelled, his eyes burning with more unshed tears. "Fuck, fuck, fuck!" he screamed, banging his hands on the wheel and sobbing like a baby.

The car behind him beeped its horn, and Cain bellowed, "*Fuck you!*" before stepping on the gas and driving the rest of the way to Woodman's place. He'd seen the little house on Main Street earlier today, on his way to the BBQ—the BBQ where Woodman had been laughing about stupid stories from the Navy, excitedly confiding that he was cleared for duty. Alive. So fucking alive, and now . . .

He stopped in front of his cousin's house and cut the engine, using the backs of his hands to wipe away the wetness on his cheeks. He didn't bother looking in the mirror. He was covered in ash and soot. His eyes would be bloodshot, his face streaked with tears. She'd know. She'd know, almost at once, that something was very, very wrong.

"Fuck," he whispered, opening the car door and stepping onto the curb. He slammed the door behind him and opened the little white picket gate, thinking, *Woodman sure keeps this place neat.* Then thinking, *kept.* And another sharp wave of sorrow took his breath away.

Suddenly the front door opened, and Ginger stood in the doorway, a smile on her face. "Woodman, you're back alrea—wait." Her eyes dropped to his filthy gear, her expression very troubled but not quite frightened when she met his eyes again. "Cain?"

It hurt like fuck, but he held her gaze as he walked toward her, his feet heavy, booted in cement made of such heavy fucking sorrow, he had no idea how he kept moving forward.

"Princess," he said softly.

"Cain?" she asked, a wild edge creeping into her voice as her eyes widened.

"Oh God, Gin," he sobbed as he reached the porch. He climbed the first step and stood before her.

She gasped, her hand fluttering up to rest over her heart. "C-Cain? What happened?"

"I'm so fuckin' sorry, darlin'."

"For what? *For what?*" she asked, her voice ratcheting up with panic. "What? *What, Cain?*" she asked, shrieking a little now. Her breathing became choppy and shallow, her chest jerking with every breath. "*What happened?*"

Cain shook his head and felt his face collapse as the tears started to fall. "I was too late."

She lurched at him, nailing his chest with her fists, and he fell backward onto the walkway, grabbing for her arms and pulling her with him.

"NO!" she wailed, beating his chest. "NO! NO! NO!"

He pulled her against him. Hard enough to trap her hands. "He got caught under a beam. Couldn't . . . couldn't get him out in time."

"*Nooooo!*" she sobbed, keening as she uncurled her fists to cover her face. "No no no no. This isn't happening. No." Then, suddenly, she wiped away the tears, lifted her chin, and looked up at Cain, her face determined. "He's goin' to be okay. There are such good doctors here, Cain. He's goin' to be fine. I know it. We're just goin' to drive over to the hospital and—"

"Ginger!" he yelled, shaking her by the shoulders until she stopped talking. "He's already *gone*! He's gone, darlin'."

She froze, staring up at him for a moment, her face contorted in disbelief and anguish. Her eyes fluttered, then rolled back in her head as her body swayed, then fell limp and heavy against his chest.

"Princess," he whimpered, the pain in his heart doubling as he watched hers break.

As gently as he could, he lifted her into his arms and carried her inside.

Chapter 22

~ Ginger ~

My eyes burn, she thought, blinking them tentatively as the early-morning light flooded her room. *And my head hurts.*

Sliding one hand over the sheets, she felt for Woodman, but he wasn't there.

And the sheets were cold.

She opened one eye and looked at his pillow, plump and full.

And then—like an avalanche of horror—her memories from last night returned. *Cain. Cain had come to tell her—*

"No!" she screamed, sitting bolt upright in her bed.

"What?" yelled Cain, from the chair in the corner of her bedroom. He jerked into a sitting position, rubbed his eyes, and looked around the room, on high alert. He was still in the sooty, filthy clothes he was wearing last night, when he came to tell her the terrible, sickening news that Woodman had . . . that Woodman was . . .

"Woodman . . .," she whispered, her eyes filling with more

useless tears, her hands twisting the sheet in her hands.

Cain closed his eyes as if hearing his cousin's name was almost too painful to bear. He clenched his jaw and leaned forward, raking his hands through the stubble of his hair.

"Oh God," she said softly. "Oh my God. It's not true."

"I wish to Christ it wasn't, but it is," he said, his voice low and beaten.

The well of tears burst, streaking down her cheeks, wetting the sheet she still clutched in her hands.

"Cain," she murmured, his name a supplication, a plea. *Cain . . . help. Cain . . . hold me. Cain . . . fix this. Cain . . . take this pain away.*

"I have to get goin'," he said, covering his mouth as a coughing fit made him reach for the arm of the chair. Finally he stood up, pulled a phone from his back pocket, and ran his finger over the screen.

"You're sick," she said between sobs.

"I'll be okay." He squinted down at his phone, scrolling through messages and wincing at whatever he was reading. "I shouldn't have fallen asleep. I have to go see my aunt . . ."

"Cain," she said, looking up at him. *Don't go.* The words sat on the tip of her tongue, drenched in sorrow, desperate for the comfort of his arms around her. Just for a little while. Just for a few minutes. They shared so many common memories, so much unique history. No one else on earth had loved Josiah Woodman like they did. No one else could share the sort of sorrow they could share with each other. And yet—

"What?" His voice was soft and dull. He was looking down at her, his face unreadable. But their conversation at the BBQ yesterday came rushing back, and she reached for her comforter, pulling it closer. *He deserves better than you.*

"Thank you for stayin'."

He took a breath, staring at her intently, like he was gathering himself to say something, but then he hefted himself from the chair and nodded. He flicked another glance to his phone before looking back up at her. "Wright Funeral Home. Today at three o'clock. You should be there."

Funeral home.

"Oh my God," she said, sobs rising up from within her as she leaned forward to rest her forehead on her hands.

She heard him move toward her, felt his palm land on her hair and rest there. "He loved you more than life, Gin. You made him happy."

"W-Woodman," she whispered, remembering his last words to her. *I love you. And I'm sorry.*

She'd never doubted his love for her. Never. Not once in her whole life.

But her heavy heart descended into perdition as she realized that, while he'd given her his whole heart, he'd never gotten more than a part of hers. He'd said that was okay. He'd always assured her that he would only take what she was willing to give. But Cain was right: he'd deserved more. He'd deserved better. And now he was gone.

Part of her blamed Cain because the reason she couldn't give her whole heart to Woodman was that such a big portion of it—rejected though it had been—had always belonged to Cain. And maybe it didn't make sense, but it made her feel angry toward Cain because, if he hadn't played with her, led her on, and eventually broken her heart, maybe she would have eventually been able to give it to Woodman.

She shrugged Cain's hand away, looking up at him with swimming eyes. "Please go."

Cain lifted his hand slowly, his expression swiftly changing from soft to hurt to cold. He nodded, taking a step away from her bed and wiping his hand on his dirty yellow fireman pants. "See you at three."

Ginger grabbed Woodman's pillow, rolled into a tight ball, and clutched it tightly to her chest as she cried until, mercifully, she fell back to sleep.

***

A soft knock at her bedroom door made Ginger turn from the dressing table mirror as she fastened the double string of pearls around her neck. "Come in."

Her mother opened the door and peeked into the room. "Baby? The kitchen door was unlocked so I let myself in."

"Hey, Momma," she said, her voice soft and flat.

Unlike Ginger, who'd woken up numb after Cain left her this morning, her mother had been crying when Ginger stopped by the manor house a few hours ago, and from the looks of it, she still hadn't stopped. Pressing a tissue to her eyes, she shook her head sadly and sat down on Ginger's bed. "I just . . . I just can't get my head around it. It's just so *awwwwwwwful*."

"Yes." Ginger caught her mother's eyes in the mirror, then looked away quickly.

"Where you goin'? To pay your respects?"

"Yes, ma'am."

"Tried to call Sophie a while ago. Howard said she wasn't takin' calls. Poor thing. I just . . . I just want to be there for her."

Much good you'd do, thought Ginger, *cryin' all over the place.*

Ginger looked at her watch. "I better get goin', Momma."

"Want me to come with you?"

"No, ma'am," she said, looking at her mother's tired, bloodshot eyes. "You rest. I'll go."

Miz Magnolia nodded sadly. "You were supposed to be wearin' white in a few weeks, not black today."

Ginger flinched but refused to examine the feelings that had elicited the instinctive response. Instead she said, "I'll be stayin' here at Gran's cottage for a while longer, if that's okay."

Her mother looked up, dabbing at fresh tears. "Can't see why not. Won't need it for weddin' guests anymore." She sniffed delicately, then got up and left Ginger's room, her face slightly dazed.

Something inside Ginger clenched in anguish at her mother's words, but again she shoved it down and ignored it, grabbing her purse from the bed and heading downstairs to drive to Wright Funeral Home.

She arrived at 2:55 to find Miz Sophie, Mr. Woodman, and Cain and his mother and her husband standing in the front foyer, waiting on their appointment. She avoided eye contact with Cain, but his mother, Miz Sarah, embraced Ginger as soon as she walked in, whispering her sympathies in Ginger's ear and holding her tight. Mr. Johnson, whom Ginger had never met, offered his hand and also shared his condolences. But when Miz Sophie turned around to find Ginger standing there, her eyes were narrow and cold.

"What're *you* doin' here, Ginger?"

Ginger blinked at her in surprise.

"I invited her to come," said Cain from behind her. "I thought she should be here."

"Are you runnin' the show now?" asked Miz Sophie, her eyes sharp and furious as she turned to glare at her nephew.

"No, ma'am. But Ginger is his fiancée, and I thought—"

"*Was*," bit out Miz Sophie. "She *was* his—"

Mr. Wright opened the double doors to the conference room, cutting off Miz Sophie's remarks. "Sympathies, Mr. Woodman. Miz Sophie. What a terrible thing."

"Thank you, Dale," said Howard Woodman, rubbing his bloodshot eyes. "Thanks for makin' time today."

"Of course. Of course," said Dale Wright, his voice soothing as he put his arm around Howard's shoulders. "Come on in and we'll talk a while."

Miz Sophie gave Ginger a look, but she didn't actually tell her to leave, so Ginger followed robotically behind Cain and Mr. and Mrs. Johnson.

They took seats at an elegant cherry table, Mr. and Mrs. Woodman sitting across from Mr. Wright, with Ginger, Cain, and the Johnsons sitting farther down. Cain took the seat beside Ginger, and for a fleeting second she was comforted by his presence there, but something about that comfort felt too raw, so she took a deep breath and focused on Mr. Wright instead.

He started discussing details. There would be a viewing on Sunday evening so that friends and neighbors could pay their respects, and the funeral would take place in two days, on Monday. Ginger half listened, half zoned out, her body exhausted, her mind fuzzy and numb, but when Miz Sophie said that Woodman should be buried in his Navy uniform, her neck snapped up and she felt words—unsanctioned, unexpected words—suddenly come tumbling out of her mouth.

"No. His lieutenant uniform."

"He *wasn't* a lieutenant," sniped Miz Sophie with a bite in her voice. "He was a seaman."

"He's a lieutenant at the fire department," she said, her cheeks burning as she stared down at the table, finally flicking a glance up at Miz Sophie to add, "And he loves it."

Miz Sophie's eye flared with fury, and she cleared her throat, turning back to Mr. Wright. "We'll bury him in his Navy whites. Like he would've wanted."

"He *wouldn't* have wanted that," said Cain.

"He was *my son*," said his aunt, completely ignoring Cain and skewering Ginger with her eyes. "Why are you even here? You aren't family. You stole enough of his time while he was alive. You don't get to have him in death!"

"*She* was Josiah's fiancée," pressed Cain, and she could feel anger being thrown off his body like heat, tightly coiled fury that he was only just managing to control. "She deserves a say."

Miz Sophie raised her palms and slammed them down on the table, making it reverberate.

"*FUCK YOU*!" she screamed, her eyes fiercely shiny with tears that didn't fall. "Are you tellin' me what *she* deserves? *I* didn't deserve to have my son *die* at twenty-four years old!" Her face was red and her voice trembled as she raised a shaking finger and pointed it at Cain. "You could have saved him! Why didn't you save him?"

"He wasn't supposed to be in there!" said Cain. "I didn't even know. I tried to find him, but . . . "

"But you *didn't.* You didn't save him, because you are a bad seed, Cain Wolfram. You are a selfish, self-servin' troublemaker, and I don't *want* you here! *No one* wants you here."

"Sophie," sobbed Sarah, shaking her head and reaching for her sister's hand.

"Don't you touch me, Sarah!" She turned on Cain again, standing up and flattening her hands on the table, shrugging away Mr. Woodman's attempts to help her sit back down. "*No one* asked you here!"

"Wrong," he said, his voice ragged and profoundly broken, but crystal clear. "*Josiah . . .*" He paused as a wheezing sound released from his throat, which spurred on a coughing fit. When he spoke again, his voice was softer. "*Josiah* asked me here. I came home because of him."

"Well," sobbed Miz Sophie, as a tenacious tear finally escaped and snaked its way down her miserable face, "I wish you'd *never* come home! I wish you'd stayed away!"

Cain didn't speak. He lowered his head and stared at the table. Without thinking, Ginger unclasped her hands in her lap, slid one of hers to one of his, took it gently from his thigh, and weaved their fingers together. She looked up at Miz Sophie, feeling profoundly sorry for her, and for Cain, and for all of them at that miserable table, suffering so terribly. *Something dreadful has happened*, buzzed her mind, but she took a deep breath and turned off the noise. She wasn't on the stage. She was in the audience watching. Only watching.

"It. Should. Have. Been. *You*!" screamed Miz Sophie, banging her fists on the table to enunciate each word. "It should have been *you*! *Not* Josiah. *You, Cain*! Always up to no good. Not half the man my son was. *You* should have died in that fire. Not my baby." She sobbed, her whole body shuddering as she collapsed into her chair and leaned forward to lay her cheek on the table, wailing with a sort of desperate, keening anguish that made tears slip down Ginger's cheeks. "My *baby*. Oh God! Oh God, my baby. My boy . . ."

Ginger leaned to her left, her lips close to Cain's ear. "Come on."

She got to her feet and tugged his hand until he stood up beside her. Without looking at each other or anyone else, they quietly left the room, walked through the foyer, and stepped outside.

On the veranda that surrounded the funeral parlor, there were several chairs and settees, and Ginger chose one, pulling Cain down beside her before releasing his hand.

"She doesn't mean it," she said softly.

"Yeah, she does," said Cain, who hadn't raised his head since his aunt's tirade.

"No," said Ginger, reaching up to swipe away tears that rolled down her cheeks. Where had they come from? She didn't feel them gather, barely felt them fall. "She's out of her mind with grief."

"She's right," he whispered.

"No, she's not."

"I didn't save him."

"But you tried."

"Yes." Cain nodded. "I was too late. He was . . . trapped. I didn't even know he'd gone in."

Her voice sounded faraway as she brushed the back of her hand over her slick cheeks again. "It's not your fault."

"He was twice the man I'll ever be." Cain rested his elbows on his knees and his face in his hands. "If one of us had to die—she's right—it should have been me."

No! screamed some primal part of her from the deepest depths of her soul, jarring her, for just a moment, from her comfortable numbness. *No, no, no!*

Her mind started racing, her voice—a desperate voice—narrating a story in her head: *Once upon a time there were two cousins: one golden like the sun, one dark as midnight, both owning equal, but different, parts of a little girl's heart . . .*

"No," she said, panting as her breathing got shallow and

quick.

She pressed a hand against her aching chest. That little girl's heart was broken all over again, shriveling in her chest, drying up, dying, changed beyond recognition from the whole, boundless place it had once been.

She stood up from the settee, placing her hands on the veranda railing and looking out at Main Street, which hustled and bustled like it was a regular Saturday, like the world hadn't ended last night.

"I shouldn't have come," she said aloud, a thought borrowing words.

"Gin," he said softly.

His words stirred something within her, and she turned to see him raise his glistening iceberg-blue eyes to her. They were so full of pain, it made something ache inside her, but the ache was quickly quieted, blanketed in dull, comfortable apathy. Her shoulders lightly brushed her ears in a slow shrug, and her tears dried—she had nothing left to give.

"I can't," she murmured, her tears ceasing as mysteriously as they'd begun.

"Gin," he said again, standing up, gesturing uselessly with his hands. "I'm . . . sorry he's gone."

I'm sorry he's gone. A ball-peen hammer to her dried husk of a heart. Four words and it was pulverized to dust.

"He's not," she said softly, walking away from Cain, dazed and dull and numb all over. *He's just away.*

PART FIVE

Chapter 23

She loves you.

 Be good to her.

 Care for her.

 Love her.

 Promise.

 Please.

 Promise.

Cain shot up in his cot, drenched in sweat and shaking as the dreamy echo of Woodman's broken voice faded.

"God," he gasped, scrubbing his hands over his face and blinking into the darkness before lowering his forehead to his bent knees.

Since losing Woodman, almost a month ago, he woke up like this every other night: seeing his cousin's frightened, blank, green eyes staring straight up, into the void of forever, feeling the weight of Woodman's head on his lap, seeing the blackish-red slickness pool at the corner of his mouth and slide over his slack and cooling cheek.

And always—*always*—he heard the handful of words that

had been Woodman's dying plea. They were Cain's constant companions—*constant torment, waking and sleeping*—and yet he had no idea how to honor them, how to make them happen.

Not that he'd really tried. He'd mostly been drunk since the funeral, and when he wasn't, he was tearing around Kentucky on his motorcycle. Seven times he'd packed his saddlebags and headed for the border, and seven times he'd stopped before crossing over to Tennessee or Virginia or West Virginia or Ohio or Indiana or Illinois or Missouri. He'd stood there at the border seven times, the adjoining state mocking his captivity. He was desperate to leave—desperate to run away and never go back to Kentucky again as long as he lived. But if he did that, he'd be turning his back on Woodman for good. He'd be taking Woodman's sacred trust and trashing it. And he couldn't. God help him, he couldn't do it.

So, seven times, at seven state borders, he'd grudgingly turned around and headed back to Versailles. Well, back to Versailles after going on a two- or three-day bender wherever he found himself.

He swung his legs over the cot he'd set up in the corner of the empty office and reached for the omnipresent bottle of vodka beside the bed. He unscrewed the top and took a nice long swig, relishing the burn on his throat. He licked his lips and took another gulp before screwing the cap back on, then stood up and stretched his arms over his head. There were no windows in the small interior office, which was a good thing since Cain was buck naked. He pulled his jeans on inside out, not bothering to zip or button them as he walked across the cold floor toward the office door. He opened it, squinting his eyes at the bright light streaming through skylights into the showroom.

On one side of the room, the three motorcycles shipped to

Versailles from Iceland and Virginia were still bungee-corded to the pallets they'd arrived on. He hadn't touched them since he signed for them.

Turning back into the office, he flicked on the light and padded over to the small refrigerator, grabbing an energy bar from the top of the fridge and throwing the wrapper on the floor. The clock on the microwave read 11:46, which meant that Kennedy's would be opening in fourteen minutes if Cain wanted to go get a cold beer and surround himself with the inanity of humanity until he returned home ten hours later and passed out in a cold stupor.

He'd done the same thing yesterday, and the day before that, after he got back from the Ohio border, where he'd turned around before crossing over, close to Cincinnati.

When he was a kid, his parents took him to the Cincinnati Zoo, and he remembered watching a wolf pace its cage. He'd asked the zookeeper why it kept walking back and forth, back and forth across the same ten or twelve feet in front of the glass, and the keeper had answered that the wolf was used to roaming a vast area to hunt and claim territory. Without the space to roam, it paced the small width of its cage in an effort to re-create its instinct to wander. It was trying to hold on to its purpose, but without the need to hunt, it had none.

He'd locked eyes with the wolf, their icy blue color identical to Cain's, and a searing sense of sympathy made his breath catch. The wolf was useless and trapped. All it wanted was to be freed, to run back to its natural habitat and rediscover its purpose.

Cain remembered the wolf with a new sense of understanding. He also wanted to run away—from Kentucky, and Apple Valley, and his dead cousin, and his devastated family, and the promises he'd made that he had no idea how to dignify. If he could just get on his bike and ride, he felt like he could outrun the unbearable heartbreak, the oppressive sorrow, the inconceivable reality of a long life spent without his cousin, his brother, his memory keeper, his friend.

And yet running also meant disgracing Woodman's memory.

So he was trapped, pacing in front of the glass, cooped up and purposeless.

Beside his cot, his cell phone buzzed, rattling on the cement, and Cain crossed the room to pick it up.

KW: Cain, call me.

Just as he'd been Cain's lifeline to home during his time in the military, his father made sure to text Cain at least once or twice a day since Woodman's funeral, checking in on him and even—several times—urging him to "come home" to McHuid's. Cain didn't respond, so his father had no idea whether Cain was even still in Kentucky. For all Klaus knew, Cain could be in California or Maine by this point.

He hadn't been back to Apple Valley since the funeral. The funeral was also the last time he'd seen Ginger, though he hadn't spoken to her since that afternoon at the funeral home. She'd hung back with her parents, as though uncertain of her place or her welcome, and though they'd locked eyes as Woodman was lowered into the ground, he didn't recognize her. Her mother wept on her daughter's shoulder, but Ginger stood stoic and calm, cold and emotionless. Like she wasn't really there. Like an empty husk. Like a ghost.

This was the girl he'd promised Woodman to love and care for.

Fuck. He could barely take care of himself.

The phone buzzed in his hand again.

KW: Cain, it's urgent. Call me.

Sighing, he reached down for the bottle of vodka when the phone buzzed a third time.

KW: It's Ginger.

Sucking in a swift breath, Cain Holden Wolfram, who'd thought just two seconds before that he was three-quarters dead, trapped in an aimless existence, suddenly realized that he was actually very much alive. His heart raced with fear—no, not fear, with *terror*. Had something *happened* to Ginger? Christ! While he'd been riding all over Kentucky and drinking himself into a stupor, had something fucking *happened* to her?

Promise.

I fuckin' promise! Josiah, I promise.

Fuck. Fuck, please no. No. No, no, no. Please, God. Please let Ginger be okay.

His hands shook and sweated as he dialed his father's number, as he heard the phone ring once, twice—

"Cain? Bist du—?"

"Papa, sag es mir!" Tell me!

"Gott sei Dank, Cain. Du lebst." Thank God. You're alive.

"Pop," he said, sitting down on his cot, his body taut and wired. "What happened to Ginger? Is she okay? Is she all right? What happened to her?"

"She is . . . *sehr traurig*."

Cain exhaled a long breath, his body relaxing. If something was seriously and immediately wrong, his father would have told him.

"Of course she's sad," he said, running his hand through his stubbly hair as he rested his elbows on his knees, shaking in relief just as he'd shaken with fear.

"I hear from Ranger. She don't eat. She don't talk. She don't leave the cottage."

Cain took a deep breath and held it until it burned his lungs.

"Cain? You are there?"

His breath came out in an exhausted sigh. "I'm here."

"You have known the princess for . . . your lifetime."

A tear snaked its way down Cain's cheek, and he reached up to wipe it away. "Yep."

"She is hurting, *mein Sohn*."

His knees bounced from the adrenaline rush he'd gotten from his father's texts.. "We're all hurtin', Pop. She ain't the only one."

His father was silent for a few seconds, then said, "She is hurting . . . *more*."

Cain looked down at the half-finished bottle of vodka at his feet and picked it up. He unscrewed the top and raised it to his lips, but his mind flashed back to her glazed face at the funeral. He lowered the bottle and walked across the small office to the bathroom, where he tipped the bottle into the sink and watched the clear liquid swish down the drain. When it was empty, he dropped it under the sink on top of an overflowing garbage can and looked up at the mirror.

He barely recognized himself.

His last buzz cut from right before leaving Virginia had grown out almost an inch, and he had a full beard that covered his jaw, cheeks, and neck with bristly, black, ungroomed hair. He'd lost weight, which made his cheeks gaunt, and his complexion had yellowed from so much drinking. Bloodshot eyes stared back him with heavy bags beneath, and his lips were chapped and cracked. He licked them tentatively.

"Cain?"

He swallowed over the lump in his throat, remembering the morning he walked into Woodman's hospital room at Walter Reed.

You look . . . rough.

Don't lie to me, huh?

I'm not a good bullshitter.

Since when?

He chuckled softly as his eyes filled with more tears, his heart aching from how much he missed Woodman. "Yeah, Pop. I'm here."

"You come home, Cain? You must come to her."

Be good to her. Care for her. Promise.

"Yeah, Pop," he said softly. "Yeah, I'll come home." He took another look at his reflection and winced. "Give me a few days, huh?"

"Don't wait too long," said his father.

Please. Promise.

"I won't. It's, uh, what's today?"

"Tuesday."

"I'll be there on Friday, okay?"

"*Ja. Gut.* And you stay? Stay for two week? For the Thanksgiving, *ja*?"

Cain nodded. "I'll stay a little while, Pop." He was hanging up the phone when he heard his father say something else. "Huh?"

"She *need* you, Cain. *Verstehst du mich*?"

He nodded. "I understand. I'll be there soon."

He pressed the End button on his phone and placed it on the shelf over the sink. Then he opened the cabinet, took out his shaving cream and razor, and turned on some warm water.

***

Some days—*most* days—Ginger pretended that he was just away. Like, on a business trip or out of town, on a fishing trip. Men did that, didn't they? It didn't matter that he wasn't a businessman and didn't especially like fishing. It was easier to imagine him alive somewhere than forcing her mind to accept the fact that Woodman was gone for good. And while some part of her acknowledged that it probably wasn't healthy, she really didn't give a shit. About much. About anything.

She picked up the remote, changed the channel from Lifetime to Hallmark, and stared at the screen. A woman was yelling at a child whose eyes were filling with tears. Yelling mother. Distraught child. Mother shaking the child's shoulders. Child's face crumbling.

And Ginger stared, unmoved, glazed over.

She didn't feel much of anything lately.

She didn't leave the cottage very much either. Not even to see Gran, whom she hadn't visited in a month, since the day before Woodman's funeral, when she'd cried so long and so hard at Gran's bedside, she'd eventually fallen asleep. The nurses hadn't had the heart to wake her, so she slept there, waking hours later in the dark with her head on Gran's bed, disoriented and frightened. She gathered her purse and walked in a daze to her car, driving back to the cottage at two o'clock in the morning and falling into bed still clothed.

Her mother periodically left bags of groceries and fashion magazines on the back stoop of the cottage. A lone cupcake appeared on Ginger's birthday, but otherwise her mother let her be.

Her father occasionally knocked on the door, looking

disappointed when she answered it wearing pajamas with limp, greasy hair framing her thin face. She would stare at his mouth, watching his lips move as he gave her a back porch speech. Some of his words registered—"fresh air," "talk to someone," "can't go on like this"—though they meant nothing, flying over her head like the autumn leaves that had started falling, blown away by chillier and chillier breezes. She would nod at the right place, he would kiss her forehead, and she'd close the door as he walked back to the manor house.

When Cain told her about Woodman's death, she'd felt her chest crack open in agony, the feelings so potent and painful, part of her wanted to die. But it was later, at the funeral home, when she'd looked into Cain's eyes, that she realized how very alone she was. Woodman, for all that she hadn't loved him the way he wanted her to, had been her very best friend, her foundation, her safe harbor, her comfortable future. She'd already lost Cain some years before, but as long as Woodman was by her side, she wasn't alone.

But now? *Now* she was alone.

Gran was sick and wouldn't last much longer.

She'd never been especially close to her parents.

She had no siblings, no real friends.

She was an island.

At the funeral—the full military honors had made it feel even more unreal to Ginger—she remembered the little girl who loved two boys. And now she had, as her grandmother had predicted on her twelfth birthday, lost them both.

Woodman was gone, and Cain hated her. And since they'd shared her heart in different ways, losing them meant that her heart was broken beyond repair, with no hope for salvation or solace. She didn't fight this realization. She quietly accepted it.

Then she changed into her pajamas, slipped into bed, and, aside from the occasional cup of tea or the need to relieve herself, didn't get out of her bed for a week. And when she finally did, she saw no reason to leave her room. And when she finally did, she saw no reason to leave her cottage. And so she hadn't. She hadn't been outside in almost a month. Nor had she cried once. And every day that passed made her feel more dead inside than the day before.

That was just fine.

In fact, it was for the best.

She pressed the pad of her thumb into the channel-return button, and Lifetime returned. Two female police officers questioned a young pregnant woman who had her elbows propped on a table, looking confused, disbelieving, then distraught. Ginger stared at the young actress who sobbed and screamed, beating her hands on the metal table. What had they just told her? That her car had been stolen? That her house had burned down? That her boyfriend had been killed?

That would be sad, wouldn't it? To be a young pregnant girl with no car, no house, and no boyfriend? That was the sort of heartbreaking story that should make Ginger cry, and yet no tears came. No lump in her throat. No burn behind her eyes. Nothing. Just . . . nothing.

She sat up, then stood up, then walked into the kitchen and poured herself a glass of water, standing at the sink for a moment.

How long will you go on like this? she wondered. *Will you just keep fading away? Until someday the ghost that you are is the ghost you become.*

"Maybe that's how it ends," she said softly, to no one. "You just fade away until you're gone."

Aknock on her door made her turn listlessly toward it. She closed her eyes and took a deep breath, willing her mother or father to leave, to go away, to just leave her the fuck alone. Couldn't they see that she was an island? Didn't they know a ghost when they saw one?

Again, a soft knock.

She leaned back from the sink and glanced at the window over the door, but her parents were smart. They didn't peek into the window. They stayed out of sight so she couldn't just wave them away.

Knock, knock, knock.

"Fine," she muttered under her breath, crossing the small kitchen and swinging open the door.

Her eyes slammed into a heather-gray waffle-weave Henley, then slid upward to a square jaw. She lingered on his lips for a moment, ruthlessly pushing down the tiny spark of a memory of those lips pressed against her own. Raising her gaze, she took in the cut-marble slashes of his cheekbones, finally meeting the arctic blue of his eyes.

"Ginger," he whispered gently.

"Cain," she answered, the sound small and stunned.

She answered his voice because she could barely see his face.

Her eyes were swimming with tears.

Chapter 24

She looked awful.

In fact, in the twenty-one years that Cain had known Ginger Laire McHuid, he couldn't ever remember her looking so terrible.

"Hi," he said, sweeping his eyes over her face.

Tired, glassy eyes stared back at him, with two sets of bags under each. Her hair, which was usually blonde, shiny, and curled, lay limp and greasy around her face. He dropped his gaze to her clothes and realized she was wearing a sweat suit or some sort of pajamas—a light pink shirt that read "Sleepy Time!" had several dried stains of different colors, mostly concentrated across the straining ledge of her breasts, and black cotton pants with white and gray fingerprint smudges on the thighs.

"What do you want?" she asked.

His eyes trailed back up her body quickly until he met her eyes. And as he stared at her, relief coursed through his body because there, behind the tears and the tiredness, the anger and the bleakness, was Ginger. The Ginger he knew. The Ginger he hadn't seen at the funeral.

"I'm goin' for a ride and you're comin' with me," he said, leaning against the doorway.

She shook her head and reached for the door as if to close it. "I'm not up for a ride."

Cain stuck his foot in the door. "You're always up for a ride, one. And two, I didn't ask if you were up for it."

She took a deep breath and sighed loudly, giving him a look that would freeze boiling water. "Cain, go away." She glanced at his foot, then back at his face. "I mean it."

"Hmm," he murmured, meeting her icy gaze unflinchingly. "No."

"Christ!" she bit out, stomping one foot. "Why're you botherin' me?"

He shrugged. "You need to get out of this cottage."

"You're not my momma."

"Thank God for that."

"I'm warnin' you . . ."

"Quit bein' a pain in the ass and go get some jeans on."

"And if I don't?"

"You're goin' for a ride either way," he said, adding a little extra steel to his voice as he recalled his promise to Woodman to take care of her. He hadn't honored his promise, and look at what had happened. He shook his head with equal parts anger at her and himself. "And if you don't get your ass up on that horse on your own, princess, I will pick you up over my shoulder, walk down the hill to the barn with you screamin' and shoutin', throw you into that saddle and smack Heath on her rump as hard as I can. Now go put on some pants. You're comin' for a ride with me."

She blinked at him.

Then she ground her jaw, her face tightening and turning

red with fury.

"Pants," he said, pointing to the stairs beyond the kitchen. "Now."

"Fine!" she spat. "But I'm *not* goin' to like it."

"Your enjoyment is optional. Your need for fresh air . . ." He leaned forward, took a whiff, and then scrunched up his nose as he jerked back. ". . . and a *shower* . . . is not. You stink, princess." He gestured to the rocking chair on the porch as he removed his foot from the doorway. "I'll wait here."

"You're a bully."

"I've been called worse."

With one last fuming look, she slammed the door, and he heard her grumbling as she walked through the kitchen and headed for the stairs.

He sat down in the rocker and looked up at the manor house. He was hoping to avoid the McHuids. Not that he couldn't hold his own with them, but he wasn't in the mood for small talk. He wasn't really in the mood for a ride either. His body was out of shape after weeks of drinking, but his promise to Woodman had tormented him over the past month, and finally, in the past few days, he'd felt some measure of peace in his heart where his cousin was concerned. At least he was doing *something* to help Ginger.

And in order to help her, he'd been forced to clean up his own act too. He hadn't touched a drop of alcohol in three days and had gone for three painful jogs. He'd finally taken his bikes off their pallets and wired some high-tech showroom lighting that made them gleam. Knowing that he had to be there for her meant that he had to take responsibility for himself first. And nothing less than a promise to Woodman—he preferred not to credit Ginger personally with any portion of his transformation—could have elicited such a change.

But mercifully, for the first time since Woodman's death, Cain felt a sense of purpose. He didn't feel like a caged animal anymore, stalking back and forth across the same trod ground. He had a purpose, and whether she liked it or not, its name was Ginger.

Standing up, he noticed that the white picket fence that surrounded the cottage had seen better days. It needed a few new pickets and a fresh coat of paint. He'd get to it. And her gran's old truck, covered with pollen from falling leaves, could use another washing. He'd get to that too. Maybe over Thanksgiving weekend, which he planned to spend with his father, he'd sneak up here for an hour or two while she was at the manor house and tidy up around the cottage a bit.

The door opened and slammed shut, and Cain looked over at Ginger.

She still looked pretty terrible, but her face was scrubbed shiny, her wet, freshly washed hair slicked back in a tight bun. She was wearing a clean sweatshirt that read " I ♥ Nursing" and jeans that hung slack on her thin frame.

"Well, you look a little less awful," he observed.

"The compliment of my dreams."

"At least you're clean."

"I even put on deodorant," she sniped.

"Thank God for small mercies." He paused, staring at her baggy jeans. "When's the last time you ate somethin'?"

"You know what? Screw you, Cain."

She turned around and reached for the doorknob to go back inside, but Cain grabbed the hand that swung back and held it tightly, keeping her on the porch.

"We're ridin'," he growled, ignoring the warmth of her

hand and the way it felt clasped in his. It was a long time since he'd voluntarily touched her skin like this. Even when he'd told her about Woodman and carried her to her room, he hadn't touched her skin. And at the funeral home, she'd reached for *his* hand, not the other way around.

She turned to look at him, flicking a quick look at her hand in his before snatching it away.

"Christ! Fine! I'll ride, but I'm *not* talkin' to you."

"Fine with me. Can't say your conversation is rockin' my world much this mornin' anyhow." He stepped off the porch, giving her a no-nonsense glare. "Now let's go."

***

Ginger had no idea what had propelled her feet upstairs and into the shower. She had no idea why—amid bitter complaining— she'd pulled on fresh underwear for the first time in three or four days and found a clean pair of jeans and sweatshirt from her month-old unfolded laundry basket in the corner of her room.

Then again, for most of her childhood, when Cain said "jump," Ginger jumped. So perhaps she'd just been shocked into autopilot by his sudden appearance on her doorstep. Besides, she had to grudgingly admit that it was a relief to *feel* something again, even if she felt manhandled, pissed off, and annoyed.

For all the murky water under their mutual bridge, Cain was still someone she'd known her whole life. Not even her parents had been able to get through to her the way Cain just had. On the most visceral possible level, Cain *affected* her— always had, and maybe, she thought ruefully, he always would. Oh, she'd never allow herself to fall for Cain again, or to feel the rush of joy she used to feel in his presence—she was too jaded by his rejection to ever be that stupid again—but their *connection*, for lack of a better word, was forged over a lifetime, and she could feel it now between them as they walked in silence, side by side, down to the barn. The snap and crackle of energy, the way their footsteps had synchronized within moments of walking, the way he felt beside her—familiar, warm, and strong, even if he hadn't been able to love her the way she'd once loved him.

Historically speaking, he'd hurt her more than any single person in her life, but there was a comfort to walking beside Cain that she recognized, that made her feel less lonely. And in that quiet fellowship, she found the smallest morsel of the peace that had been denied her since Woodman . . .

Since Woodman had gone away.

"We may not be the best of friends, Gin," said Cain, as though sharing the same wavelength on which her thoughts were traveling, "but Woodman loved you. So I'm not just goin' to—"

She spoke through clenched teeth. "I don't want to talk."

"I get that, but I just wanted to say—"

She stopped walking, put her hands on her hips, and watched him continue down the driveway until he realized that she wasn't beside him and turned back around to face her.

"Don't talk about him," she whispered, her voice a hair short of crazy. "I mean it."

Cain flinched, his eyebrows furrowing for just a moment as he stared at her, searching her face. "At all?"

She was clenching her jaw so hard, she was afraid it would pop. She couldn't speak, but she managed a jerked shake of her head.

Cain nodded slowly, holding out his hand to her to coax her along. "Okay."

She glanced down at his hand, then back up at his face, and stepped around it, refusing to touch him, but was relieved when he fell back into step beside her.

After two hours of riding side by side in utter silence, they returned to the barn. Ginger slipped down from Heath and led the mare into her stall, quietly removing her bridle and saddle and hanging them up. She nuzzled the horse's nose gently.

"I promise I'll come back tomorrow, pretty girl. I'm sorry I've been away so long."

Cain peeked through the stall slats at her. "Want a cup of coffee?"

She shook her head, still looking at Heath. "No, thanks."

"Tea?"

"No."

"Hot chocolate?"

Sighing with annoyance, she turned from her horse and left the stall, locking it behind her. "No."

Cain nodded. "Okay. Then I guess I'll see you on Tuesday. How about I pick you up at ten?"

She wrinkled up her nose, facing him. "What are you talkin' about? For what?"

"Pop told me they're layin' a wreath on Woodman's grave for Veterans Day," he said, watching her face intently. "We should be there."

Her chest compressed, squeezing the air from her lungs, and she squeaked, "I'm not goin' to that."

Cain took a step toward her, his eyes lasering into hers. "Oh, yes you are, Ginger McHuid. You be ready, or I'll come up to your room, pull you out of that bed, and you'll stand there by his grave in your dirty pajamas, you hear?"

"No, I *don't* hear. I'm not—"

He turned to walk away, throwing, "See you on Tuesday, princess," over his shoulder before disappearing into the tack room and kicking the door shut.

"Oooofsh!" she grunted, her eyes burning as her nose flared. "Who the *hell* do you think you are?"

"Cain Holden Wolfram," she heard him say, his voice muffled from the other side of the door.

She balled up her fingers into fists by her sides. *I'm not going. I'm not. He can't make me. He can't fuckin' make me!*

"Now go on home, princess."

"Go to *hell*, Cain!"

"Just got back," he said, his voice fading as he walked farther into the tack room, away from the door.

Her feet started moving, away from Cain, out of the barn, onto the gravel, which crunched under her furious footsteps as her arms swung by her sides. She kept walking until she stomped into her kitchen, pulled out a loaf of bread, a jar of peanut butter, and two bananas, cursing Cain a mile a minute as she made herself a sandwich, then ended up eating two.

***

"God *damn* it!" she muttered, throwing a dark gray dress on top of the navy blue and black ones already scattered on her bed.

Over the past three days, her appetite had gotten better, but every dress she had still hung unattractively loose on her thinner frame.

She sat down on the bed and flicked an unhappy glance at the clock: 9:48. He'd be here any second, and she knew Cain well enough to know that he was completely serious about hauling her to the cemetery regardless of what she was wearing.

And what was her recourse? To scream at him? Sure. Much good it would do her. He'd pick her up screaming and kicking and toss her in Klaus's truck one, two, three.

Lock all the doors? Great idea . . . if Cain hadn't taught himself how to pick locks when he was eleven. And if memory served, he hadn't yet met a lock he couldn't pick.

Call the police and have them stand guard at her door? Theoretically this was an option, but one, it would cause a major scene in Apple Valley, and two, calling the police on Cain was a line not even Ginger could cross. As angry as he made her feel, she just . . . couldn't.

Which really left her only two options: to call his bluff and let him haul her out to Woodman's grave wearing her pajamas, or find something decent to wear and get dressed.

Standing up, she crossed back over to her closet and took out a pair of dark, dark blue jeans and pulled them on. They'd always been a little snug, so they fit just fine now. Taking a white silk blouse from her closet, she pulled it over her head and added a periwinkle-blue cardigan. Then she twisted her hair into a modest bun and fastened it with a plain old navy blue scrunchie. She skipped looking in the mirror—half of her simply didn't care how she looked, and the other half didn't want to look at the deep grooves under her eyes and the hollows in her cheeks.

As she headed downstairs, she heard knocking at the back door and slowed her pace deliberately. He was five minutes early and he could damn well wait. She picked up her purse from a table at the foot of the stairs and rifled through it for ChapStick, running it over her lips slowly, like she had all the time in the world. She smoothed back her bun and stepped into the kitchen as he knocked again, louder this time.

Just as she was about to open the fridge and peruse its contents for a snack, she heard him bellow at the top of his lungs, "Virginia Laire McHuid, you get your ass down here or I'll—"

"Cain!" She whipped open the door and clapped her hand

over his mouth. "Quiet!"

She could just imagine her mother's pleasure to find Cain Wolfram screaming "ass" at the top of his lungs on her daughter's doorstep, and she was not in the mood for her mother's attitude this morning.

His eyes looked down at her, but he didn't move, and it took another second for Ginger to realize that his lips were pressed to her hand. His mouth was open, and she could feel his warm breath against the skin of her palm. Staring up at him, she blinked and pulled her hand away.

"If you wanted me to kiss your hand hello," he said, "you could have just asked."

"Don't be cute," she said, fisting her hand to get rid of the lingering warmth on her skin and trying desperately to ignore the way her chest had fluttered when Cain drawled the word *kiss*.

"Okay," he said evenly. "I won't be cute today."

For the first time, her eyes slipped from his face, and she realized that Cain wasn't dressed in his usual jeans and Henley. Today, for the first time ever, she was seeing him in his uniform, and it fairly took her breath away.

He wore a navy blue top with three white stripes at the collar and another three at the cuffs, and a black, knotted neckerchief at his tanned, muscular neck. Her eyes traveled over his broad chest, and she raked her teeth over her bottom lip as her eyes dropped to the matching blue pants with a front flap fastened with thirteen buttons. On his feet he wore black formal shoes, buffed to a high shine, which touched her heart for some reason, imagining the time it had taken to get them that shiny. In his hand, he held a starched snow-white cap, which he lifted and placed on his stubbly black hair.

"I look okay?" he asked softly, his eyes

uncharacteristically earnest.

She nodded, blinking back tears. The last time she'd seem someone in full service blues, it was . . . it was . . .

He's not gone. He's just away.

Her vision became blurry as she stared miserably at Cain's chest, decorated with various pins and ribbons. He raised his arm and offered it to her, as though to formally escort her from the kitchen.

He's not gone. He's just away.

"No, thanks," she said, refusing his arm as she finally exhaled and took another deep breath. "I'm only goin' to this because you're forcin' me to."

"Well, that's too bad," said Cain, stepping around her. His voice held a small but certain measure of censure as he added, "It'd be nice if you actually *wanted* to go."

He preceded her out of the cottage and stopped at the passenger side of his father's truck. He opened the door and held it for her, his eyes straight ahead, his body at full attention.

She felt mean, suddenly, for what she'd said, and flinched from the disappointment of his tone. But the feeling didn't linger. Anger hip-bumped it to the side. She stepped over to the truck and climbed inside.

"Don't judge me, Cain."

He didn't answer. He didn't even look at her. He just slammed the door shut, walked around the truck, and sat in the driver's seat without a word. He was giving her the silent treatment, and it infuriated her further.

"You know what I've been wonderin'? Why are you even *here*? Why haven't you left yet? When the goin' gets tough, Cain gets goin'. Why are you even still *here*?"

He looked at her with side eyes as they rolled down the

driveway of McHuid's. "Hell, princess, maybe I'm just stickin' around to annoy you. You ever think of that?"

"Often," she snapped.

Staring out the window, her lips twitched because, even though she'd said the words as bait, she found she actually wanted an answer. She adopted a gentler tone. "I mean it, Cain. I thought you left after the . . . the . . ." Somehow she couldn't choke out the word *funeral*. "*Why* are you still here?"

He shrugged. "Promised my pop I'd stay through to Thanksgivin'."

Ah. So he *did* have a departure date in mind. He wasn't staying here forever.

It was the moment that Ginger realized that, however much Cain had hurt her in the past, she was very, very sorry to learn that he was going to leave again so soon. She didn't know what to make of his sudden visits—the way he'd forced her to take a ride or to go to this wreath laying today. She didn't like it, and yet some part of her—small though it was—had to admit that Cain was likely the only person who could have forced her out of her destructive style of mourning and back into the world. She didn't want to depend on him, but she was comforted by his presence nonetheless.

And to her great surprise, her heart, which she'd been so certain was dead, flickered to life and ached at the thought of him walking out of her life yet again.

***

Cain watched her at the wreath-laying ceremony: the impassive expression on her face, the way her eyes didn't tear up. She didn't sniffle or cry, just stood stoically beside him, accepting condolences politely, her voice devoid of emotion.

Across from them, his Aunt Sophie stared daggers at Cain,

still wishing him dead, and he wished it didn't hurt, but it did. He and his aunt had never been close, but losing Woodman had been a blow to both of them, and they could have been a comfort to each other. Instead his aunt kept her anger trained on him, which kept her an island of sorrow, isolated by fury.

Much like Ginger.

What will it take for you to break? he wondered, stealing a glance at her neat blonde bun. *Because you're going to break, princess. Eventually you're going to have to say his name; you're going to have to acknowledge that he's gone. You're going to have to scream and cry or you'll never be able to grieve. You'll never have any relief from the terrible sadness that's weighing you down.*

Not that Cain felt light as a feather. He didn't. Most days he still struggled wildly with Woodman's death and felt the sharp heartbreak of his cousin's loss. Five weeks hadn't softened the images of Woodman dying, nor erased his final words from Cain's head, though Cain had noticed that, ever since he'd started honoring his promise to Woodman, he'd felt the very beginnings of a peace he'd been missing when he was drinking and raging. He wanted Ginger to know that peace for two reasons: one, because without it, she'd never find her way toward healing, and two, because it's what Woodman desperately would have wanted for her. Cain intended to do whatever he had to do to help her find it. He'd promised.

After the ceremony, they stood with Mary-Louise and Scott Hayes for a few minutes, but Ginger looked pale and tired, so Cain finally excused them so that he could take her home. He debated what to say to her—he felt a responsibility to get through to her, but he wasn't sure how.

Just be yourself.

The words skated through his head, and he decided to give them a try.

As soon as they pulled away from the cemetery, she sighed audibly as he looked over at her.

"You okay?

"Fine."

"They did a nice job."

She didn't answer, just stared out the window.

"It was good that you went."

Still nothing. No reaction.

"I been meanin' to ask," he said, an edge creeping into his voice. "How's your gran doin'?"

"Haven't been out much." She looked over at him, her eyes flashing.

"She's old, Ginger."

"What do *you* know about *my* gran? Besides, it's none of your business where I go and what I—"

He pulled the truck over to the side of the road, and the brakes screeched as he stopped in a cloud of dust and swirling fall leaves.

He cut his eyes to her, trying to keep his voice level but failing. "You know what, Gin? I understand that you're hurtin'. I'm hurtin' too. But Woodman would be *ashamed* of the way you're behavin', and that's the truth. Refusin' to see his grave honored? Not visitin' your gran? Lyin' around all day in your pajamas? Not showerin'? Not takin' care of yourself?"

"Oh, I'm sorry I'm not keepin' myself to your high standards of feminine—"

"This has *nothin'* to do with *me*. I could give a shit whether or not you deck yourself out to the nines every day, princess. This has to do with honorin' *his* memory by livin' *your* life with dignity. By bein' the woman he loved even though he's gone. That woman was spunky and strong. She was gorgeous and smart, sweet and carin'. Even when people thought she was breakable, she proved to all of them—to this whole goddamned town—that she wasn't."

Her nostrils flared, which was the only indication she'd heard him since she still stared out the windshield, expressionless. Finally he huffed out a long breath. "And you know what else? If *that* Ginger shows up—the one who my cousin loved so fuckin' hard, the lionhearted l'il gal who didn't let a broken heart keep her down—maybe let me know, huh? Because I'd surely like to see *her* again."

He put the car in drive, burning rubber as he pulled away from the shoulder, and neither of them said a word until they reached her cottage. As soon as the truck came to a stop, she reached for the door, but Cain grabbed the hand closest to him and held it and squeezed it gently, trying to soften the blow of his words, trying to let her know that they came from a place of caring.

But she nailed him with furious eyes and jerked her hand away. "Don't you touch me."

Aw, Christ, he thought, shaking his head in frustration. *Fine. Have it your way.*

He narrowed his eyes at her. "Go see your grandmother, for fuck's sake. She don't have forever."

"Screw you," spat Ginger, hopping down from the truck and slamming the door behind her.

Chapter 25

The next day, instead of sleeping until noon, Ginger woke up early, took a shower, blow-dried her hair, and changed into clean clothes. Then she climbed into the SUV she hadn't used in over five weeks and drove to the Silver Springs Care Center to see her grandmother.

As she drove there, she promised herself that this decision had nothing to do with Cain's pep talk yesterday, though her heart knew a lie when it heard one. His words had hurt her, made her feel self-pitying and weak, and he was right: Gran *didn't* have forever, and Ginger *had* neglected her.

She stopped by a florist on her way over, picking up a peace offering of pink roses, but found when she entered Gran's room that she'd been beaten to the punch. On her grandmother's dresser and bedside table were vases of fresh wildflowers, cheering her room with their vibrant fall colors.

She shrugged. *Daddy must have come by recently.*

She set the roses on the blanket at the foot of Gran's bed and pressed her lips to her grandmother's forehead. It was smooth and warm, and Ginger inhaled deeply, the scent of marshmallows and coconut filling her with comfort.

"G-Gin?" Gran whispered, waking up slowly. "That . . . you, d-darlin'?"

"It's me, Gran," she said, sniffling as she wiped a tear away.

Her grandmother looked more frail since the last time she'd seen her, after Woodman's funeral, and Ginger had a sudden burst of gratitude toward Cain, for his harsh words, which had challenged her to get up, get dressed, and go see her gran.

"D-doll baby," said her grandmother, "it's b-been . . . an . . . age."

"I know, Gran. I'm so sorry," she said, wiping away a tear. "I think I lost my way for a while there."

"Are you . . . f-findin' it . . . again?"

She managed a small smile as she sniffled again. "I think so. I hope so."

"Isn't easy . . . losing s-someone . . . you l-loved."

He's just away. He's just away. He's just away.

She clenched her jaw. "I'm not ready to . . . to talk about him, Gran. Not yet."

"If you . . . d-don't, you're g-gonna . . . c-c-collapse under . . . the w-w-weight . . . of your s-sorrow."

Ginger stood up and plucked the bouquet of flowers from Gran's blanket, fixing a bright smile on her face. "I brought you flowers, but it looks like someone else had the same idea. Daddy stop by recently?"

"Yes, but they're not from him," said Gran, her alert eyes searching Ginger's face carefully.

"You got a new beau? A new admirer?"

Gran chuckled softly, which led to a fit of coughing.

Ginger poured her grandmother a cup of water and held the straw to her lips. Gran had long since become dependent on others to feed her and help her drink. Her hands shook so violently now, the water would slosh all over the place if she tried to hold the cup herself.

"Th-thank you, d-doll b-baby."

Ginger placed the cup back on the bedside table and sat down on the bed. "I don't want to tire you out, Gran. But I promise you I'll be back more often now. I'm so sorry I checked out for a while."

"I un-derstand."

"Thank you," she said, leaning down to kiss her grandmother's parchment-paper cheek.

"G-Gin?" whispered Gran near her ear.

"Yes, ma'am?" she asked, staying close to her lips.

"P-people . . . c-can . . . ch-change."

Ginger leaned back and looked down at her grandmother's face. "Well, sure they can."

"C-completely. F-from who . . . th-they were . . . t-to who . . . th-they are."

"I know that," said Ginger, cocking her head to the side, trying to understand where Gran was going. "What are you tryin' to say? Are you talkin' about someone in particular?"

Gran's lips were open, and her eyes seemed to be begging Ginger to understand, but they grew heavy and finally flitted closed, like the conversation they were having was too much effort to continue.

"Gran?" she whispered, but her grandmother's breathing was slow and deep. She was asleep.

Ginger took the roses into the bathroom, found a vase under Gran's sink, and placed the stems in the water. Then she brought the vase back out and put it them on top of the bureau across from Gran's bed, beside the vase of wildflowers. She grinned at the contrast: polite hothouse roses next to primitive, wildly colorful weeds.

"He . . . loves . . . you," Gran whispered in her sleep, her words just short of a sigh.

Ginger nodded, tears stinging her eyes because everyone else used the past tense, but in her dreams, Gran still talked about Woodman as if he were alive.

Yes, he does, she thought sadly, turning to leave. *He loves me very much.*

***

Thanksgiving Day was inauspicious at the manor house this year, with just the three McHuids and Pastor and Mrs. Greenvale in attendance. Ginger's mother had included the Woodmans in her annual invitation, but Howard had called to say that he and Sophie were spending this year with Miz Sophie's sister, Sarah, and her husband over in Frankfort. It had left Miz Magnolia feeling forlorn and missing her friend, but Ginger had suggested inviting the new pastor, which had cheered her mother right up.

For most of Ginger's life, Miz Sophie and her mother had been thick as thieves, giggling with each other behind their wineglasses, attending every social function in Apple Valley together, and coordinating beautiful parties and events. But since Woodman's passing, they'd seen very little of his parents— almost as though seeing Ginger's family was too painful to bear. They were a reminder of Woodman's lost future, of the good times they'd all spent together. Plus, Ginger perceived that Miz Sophie, who'd always been a little jealous of her, had turned that jealousy to ripe anger. She seemed angry that Ginger had ever claimed any part of Woodman's heart, as though his love for her had somehow lessened his love for his mother.

The well of friendship had been poisoned by Woodman's absence, and though her mother still talked about Sophie like they'd resume their friendship one day ("When Sophie's up for it, we'll have to plan another casino night at the club"), Ginger felt sure that the longtime friendship between the Woodmans and the McHuids was over.

Though she didn't really want to see the Woodmans, their absence after twenty years of Thanksgivings spent together was hard to ignore, and it made Ginger feel lonesome in a way she hadn't anticipated. Her mother, however, was in full-blown hostess mode.

"Ginger, I have to say, you're lookin' so much better," she said, reaching over to pat her daughter's hand as a hired server stopped by each place setting with a platter piled high with turkey. Miz Magnolia turned to Monica Greenvale and loudly whispered, "The fireman who died in early October was Ginger's fiancé."

"Yes," said Mrs. Greenvale, looking sympathetically across the table. "I'm so sorry, Ginger."

"Thank you, ma'am," said Ginger, pulling her hand away from her mother's.

"Now, Pastor Greenvale, did you tell me that y'all have a son down at Em'ry?"

"Yes, Miz Magnolia," said Stuart Greenvale. "Our youngest, Colin."

"Colin Greenvale," said Ginger's mother, giving her daughter an encouraging smile. "Isn't that a fine name?"

Ginger grimaced at her mother, wondering where this conversation was going and dreading her suspicions. "Yes."

"Tell us more about Colin, won't you?" her mother asked

Mrs. Greenvale.

Monica Greenvale nodded. "He's a senior, just twenty-one last month—"

"Well, my goodness! Just like our Ginger!"

"Are you twenty-one, dear?" asked the pastor's wife.

"I am. Yes, ma'am. Just."

"Our Colin is studyin' to be a doctor, so he has many more years—"

"Well!" gasped Miz Magnolia, pressing a flattened palm to the front of her Tory Burch silk wrap dress. "Our Ginger's a nurse!"

"What a coincidence!" exclaimed Pastor Greenvale, helping himself to another scoop of green beans. "Medical children, eh, Ranger?"

"I guess that's so," said Ranger, flicking a glance at Ginger, who felt her cheeks flushing with heat.

"Is your son spendin' Thanksgivin' with his girlfriend?" asked Ginger, feeling more and more uncomfortable and trying to waylay her mother's interest in Colin Greenvale.

"No, no," said Miz Monica, "he's volunteerin' at a hospital in Guatemala for six weeks. We'll have him back in the States after the New Year."

"January, Ginger," said her mother, with a knowing smile. "And since he'll be new to Apple Valley, I expect you could spare an evenin' to show him around?"

Ginger's breath caught, anxiety seeping into her veins.

"Virginia," said Ranger, suddenly commanding his daughter's attention. "I asked Nina to set aside a pumpkin pie for Klaus and Cain. If you're finished eatin', perhaps you wouldn't mind takin' it down to the barn for them?"

"Ranger!" exclaimed Miz Magnolia. "We're still dinin'."

Ginger's father ignored her mother, keeping his eyes fixed, with compassion, on his daughter. "You wouldn't mind, now, would you, dear?"

"No, sir," she said softly, placing her napkin beside her plate and standing up from her seat. "With your permission?" she said, smiling serenely at the Greenvales and her mother before giving her father a genuine and grateful nod.

And Ranger McHuid, whom Ginger could never remember denying anything his Magnolia, winked at her conspiratorially before she slipped away.

***

"*Noch ein Bier?*"

"*Ja, Papa,*" said Cain, standing from the warm leather chair beside his father's. He took the two empty bottles from the table between them. "I'll get us two more."

The tack room apartment smelled of roasted chicken and vegetables that would be ready in about an hour, and though it wasn't the traditional American Thanksgiving menu that his mother would be serving today, Cain had decided he'd prefer to spend the holiday with his father. The idea of Aunt Sophie's vitriol, however contained, would have made his mother's table uncomfortable. Plus, his mother had her husband and sister. His father had no one, and Cain was perfectly happy watching football with cold beer and pretzels. It was relaxed and companionable.

As he threw the empties in the recycling bin and grabbed two more bottles of Grolsch from the refrigerator, he was surprised to hear knocking at the tack room door. His father turned from the TV, his eyebrows furrowed in question.

"You expect someone?"

"*Nein, Papa,*" said Cain, handing his father one of the two beers, then heading for the door. And damn if his heart didn't roar to life to find Ginger on the other side.

"Hi," she said, her voice considerably warmer and softer than it had been a week and a half ago, when he'd dropped her off after the wreath laying.

"Hi," he said, taking in the pretty wave of her shiny blonde hair, the glossy bit of pink lipstick that drew his attention to her mouth.

"My, uh . . ." She cleared her throat, her big brown eyes holding his captive. "My father asked me to bring down a pie."

"Wunderbar, Ginger! Danke!" said Cain's father, hopping up from his chair with his arms outstretched. *"Bitte schön!"*

"He's so excited for the pie, he's forgettin' his English," said Cain, chuckling good-naturedly at his father's wide grin. "Wonderful, thank you, and come in."

Ginger handed the pie to Klaus with a small smile, then looked up at Cain, her lips flattening just a little, the warmth in her eyes cooling just a bit, like she didn't trust him, like she wasn't sure of him.

He raised his bottle. "Can I get you a beer?"

"Umm," she hummed, and two spots of crimson suddenly popped out on the apples of her cheeks. He watched her for a moment, the way she lowered her eyes and looked at her shiny tan high-heeled shoes. And then he remembered—the last time she had beer, she'd vomited on the firehouse floor.

His father, however, only knew Austrian hospitality, nothing of Ginger's erstwhile overindulgence. When he returned from placing the pie safely in the fridge, he was holding another bottle of open Grolsch and offered it to her.

"Happy Thanksgiving!" said Klaus, clinking her bottle with a cheerful grin.

She laughed softly and nodded, putting the bottle to her lips and tilting it up to take a sip as she grinned at Klaus.

And Cain, who watched her, felt his own rising arm still. For just a moment—a short, perfect moment—she looked happy. She looked young and lovely and open, without any sorrow weighing down her small shoulders. His breath caught, softly, without incident—his father and Ginger both oblivious—and his heart thundered inside its cage at the most beautiful woman he'd ever seen in his entire life.

Almost in slow motion, her stunning face turned, and as her eyes met his over her bottle, he raised his own quickly. The cold glass connected with the warm flesh of his lips, and the beer sluiced down his throat as he watched her lower hers and say, "Yes. Happy Thanksgivin', Klaus."

Klaus looked back and forth between his son and Ginger. "You know? I need to water the horses and check on . . . things. I be right back?"

Before they could respond, Cain's father slipped out the door, leaving them alone.

"Do you like football?" Cain asked her, squelching a wince, feeling—for the first time in more years than he could remember—young and self-conscious around a woman.

"Um, honestly? It's not my favorite."

He gestured to the chairs. "You came all the way down here. Stay a few minutes. You have to finish your beer."

She looked wary for a moment, then grinned at him. "Sure. Just for a few minutes."

They sat down side by side, but Cain was so aware of her—of her slight citrus scent, her plum-colored dress, her pretty shoes—he couldn't help but notice her transformation. Besides, the last time he'd seen her, she was spitting mad at him, and today she seemed much more gentle, like her old self, like the girl he'd once loved so desperately.

"You look nice, Gin," he said, forcing his glance away from her. He stared at the TV and took another sip of beer.

"Thanks," she said. "I, well, if you want the truth, an old friend of mine told me to stop feelin' sorry for myself."

"Sounds like a total bastard. I'll beat him up for you."

She burst into a small laugh, shaking her head at him.

"I'm sorry, princess," he said, wincing to recall the harshness of his speech.

Her smile faded, but her voice remained gentle. "I hated your words, but I needed to hear them."

He nodded, looking away from the aching sweetness of her face, reminding himself that he was an emissary on Woodman's behalf. Looking after her was fulfilling a promise to his cousin. Nothing less, but nothing . . . more.

"So, uh," he said, "I tried out your Presbyterian church, and I think it's a real nice service."

"Wait, um, did you just say you went to church? And enjoyed it?"

"I'm not utterly godless, Gin."

"That's up for debate," she shot back.

"Damn," he said, chuckling softly as he took another sip of beer.

"And nice compared to what? The Church of Motorcycles, Sluts, Cussin', and Beer?"

"Fuckin' sassy," he whispered, looking at her out of the corner of his eyes and enjoying her immensely.

She was right. He didn't especially like going to church, but in the two weeks he'd been going to hers, she hadn't show up, which bothered him. It had been an important part of her life when Woodman was alive, and he was anxious that she start going again. She needed the community—she needed to feel less alone. "They're doin' a, uh, a carolin' thing at your gran's place."

"A *carolin'* thing?"

He nodded. "Friday night next. I'll pick you up at six and we can go together."

And suddenly all that gentleness and sass jumped ship. She sat back in her chair, her face pinched. "I don't think so. I'm not . . ."

"Oh, I'm sorry," said Cain, "is there a very important Lifetime movie that requires your attention?"

She whipped her face to the side, her eyes narrowing in annoyance. "No, I just don't—"

"Great. You're free. I'll pick you up at seven, and if you're not dressed—"

"I know. I know. You'll haul my ass out of bed and throw me in your dad's truck."

He couldn't help grinning at her. "You're a fast learner."

Her nose twitched. "Fine. I'll go. But I don't promise to have a good time."

"I think we've already established that your pleasure is irrelevant."

"Sweet talker." She rolled her eyes at him before turning back to the TV. "This how you got all the girls?"

"Nope," he said, placing his empty bottle on the table between them. "My personality sucks. It was my dimples. And my ass."

"Ha!" she chortled. "So full of yourself."

He raised his eyebrows and grinned. "Can't change a wolf's howl."

"Or an ass's hee-haw," she returned, taking a big gulp of her own beer before placing it next to his.

Damn, but she was quick. And funny. And gorgeous. But around her eyes, he still saw deep, deep lines of sadness. Church once a week wasn't going to be enough. She needed somewhere to go, more to do. She needed to get the fuck out of her goddamned cottage.

"What you been doin' with yourself?" he asked.

"Visitin' Gran." She took a deep breath and sighed. "And I've gone ridin' a couple times."

"When are you goin' back to work?"

She shrugged, avoiding his eyes, though they were trained on her. "I don't know."

"You loved nursin'. I remember you tellin' me."

"I *did* love it," she said. "But, I don't think I'm ready to—"

"So you're just sittin' around at home all day? Goin' to be a lady of leisure like your momma?"

"No! I just . . . I'm . . ."

"You're what?"

She blew out an exasperated breath "Know what? It's none of your business what I'm doin'! What are *you* doin'? Loafin' around this tack room drinkin' beer?"

In fact, he'd been doing a great deal of work at Wolfram's Motorcycles. He'd finished all the electrical wiring of the lighting in the showroom and service bays, and he'd ordered some of the more expensive equipment he needed to offer top-notch service on European bikes. He'd purchased a desk, two guest chairs, and a nice Persian rug for the office, and found a townhouse to rent in Lexington, halfway between Apple Valley and Versailles. It was in a gated community with lake views and a swimming pool, far nicer than *he* required. All that had mattered to him was that it might appeal to Ginger. And he had less than zero interest in exploring why she'd been on his mind so much as he'd signed the lease.

He still wasn't ready to tell her that he was putting down roots in Kentucky, however.

"I'm stayin' busy," he said, keeping his eyes on the TV. "By the way, the hinge on your back gate is busted, and some of the pickets are rottin' on the fence. I'll be by to fix it tomorrow. If you don't relish my company, be scarce, huh?"

She stood up. "Cain, I don't need your help. I'm perfectly capable of—"

"Maybe a good excuse for you to go see your gran," he said, looking at her meaningfully.

Her eyes narrowed again, and her voice took on a seriously irritated edge. "How much longer you stayin'?"

"I haven't decided yet," he said, looking back up at the TV dismissively. "Does it matter?"

She took so long to answer, he shifted his face to look up at her. She was watching him, her face thoughtful, her bottom lip caught between her teeth. His eyes zoned in on her mouth like a beacon, and his body unexpectedly tightened.

"No," she finally said, shaking her head. "Not to me."

Without another word, she walked to the tack room door and slammed it shut behind her.

Chapter 26

Damn Cain anyway, she thought, pulling into a parking space at the Silver Springs Care Center and cutting the engine of her SUV. He had arrived bright and early to work on her fence, and of course her mind had immediately segued back to three years ago, when she'd woken up to find him washing Gran's truck. A flood of memories had engulfed her—his smile when she'd said "Hey!" from her bedroom window, the way he'd caught her gaping at him from the kitchen as she made them eggs, how they'd gone riding afterward, how she'd fallen even more in love with him.

On the one hand, it felt warm and innocent to remember those fleeting, golden days with Cain—her heart had been so full and hopeful that she and Cain might finally find their way to each other. But on the other hand, it made her heart twist with pain, with embarrassment and regret. The following day she'd declared her feelings to Cain and been ripped to shreds for her honesty. And to console herself, she'd made the abrupt, impulsive decision to be with . . . to offer her body to . . .

Her heart started racing, and she jerked the rearview

mirror to look at her face.

He's just away. He's just away.

"He's just away," she whispered, wetting her lips and blinking her eyes against an unexpected burn.

She'd noticed over the past couple of days that it was becoming harder and harder to block out her memories of Woodman and trick herself into believing that he was only temporarily gone. She never allowed herself to think of him as gone forever—*never*—but as she spent more time with Cain and her heart came back to life little by little, it was more difficult to stay cold about Woodman's loss. She felt a growing pressure to confront it—to put a name to it and deal with it. Like water behind a dam, the pressure was growing and growing, and someday the dam wasn't going to be able to handle the volume anymore. The high walls would eventually crumble. The floodgates would open. And Ginger would have to come face to face with what had happened to Woodman, and the myriad complicated feelings that accompanied the reality of his loss.

"Not today," she said softly in the quiet of her car. "Not yet. For now . . . he's just away."

Lifting her chin, she grabbed her purse and headed into the care center, where she signed in at the front desk. As she headed for the elevator, she heard someone yell, "Hold it!" and she just managed to keep the doors open for Nurse Ratch—*Arklett*—to rush inside.

"Miss McHuid," she said politely, offering Ginger a tight smile. "Good morning. Here to see your grandmother?"

"Yes, ma'am," said Ginger, giving the starched, white-haired lady a small smile.

Nurse Arklett opened her mouth as though to ask Ginger something, then said, "No. I don't suppose . . . no."

"I'm sorry?" asked Ginger.

"Miss McHuid, this goes against everythin' I teach my girls here—fraternizin' with the visitors—but I am in dire straits. We are losin' four nurses come New Year's, and I just haven't had time to replace them yet."

"Four at once? Why so many?"

Nurse Arklett huffed through her nose. "New retirement center just opened in Paris. State-of-the-art. Hirin' anyone with an RN degree."

"Ahhh," said Ginger. "Well, no one runs as tight a ship as you, ma'am. I learned more from you durin' my trainin' and employment here than, well, than I learned durin' all three years at nursin' school. They'd be silly to leave you."

"Miss McHuid," said Nurse Arklett, following Ginger out of the elevator on the fourth floor, "I don't suppose you'd consider comin' back in January? Three or four days a week? Until I can hire a few new nurses and train them?"

"Come back here to work?"

The older woman winced and shook her head. "No, I guess not. I'm terribly sorry I bothered you. Regards to your—"

"Wait! Yes!"

"What?"

"Yes, ma'am. Yes, I'll come back to work. Three weekdays and every other Sunday sound okay?"

"Mondays, Wednesdays, and Thursdays?"

"That sounds fine. I can start on January second."

Nurse Arklett smiled. "I'd be so grateful. Nine a.m. on January second, Nurse McHuid. In scrubs. Ready to work."

"Yes, ma'am. I'll be here."

"Stop by HR on your way out today. I'll tell them to expect you."

"Thank you, ma'am."

Her boss nodded crisply, then headed quickly down the hallway to parts unknown. Ginger waved to Teresa, a nurse she knew, at the fourth-floor nurses' station.

"Hey, Gin— I'm sorry. Hello, Miss McHuid."

"It's Ginger again," she said with a grin. "I'm comin' back to work in January."

"Aw, Ginger!" said Teresa, coming around the counter to give her a big hug. "I'm sure glad to hear that, honey. I'll let the girls know too! We missed you!"

And that'll show you, Cain Wolfram, that I am *gettin' back on my feet again and I do* not *require your assistance or goadin' or interference anymore.*

Pushing open the door to Gran's room, Ginger was surprised to find the room festively decorated for the holidays: a small boxwood with tiny red velvet bows, flanked by two poinsettias, sat on the dresser. A dark green, bright white, and red afghan was neatly folded at the foot of her bed, and a statue of a Santa Claus with a little blonde girl on his lap sat on her bedside table.

"Well, Gran!" she said, leaning down to kiss her grandmother hello. "What little elves have been here to visit you?"

"Gin-ger," she said, her lips attempting a wobbly smile. "Hel-lo, d-doll baby."

"Hello, beautiful," said Ginger.

"You're . . . in high . . . s-spirits."

"I'm comin' back to work," she said. "Three days a week and every other Sunday."

Gran's eyes lit up, and Ginger could hear her small gasp of pleasure. "I'm s-so . . . p-pleased."

"I'll spoil you tons, Gran. Sneak you contraband ice cream and the like," she said, flicking an eye around the room. "Now are you goin' to tell me who keeps bringin' you flowers?"

"N-no."

"Why not?"

"It's m-my . . . s-secret for . . . now."

Ginger pulled a book off her grandmother's bedside table. "*The Christmas Box.* May I read it to you?"

Gran looked up at Ginger thoughtfully, then made a small sound like laughter and said, "Yes, b-baby . . . start on . . . the b-bent page."

"Oh. Someone's already readin' it to you?"

Her grandmother nodded, leaning back on her pillow and closing her eyes, a rare look of composure and contentment relaxing her face. "Started it . . . l-last n-night. B-but . . . you can . . . r-read it t-to . . . me . . . t-together. In f-fact . . . that'd b-be . . . p-perfect."

***

When Cain pulled up in his daddy's truck on Friday night, Ginger was *reluctantly* ready to go caroling and stepped out onto the porch in jeans, a white turtleneck, and a bright red cardigan halfway buttoned. She wore her gran's pearls around her neck and had a red velvet hairband in her blow-dried hair.

Cain rolled down the window. "Would've come to the door. I'm not a total caveman."

"Yes, you are . . . and besides, I didn't need you to," she said, walking around to the passenger side and opening her own door. She stepped up into the truck and pulled the door closed, giving Cain a saucy look. "*And* for your information, I'm goin' back to work in January."

He nodded, his dimples deepening, respect or pride

shining in his eyes, and it meant so much to her, she felt her own lips tilt up in return.

"Goin' back to work. Way to go, princess. Big step."

"Yes, it is." She buckled her seat belt as he backed up and headed down the driveway of McHuid Farm. "What exactly did you think? That I'd just sit around in my house forever watchin' Lifetime?"

"You were doin' a real good imitation of makin' that your life's mission."

"I just needed some time, Cain."

"I can understand that," he said softly, turning out of McHuid's to head into town. "I'm glad to hear you're movin' forward, Ginger . . ." He glanced over at her and sniffed experimentally. ". . . and showerin' regularly again."

"Always such a flatterer," she said, giving him a pissy look.

"If you're lookin' for someone to blow sunshine up your ass, I ain't a contender for the job. Ain't never seen you as a china doll, princess. Sorry."

His words sank in, and she felt the stark and utter truth of them. Cain had *never* treated her like she was fragile. Hell, her mother barely let her leave the house after her heart issues, but there was Cain, goading her into jumping from a two-story barn window. There was Cain, who didn't soften the blow of his rejection when he told her he didn't want her. And now here was Cain, threatening her, forcing her out of her house, back into the world, when, truth be told, she would have kept watching TV in dirty pajamas for a much longer time.

This was textbook Cain for as far back as she could remember—challenging her, getting under her skin, but treating her like an equal, even though he called her princess. There were times when he had her back, as he had at the funeral parlor, when Miz Sophie jumped down her throat, but as a rule he didn't mollycoddle her, and unlike everyone else, he didn't underestimate her either. Somehow the way Cain treated her made Ginger want to be more, to be stronger, to be better. Maybe because he believed in her in a way that nobody else did. He *believed* she was strong, and that made her strive to *be* strong.

"Don't be sorry," she said, straightening her spine and raising her chin as she looked out the windshield. "Because I'm *not* a china doll. Never was."

Cain nodded. "Don't have to tell me. I've always known that."

"How?" she asked, turning to him. "How did you always know that when everyone else always treated me like . . ."

She gasped, realizing where her question, where her train of thought, was headed. It would betray Woodman, wouldn't it, to admit that he didn't see her as strong? He didn't see her as an equal. He saw her as delicate and fragile. He saw her as someone to protect and manage. Wait. Not *saw* but *had* seen her as someone to . . .

She inhaled sharply and squeezed her eyes shut as her mind tried to change the tense of her thoughts to the past.

No!

"Stop," she said quickly. "I mean, f-forget it!"

"Actually, I'd like to answer you, if that's okay," said Cain, glancing at her as they stopped at a red light close to Silver Springs.

"Cain, please just . . ."

He spoke over her. "When your heart got all screwed up, when you were a kid, the whole town knew about it. *The little princess at McHuid's was airlifted to Vanderbilt*, they said. *Maybe she'll die*, they said. *Poor little thing*, they said." He stopped talking, clenching his jaw for a moment and staring at her, his eyes fierce. "I *hated* it. I hated every word. I hated the thought of losin' you. I was only eight, but I told myself that if you came home, then you were stronger than death, Gin. Stronger'n death, with the heart of a lion. And I told myself that if you could beat death, that would make you the strongest little girl in the whole world."

"Cain . . .," she said softly, moved to tears by a version of her story she'd never heard before.

A car beeped at them from behind, and Cain thrust his middle finger into the rearview mirror before shifting back into drive. He stared out the windshield as they pulled into the care center.

"And then you came home," he said, pulling into a parking space and turning to face her. His face, his beautiful face, was trained on her, his eyes soft, his lips tilted up just a touch. "You came home. And you were runnin' around and yellin' and playin' and ridin' just like always, and I said to myself, *My God, it's true. She's stronger than death. She's stronger than anythin'*. And it was so strange to me because no one else seemed to see it. Your folks pulled you outta school and got you a tutor, and your momma tried her best to keep you quiet, keep you inside. No one else seemed to see that you were so strong, you'd beaten death. No way life was goin' to take you down if death couldn't finish the job."

Ginger took a deep, shaking breath and lowered her chin to her chest, which tightened with emotion. "But life *does* get me down."

"Course it does." Cain nodded. "I know it does. I know

that, Gin." He shrugged. "Still doesn't change the fact that when the clouds part, you're goin' to be okay. You've got the heart of a lion, princess. And you've got the fightin' scars to prove it."

She thought of all the times in her life he'd called her "lionhearted l'il gal," and suddenly it made sense to her. He was referring to her strength. He'd been talking about her survival.

The heart of a lion.

The scars to prove it.

Literally speaking, she did have a white scar over her heart, where the doctors had operated on her so long ago.

Figuratively speaking, she had other scars on her heart, and many of them belonged to Cain.

Cain, who never stuck around.

Cain, who always left her behind, brokenhearted.

"*Why* are you still here?" she asked him, her voice low and breathless.

"I have my reasons."

"Tell me, Cain. Thanksgivin's come and gone. *Please* tell me why you're still here."

"Does it matter?" he asked.

She didn't want it to matter. She desperately didn't want it to matter.

She nodded.

He leaned back from her and searched her face as though trying to determine something—if she was ready to know something, if he was ready to tell it.

"I tell you what, if you want to know why I'm still here, I'll *show* you, but you need to take a ride with me."

"Where to?"

"Not tellin'." He paused. "You trust me?"

She shook her head. "No. " She shrugged, sniffling softly.

"Kind of."

"We got a lot of water under the bridge, don't we?" he said, looking away from her. He shrugged. "Well, it's up to you."

A good thirty seconds passed in silence as she struggled to make a decision. Part of her felt like running as far away from Cain as she could possibly get. The other part, however, needed him like a lifeline.

Survival won the draw.

"When?"

"Next Saturday."

"What time?"

"Five," he said. "And dress warm. I can't keep borrowin' my pop's truck. We'll take my bike."

"Your bike. Oh, okay," she said, watching as he opened his door and waiting as he walked around the truck to open hers.

She'd never ridden on a motorcycle before, but she was too intrigued to say no.

And Saturday felt like a very, very long way away.

***

For most of his life, Ginger McHuid had been forbidden fruit to Cain Wolfram. He hadn't respected much of anything in his adolescence, but one thing he had *tried* to respect was his cousin's early and undying love for Ginger.

When he'd realized, at fifteen, that he was attracted to her . . . or at eighteen, that his feelings for her ran far deeper than the childhood friendship they'd shared . . . or at twenty-one, that he was in love with her . . . he'd *still* denied himself having her in deference to Woodman. Even five weeks ago, when he'd showed up at her doorstep threatening to haul her out of bed and throw her on Heath's back in pajamas, he'd still maintained that walking back into her life was the only way to honor his promise to Woodman, and not because he had any tender feelings for Ginger. He *couldn't* have any. He wouldn't allow it.

But the thing he hadn't expected was that being forced to care for her and be good to her also meant, by default, investing personally in her happiness and well-being. And that investment was causing an unintended shift in his heart—the hate and hurt he'd held on to for three years was shifting back to love so quickly, he didn't know how to stop it. And without Woodman's presence in his life, there was nothing stopping Cain's conscience from loving Ginger all over again. And this time, forever.

Well, there was *one* other thing stopping Cain: the fact that she'd told him that she loved him, then turned around and slept with his cousin a few hours later. It had hurt like an unimaginable bitch to find her naked body entwined around Woodman's. If he let himself think on it, it *still* hurt like hell. And if she'd hurt him once, certainly she could hurt him again.

After a lifetime of keeping his heart safe from harm, he'd be a fool to give it to the only girl who ever broke it, wouldn't he? Yes. And Cain Wolfram was no fool.

Which was why the feeling of her body pressed up close to his, with her arms around his waist and her cheek resting against his leather-clad back as they raced through the darkness toward Versailles, was perilous to his heart and his sanity and his reason.

He was unprepared for the rush of emotions he felt as she held him tight, or for the way his cock swelled uncomfortably in his jeans, twitching and throbbing with every mile they rode, the vibration of the engine only making the torture worse.

It had been months since Cain had been with a woman—

ten weeks, in fact, since he'd fucked a girl he met in a Norfolk bar before leaving for Versailles. Ten fucking weeks. He'd never gone that long without a woman since he'd given up his V card to Mary-Louise at the distillery when he was fifteen. And since the only woman with whom Cain had spent a significant amount of time in those ten weeks was Ginger, maybe it wasn't so surprising that he'd get wood when her pussy was pressed up against his ass—*clothes be damned*—going sixty miles an hour into darkness.

But he was lying to himself if he pretended that's all it was.

The uncomfortable reality was that the more time he spent with Ginger, the less he wanted to wander, the less he wanted a taste of random snatch. Though she'd been his cousin's woman, and though he would miss Woodman every day for the rest of his life, Ginger was a growing ache inside. Not only in his heart, which could prove lethal, but to his traitorous fucking body too.

Exiting the highway, he pulled up to a red light and felt Ginger's warm breath on the back of his neck behind his ear. He clenched his eyes shut for just a moment.

"Where in the world are we goin'?" she asked.

"Ten more minutes," he said, surging forward, allowing himself to enjoy the rush of adrenaline he felt from having her on the back of his bike.

He'd spent the last week whipping his place into shape for her visit. He'd had a neon exterior sign made a few weeks ago, but he'd finally mounted it and turned it on before leaving to pick her up. He'd purchased a few bikes from a Lexington distributor so that he had some inventory on the floor. The cot in the office was gone, and the refrigerator was on top of a file cabinet that also held a Keurig machine for coffee, tea, and hot chocolate. He'd cleaned up the bathroom, installed a new sink and toilet, and placed a bar of orange-scented soap in a little white dish.

He couldn't wait to show it to her.

For the first time in Cain's life—the very first time—he felt like he had something worthy of Miss Ginger McHuid, and although he had no expectations, he'd be crushed if she didn't like it.

And that was the God's honest truth.

***

Ginger had never ridden on a motorcycle before, and at first she was uncomfortable, in an *embarrassed* way, pressed up against Cain so intimately. Surprisingly, it didn't take long for her to close her eyes and relax, relishing the contact and enjoying the ride.

Relish, not because she had any designs on Cain—she wasn't stupid enough to fall for him again, nor did she feel herself available—but it simply felt nice to hold on to him.

Once upon a time, she'd had a safe haven, a fiancé to whom she ran whenever she was sad or down or confused, and he would hold her close, kiss her and hug her, give her unlimited comfort and unconditional affection. For weeks now she hadn't been touched very much by anyone. At first she'd been deliberately housebound, but then, even as she came out of her self-imposed shell little by little, there just weren't that many people in her life who kissed and hugged. Her parents weren't affectionate, and her gran didn't have enough muscle control to embrace her anymore. Her safe, warm harbor was gone. And she missed the physical contact. She missed it desperately.

So she held on fiercely to Cain, resting her cheek against his leather jacket and feeling the tight muscles of his stomach clench and release as they zigged into turns and zagged through valleys. She closed her eyes and held on and basked in the warmth of human contact.

When he finally stopped the motorcycle, it took her a moment to open her eyes, and once she did, it took another moment to realize that she needed to unclasp her hands and let go of him. An audible sigh of regret passed through her lips like a whisper, but she hoped he hadn't heard it, and she tried to comfort herself that she'd get to hold on to him again all the way home.

"You okay, princess?" he asked over his shoulder, his voice gentle.

She reached up for the helmet he'd fastened under her chin and unclasped it, pulling it from her head as he dismounted from the bike and offered her his hand.

"Uh-huh. Where are we?" she asked, letting him help her off the saddle.

His eyes sparkled in the darkness—pools of obsidian outlined in light blue. He tugged her hand, and they walked out from under a garage roof and onto the sidewalk, under the stars.

"Turn around," he said.

She did. And she gasped softly when her eyes found the bright white sign over the garage that read "Wolfram's Motorcycles." She blinked twice, taking in the double-bayed, open garage they'd just walked from and the shiny glass of the adjacent showroom. The floor inside was gray and glossy, and five or six motorcycles gleamed in the bright blue and white fluorescent track lighting that shone down from the showroom ceiling.

"Cain," she murmured.

"What do you think?" he asked from beside her.

She looked up to find him staring down at her, his face

expectant but uncertain, his eyes searching.

"It's yours?"

He nodded. "Uh-huh. *All* mine. My own business."

"But I thought . . ."

I thought you were leavin'.

Suddenly her eyes filled with more tears than she could handle, and she dropped her head and looked down at her shoes. It was basic and visceral, the feeling that swept through her like a flash storm. *Relief.* She was so relieved, so *unbelievably* relieved, she almost couldn't breathe.

"You don't like it," he said softly, his voice low, edged in hurt.

She shook her head, pressing her palm to her chest, unable to speak.

"Huh. Well. I guess motorcycles aren't for everyone." He stopped talking and dropped her hand. "Fuck," he hissed. "I'll take you home."

As he started to move away, she grabbed his arm, her fingers viselike around his wrist as she raised her glassy eyes to his.

"I'm so proud of you," she sobbed. "So damn proud."

His face was transformed by her words. Hurt and angry at first, he furrowed his brow in confusion as he stared at her, and when he had confirmed the truth of her words from looking deep into her eyes, his dimples sprang out at her, and his smile—so wide, so happy—was blinding.

He laughed softly, shaking his head at her. "I thought . . . oh, man, I thought you didn't like it."

"I don't," she whispered. "I *love* it."

"You *love* it?" he asked, looking down at his wrist still captured in her hand before sliding his eyes back to her face.

"You're stayin'," she said, her eyes locked on his.

He nodded. "I'm stayin', Gin." He reached forward with his free hand and gently wiped a falling tear from her cheek. Then he adjusted her grip on his wrist so they were holding hands, and he pulled her back up the driveway. "Come and see!"

She smiled and nodded at all the right places as he gave her a tour of his new business. And truly she *was* proud of him. He had a sort of rustic-industrial thing going on that worked well with his motorcycles—rough-hewn wood walls, gleaming gray floors, funky lighting on modern tracks, and tin signs with motorcycle logos and neon lights decorating the walls.

But even as she noted the details, and truly admired them, her mind whirred with more important matters.

He's stayin'.

Cain's stayin'.

Cain's finally stayin'.

It was all new territory for her. With the exception of two weeks, Cain had essentially left Kentucky when she was fifteen years old. And now, six years later, he was home. For good. Her mind flew back to the wild yearnings she'd had three years ago—the desperate hope that he'd sleep with her and suddenly find a way to make Apple Valley his home. He'd been a wanderer then, and she had been sure he was still a wanderer now. But some significant part of him must not have wanted to wander anymore. He had purchased a business not forty-five minutes away from Apple Valley. Cain Wolfram was finally settling down.

It was jarring and confusing for Ginger because it didn't correspond with the man she thought him to be. It was also a relief because he'd become important to her again over the past few weeks and she wasn't ready to lose him. And it was a little sad because her onetime dream had finally come true, but it was too late for them now.

Too late because she'd already made her choice, and it hadn't been Cain.

It had been . . .

"Woodman," she said.

"Huh?"

He'd been gesturing to one of three motorcycles raised up on small, foot-high, black-lacquered platforms. But now he turned to her, his smile fading.

"I chose Woodman," she said, her voice faraway.

Cain nodded. "Yes, you did."

She tugged her bottom lip into her mouth, her brain spinning, the past and the present colliding. *Woodman's gone and Cain's here. Cain's settling down and Woodman's wandering. Wait. No. That's not right. That can't be right.* Confusion and dizziness made her blink, and she reached her hand out to steady herself. She felt Cain's arm snake around her waist, and he walked her into his office, helping her into a chair.

"I'll get you some water."

"Woodman," said Ginger again, closing her eyes and trying to take a deep breath. "I want him to come back."

She felt the cold glass press against her lips, and she opened them to let the cool water slip over her tongue and down her throat. When she was finished, Cain pulled the glass away, and she heard him set it on a nearby surface.

"Ginger," he said gently but firmly, "open your eyes."

She opened them on command, still feeling deeply unsettled as she looked up at Cain. He reached out to cup her jaw, forcing her to hold his gaze. "He's gone, darlin'."

She flinched, trying to escape his grip, but he increased the pressure of his fingers and kept his eyes glued to hers.

"He's gone, and no amount of pretendin' he's comin' back will make it so. You need to face his loss, Ginger. You need to deal with it."

She didn't fight the way he held her chin—it wouldn't have done any good since he was much stronger than she—but she felt a coldness sluice through her veins as his words sank in, and she welcomed it. It felt good. It felt like a shield, like protection. It helped her tears dry and kept her voice low and steady when she finally spoke.

"You can force me to go ridin' or to a wreath layin' or even carolin', but you can't force me to grieve on your timeline, Cain."

He flinched, his blue eyes sad and concerned. His voice was deep and rough with emotion. "I know what you're doin', and it ain't healthy, darlin'."

"*I don't care*," she growled. She jerked her face away and left his hand hanging in midair for a moment before he lowered it.

"*I* do," he said intently, squatting down in front of her, "and Woodman would've too."

His name. Hearing someone else say his name hurt. So much.

She took a shaky breath, sobbing softly when she let it go. "I'm really grateful to you, Cain. I'm goin' back to work. I'm back on my feet. And this place is great. I wish you a lot of luck with it." She paused for a moment, holding his eyes as she stood up, looking down at him. "But I want you to take me home now. And I need you to leave me alone."

He stood up too, which changed their positions and forced her to look up at him.

"I'm only tryin' to help, Ginger."

"I know that," she said, the coldness inside keeping her voice stoic and calm. She turned away from him and headed back to his motorcycle. "Now, please take me home."

Chapter 27

For the next two weeks, grubby pajamas and greasy hair reigned once again, but this time there was no Cain stopping by to threaten and force her out of her comfrt zone, which, if she was honest, bothered Ginger to hell and back. And she finally discovered—or had to face the fact—that the reason she was keeping herself so low was almost as bait for Cain, or out of protest for the way he'd tried to force her process. Yes, she'd told him to leave her alone, but she hadn't meant it. What she'd *really* meant was *"You can come and bother me, and we can spend time together, but only if we both pretend that Woodman went on a long trip and someday he'll be home again."*

It was crazy. The logical part of her brain *knew* it was crazy, even knew that she couldn't go on like this forever, but as long as she could keep her grief at bay, she would. She was terrified of what would happen once she was forced to face it.

By Christmas Eve, she'd had enough cheerful Lifetime and Hallmark Christmas movies to last a, ahem, *lifetime* and decided it was high time to shower and go for a ride. Clearly Cain wasn't coming to harass her, and while that frustrated her and hurt her feelings, she had also recognized that at some point she'd left behind the phase of grief when dirty hair and pajamas didn't bother her.

And Cain or no Cain, she didn't like being dirty and smelling bad.

When she found the tack room cold and dark on Christmas Eve, and didn't see Cain in the last pew at church for services, her heart sank a little lower.

Christmas Day came and went quietly, with the Greenvales once again joining the McHuids for modest festivities, and Ginger's mother forcing Miz Monica to talk ad nauseam about Colin, the *Wunderdoktor*. Ginger saw right through her momma's wiles but didn't have the energy to be sassy so she nodded and smiled and agreed to have dinner with her parents, the Greenvales, and Colin in January. *Yes, ma'am, I'd love to come to dinner.* The words barely registered in her head as she said them aloud.

Where were Cain and Klaus? she wondered. While Cain might have decided to spend Christmas with his mother, why wasn't Klaus around? Perhaps they were at Cain's place, assuming Cain had a place, and suddenly she found herself at Christmas dinner staring at her plate, wondering where Cain lived and what it looked like and why he hadn't shared it with her. Is that where he was? At his new place? With his dad? Or maybe with some new girl he'd met? Or—

"Ginger! Monica just said that Colin absolutely loves to ride. Did you hear that?"

"Oh?" asked Ginger, looking up, jolted from her internal dialogue.

"But I s'pose he's not half as good as you are," said Miz Monica with a wink.

Oh Lord, thought Ginger. *The poor woman's drinkin' the Kool-Aid.*

She sighed, excused herself from the table, and headed back to her cottage early.

By New Year's Eve, Cain still hadn't come around or been in touch, and the ache inside Ginger was getting sharp. Really sharp. She thought about his coming by to take her riding, about the wreath laying, and about the beers on Thanksgiving Day. She thought about going caroling with him and what he'd told her about her lion's heart. And she thought about Wolfram's Motorcycles, his beautiful new business. She stopped herself half a dozen times from driving down to Versailles to see if he was still there.

But some part of her knew she wouldn't be welcome. Not yet. Not until she'd faced all the realities of her life head-on and started making peace with them. Not until she'd faced the truth of Woodman's loss.

On New Year's Eve, she stopped by Silver Springs to see her gran.

"D-doll baby," greeted Gran as Ginger stepped into her room and kissed her cheek. "Where . . . you b-been?"

Ginger took a deep breath and sighed. "At home. Feelin' sorry for myself."

"You've had . . . a t-tough t-time . . . of it." Ginger didn't answer so her grandmother continued. "Are you . . . r-ready to . . . t-talk 'bout . . . W-Wood—"

"Oh, Gran," she said, shaking her head. "I'm a terrible, terrible person."

Her grandmother winced, her eyes sad. "N-no. N-no, b-baby."

She sniffled. "I didn't . . . I didn't love him the way I

should have. He deserved—" She grimaced at the sharp and sudden pain near her heart, and pressed her hand against her breast. "I can't. I can't talk about him. Please don't make me."

Her grandmother's eyes flicked to Ginger's hands, folded in her lap. "S-still w-wearin' . . . your ring?"

"*Please*," she begged.

She refused to look down at the engagement ring Woodman had given her on New Year's Eve last year. New Year's Eve. Oh my God. A year ago today.

Don't think about it. Don't think about it.

Her heart started pounding uncomfortably so she stood up, looking around the room to distract herself.

Don't think about it.

The little boxwood had been carefully watered because it was still bright green, and the poinsettias looked healthy too. There was a "Merry Christmas & Happy New Year" banner in silver, red, and green foil letters hanging over Gran's double windows, and a new bookcase under them.

"Did Daddy bring you that bookcase?" she asked, grateful that her heart was slowing down to a normal rhythm.

Gran smiled as best she could. "A f-friend . . . m-made it. F-for C-Christmas."

"What friend, Gran? What friend is bringin' you flowers and decorations and furniture and readin' *The Christmas Box* to you?"

Her grandmother's eyes held hers for a moment. "S-someone . . . n-new."

"New? Someone new in town? New to Apple Valley?" She shook her head. "Who, Gran? A volunteer?"

"Old s-someones . . . c-can b-be . . . n-new, G-Ginger."

She looked back at the bookcase. "Did that someone

refinish this for you?" She placed her hand on it, running her fingers over the layers of glossy finish that made it as smooth as lacquer. "It's lovely."

"Y-yes. It was . . . f-fixed up w-with . . . l-love."

Ginger's eyes shot up, and she plunked down on Gran's bed. "Kelleyanne McHuid, you tell me once and for all: do you have a beau?"

Gran's eyes rested tenderly on Ginger's face, scanning it as though for remembrance. "T-tell me . . . 'bout C-Cain." She paused, watching Ginger's expression carefully. "Y-your d-daddy . . . told me . . . he's home n-now."

Ginger took a deep breath and lay back on the bed beside her gran's petite frame. "He is."

"And?"

"I . . ." Ginger sighed. "I don't know, Gran. Cain . . . Cain and me are so mired in old . . . grievances and hurts and anger. I hated him for years. I hated him when he came home in October. But then . . ."

"H-hate is . . . real c-close . . . to l-love, G-Gin."

Tears sprang into Ginger's eyes because she'd been learning this truth, day by day, since Cain had been leaving her alone, at her request. She missed him. She missed him something awful.

She turned onto her side, resting her head on Gran's pillow and speaking into the papery skin of her grandmother's neck.

"But th-then . . .?" prompted Gran.

Ginger swallowed. "He's like a paper cut, comin' into my life and openin' up a painful wound that doesn't bleed, but I'm aware of it all the damned time because it's deep. And then it heals, and when it does, I miss it. I miss the stingin' of the cut." She inhaled sharply. "I miss Cain."

"B-but he's . . ." Her grandmother paused. "Isn't he . . . r-right d-down there . . . in V-Versailles?"

Ginger nodded.

"Then you d-don't . . . have to m-miss . . . him, d-doll baby."

"But I don't know how to be friends with him, Gran. We were friends when we were children, then I was in love with him, then I hated him. Now? Now I don't know where he belongs. And honestly I'm thinkin' he doesn't belong at all. I don't want to care for Cain, Gran. I don't want to care for anyone. Just you and Momma and Daddy. And that's it. Carin' about someone . . . *hurts*," she sobbed, burrowing her forehead into her gran's neck.

"It sh-shouldn't," said Gran, reaching over to run a trembling hand through her granddaughter's hair. "L-lovin' someone . . . shouldn't . . . h-hurt so b-bad."

"But it does," she whispered. "Every day."

"Woodman," murmured her Gran, still stroking her hair. "But that's . . . l-losin', not . . . l-lovin'."

"What's the difference?" Ginger sighed, closing her weary eyes. "If you love someone, you could lose them. It's a risk. You're openin' yourself up to hurt."

"Or . . . t-to joy."

Joy. Something Ginger didn't feel like she'd known for a million years.

A while later, when her grandmother's hand stopped moving, Ginger knew she had fallen asleep so she put on her coat and wound her scarf around her neck. Leaning close, she kissed Gran's cheek, then slipped quietly from the room.

It wasn't too cold outside so she left her car in the parking lot and walked into the little town center of Apple Valley, breathing in the fresh winter air and trying to make sense of everything.

Her heart, which was coming to life again—*felt* more, *wanted* more. Like the buds that break through the earth in early spring, there was energy spent and work involved in coming back to life, and Ginger felt it. It was tiring and frightening, but she couldn't seem to stop it: the longer Cain stayed away, the more she couldn't think about anything *but* Cain. Being around Cain comforted her and made her feel alive. But being around Cain came at the price of confronting the loss of Woodman. It wasn't possible to have the former in her life without reconciling the absence of the latter.

If she wanted Cain, she needed to start the process of saying good-bye to Woodman.

It shouldn't have surprised her that her feet stopped walking suddenly in front of Woodman's house, but it did. Her breath caught as she turned and looked at the little house he'd purchased with so much hope and cared for with so much love. There was a little For Sale sign on a post just inside the white picket fence, and Ginger watched it swing back and forth in the light winter breeze.

Over a month ago, Mr. Woodman had stopped by the McHuids' with two boxes for Ginger, and her father had brought them over that evening. She'd asked him to place them in her front hall closet and hadn't opened the closet door since. She didn't even know what they contained—some clothes, maybe, her running shoes, a nightgown, a few toiletries. Because her own house had been so close, she'd never left much at Woodman's, opting to shower and dress at her own house most days. But there would be things, of course. Leftover things that would remind her of the life they'd shared.

Placing her gloved hand on the white gate, she unlatched it and pushed it open, stepping into the courtyard that Woodman had tended so lovingly. He'd planted flowers along the footpath she walked on now—they'd be bright and vibrant in a few months—and two cheerful flower beds in front of the porch. She stepped up the three stairs and onto the porch, where they'd rocked side by side many a Sunday evening. The paint was still as bright white as it had been when Woodman painted it, and the ceiling was still sky blue, just as she'd suggested. Putting her hand into her purse, she found the solitary key still at the bottom and pulled it out, placing it in the lock and twisting. The front door opened easily, and Ginger stepped inside, where thousands of memories bombarded her with enough regret to make her tears finally fall.

***

"Fuck!" Cain yelled as he threw the wrench across the bay and popped his thumb into his mouth. He'd pinched it badly because he wasn't concentrating. But damn it, it was just about impossible to concentrate on *anything* lately.

He'd pushed her too hard.

Too fucking hard.

Before driving her home two weeks ago, she'd asked him to please leave her alone, and because his head was so fucked-up over the way he felt about her that night, he'd agreed. His reality? He couldn't honestly say that he was pursuing her only for Woodman's benefit anymore. It had started like that, yes. He'd shown up at her door out of obligation, to fulfill a promise to his dying cousin. But things had changed so quickly; he found himself living for the moments he spent with her, hoping she'd like his place, be proud of his business. He was coming up with ways to cross paths with her, to spend time with her. He was fucking falling for her, and the timing was shit. Total shit. She wasn't even over Woodman yet. Not by a fucking mile.

And hell, he wasn't a grief counselor, for fuck's sake! He didn't know what the fuck he was doing. He was trying to help her get her old life back—church, job, riding—but the reality was that her old life was gone. G-O-N-E. And he had no right to tell her how to mourn her dead fiancé.

What the fuck did he know? Maybe it was okay that she didn't seem to acknowledge that Woodman was actually gone. Maybe it was okay that she seemed normal except when Woodman's name came up. Maybe it was better that she didn't face it yet if it was too painful for her.

"I don't know," he growled, huffing out a breath and feeling like shit.

He missed her.

That was his fucking reality.

He missed her, and he thought about her nonstop, all the time.

Klaus had visited his family in Austria while Cain spent Christmas Eve and Day with his mother, thanking the Lord that his aunt and uncle had opted for Barbados instead. He'd been to his pop's a time or two over the past week since he'd been home, and saw her white SUV going up and down the driveway from time to time, so at least she wasn't staying holed up in her house again, which was good. And if she hadn't backed out of the job, she'd be returning to work on Wednesday, which was also good. But none of that helped with him missing her.

He'd tried going out in Versailles, and even met a woman who seemed pretty nice. Cain didn't have a whole lot of experience with dating—fucking was far more his style—but he was enough of a man to admit that he was lonely and needed some friends. Cassidy was a waitress at Kennedy's, and last week he'd taken her out for dinner, but when she invited him into her apartment at the end of the night, he did something he'd never done before—not ever in his entire life. He said no. He thanked her for the date without even kissing her. And he left.

Since then, he didn't have the balls to show his face at Kennedy's.

Why had he turned down a perfect opportunity to fuck a good-looking woman?

Because Ginger's face had appeared front and center in his mind. Blonde hair. Deep brown, sad eyes. The feeling of her arms around him. The soft skin of her fingers clasped in his. She hadn't even come to terms with Woodman's death, let alone gotten over it enough to be with someone else . . . but her availability didn't seem to matter. Cain *wanted* Ginger. And though wanting Ginger in the past hadn't prevented him from being with someone else, now it did. He wanted her, and only her.

To try to make friends outside Kennedy's, he'd stopped by the Apple Valley Fire Department a couple of times to see the guys, and went out for a beer with Scott Hayes. Scott had come down to Versailles to help Cain attach an especially sweet antique bike to bolted cables and extend it from the showroom ceiling. It made him shake his head to imagine that he'd end up friends with Mary-Louise Walker's husband, but he guessed that weirder things than that happened in real life.

As he readied Wolfram's Motorcycles for his grand opening next week and furnished his townhouse little by little, his thoughts always returned to Ginger, and lately his mind had concentrated greatly on the fateful day he'd found her in bed with Woodman, three years ago.

But instead of letting his anger blind him, he tried to really examine what had happened that day. The way she'd poured her heart out to him. How he'd rejected her, not because he didn't want her—*he had wanted her desperately*—but because he couldn't take her away from Woodman when he felt she was integral to his cousin's wellness. Nor could he betray his cousin by sneaking around with Ginger behind his back after Woodman had made his feelings so clear. But Cain recalled the devastated look on her face when she said, *I know you love me, Cain. I can see it. I can feel it. I know it's true.* And it made him ache.

It *was* true. She was right. He had loved her so much at the time, it was killing him, and yet he'd let her walk away from him. No. Not just *let* her walk away. He'd called her disgusting names and insulted her. He'd *pushed* her away with all his might. And not just away. Into Woodman's arms.

Finding her with Woodman had hurt Cain, but for the first time in years, he questioned whether he had a right to that hurt. He'd taken her tender, beautiful feelings and smashed them to smithereens. It didn't really matter that hours later he'd had a change of heart and decided to apologize to her. The damage had already been done. There was every chance he had broken her heart that day, which was the very thing that had made her run to Woodman for comfort. Seen in a certain light, Cain was responsible for the fact that Woodman and Ginger had ended up together.

He sighed, crossing the concrete floor to retrieve the wrench he'd thrown, when his cell phone buzzed in his pocket. Swiping the screen, he looked at the incoming number but didn't recognize it.

"Hello?"

"C-Cain?"

"Ginger?" he said. She was crying, and the hairs on his arm stood up as a shot of adrenaline made him freeze where he stood. "Princess, are you okay?"

"He's g-gone."

Cain's eyes closed slowly as his heart ached for her. It had finally happened. She'd finally broken.

"He is, baby," he said tenderly. "He's gone. I'm so sorry."

"C-Cain," she sobbed. "C-can you . . . can you c-come? C-come to me?"

"Where are you?"

He threw the wrench into his toolbox, locked the showroom door, and grabbed his helmet from the back of his bike. Shrugging into his leather jacket, he straddled the motorcycle and twisted the key in the ignition.

"W-Woodman's place."

Woodman's place? Shit. Shit, shit, shit.

Be strong, lionhearted l'il gal. Be strong for me.

"I'm leavin' right now," he said, his voice raspy and urgent. "You stay put, darlin'. I'm on my way."

Chapter 28

All the sadness.

It was like all the sadness in the world had suddenly engulfed her, swept her out to sea, and marooned her in a place of utter despair. Everywhere she turned in the sweet little house, Woodman was there: laughing as he showed her around for the first time, sitting across from her on the empty living room floor as they ate pizza on a moving box, pulling her hand up the stairs to his bedroom, exercising his leg in front of the TV, waiting for her with dinner when she'd had a bad day at work, kneeling before her—backlit by their first Christmas tree—when he asked her to be his wife.

Finally she lowered herself to the stairs and hunched over, weeping. She could barely catch her breath and couldn't remember a time when she'd ever felt such intense and debilitating sorrow. And yet, through the bleak darkness, there was one unlikely point of light: Cain. Cain would come. Cain would come now. He would hold her and help her and remember with her. He would mourn with her—just as hard and just as deep as she. Because Cain, above all others, had known and loved Woodman as Ginger had.

As she recalled the poignancy of Woodman's proposal, a year ago today, she pulled the engagement ring from her finger for the first time. She clutched it in her palm until the prongs drew blood as a slide show of Woodman—of the Woodman she'd loved deeply her whole life—played through her mind:

At six years old, holding her chubby three-year-old hand and leading her around a paddock to "say hey to the horsies."

At eight years old, screaming for her mother when Ginger's heart seized. He'd saved her life that day and was waiting on the front porch of the manor house when she came home, two weeks later.

At ten years old, sneaking her into the barn to see Cain on her seventh birthday. She didn't know it until they'd gotten down there, but he'd hidden a big piece of cake and three forks under his sweater, and the pale skin of his belly was covered in frosting.

At twelve years old, taking her to the tack room for a Band-Aid when she'd fallen off her bike and scraped her knees. He cleaned them and blew on them and covered them up as Cain stood off to the side making her giggle.

At fifteen years old, on her twelfth birthday, giving her the prettiest bracelet she'd ever seen—with a horse and an apple and a banjo and his heart.

At eighteen years old, saving the day when he came to take her to the homecoming dance, bearing a fistful of forbidden flowers. He'd kissed her for the first time that night, and though she knew they'd never have the chemistry she shared with Cain, he'd proved his love for her in a way that Cain never had and—seemingly, at the time—never could.

At nineteen years old, coming home for his first extended

visit after a long year apart. He'd swung her into his strong arms, holding her close and whirling her around before dropping a sweet, quick kiss to her lips. "Ginger!" he cried. "You grew up, and you're so beautiful!"

At twenty-one years old, with every right to self-pity and anger, he'd come home ready to love her. And she let him. She gave herself to him, and he called it the best night of his entire life, holding her body next to his.

It was true that her feelings for him had never truly evolved from a place of profoundly loving friendship to romance, but memories of being held in Woodman's arms would always twist the bindings of her heart. Until the day she died, she would remember how tenderly he'd held her, how safe she'd felt leaning into him, and how much he'd loved her. Truly, deeply, forever loved her . . . in a way she'd never been able to love him in return.

"Oh God, Woodman," she sobbed. "We were never supposed to happen like we did. We were never supposed to end like we did. I'm so so-o-o-orry. So f-fuckin' sorry."

Woodman was such a good man—such a kind, loving, protective person, such a good friend—surely there was a woman in the world who would have been lit on fire by the way his eyes could turn dark green with want, by the careful touch of his lips on her breasts, by the way his voice would get raspy when he told her he loved her. It just wasn't *her*. And she'd lost him before she could let him go, before she could set him free to find a woman who could have loved him the way he deserved.

Resting her forehead on her bent knees, she cried—for Woodman's loss and for not being able to give him what he wanted; for his sweetness, which she would miss forever; for his friendship, which she would die grieving. She cried all the tears that hadn't fallen for three long months, and then she cried some more—tears of guilt, of regret, of loss, and of sorrow, all the while wondering how she would ever feel whole again now that he was gone.

She heard the front door open and felt Cain's boots vibrate across the hardwood floor before she heard his voice bark, "Ginger?" with so much growly urgency, it made her gasp.

Cain. Her shoulder slumped with relief to hear his voice.

"Here," she said, raising her head and swiping the back of her hand across her weeping eyes and runny nose. "I'm over here on the stairs."

In a second he was standing before her, his helmet clutched in his fist, his coveralls covered in grease, with matching smudges on his face. He squatted down and placed his helmet on the floor by her feet.

"How you doin', princess?"

She tried to take a deep breath, but it was ragged and sobby. "Not good."

"Let me take you home," he said, offering her his hand.

She took it without thinking, her eyes fluttering closed for a moment as the rough, warm skin closed around her cold fingers.

"Stay with me," she whispered.

She wasn't looking at his face, so she couldn't see his expression, only hear the coarse gravel of his voice when he said, "I won't leave till you're feelin' stronger."

"I hope you have nowhere to be for a while," she said, opening her burning eyes.

"You underestimate yourself, Gin. Worst step of all was facin' it. You did that tonight."

Her face crumpled, and she threaded her fingers through

his, clasping them. "You were right. He deserved so much b-better than me, Cain. So much better. So much more."

With his free hand, Cain cupped her cheek, forcing her eyes to meet his. "I had no right to make that comment. Only you and Woodman know what you had together. All I know is that you made him happy. Really, really happy, Gin. You, well, dreamin' of you made Woodman who he was—made him strong and good. He wanted to be the best-possible version of himself for you. I know that. You should know it too."

His words only made her shoulders shake harder as more tears poured from her eyes, and she felt Cain's hands slip under her arms and pull her up. For a moment he seemed to debate what to do, holding her limp body against his chest before sweeping her into his arms. He walked over the threshold of the little house that had held her future with Woodman, and into a dark and lonely world that felt bearable only with Cain's arms around her.

"Where's your car?" he asked close to her ear.

"At Gran's," she said, burrowing her forehead into Cain's neck.

He jerked in a quick breath, as she would if she'd burned herself. "I've only got my bike. Can you hold on to me for the ride home?"

I'm so tired. So very tired.

"Yes," she managed as he set her down on her feet beside the bike, a gentle hand on her shoulder to be sure she was steady.

"I'll be right back."

She watched as he ran back inside and returned a second later with his helmet, turning off the light in Woodman's living room and closing the front door. He strode down the walkway to her, carefully to shut the white gate behind him. Then he placed the helmet on her head, buckled it under her chin, and helped her straddle the bike before swinging his leg over the saddle and turning the key.

"Hold on to me, Gin. Don't fuckin' let go."

As if he didn't quite trust her, he covered her small, cold hands with his, then zoomed off into the night toward McHuid's.

***

When they got to her cottage, he didn't bother helping her off the bike. He pulled her back into his arms and carried her inside the unlocked house, through the kitchen, down a dark hallway, and up the stairs to the bedroom he'd visited only once, the night he'd found her with Woodman. Once there, he placed her gently on the bed, where she sat listlessly as he pulled her coat off one arm at a time. Underneath she was wearing jeans and a soft fleece top, which seemed as comfortable as anything.

"Lie down, baby."

As though on autopilot, she twisted her body and leaned back against the pillows, with her feet still on the floor. Cain leaned down, untied and unlaced her boots, pulled them from her feet, and lifted her legs onto the bed.

And as he worked, she stared up at the ceiling, sniffling and weeping, almost in her own world of pain and sorrow, and it just about killed him that he couldn't take the anguish away and carry it for her.

He'd felt the dead weight of her body when he picked her up off the stairs at Woodman's house, and the only comparison he could think of was the way a marathon runner feels when she reaches the finish line and falls into the arms of someone waiting for her. Her body was exhausted in that same way—completely spent, boneless, and limp—as though she'd run and run and run for weeks on end, only to fall into his arms in exhaustion tonight, when she had reached the end of her own emotional marathon.

Cain grieved her pain. He wished he could take the ache away from her, take it *for* her, but he couldn't. The very stark difference between them was that Cain had gotten a chance to say good-bye to his cousin and a mission by which to serve him after his death. Further, Cain had not only been given permission to love Ginger but encouragement. Cain loved his cousin, and he would mourn him for the rest of his life, but Cain had peace.

Ginger, on the other hand, didn't. Cain had no idea of the state of their relationship when Woodman died, but among Woodman's last words were *She loves you*. And he'd only stayed alive to hear Cain promise to love her back. She had to be living with the weight of guilt and regret on her shoulders, and as much as Cain wanted to take that pain away for her, he couldn't. Not without telling her that Woodman had placed her in his care before dying, which was something he wasn't prepared to do.

The reality was that he needed to keep the secret until she believed, beyond any doubt, that Cain loved her. If he told her too soon, she'd always question whether or not he loved her only because Woodman had told him to, when the truth was that he owned the love he felt for her in the same way he owned his heart or his lungs or the blood in his veins or the thoughts in his head. Loving Ginger was as effortless as breathing, and no less fundamental. Had been since he was a kid, would be until he died.

A lump rose in his throat, and he tried to clear it away.

"Gin," he said softly, running the backs of his fingers across her damp cheek. "You want some tea or somethin'?"

She opened her eyes, which were glassy and tired.

"Just h-hold me awhile?" she whispered, her soft, sad voice shredding his heart.

Cain gulped. He'd fucked hundreds. He'd willingly held almost none.

"I'm . . . I'm filthy, Gin. I didn't change before I left the garage. I'll get your bed all dirty. I could just sit on the floor beside—"

"I don't care," she murmured. "P-please, Cain."

He wasn't sure how good he would be at emotional intimacy—he hadn't had a very good example in his parents— and he'd never allowed himself to become attached to any of the girls he'd been with, purposely wandering, never making a connection. But, fuck, if there was one girl he was willing to figure it out for, it was Ginger.

He sat down in the curve of her body and leaned over to untie the laces of his boots, his heart racing like that of a teenager about to touch a tit for the first time. His fingers trembled lightly, which made the job harder, but he finally managed to shuck them off. His hands were rough, smudged with grease, and for just a moment he considered going into her bathroom and washing them before he lay down beside her, but he sensed that his presence was what she needed more than clean hands, and he promised himself if he ruined her clothes or comforter, he would buy her something new.

He stood up, walked around the bed, then paused a moment as he stared down at her small body. She was a perfect S, with her head bent forward and her legs tucked back. As he sat down on the other side of the bed, the mattress depressed and his breathing quickened. Swinging his legs up, he lay down, rolled onto his side, and scooted closer to her. He wrapped his arm around her waist and, inhaling the warm woman scent of her body, pulled her against his chest. He slipped his other arm under her head like a pillow and bent his knees into hers. She reached for his hand, covering it with hers and backing up against him until they were so close, he could feel her lungs expand and release with every breath she took and gave. Instead of concentrating on the feeling of her body in his arms, he closed his eyes and synchronized his breathing to hers. Little by little, his heart stopped racing, and his body, which had been so wired a few minutes before, calmed down.

Soon he heard her softly snoring and realized she was asleep. He leaned forward to press his lips to her hair.

I'm in love with you, he thought, flinching even as he held her closer. *I've been in love with you for most of my life, princess. And I promise you, here and now, there's only you for me. I'm not sayin' I'll be good at this, because I don't know what the fuck I'm doin' when it comes to stickin' around. But no matter how long it takes, I promise I'll wait for you. I'll help you find the peace you need. I'll do anything, darlin'. Just to be with you.*

"Cain," she whispered into the darkness, her voice so tired and small, he wasn't sure if she was awake or asleep.

"What, baby?"

"Don't leave me again," she murmured, sighing deeply before falling back to sleep.

He had no idea if she was aware of her words or what they did to him—the hope they lit inside him, the longing they assuaged, the beautiful dreams they set in motion.

"I'm not goin' anywhere, darlin'," he said softly, near her ear. "I'm stayin' with you."

She didn't speak again, but she snuggled a little closer to

him, and he adjusted their hands so that their fingers were woven together. Ginger. Cain. Ginger. Cain. Ginger. Cain.

Be good to her.

Care for her.

Love her.

"Thank you, son," whispered Cain into the darkness before falling asleep beside her.

***

Warm.

Safe.

Cain.

Early-morning light streamed through her bedroom window, which was a very good excuse to keep her eyes closed and pretend that she was still asleep. Their fingers were still loosely braided together, and the front of his body was still pressed flush against the back of hers. She felt his breath on the back of her neck, deep and even, warming the skin and causing goose bumps to rise on her arms. She moved experimentally, shifting against him, and was rewarded with a low groan and the tightening of his arm around her.

She had no disorientation or confusion. She didn't wonder if she was still dreaming. She knew where she was and with whom, but what she could barely contain was the rush of feelings that accompanied waking up in Cain's arms because there was an immediate rightness to it, an organic yes to it, a sense of coming home that she'd never experienced in her life. Not with Woodman. Not ever.

Turning in his arms, she stared at his sleeping face.

The angles of his cheeks were as cut as ever, and his square jaw was covered with overnight scruff growth that was jet black against his pale complexion. She stared at his lips for a moment—they were pink and pillowed, slack with sleep, and she flashbacked to the feeling of them moving over hers. So carefully when she was fifteen, so hungrily when she was eighteen. How would they feel now? The same? Different? She took a deep breath, her breasts pushing against his chest and her nipples pebbling under her fleece sweater. His eyelashes, obsidian and long, fanned out from his eyes, and his eyebrows were thick and dark over his closed eyes.

He was so beautiful, her breath caught, and feelings that she didn't expect crashed over her in waves. For her whole life, Cain had been a dark angel on her shoulder: the voice of recklessness, the ice-eyed charmer, the shatterer of her heart and executioner of her dreams, throwing shade on whatever felt safe and defying her to choose spectacular. And in return, she had loved him in different ways—passionately, fiercely, furiously— for almost as long as she could remember.

And now here he was, beside her, all grown up, sticking around.

Old someones can be new, Ginger.

Cain had served his country. Forgiven his father. Traveled the world. Lost his cousin. He was no longer a swaggering boy or an angry teen or a rootless, roaming young man. He was a new man, a new person. And yet, if she squinted her eyes and tilted her head so that the sun kissed his inky hair, she saw Cain from forever, in all his forms, in all his phases, right up until this morning, holding her in his arms.

Nothing—*no, not anything*—had ever felt so right.

Felt right to her heart.

Felt wrong in her head.

Woodman had died only three months ago. Wouldn't it be wrong to switch her affections so quickly to Cain? It would be.

But she'd never loved Woodman the way she'd loved Cain. She'd never been *in love* with Woodman. The cold reality that made her a terrible person was that she hadn't been engaged to the love of her life. The love of her life held her in his arms now. She hadn't lost her soul mate. Her soul mate was lying beside her.

Was it possible that *their time* had finally arrived?

She winced.

How could they embrace it at the cost of Woodman's life? Could they truly have a future together? Was she even what Cain wanted? How could she even know? The Cain he was now—coming when she called, staying when she asked—was a new Cain. She had no idea what he wanted.

But hadn't he hated her when she confessed her feelings to him three years ago? Hadn't he hated her when he came home in October? What had changed? Losing Woodman? Was it a common bond of grief that bound them now? But their grief would fade. It wouldn't be this wrenching forever. And then what? What would happen when the sorrow that bound them together faded away?

She took a shaky breath, raking her teeth over her bottom lip as she stared at him, a mountain of emotional detritus suddenly making her feel much further away from him than she had moments before. Too many hard questions. Too much to sort out to clear a path to any kind of future. It felt hopeless.

Cain, however, was oblivious to her struggle.

"Mmmm," he groaned, pulling her closer, arching against her and fitting them together in his sleep. Beneath his coveralls the hard bulge of his erection found the valley between her thighs, and he rubbed, a low growl slipping from his throat. His hands, which were around her, slid down to her hips, and he pulled her against him, holding her sex perfectly aligned against his and gyrating deliberately against her, into her.

And damn it, but it felt good. So good, her breath caught and a small whimper escaped from her lips.

"Baby," murmured Cain, his eyes still closed as he leaned his head forward to nuzzle her throat.

She gasped in surprise. "Cain. Cain, that's enough."

His lips razed her skin, the tip of his tongue darting out to circle her throbbing pulse. "Aw, let me, baby," he drawled, his voice still thick with sleep.

"Cain!" she said louder, leaning her head back. No matter how good it felt, she didn't feel comfortable letting it continue. She had no idea where they were. She had no idea where they were going. There was too much for them to sort out before they could even consider the possibility of more. She pushed at his shoulders. "Cain, quit it!"

His eyes popped open, and he jerked his head back, his eyes wide open. "Gin? What the hell? Where am—?"

She blinked at him, watching his face as he remembered last night and put together where he was waking up. "Good mornin'."

He rolled onto his back, scrubbing his hands over his face, which was turning very, very pink. "Mornin'. Fuck, I'm . . . sorry."

Cain, the big bad wolf, who'd been with more girls than she could possibly imagine, was blushing like a preteen found looking at a nudie magazine. She giggled softly and shook her head as she swung her legs over the side of the bed. When she looked over her shoulder at him, he was still staring at the ceiling like his life depended on it.

"Want eggs?"

He turned to her, his eyes dark and rattled, yet somehow soft, and she felt her heart skip a beat as he stared up at her and nodded. "Yeah."

***

Fuck. *Fuck.*

You were fuckin' *dry-humpin'* her, man! Get it the fuck together!

Wincing, he felt his cock flinch in his shorts, hot, thick, and throbbing. He had a massive boner, and she was downstairs making fucking eggs for breakfast.

He took a shaky breath and tried to think of football, baseball, snowfall, vomit, but nothing worked. All he could see was her big brown eyes less than an inch from his. All he could feel was her delectable fucking body fitted against his like a second skin, like she was made to be with him, and *only* him. Sitting up, he looked over at her bathroom and considered heading in there to rub one out, but she called upstairs, "Cain! Breakfast is ready."

There were two solutions: jog in place for five minutes to get the blood flowing elsewhere, or force himself to piss. Option two won out but put Cain in a fairly foul mood that he attempted to fix between her toilet and kitchen.

Three months without a woman sucked.

That *was* the fucking truth.

Or it was the fucking truth until he found himself standing in the kitchen doorway watching Ginger McHuid putting eggs on two plates. She turned from the stove, surprised to find him standing behind her, and her sweet lips tilted up into the most beautiful fucking smile he'd ever seen. And suddenly he didn't give a shit about three months of abstinence. All he could think was the same thought he'd had last night before falling asleep:

There's only you for me. I'll wait for you.

Which meant he had to figure out a way to see her. Regularly. And if that meant coming up to McHuid's every weekend, so be it, but he wished he could figure out another way.

"Hungry?" she asked, putting the plates at the little table where he'd shared breakfast with her three years ago, after washing her gran's truck.

Un-fuckin'-believably hungry, darlin'.

"Uh, yeah," he said, sitting down across from her.

"I can't believe I go back to work tomorrow," she said, spearing a plump piece of scrambled egg with her fork.

Fuck. That's right. That's just goin' to make seein' her that much harder. Who was the fuckin' genius who encouraged her to go back to work? Oh, right. Me.

"What days you workin' again?" he asked, taking a bite of eggs.

"For now? Mondays, Wednesdays, Thursdays, and every other Sunday."

"What're you doin' on Tuesdays and Fridays?"

"I don't know. Maybe I'll try to pick up some extra hours." She shrugged. "You want orange juice?"

"Sure," he said. Then, "Huh."

"What's 'huh' mean?" she asked, taking the juice out of the fridge and grabbing two glasses from the cabinet. She sat back down, pouring them each a glass and sliding his glass over to him. "Huh?"

Is this a good idea? Bad idea? Fuck, I don't know. I don't know how this fuckin' works. I just know I need to see her. A lot.

"Why don't you come work for me?" he asked.

Her eyes widened, and she grinned at him in surprise.

"*Work* for you? You mean . . . fix motorcycles?" She wrinkled her nose in a way he'd always thought was fucking adorable. "I don't know the first thing about—"

"I need someone to answer the phones, don't I?"

"Oh . . . you mean, be your secretary?"

He shrugged. "I don't know what you call it. Answer the phones. Say hi to people."

"Receptionist."

"Yeah. That," he said, taking a gulp of orange juice.

She rolled her lips between her teeth for a moment, then licked them. *Oh, fuck, Gin, I'm a weak man, please stop.* He looked away from her, back down at his plate, and speared another cluster of eggs with a little too much force.

"Whoa! What'd that egg do to you?"

This egg is on a plate that's on a table that's between my body and your body so I fuckin' hate this egg. I want to lunge across this table and kiss you senseless until you're beggin' me to fuck you until the sun sets and rises all over again. That's why I hate this goddamned egg.

"So?" he prompted her, frowning at his plate before looking up at her.

"What're the hours, boss?" she asked, raising an eyebrow.

Sassy. Damn, but he fucking loved her sassy.

"Twelve to seven."

"Late hours."

"I like sleepin' in," he growled. *And I'd like it even better next to you, princess.*

She grinned. "And how much you goin' to pay me?"

And that's when it occurred to him: *She's sayin' yes. She's fuckin' sayin' yes. I'm goin' to see her every Tuesday and every Friday.*

"Seventy-five bucks a day."

"Ninety-five," she countered.

"Done."

"Done," she said, her smile blinding.

He stared at her—at her blonde hair, golden in the sunlight that streamed through the window over the sink, and at her pink lips that he was dying to taste again. *Soon, brother. Soon.*

She held out her hand, giggling softly. "Shake on it?"

Reaching across the table, he took her hand and clasped it. "Happy New Year, princess."

"Happy New Year, Cain."

Chapter 29

As she pressed the button for the fourth floor, Ginger sighed contently. Her feet ached after an eight-hour shift, but she felt energized and invigorated . . . *and* that much closer to tomorrow, when she would see Cain again.

Yesterday, after breakfast, she asked Cain if he would visit Woodman's grave with her, and he'd agreed, driving her to the cemetery and holding her hand as she wept. After a moment, he dropped her hand and wandered away, giving her some privacy, and she talked to Woodman for a while, telling him how sorry she was and how much she missed him. When she had no more words to say, she found Cain standing twenty yards away, under the bare winter branches of a tree, watching her, and she walked over to him.

"You okay, princess?" he asked, leaning away from the trunk and opening his arms.

She stepped into them gratefully, her own arms limp at her sides as she rested her cheek over Cain's heart and closed her eyes. Seconds turned to minutes, and he never said a word, just held her in his strong arms, his chin resting on top of her head for as long as she needed him.

With every breath, his chest, hard and broad, pushed into hers, a reminder of his strength, of the strength he was sharing with her. And with every breath, she felt more and more certain that she could bear the loss of Woodman, provided she'd never have to bear the loss of Cain.

Finally, almost on the brink of sleep, she raised her head from his heart, and he raised his chin from her head, looking down at her.

"Better?"

She took a deep breath and nodded. "A little."

His eyes, bright blue and sad, searched hers. "A little's better than nothin', right?"

"I miss him," she said softly.

"Me too."

"You think we'll always miss him?"

Cain sighed. "It won't hurt this much forever, but yeah. I think we will."

He let his arms fall from around her, and though she instantly missed their warmth, he made up for it by taking her hand.

"Why don't I take you to get your car?"

"Okay," she said, letting him lead her down the path from Woodman's grave to the parking lot. "You know, before he left for the . . . the fire that night, we had a—I don't know what it was, exactly—a little fight, I guess."

"You and Woodman?"

She nodded. "Yeah. And I just . . ."

"You what?"

"I wish we hadn't. I wish I'd kissed him good-bye and told him I loved him."

"He knew," said Cain softly, dropping her hand as they reached the motorcycle. "And he loved you more than anythin', Ginger."

The elevator opened to the fourth floor, and her thoughts of yesterday scattered as she stepped out, looking forward to seeing her grandmother for a few minutes before leaving for the day.

As she approached, she realized that Gran's chart was still in the clear plastic box on the wall outside her room. Ginger wasn't assigned to the fourth floor, but she couldn't resist taking a peek at the chart. Almost instantly she wished she hadn't.

January 2nd: Palliative care recommended. Patient not advised, per her son.

Palliative care, otherwise known as end-of-life care, was recommended when curative care, or active medical treatment, had ceased working. It meant that Gran's body was no longer responding to the medication meant to slow the Parkinson's. It meant that she was coming closer to the end.

Had Ginger failed to notice, as she grieved Woodman, how rapidly Gran was declining? She could still speak pretty well, even though she was in the advanced stages of Parkinson's. She hadn't experienced any dementia or blatant forgetfulness. But her chart noted incontinence, constipation, breathlessness, and problems swallowing. She would be given certain medications to manage stress and pain, but her body was failing, and apparently Ginger's father had advised her grandmother's medical team not to make his mother aware that time was dwindling, which meant that Ginger needed to put on a brave face whenever she was around Gran.

She'd known, of course, that her grandmother's disease would take over eventually, and she'd observed enough to know that Gran was in the advanced stages of the disease. She just hadn't considered that it would be so soon.

Then again, she reminded herself of what she knew about Parkinson's: a patient could live on for years with palliative care. Parkinson's was a complex disease, and by itself it wasn't enough to take a life. It would take complications to jeopardize Gran. As long as she stayed at Silver Springs, cared for by the staff of nurses and doctors, she could still have some time left. And Ginger chose to concentrate on that time rather than on the prospect of losing someone else she loved.

Lifting her chin as she placed the chart back in the holder, she swiped at her eyes with the backs of her hands and fixed a smile on her face. If anyone in the world deserved her bravery, it was Gran.

"Hello, beautiful," she said, walking into the room and immediately noticing the bouquet of wildflowers that hadn't been there when Ginger visited on New Year's Eve.

"D-doll baby," said Gran softly.

Ginger leaned down and kissed her grandmother's cheek. "More flowers?"

Gran's eyes flicked to the flowers, then back to Ginger. "How w-was . . . w-work?"

"It was good," she said, reaching for her grandmother's trembling hand.

"W-will I . . . see you . . . t-tomorrow?"

"I can come by in the morning if you like, but I'm working at Cain's new business on Tuesdays and Fridays."

Was it Ginger's imagination, or did Gran's eyes light up at this news?

"How is . . . C-Cain?"

"Confusing. Wonderful. Terrible. Amazing." Ginger scoffed softly, tracing the blue veins on the back of Gran's hand before lifting it to her lips for a kiss. "Remember when I was fifteen? You warned me against him."

"I didn't . . . t-trust him . . . then. B-but d-doll b-baby . . ." Gran struggled to take a deep breath, and when she finally did, she sighed a long breath before continuing. "P-people can ch-change . . . Has C-Cain . . . changed?"

"Yes," said Ginger, lying down beside her grandmother's constantly trembling body. "He *has* changed. He's, well, he's settled down, for one. He isn't drinkin' and angry. He grew up, Gran. He isn't a boy anymore. He's . . . he's a man now."

"A g-good man?"

Ginger considered this. She thought of how he'd come to tell her about Woodman, how he pulled her out of her deep and dark depression and back into the world, how he risked her feelings by telling her the truth, how he came to her on New Year's Eve when she'd called and kept her company for most of yesterday.

"I think so . . . but Gran, I loved him once before, and he couldn't love me back. He didn't want me."

"Cain al-ways . . . w-wanted you."

She shook her head. "No. That's not true."

"Yes, s-sweetheart. Always. He j-just . . . d-didn't feel . . . w-worthy of you. And m-maybe he w-wasn't . . . racing all a-around . . . the c-countryside . . . w-with God . . . knows who."

"He isn't like that anymore," said Ginger quickly. "He has a business now, Gran. He's changed. I promise you." She took a deep breath and released it carefully. "Since Woodman . . . since Woodman . . . *died*, he's changed." She exhaled shakily, as acknowledging Woodman's passing was still new and painful. "He's still ornery. He cusses a streak. And he's bossy as anything. But I think . . . I mean, I feel like I might still be wastin' away without him. In his own way, he saved me, Gran. He saved me from grieving my life away."

"You said . . . you l-loved . . . him once?"

"Very much," said Ginger, remembering the courage it had taken to find him at the old barn and confess her love to him. His hands cupping her face. His body pressing hers against the barn wall. Their kiss. His hands. *Cain, Cain, Cain . . . I love you. God, I love you so much.*

"D-does that . . . k-kind of l-love . . . d-die?" asked Gran.

No. It doesn't. Don't lie, Ginger. Don't say it's dead when you can feel it alive inside you right this minute.

She bit her bottom lip in thought, finally answering, "It becomes cautious."

"Then t-t-t-take . . . your t-time," said Gran.

She was slurring her words, and her voice was becoming softer and softer even as her body kept moving and jerking. Ginger rolled to her side and gathered her grandmother into her arms as best she could.

"I'll miss you . . . someday," said Ginger as a tear slid down her face.

"You'll . . . h-h-have . . . C-Cain."

Will I? Is it possible, after everything, for Cain and I to be together?

Gran's eyes were closing. "C-consider . . . who he *is* . . . not who . . . he *was*."

A new man. A good man. A tender man. A man who stays. A man who sets her blood on fire. The man she'd always wanted, and yet . . .

"If I let myself love him, I don't think I could stand to lose him. Gran, it would take so much courage to fall in love with him again."

"L-lionhearted l-l-l'il . . . g-gal," murmured her grandmother, drifting off to sleep.

Ginger started, wondering when in the world Gran had ever heard Cain call her that . . . but then, Cain had been calling her that forever. Certainly Gran could have heard it at some point or another.

Stronger'n death, with the heart of a lion.

But was she strong enough to give love, and Cain, another chance? And was that a chance he was interested in taking?

***

It was only his second day open, but nothing was going right.

Cain had bought two laptops—one for himself and one for Ginger—but the guy he'd hired from Geek Squad to set them up basically told him they were both shit. Great. So Cain had to run up to Best Buy in Lexington and get two new ones, at twice the price.

Upon returning, he noticed the flowers on her desk were gone, and the IT guy sheepishly admitted he'd knocked them over and the vase had shattered. He'd thrown them in the bathroom garbage bin. So Cain had to take out the trash and make another trip out—this time to the Piggly Wiggly—for a fresh bouquet.

When he came back from that trip, the phone was ringing. Someone was calling about a funny noise on his custom chopper's suicide clutch. Could Cain take a look? Sure, he could. Would twelve work? He made a face. He definitely didn't want to turn down new business, but he'd really hoped to have a little one-on-one with Ginger when she first arrived.

"Sure," he said, feeling grouchy but keeping his voice professional. "Twelve is great. Bring it in. I'll take a look."

"Mr. Wolfram," asked Linus from Geek Squad as Cain

hung up the phone, "you want Wi-FI, or were you plannin' to use DSL? Or cable?"

Cain, who'd been a rebellious teen, then a naval firefighter, had very little knowledge of computers. "Uh, I need the Internet."

"Yeah. But to connect: cable, DSL or Wi-Fi?"

Cain clenched his jaw. "If you were me, what would you do?"

"DSL or cable hardwired to your laptop, Wi-Fi to your assistant. Then you can offer it to your customers when they're waitin' on service."

"Fine. Great. Do that."

"The DSL or the cable?"

"Whatever!" yelled Cain, picking up the phone. "Wolfram's DSL."

"Oh, sorry. Wrong number."

The caller hung up before Cain realized his mistake, and he groaned, slamming down the phone.

I have to get out of here for a few minutes.

Except that just then, as he was about to pull out his hair, the bell jingled over the door signaling that someone had walked into the showroom.

"Hello? Cain?"

And fuck if every bit of stress from the morning rolled off his shoulders and faded away. She was here. He looked down at his clothes and made a face. He hadn't been able to change from his coveralls back into jeans and a T-shirt, but he hoped like hell that she didn't give a shit.

"Get them workin'," he growled at Linus, who shrank back nervously, busying himself with the two computers.

Cain crossed the office and stopped in the doorway,

looking across the showroom to where Ginger stood in a beam of sunlight checking out his favorite bike. Her blonde hair was up in a ponytail, her perfect ass was tight and high in jeans, and her hand caressed the shiny chrome fender of a fully restored 1952 Zündapp K800. Cain took a moment to burn the image—way hotter than the hottest porn—into his mind before clearing his throat.

"You like it?"

She turned around, and her face broke into a smile. "It looks real old."

"It is. Almost sixty-five years old."

"Wow. It's beautiful, Cain."

He looked down at the early-model motorcycle. "I met this guy in Sweden . . . his name was Sven, and he was from Iceland. He restored old bikes, and when I finished riding across Europe, I headed over there to check out his shop. Ended up staying for a couple of months. That's how I got the idea to open my own place."

"Was this motorcycle his?"

Cain shook his head. "I found it in England and had it shipped to Sven's shop. We restored it together. It's worth a lot now to a collector; it's in mint condition."

She put her hands on her hips, tilting her head back to look up at him. "What *happened* to you?" She shook her head and laughed softly. "Sometimes you don't even feel like the boy I grew up with."

"Shouldn't that be a good thing, princess?"

"Maybe," she said, her voice soft and wistful, her smile warm. "You're all grown up now."

"Had to happen eventually."

"I guess so."

"Any complaints?"

She bit her bottom lip like she was trying to decide whether or not to ask him something. Deciding against it, she shook her head. "Nope."

He knew it was brash, but he let his eyes drop to her lips and linger, then to her neck, to her breasts, full and firm in a light blue sweater. Lower, to her tight waist and lightly flared hips. Her legs in jeans, probably strong from a lifetime of riding. He let his gaze travel back up her body slowly, reverently, and found her brown eyes dark and wide when he met them again.

"You grew up too, Gin."

She swallowed. "Any complaints?"

He shook his head slowly. "Nope."

"Uh, Mr. Wolfram?" called Linus from the office. "I have a question about your cable plan, sir."

Fucking Linus.

"Ready to work?" Cain asked Ginger.

She nodded, but he could have sworn he saw a hint of disappointment in her eyes, like maybe she was just as curious about where that exchange would have gone if they'd been alone, with plenty of time.

"I guess so."

He showed her into the office and introduced her to Linus.

"Linus, Ginger. Ginger, Linus. He's from Geek Squad. Obviously," he muttered.

"Hey, Linus," she said, offering scrawny, bespectacled Linus her hand.

Over her head Cain gave Linus a look that told him Ginger was absolutely, positively off-limits unless Linus was interested in getting beat up with his own laptop.

"Afternoon, miss."

"Ginger's the, uh, the receptionist, or, uh, secretary, so maybe show her how all this works, okay?"

A loud motor pulled into one of the drive bays, and a moment later the showroom door opened to a cheerful jingle.

Ginger flashed her eyes at him. "Should I go . . .?"

"No," said Cain. "Stay here and get these computers workin', okay?" He gestured to a mountain of unsorted paperwork. "And maybe make sense out of that? I'll come check up on you later."

And he meant to. Hell, he would have liked to spend the whole fucking day just staring at her. But the suicide clutch guy was part of a motorcycle hobbyist club two towns away, and he called a guy who called a guy who called a guy, and Cain was lying under an antique British motorcycle called a Vincent Rapide C when he noticed Linus walking back to his black, white, and orange VW bug.

"Linus!" he called. "Already done for the day?"

Linus turned around, looking perplexed. "*Already?* It's a quarter to seven. But yeah, I'm finally done. I'll send a bill."

Cain glanced at his watch and blinked when he saw the time. *Holy shit.* She was leaving in fifteen minutes.

Three motonuts were still hanging out with Cain in the drive bay, but he rolled to his knees and stood up. "You know, boys, I gotta close up shop in a few. Vic, I don't think you'll have any more trouble with that clutch. Frank, can you leave the Vincent with me for a few days?"

"Sure thing, Cain," said Frank, giving Cain an appreciative nod.

"I'll, uh, I'll give you a call when I fix the front forks. Might need to send for some parts."

"Dang, son, but you know your way around a bike."

Cain grinned at the older man. "Been tinkerin' with 'em for as long as I can remember."

He waved good-bye to the men, welcoming them back anytime, then turned and headed inside to salvage a few precious minutes with Ginger.

He knocked lightly on the open office door and watched as she looked up at him from the desk, which was now twenty times more organized than it had been that morning. All his bills and receipts had been replaced by a neat stack of folders, and the two laptops sat back to back on the desk, with an office chair pushed into one side and a guest chair pushed into the other.

"Hi," she said.

"Hi," he said, wiping his greasy hands on his coveralls and stepping into the room. "How'd it go today?"

"Good." She gestured to the files. "Purchases and receipts categorized and filed." She pointed to a small pile of pink notes. "Phone messages." She picked up the laptop before her and turned it to face him. "A simple bookkeepin' system that Linus helped me download."

"It looks great in here, Gin. Thanks for gettin' me organized."

She smiled. "You're welcome. I decided to take messages rather than disturb you. Seemed like you had enough work to keep you busy for today."

"Thanks."

"And from the look of that pile, I don't think you'll be wantin' for work tomorrow either." She took a deep breath and sighed. "Well, it's just about seven. I guess I'll be goin'." She pulled her coat from the back of the chair and shrugged it on. "So I'll see you again on Fri—"

"Hey, um . . ." He put his hands on his hips, feeling a

sudden heat warm his cheeks. "Would you, uh . . . would you want to have dinner with me on Friday? After work?"

"Sure." She grinned at him. "But won't your girlfriends be jealous?"

"I don't have a girlfriend," he said, keeping his expression stone cold sober.

"Well, if we're bein' honest, you never did have a *proper* girlfriend," she said lightly, "What you had was a boatload of—"

He held up his hand to stop her. "There's only one girl I'm interested in right now, Gin. And she's standin' in front of me."

Her eyes widened, and he watched the pulse in her neck spring to life. Her lips parted in surprise, and she searched his face, pressing her palm to her chest.

"Me?"

You stakin' a claim here?

He nodded. "Ain't no one else here, princess."

"Wait. Um." She cocked her head to the side, her face set somewhere between shocked and confused. "I'm sorry, but Cain . . . are you askin' me out on a *date*?"

"I don't know much about datin', Ginger. But yes," he said, nodding his head, "you could call it that, I guess."

"I'm more curious about what *you'd* call it," she said, lowering her chin and raising her eyebrows.

Sassy. His heart thundered. His balls tightened. *Damn.*

He nailed her with his eyes, unable to keep his lips from twitching into a grin. He rubbed his bottom lip with his thumb, staring at her—staring at her the way he would if she was naked on his bed and he had all night long.

"I'd call it a date," he finally said, his voice gravel.

"Oh," she murmured, blinking at him. "Huh. I wasn't, um, I wasn't . . ."

Shit. Was she turning him down? *Oh, fuck.* He'd read this situation for shit, and then some.

"You know what? Just, uh, just forget it," he said, taking a deep breath and trying to hold back the overwhelming wave of disappointment that threatened to flatten him where he stood.

"No, thanks."

"Right."

His neck bent forward until he stared at the floor, blinking, wondering where he'd gone so wrong. He'd thought . . . fuck, he'd sort of thought that maybe she was into him too. But he must have misunderstood. She wasn't interested in him. She just wanted his friendship or comfort or—

"No, thanks. I don't want to forget it," she said softly. "I'd . . ."

He jerked his head up, his eyes locking with hers as he held his breath.

"I'd *like* to go out to dinner with you on Friday. I'd like to go on a date with you, Cain."

"Oh, yeah?" he asked, exhaling in a rush and running his hand through his bristly hair. He felt his lips tilt up into a relieved smile. "You would?"

She nodded, answering his grin with a sweet one of her own. "I would."

His chest tightened, aching a little because she looked so clean and soft and pretty standing there behind his desk . . . and because she'd said yes, when he truly thought she was saying no. He held her eyes, smiling at her, wondering if this was how Woodman had felt around Ginger, and understanding—*really* understanding—why Woodman had staked a claim so long ago and clung to it so fiercely.

She licked her lips and raked her teeth across her bottom

lip, staring back at him, a goofy smile covering her face and making her eyes sparkle.

Oh, my heart, princess. I ain't never given it to anyone before, but it's yours now. It's all yours.

"All right then." He gulped. "I guess I'll see you Friday."

"It's a date," she said, giggling softly, like she couldn't believe it. She picked up her purse and walked around the desk, stopping beside Cain to lean up on tiptoe and press her sweet lips to his cheek. "Good night, Cain."

He froze in place, his breath held, his body taut and still. He listened as she passed by him and walked away, heard her car engine start and the sound of her wheels turning out of his driveway. The office still smelled lightly of lemons, his cheek burned like she'd branded him with a poker . . .

. . . and Friday was three long days away.

Chapter 30

On Friday Ginger arrived at Cain's place at noon in a pair of jeans, a long-sleeved T-shirt, and sneakers, but out in her Jeep she'd left a black scoop-neck blouse and black boots. As she had on Tuesday, she spent most of the day alone, in the little office, answering the phone and making coffee for the folks waiting on Cain to service their motorcycles. She chatted with many of them as they sat in the guest chairs waiting for him to come and tell them the work was done or how much more time he'd need, and found she enjoyed the company and good-natured small talk. But what she loved the most was that whenever Cain came into the office, he'd cut his eyes to her first, right away, and she came to long for those intimate nanomoments, which quickly became the peak of her whole day.

She'd talked to Gran about Cain after work yesterday, sharing that they had a date set for after work on Friday, and Gran had seemed pleased as punch. Ginger would be just as excited as Gran if an idea stuck in the back of her head wasn't bothering her so much.

Were she and Cain only bound by grief?

Like most relationships that started under pressure, she worried that it wouldn't end well in the long run, and losing Cain again was not something her heart would be able to bear.

Three years ago Cain had hurt her, and in response, she'd shifted her attention, if not her romantic affections, to Woodman. After she chose Woodman so soon after declaring her affections to Cain, Cain had come to think of her as fickle, believing that Woodman deserved far better than her. When he'd sought her out at the fire department BBQ that fateful day, their reunion had been full of caustic, biting anger. A few hours later, Woodman had tragically died, and a month after that, Cain had started coming around. Now here they were, going out on a date. And if there had been any confusion about the purpose of the date when he asked, Cain had made it very clear, with a searing-hot expression, that he was interested in her.

But why?

Or rather . . . how?

They'd been archenemies at the BBQ.

Then Woodman died.

All vitriol was suddenly gone.

It was a strange equation, and deep down inside it didn't add up for Ginger, which worried her. Was the fury they'd both felt truly gone for good? Or was it temporarily gone, to make way for grief? Had they made quick amends only because they'd both lost someone they loved? Because didn't that mean that when their grief mellowed, the baggage of anger and hurt feelings would resurface? Didn't they have to deal with the baggage between them at one point or other? If not, how could they possibly move forward?

She didn't know. But all of it worried her.

At seven o'clock she went to her car and grabbed her bag

with her blouse and boots, then headed back into the office, locking the bathroom door and changing. She put on some mascara and lipstick, took her hair from its ponytail and brushed it out until it lay wavy and shiny on her shoulders. When she was ready, she opened the door to find Cain waiting.

"Princess," he murmured, his eyes scorching a path from her eyes to her lips to her throat to her breasts to her boots and back up again. "You look . . . *beautiful*."

"Thanks," she said, smiling at him. Tucked under his arm she saw a rolled-up pair of jeans. "Looks like we had the same idea."

"Give me a minute or two to change?" he asked.

She nodded. "I'll shut down the computers and forward the phones to voice mail. Meet you in the showroom?"

"Sounds good," he said, unmoving, his dimples deep and sweet.

Her heart fluttered wildly as he approached the bathroom, closer and closer, until his hip nudged hers. He leaned down and whispered in her ear, "You look beautiful, princess, but you also look fuckin' *hot*."

She didn't know how, but she kept herself from whimpering aloud as he edged past her and closed the bathroom door. Her skin tingled and her heart hammered, and she knew that, if she looked in a mirror, her eyes would be as wide and black as a midnight sky.

"Gin," he called from the bathroom. "You still frozen in place?"

Her lips parted in surprise, and as quietly as possible, she tiptoed to the desk. *Cocky so-and-so.*

"Did you say somethin'?" she called.

She heard him chuckle, a low rumble that made her cheeks

flush as she programmed the phone to go to voice mail and shut down the two laptops.

"You're a bad liar," he said.

"I have no idea what you're talkin' about," she said, putting her hands on her hips and sticking her tongue out at the bathroom door.

He laughed again, and this time she couldn't help herself—she laughed right along with him. The sound of Cain happy was too infectious to ignore.

He spoke through the bathroom door again. "So I thought I'd drive your car back up to Apple Valley tonight and we'll get some dinner, and when I take you home, I can stay over at my pop's."

Huh. He'd put some thought into this. And she found herself strangely touched that Cain had come up with a plan. She knew he was telling the truth when he said that dating was new for him. He'd screwed around plenty in high school, but she never remembered him having a steady girlfriend. And Woodman had never mentioned him having a girlfriend while he was in the Navy. She wouldn't lay bets on him *never* having gone out on a proper date in the whole of his life, but she knew it wasn't commonplace for Cain, which made his efforts for Ginger all the sweeter.

That said, she was absolutely, positively not ready to go out on a date in Apple Valley with Cain Wolfram.

"Umm," she said. "How about maybe we stay down here in Versailles?"

Silence. Water running for a good thirty seconds. More silence.

"Cain?"

"Why don't you want to go to Apple Valley?"

She winced. "Woodman and I lived there, Cain. It was, you know, our home. How would it look if—"

The bathroom door swung open, and Cain appeared in the doorway, his eyes black, his gaze hard. "Are you embarrassed to be seen with me?"

"What?" she gasped. "What are you—no! No, not at all!"

He grabbed a towel from beside the sink and wiped away the remaining white foam on his freshly shaved jaw. He'd changed from his coveralls to jeans and a white button-down shirt, and he looked so handsome, she wasn't able to totally squelch her little moan of pleasure this time. But maybe that was a good thing because Cain noticed, and it softened his thunderous expression.

His voice was warmer when he said, "Gin, talk to me. Tell me what's goin' on in your head, baby."

"I don't want to be the source of gossip," she said, leaning back against the desk and crossing her arms over her chest. "No. It's more than that. I don't want to . . ." She gulped. "I don't want to dishonor Woodman's memory by steppin' out with his cousin just three months after his passin'."

Cain's chest expanded as he took a deep breath, still staring at her, measuring her words. Finally he nodded slowly. "Okay. But if you don't want to go out with me, why'd you say yes to the date?"

She took a deep breath, hearing the words in her head and gathering the courage to say them aloud.

"I *do* want to go out with you. It doesn't feel *wrong* to spend time with you," she said softly, holding his eyes.

He flinched slightly, then softened, throwing the towel back into the bathroom and taking a step toward her.

"But it doesn't feel totally right either?" he said. "I mean, you'll only go out with me as long as no one knows? I don't like that. It feels like a dirty secret or somethin'."

She lowered her hands and took a step forward, closing the distance between them. As she stood before him, she reached up to palm his smooth cheek with her hand.

"It's not a dirty secret. It feels right," she assured him softly. "When it's just you and me, I promise it feels right, Cain."

"Then . . .?"

". . . but it's also complicated."

Cain rotated his face so that his lips kissed her hand, then he reached for it, fisted her fingers gently around the kiss, and let go. "I tell you what . . . I'll take you somewhere that isn't Apple Valley tonight if we talk about what makes this so complicated. Okay?"

"Okay," she said, following him out of the office but wondering where in the world to begin.

***

She gave him her keys so he could drive, and because he wanted a chance to really talk to her, he decided to take her to his townhouse. For one thing, it was halfway between Versailles and Apple Valley, but for another, he wanted her all to himself, and what better way to ensure that they had privacy and quiet to talk than going to his place?

However, now that they were in the car, Ginger had clammed up. She wasn't saying much of anything.

"Gin?" he said as they drove away from Wolfram's Motorcycles. "Tell me why it's complicated."

"Where do I even start?"

He shrugged. "Wherever you want."

"You're Woodman's cousin."

"Yes, I am."

"It looks bad for me to be datin' you a few months after he died." She sighed, turning away from him. "He only died in October. It's January. And if you and I start datin', it'll look like I didn't really love Woodman."

"Of course you loved him."

When five seconds of silence had passed, Cain looked over at Ginger.

She was worrying her bottom lip between her teeth, her eyebrows furrowed, as she stared down at her lap.

"Of course you loved him," he repeated slowly, staring at her profile.

Her jaw was granite, but she blinked several times.

He pulled over, cutting the engine and turning to look at her.

"Tell me you loved him, Gin," he murmured.

"Not like I was supposed to," she finally whispered.

"What does that mean?"

She turned to face him, her eyes swimming, her lips tilted down. "I loved Woodman. He was my best friend, but I . . . I was never . . ." She took a deep breath and held it as she finished, "I was never *in love* with Woodman."

I was never in love *with Woodman.*

Cain stared at her, letting the words sink in, letting their full meaning unravel. "Wait, what? What do you mean?"

She swallowed, looking away from him, a tear slipping down her cheek. "I loved him like a friend. I wasn't in love with him. Ever."

"You were goin' to *marry* him."

She nodded, a small jerking movement. "I tried to love him like he wanted me to. God, I swear I tried. I wanted to. I wanted to love him just as much as he loved me." Her voice was hushed and low as the tears cascaded down her cheeks. "But I couldn't."

His eyes, unfocused as he stared straight ahead, closed slowly.

"Why not?"

He knew. He knew why. He knew because the same feelings that had survived in her broken heart had also survived in his.

"There was always s-someone else in my heart," she said, her voice breaking.

He clenched his eyes shut tighter as the implications of her words took root in his head. *My God, is it possible she's still in love with me? Please.*

"And I couldn't let that someone go," she sobbed softly. "I wanted to hate him. Christ, I wanted to hate him so badly, and part of me did for a long while. But I couldn't get him out of my heart no matter how hard I tried."

"Princess . . .," Cain whispered into the darkness, opening his eyes and facing her. "Ginger."

"I know you didn't want me, Cain. I know you didn't love me like I loved you, but I—"

"I did, Ginger," he said. "I *did* want you. I *did* love you. I just—"

"What?" she gasped, her eyes wide, her mouth gaping open. "What are you *talkin'* about? You called me a bitch. You told me to go. You *left* that night. You—"

"I didn't leave. I mean," he gulped. "I did eventually, but not at first—"

"What are you—"

"First I came to tell you that I was wrong." He winced, his

own eyes burning from the terrible and still-vivid memory. "I went to your place to tell you that I didn't mean what I'd said at the old barn. That I loved you just as much as you loved me. That I had for years. That I was only pushin' you away because Woodman loved you so much and I didn't want to hurt him after everythin' he'd been through. But I loved you, Gin. I did. I swear to God, it's true. I came after you later that evenin'." He paused, staring at her stricken face. "Your door was unlocked. When I knocked, it opened. I walked into your house, I climbed up the stairs, down the hall, and—"

"No!" she screamed, putting her hands over her ears. "No! No, no, no!" She stared at him, her eyes wild, tears coursing down her face as her breath came and went in jagged spurts punctuated by broken whimpers. "Stop it! Stop talkin'! Please, stop . . ."

She slid her hands to her face, covering her eyes as she wept—long, hard sobs that racked her body and made her seat tremble. And it was fucking unbearable for him to watch.

Cain lifted the bolster between them, unbuckled her seat belt, put his hands under her arms, and lifted her from her seat onto his lap, wrapping his arms around her as she buried her face in his neck and cried with long, wrenching sobs of sorrow, of anguish, of lost chances and terrible revelations.

He closed his burning eyes, pressing soft kisses to her hair.

"You're wrong," he murmured. "It isn't complicated, darlin'. It isn't complicated anymore."

She took a ragged breath. "You saw. You saw me with him."

Cain clenched his jaw before pressing another kiss to her head. "Yes, I did."

"That's why you left a week early three years ago?"

"Yes."

"That's why you hated me so much . . . at the . . . the BBQ."

"Yes."

"That's why . . . that's why you said that Woodman deserved better than me."

He nodded. "But it was my fault too," he said softly, holding her tighter. "I was so cruel to you, princess. The things I fuckin' said to you." He winced. "When I think of your face—the way you looked at me when you told me I'd never hurt you again, then turned and walked away. I wanted to kick my own ass. Part of me wanted to die for hurtin' you like that."

She looked up at him with glassy eyes. "I was so devastated, and . . . he was s-so good to me. My heart was sh-shattered, and Woodman—"

"Princess."

He stopped her because it hurt. He wished it didn't, but it was painful to remember her limbs entwined with his cousin's so soon after telling him she loved *him*. And yes, he understood his part in pushing her away, in pushing her back to Woodman, and he regretfully owned it. But the loss he'd felt at the time, the betrayal, the sickening sense of "too late" wasn't something he was anxious to relive.

"If it's all the same to you? I get it. I do. I know why you ran to him. But I just . . ." Cain scrubbed his hand over his face, looking down at her face, which was cradled on his bicep. "I want to move on from that day. I don't want to look back."

She sighed, leaning against him. "Me too. I want to move on, but . . . Cain?"

"Yeah, baby?"

"You think we're only bound by grief?"

He pressed his lips to her forehead. "Darlin', I'm not even sure I know what that means."

"Remember at the BBQ? We were spittin' mad at each other. We could barely be civil. Now here we are, goin' out on a date. Are we just doin' this because we both miss Woodman and we're sad and we lost him and we're turnin' to each other in our grief?" She gulped and he felt it against his chest. "And then, one day, we won't be as sad anymore, and then you'll remember I was the whore who told you she loved you and slept with your cousin, and I'll remember you were the heartless bastard who threw my love back in my face."

"Is that how you feel about me?" He knew his voice was rough, but it ached to hear her describe herself and him in such stark and awful terms.

She looked up at him, held his eyes in the dim light, and shook her head. "No. Not anymore. Not at all." She sucked her bottom lip between her teeth and held it for a moment. Her voice was barely a whisper when she asked, "But is that how you still see me? On some level?"

"Not even a little," he said sadly, "and I fuckin' hate it that we ever felt that way about each other at all."

She was quiet for a moment before saying, "Maybe . . . maybe we had to be there to get here."

He nodded, leaning back so he could at her face, just inches from his own. "We're bound by somethin' much stronger than grief, Gin. We're bound by memories and dreams and rides in the rain and skippin' stones. By knowin' each other as little kids and stupid, dreamy teenagers. By destroyin' each other but still not bein' able to let go. *I can't stop thinkin' about you.* And some of the time—fuck, *most* of the time—I'm pretty sure that I was *made* for you and you were *made* for me because there ain't another woman in the world who affects me like you do. Maybe you're right. Maybe we had to go through the bad to get to the good."

He searched her eyes, his heart hammering as he lost himself in her gaze, surrendered himself to her warmth, which took the icy shards of their broken hearts and was somehow putting them back together. "I don't know why or how. I only know this: We're *bound*, princess. That's all I know."

He watched her eyes as he leaned forward, as he kissed Ginger McHuid for the fourth time in his life.

The first time she'd been a twelve-year-old kid, and he'd kissed her cheek on her birthday, stunned by the unexpected jolt of electricity between them . . . and he'd run from her, unable to process his sudden feelings for her.

The second time had been her first kiss. *You still want that first kiss?* Her sweet, untried lips had parted for his, and it was like no one had ever come before and no one could ever come after. And yet again he'd run away from the overwhelming feeling of want, of more, of knowing that no other woman could ever be what Ginger was to his heart. He'd known it with every mile he'd placed between them.

The third time? *Cain, Cain, Cain . . . I love you. God, I love you so much.* His kiss had been desperate, had been angry, fierce and wild and unrestrained, because he loved her madly but he couldn't have her. Because she was sweet and open and offering him everything his heart had ever wanted. He had kissed her knowing he couldn't have her, and it had just about broken him as he pushed her into Woodman's arms and rode off into the night.

But Cain was no longer a child or a cocky kid or an angry young man who couldn't have his heart's desire. And there would be no running this time. Or ever again.

He cupped her face between his hands, staring into her dark eyes until they closed, until his lips touched down on hers, pursing gently as he groaned in a frustrating mix of satisfaction and hunger. Softly she licked his top lip, then pulled back. As he leaned in again, she gently bit his bottom lip, and Cain's self-control snapped. He threaded his fingers through the soft strands of her golden hair as she leaned her neck back and opened her mouth for him. As his lips sealed over hers and his tongue slid slowly against the velvet heat of hers, she released the breath she'd been holding—he heard it and he felt it and he tasted the sweetness of it as it slipped from her body into his and became part of him.

She'd been sitting on his lap with her back against the driver's door and her feet on the passenger seat, but now she turned into him, pressing her breasts against his chest as her hands slid up the front of his shirt and flanked his throat, pulling him closer.

Ginger, Ginger, Ginger . . . I love you. God, I love you so much.

He tilted her head back and leaned forward, running his lips along her jaw to her throat. Pausing over her raging pulse, he listened to the rapid in and out of her breathing, the tiny whimper that told him she liked what he was doing, the way she arched into him and leaned her neck back farther, straining the muscles of her throat so he could kiss the smooth planes.

"Princess," he murmured against her skin, a plea, and she guided his head still lower. He pushed the elastic hem of her blouse down, kissing along the edge of her black bra as he wrapped his arms around her.

"Cain," she moaned. "Cain . . ."

"Fuuuck, I want you, Gin," he groaned, skimming his lips back up to claim hers again, this time harder, more insistent.

He wanted her naked and panting beneath him. He wanted to drive into her soft cunt with his rock-hard cock and watch her eyes roll back in her head while her nails drew blood from his back. She met his hunger with her own, clutching at his face as he pulled her closer. Except he couldn't get her close enough. He couldn't feel her flush against his body, couldn't feel her soft places cradling his hardness, couldn't feel the soft warmth of her skin pressed against him, and it wasn't enough. Not by a fucking mile.

"This fuckin' car!" he burst out, leaning away from her and staring into her surprised eyes, which popped open when he barked in frustration.

Suddenly her whole face split into a smile, and she licked her slick, swollen lips as she stared at him, caressing his throat as she gently slid her hands back down.

"You just kissed me. Again."

"Get used to it," he growled.

She took a deep breath and released it, leaning forward to kiss him again. As she pulled back, she searched his eyes with a wonder he shared.

"I'm goin' to do that whenever I want to," she promised.

Her eyes sparkled with happiness, and he couldn't help smiling back at her, even though his heart ached with love for her and his body was taut and raging with longing.

"You better."

Easing herself off his lap, she scooted back over to her seat. He reached across her body, grazing the tips of her very erect nipples with the back of his hand, to grab her seat belt and buckle it, smirking with satisfaction when she gasped from the contact.

"Fuuuuuck," he hissed, shaking his head and feeling slightly sorry for himself. He couldn't keep his fucking eyes off her now, and his body was so hard and so hungry, it was almost painful. But they were in a car and needed to get somewhere private before he could take what he was sure she was offering. "I was goin' to take you to my place and order some takeout. Does that still sound okay?"

Or how about we skip the takeout, get in my bed, and fuck all weekend?

"Ummm . . ." She did a nod–shrug combination. "Or we can go to my place. I don't care where we go. I just want to be with you."

He would have thought that words like that—*I just want to be with you*—from the princess, from the forbidden girl of his dreams, would make him even needier, even greedier, but it did just the opposite: it soothed the starving beast inside him. She wanted *him*. The princess wanted *him*, the little boy who wasn't allowed at the parties, whose father scrubbed her father's horse stalls, whose cousin had been the golden boy, who had been the hell-raiser and troublemaker.

She still loved him after all this time, and Cain, who'd lived most of his life fucking without loving, suddenly understood that he stood at the precipice of *making love* for the first time in his life, and his heart quaked with the knowledge that whatever was going to happen between him and Ginger would be a first for him, would be a new beginning.

"Cain? My place?"

He grinned at her. "You still have those frozen pizzas fillin' up your freezer?"

She lowered her lashes and peeked up at him. "And here I

thought you might be hungry for somethin' else."

He tightened everywhere, his swollen cock pressing painfully against the zipper of his jeans and his breathing going all shallow and sharp. Was she offering him sex? Now? Tonight? Already? His heart thudded dangerously. "Gin . . ."

"You know . . ." She winced before shaking her head and grinning at him sheepishly. "I shouldn't have said that. I mean . . . I want you to come over. S-stay over. I want us to be toge— um, oh, God, I don't even know if we're . . ."

"Together? Is that what you were goin' to say?"

She full on cringed. "Sort of. Yeah."

"Fuck, Gin, after makin' out like that? With the thoughts goin' through my head right now? I fuckin' *hope* we're together, even if it has to be a goddamned secret for now."

"But Cain, I'm not ready to . . . I mean, I need some—only a little—time. I've only been with . . . um, maybe we could just . . ." She sucked her bottom lip between her teeth, and his eyes darted to it greedily. ". . . fool around tonight?"

"Oh." His eyes widened with understanding, and he looked up and grinned at her. "Whatever you want, princess." He chuckled softly because she looked so adorable and he loved her so madly. "How 'bout this? I'll keep my jeans on."

Her lips widened into a relieved smile as her shoulders relaxed. "Me too."

"But that's *all* I'm keepin' on," he warned her.

She lifted her eyebrows, all sweet and sassy. "Me too."

Fuuuuuuuck.

He turned the key in the ignition, and fuck if his cock *and* his foot weren't suddenly made of lead at the exact same time.

Chapter 31

When she walked into the office at Wolfram's Motorcycles on Tuesday morning, a massive bouquet of wildflowers was waiting for her on the desk. Cain looked up from his laptop, waiting for her, his eyes hot and liquid.

"Close the door and lock it."

She blinked, her breath catching, and her panties flooded with wet warmth.

She pushed the door closed and turned the lock. As soon as it clicked shut, she felt the heat of his body behind her, watched his hands slap the wood of the door, landing flat on either side of her head, caging her in. She inhaled sharply when she felt the bulge behind his jeans grind into her ass, but turned around slowly so that her breasts purposely raked across the hard planes of his chest.

"I missed you," he said, pressing her against the back of the door with his body and slamming his lips into hers.

They'd made out all weekend, but Cain had been as good as his word, keeping his jeans on the whole time, though he'd been so swollen and hard behind the zipper, she was fairly sure she would have seen teeth marks on his cock given the chance.

She had also kept her jeans on, though her shirt, like his, had come off, and he'd spent the weekend proving to her that it was possible to orgasm from having your breasts loved, which was something she'd never known before. Something that made her nipples bead with anticipation now.

His tongue, so skilled in making her boneless and pliant, swept into her mouth like he owned it, and the thing is, he did. He owned just about whatever part of her he cared to claim, and she was almost out of the strength it would take to make him wait much longer to take everything.

Hands.

Over the weekend she'd learned that his hands were warm but coarse, chapped and dry, the rough texture wringing more pleasure from her sensitive, silky skin than they would if they were soft like hers.

He ran his hands from her throat, slowly and deliberately over her breasts, to the hem of her sweater, slipping underneath it to land on the bare skin of her waist. While his tongue savaged her mouth, his hands met on her back, his fingers unfastening her bra with a practiced flick, and she raised her arms without being asked so he could pull off her sweater and toss it, along with the bra, on the floor.

"Ginger," he groaned, wedging his knee between her legs and dropping his lips to her nipple. "A day away from you is too long . . ."

"Ahh," she whimpered as he latched onto the erect bud, sucking it into his mouth and rolling it between his upper lip and tongue. "Caaaaaaain . . ."

"You taste like sugar, darlin'. You make me crazy."

As he laved his tongue over the slick nub, he cupped her cheek and slipped his thumb into her mouth, and she sucked it eagerly, imitating the pressure he used on her nipple and finally releasing it with a pop.

He dropped the glistening digit to her already slick and distended nipple, circling it slowly as he circled the other with the tip of his tongue. Maddeningly slow, his tongue traced her areola, and she arched her back, desperate for him to take her nipple between his lips and suck. Just when she thought she might go crazy, he licked the hard bud, then blew on it softly, and she cried out, not quite in orgasm, but because the sensation was so strong and so good and so frustratingly not enough. Her hunger was increasing. What had made her come on Sunday wasn't enough on Tuesday.

"Cain," she whimpered as he flicked his thumb over her nipple. "I need . . . I need more . . ."

"I know, baby," he said, dropping one hand to the button of her jeans and twisting it open with his fingers. He flattened his hand over the zipper and murmured close to her ear, "Weekend's over. Are you okay with the jeans comin' off? If you want me to stop, say stop."

She was wet and aching, and her jeans were going to have to come off to relieve the pitch of her desire.

"Don't stop."

"I'm goin' to love you with my tongue, baby."

"Oh, my God . . ."

"You've done this?"

"N-no, but I need you."

"You're sure, baby?"

"Cain, *please*."

Her breathing quickened to a pant as he dropped his hand, releasing the fullness of her breast, and fell to his knees before her. He yanked her jeans and panties to her knees, then cupped her ass and jerked her forward, keeping her back braced against the door as he pulled her legs over his shoulders. She let her hands slip over her damp, erect nipples, over the soft skin of her stomach, and reached down to part the folds of her sex with her fingers. Cain leaned forward, and Ginger's head fell back against the office door as his tongue licked her clit in one long, slow stroke.

"Ohhh," she moaned, the sound like dying, like crying, like shock and surprise and heaven.

With her hands on either side of his head, she guided him gently back and forth, up and down, his tongue brushing against her with increasing pressure as his fingers kneaded her ass, pushing her sex into his face and then letting her slide away.

The muscles deep inside her body were stretched taut and tight, like violin strings twisted to a hair's breadth of snapping, when he leaned his head all the way back and fucked her with his tongue, one hand holding her up as the other reached around and pinched her clit.

"*Cain!*"

She screamed his name as she exploded in wild waves, trembling and shaking, her insides flooding hot and wet, coating his tongue and his lips as she rode out the most complete and profound orgasm of her life.

Finally, as the tremors began to subside, she felt her feet hit the floor and his arms anchor her to his body as he stood up. She leaned against him, limp and loose and utterly sated.

"Catch your breath, baby. I'm doin' that to you again in ten minutes."

Her eyes fluttered open, and she looked up at him, laughing softly at the lazy, self-satisfied look in his clear blue eyes as he gazed down at her.

"Promise?" she asked, breathless and trembling.

"Fuck, yeah. That was the hottest fuckin' thing I've ever seen in my life."

She took a shaky breath and smiled at him, leaning up on her tiptoes to kiss him, when the phone rang.

"Ignore it," he growled.

"Cain," she said, gasping as he rolled her nipple between his thumb and forefinger. "I should answer it."

"No. We should kiss again."

She covered his hand, pressing it against her sensitive, bare skin but gently stilling his movements. "You'll lose business."

"Good. I have enough." His eyes were so dark, she could barely make out the ring of ice blue. "What I don't have is enough of you, princess. I'll *never* get enough of you."

The phone rang again, and she leaned forward to press another kiss to his lips, then reached down to pull up her panties and jeans. She grabbed her sweater off the floor to cover her breasts as she stepped over to the desk and picked up the phone.

"Wolfram's Motorcycles . . . Uh-huh. Yes, I see." She covered the mouthpiece, turning to Cain, who looked fiercely annoyed with her. "Are you gettin' any new Harleys in stock?"

He shook his head, swiping at his bottom lip with his thumb, then sucking it into his mouth as he stared at her.

"Cain?" she prompted, refusing to be distracted by him, refusing to let him lose business because he was distracted by her.

He huffed, glaring at her in surrender. "No, but I can place a special order. Take a message. I'll call them back."

"Why don't I take your name and number and have Cain call you back?"

She tucked the phone between her shoulder and ear and

jotted down a quick message, overwhelmingly aware of Cain's eyes boring into her back and loving how much she affected him.

"Thank you. Yes. Later today. Good-bye."

She turned around to find Cain still standing where she'd left him, a troubled expression on his face. He was unsatisfied, and he was running low on patience. And hell, if she was honest, so was she.

"Soon, Cain," she said, understanding him just as well as she always had. "I promise."

He exhaled, stepped toward her, taking the bra out of her hands. "Hold out your arms."

He threaded her arms through the loops and pulled them up to her shoulders, then dipped his head and kissed each swollen nipple gently before fastening her bra in the back. He took her balled-up sweater from her hands and shook it out, placing it carefully over her head and holding the arms out for her.

"Never had to wait . . .," he said softly, almost more to himself than to her as he helped her get dressed.

A tiny part of her bristled, and she almost said, *Well, sorry I'm not one of your high school sluts, ready and willin' on a moment's notice.*

He watched her eyes flare, and she watched the sexiest mouth in the world turn up in a slow grin as his arms wound around her waist.

"Don't get your back up, princess. I didn't finish."

"So finish," she said pertly, smoothing her shirt and giving him a pissy look.

He pulled her closer so that her breasts were crushed against his chest, and the long length of his erect cock pressed against the valley of her sex. But despite their shared arousal, his stormy eyes were focused and intense, holding hers captive with the sort of longing that made her heart thunder with love for him.

"I never had to wait," he said softly, "until you. And for you, darlin', I'd wait until I ran out of days. And when I ran out of days, I'd wait for you in heaven. And when you got there, through every eternity, I'd wait for you and your lion's heart to give me another chance, to choose me again."

"Cain . . ."

"I love you," he said in a gravelly whisper, furrowing his brow like it hurt a little to say the words. "I've loved you for so long, I don't know how to stop. I don't want anyone else, princess. Not ever. When you're ready, I'm ready. And until then . . . I'll wait."

Her breath caught.

Her heart clutched.

I've loved you for so long, I don't know how to stop.

She'd waited for words like these for most of her life, and now—suddenly here and now—they'd arrived.

Before she could answer, he leaned down and kissed her lips, gently, tenderly, slowly, and then he dropped his arms, stepped around her, and left the office.

She looked over her shoulder to find him gone, then moved slowly, in a semidaze, to the desk chair. Plopping down, she leaned back as tears filled her eyes and a laugh born of unexpected happiness started deep in her belly and rumbled up through her throat, to her lips, filling the room with a sound of disbelief and joy.

He loved her.

Cain Holden Wolfram, whom she'd loved every day of her life since she was eleven years old, finally loved her back.

"*He loves me*," she whispered. She giggled, stomping her feet on the carpet under the desk, and then said it louder, "He loves me!"

"Yes, he does!" he barked from the showroom. "Now do some damn work, or I'm comin' in there, and this time we're not unlockin' the door until tomorrow mornin'!"

Her face flamed red, but she grinned, whispering, "Yep. He loves me" one more time for good measure and just to hear the words aloud.

Her body still quaked and trembled deep, deep inside, where he'd set off a chain reaction after owning her with his fingers and his tongue, where he'd loved her until she'd screamed his name. And a dreamy smile was plastered on her face for the remainder of the day. Well, for most of the day.

It was the third week since Wolfram's Motorcycles had opened, and clearly the word was out that a superhot young motorcycle mechanic was in town because every local female with a car, and several with bicycles and scooters, had stopped in with a "problem." At present, she had four women waiting to see her boss.

Flirtatiously: "Can Cain take a look at my gears?"

Conspiratorially: "Is Mr. Wolfram as hot as they say?"

Insecurely: "So is he single, or does he have a girlfriend?"

Queen Bee: "I heard Mr. Wolfram is here today. Tell him I need to see him. Now."

That last one made Ginger roll her eyes, but she'd asked the strawberry-blonde bombshell in the ridiculously short miniskirt to take a seat as she went looking for Cain, and found him in the supply room behind the showroom, looking for a ball bearing.

"Cain?"

He turned to face her, his beautiful face lighting up. "Please make my day and tell me you want a quickie in the supply closet?"

"You want our first time to be in a dingy supply closet?" she asked, putting her hands on her hips and arching one eyebrow.

He snaked an arm around her waist and pulled her against his body. "I *want* our first time to be three years ago, but I fucked that up so . . ."

"So a supply closet will do?" She hooked her thumb to the left. "What? Up against the spare tires?"

He made a face and huffed softly, letting her go. "Well, if you came here to torture me, go on back to the office. I'm goin' crazy as it is."

"Poor baby," she said, dropping her voice and keeping it kitten soft and smooth. She reached for his face and caressed his jaw.

"Gin," he groaned. "Don't tease me. My heart can't take it, and my cock's about to break off."

He looked so pitiful and adorable, she leaned up and licked his lips, meeting his tongue with hers as they opened. His arms came around her again, holding her fiercely as he dropped whatever was in his hand, and the soft ping of metal hitting the floor competed with their sighs and moans. When she was dizzy and breathless, she broke away, leaning her head on his shoulder, marveling at the way her body responded to his as she'd never been able to respond to his cousin's. She was primed and ready for him. Waiting was painful, but she couldn't help it. She wanted her first time with Cain to be special.

"Come home with me later," he said, sliding his lips down her neck, pursing them over her skin, his tongue darting out to lick tiny circles that made her shiver. "Stay over tonight."

"I wish I could," she half whispered, half moaned. "But I have an early shift tomorrow, and Gran's not doin' well. She's havin' some tests. I want to be there for her."

"I'll come up tomorrow and stay with you."

"I have to concentrate on her for a day or two, Cain, and you are way too distractin'," she said, smiling into his eyes with all the old and new love filling her heart. "But I'll be back here on Friday. I promise. And . . ."

"And?" He stopped, pausing his tender ministrations, his lips hovering over her skin and his hot breath making her shiver.

"I don't have to work this Sunday." She swallowed. "I'm free this weekend."

"Okay," he said, leaning away from her, his wide eyes black and blue. "But pack a bag and stay with me till Monday morning. *All weekend*, Gin. I want you all weekend long."

She saw it in his eyes, what he meant, what it would mean for her to stay with him all weekend. Their bodies fused together as every last barrier between them finally came down forever. That's how they'd be, and that's what she wanted too . . . all weekend long.

She shivered in anticipation, then nodded. As she turned to leave, she remembered why she'd come looking for him in the first place.

"By the way, there's a horde of women in the office. They all want to see you."

"Legit business?"

Nope. Ginger shrugged.

"Okay," he said. He looked down at his crotch, which looked bulging and strained. "Give me a couple of minutes to think about baseball, huh?"

"Friday," she whispered, grinning at him before walking back to the office with an ache of her own.

"Mr. Wolfram will be here in a minute, ladies. May I get you coffee?"

When they all declined, she sat down at her desk and looked them over. They were all pretty in their own ways, though the Queen Bee was the prettiest, and Ginger had a sudden pang of worry that Cain would see her and run off, leaving her in the dust. She looked about ten times more experienced than Ginger too, confident in her own skin, and Ginger bet that she'd had about a million orgasms from enthusiastic lovers, and knew exactly what to do in bed to pleasure a man.

Cain? He loved pleasure.

And Ginger? She'd never known anything but mediocre sex with a friend.

What if she wasn't enough for him? She certainly wasn't anywhere near as experienced as he was. He'd been bedding women since his early teens, and Ginger had only ever been with Woodman. What if she wasn't good in bed? What if she and Cain had sex and it was just as bland and boring as it had been with Woodman?

She got up and made herself a cup of coffee, covertly looking at the Queen Bee, who flipped through a magazine, looking up at the office door every few minutes and sighing her annoyance. Ginger's breasts weren't as large, her waist wasn't as small, and she wasn't anywhere near as tall.

"Humph," Ginger muttered, pouring a little milk in her coffee and sitting back down at the desk.

Wait until they see him up close and start batting their eyes at him. She was making him wait until Friday, when she was positive that any woman in this room would have let him take her against the spare tires in the supply room with a great big grin on her face. Shoot. Damn it. Why was she making him wait? Why was she risking what was growing between them?

And then suddenly there he was, standing in the doorway of the office. She felt him, but she also heard the dreamy sighs from at least two of the four women waiting.

"Afternoon, ladies," said Cain, standing in front of the four women waiting in guest chairs. "My *girlfriend*, Ginger, here, told me y'all were lookin' for a motorcycle mechanic. That right?"

Ginger's lips trembled as she watched two of the women—Conspiratorially and Insecurely—quickly deflate at the news of Cain's "girlfriend." One of them made an excuse about needing a car mechanic, and the other said she thought he serviced bicycles too. When he politely referred one to a garage down the street and the other to the local bike shop, he was left with two.

Flirtatiously stuck out her boobs, sucked a finger into her mouth, and asked if Cain would check her gears.

"Sure," he said, nodding. "For gear problems, I charge four hundred dollars an hour. If you'll go ahead and give Ginger your credit card, I can schedule you for a—"

"*Four hundred dollars?*" she cried, her finger falling forgotten to her side. "Forget it!"

She stomped out of the office, leaving Cain, Ginger, and Queen Bee alone. Ginger braced herself. Queen Bee was five-foot-nine, tan even though it was winter, with straight reddish-blonde hair and bright green eyes. She was stunning and she knew it.

"Mr. Wolfram," she said, holding out her hand. "I'm Saffron Barnett. But my friends call me Saffy."

"Miss Barnett, I'm Cain," he said warmly, taking her hand and shaking it.

Ginger tightened her jaw, her fingers curling into fists, her eyes fixed on Cain's hand in Queen Bee Saffy's grasp.

"Seein' as how you're new in town and I'm the assistant to the head of the Versailles Chamber of Commerce, I thought that maybe we could grab some dinner on Friday and . . ." She chuckled, her low, sexy voice a suggestive rumble. ". . . you know, see what happens."

Cain smiled at her, pumping her hand one more time before dropping it.

"Miss Barnett? You see that gal sittin' over there? You couldn't have missed her. She's the prettiest, sweetest girl in the whole world, and I've been in love with her for as long as I can remember. You see her, right?"

Miss Barnett gave Ginger a frosty glance, then cleared her throat. "I noticed her, yes."

"Well, I don't go out to dinner unless she's doin' the arrangin' and ends up sittin' beside me while we dine. So I'm goin' to get back to work now. And if you'd like to schedule that dinner with Ginger, I'm sure she'd be glad to accommodate you on *our* schedule." He looked at Ginger. "Right, baby?"

With that, Cain gave Ginger a sexy smile, winked at her, then turned and left the office.

"Did you want to schedule—" started Ginger, squelching a grin and opening Cain's calendar.

Miss Barnett picked up her purse and gave Ginger a snotty smirk. "It'll keep for another day. Take care, now."

As she flounced away, Ginger's heart swelled with so much love, it spilled into every crack and crevice of her body, until she was warm all over, and she knew—beyond any shadow of doubt—it didn't matter how inexperienced she was. She wouldn't disappoint Cain, because he loved her. And because some things—no matter how long they take to finally happen—are simply meant to be.

Chapter 32

"Ranger, Miz Ginger, good to see y'all. Why don't you come on into my office and we'll have a chat about Kelleyanne."

Ginger followed her father into Dr. Sheridan's office and took a seat across from him at one of three guest chairs.

The doctor opened the file on his desk and sighed, looking up at the McHuids with sympathy in his eyes.

"Kelleyanne has entered what we call the end stage of Parkinsons. Ranger, I know you've noticed that she's become more disoriented lately."

Ginger's father cleared his throat. "Just lately, in the past couple of weeks. She asks about my sister, Amy, who passed away as a child. Asks to see her."

Dr. Sheridan nodded. "That's common. Even expected. I fear it's goin' to go quickly now." He turned to Ginger. "She's been incontinent for a while now, and we've had some issues with chokin'. I need to recommend . . ."—Ginger's heart dropped—". . . a feedin' tube. It's just safer."

Safer, but it meant that Gran wouldn't be able to talk very much anymore. It would tickle her throat and bother her to talk, which essentially meant that their wonderful, long talks would be over.

"When?" she asked.

"I've scheduled it for tomorrow. Kelleyanne knows. Can't say she was pleased, but she's been fadin' in and out lately, as you've noted, Ranger. I won't beat about the bush. She's gettin' weaker, folks. It's gettin' harder for her to breathe, harder for her to swallow. You need to prepare yourselves." Dr. Sheridan's voice was kind and level, but Ginger felt the words like a vise around her heart. Her two most beloved friends—one gone, one almost gone—and she'd be so terribly lost without both of them.

"How long does she have?" asked Ranger, blinking furiously.

"A few weeks, I think," said Dr. Sheridan. "Maybe a month. Not much more'n that. And she'll be more and more out of it, I'm afraid. But we can keep her comfortable. Make her final days as easy as possible."

Ginger's father swiped at his eyes, then slapped his hands on his knees. "Thanks, doc. I know you did all you could for her."

"Take some time with her tonight, Ranger. You too, Ginger. Talkin' will be harder after tomorrow."

Ginger gulped, nodding at the doctor before turning to her father.

"Why don't you go first, Ginger?" said Ranger. "Doc, if it's okay with you, I'll stay with her tonight. Until the procedure tomorrow."

"Course," said the doctor. "If Ginger wants to spend a bit of time with her grandmother now, you could go get somethin' to eat and come back in a few hours. I'll let the nurses know you'll be stayin' over. They can bring in a cot for you."

"I'd appreciate that."

"Daddy, I can stay too," said Ginger, but her father shook his head and reached over to squeeze her hand.

"No, baby. She's my momma. It'll just be me and her."

Ginger nodded. "I understand."

Ginger left her father and Dr. Sheridan to discuss the details of tomorrow's procedure and headed to the elevator. She'd go on up to Gran's room and stay with her for a while, hopefully have one last conversation.

When she entered the room, Gran was sitting up in bed, her face slack, staring straight ahead.

"Gran?"

"Amy," she said, her voice soft and breathy.

"No, Gran. It's me. It's Ginger."

"Oh, Ginger." She looked up at her granddaughter, her eyes taking a moment to spark recognition. "*Ginger*. How . . . are you, d-doll b-baby?"

Ginger pulled a chair over to Gran's bedside and sat down beside her. She reached for grandmother's bony hand and held it gently.

"I'm fine. How're *you* feelin'?"

"Tired," she sighed, closing her eyes for a moment.

Ginger gulped softly, blinking her eyes to hold back the tears.

"You look . . . m-miserable," said Gran.

"I'm goin' to miss you so much," said Ginger, laying her head on the bed beside her grandmother's frail body.

"We been . . . g-good friends . . . you and me."

"The best."

"B-but," she said, each word coming slowly and softly and taking strength Gran probably didn't have to spare. "You're . . . g-gonna b-be . . . okay." She paused for a moment, then Ginger heard her gasp softly. "C-Cain . . . y-you're here."

Ginger lifted her head and turned around in shock to find Cain, dressed in jeans and a button-down shirt, standing in the doorway of her grandmother's room with a bouquet of flowers by his side. His face was concerned, almost grave, but he managed a smile for Gran as he approached the bed, and Ginger had to physically restrain herself from launching her body into his arms and sagging against the strength he could offer.

"Came to see you, Miz Kelleyanne."

"You are . . . t-too handsome." She looked at his hands. "F-flowers."

He nodded, laying them on a rolling table at the foot of her bed.

"What are you *doin'* here?" asked Ginger, wiping away the tears that spilled down her cheeks. She looked up at his face, her gratitude so overwhelming, it almost made her light-headed.

"You said your Gran was havin' tests. Thought maybe . . ." He shrugged, squatting down beside the chair where she was sitting and resting his hands on her knees. "Thought maybe you could use a friend."

"A friend?"

His eyes flared with heat for a moment before he nodded. "A friend. Tonight you don't need a distraction. You just need a friend who loves you."

The word *friend* had worried her for a moment, but chased by a reminder of his love for her, it meant that he was restraining his desire for her tonight, and was here just as support. And it meant more to her than he could ever know.

"Thank you," she managed to whisper, her tears breaking the words.

He leaned forward and planted a quick kiss on her lips

before drawing back.

"You look . . . g-good together," said Gran, watching them from her hospital bed. "Like you . . . f-finally f-found . . . your way."

"I think we have, Gran," said Ginger, no longer trying to stop the tears that were rolling down her cheeks.

Cain took her hand, threading their fingers together, and Ginger fairly sighed at the unconditional love and gentle support he was offering her tonight. She didn't know how desperately she'd needed him until he arrived, and now that he was here, she felt that she could handle anything.

"W-why you c-cryin' . . . Ginger? Is . . . someone . . . d-dyin'?" Kelleyanne couldn't smile anymore, but Ginger could almost hear the familiar lilt of a smile in her tired, breathless voice. "Whoever it is . . . I hope . . . they had . . . as g-good a . . . l-life as m-me."

After such a long speech, she sighed, long and hard, and it almost broke Ginger to see her strong, resilient grandmother fading so fast.

"Now, y'all . . . send in . . . R-Ranger and Amy . . . t-to see their . . . m-momma." Her eyes fluttered closed as she sighed with a long, labored breath. "C-Cain . . . t-take care . . . of m-my . . . l-lionhearted . . . l'il g-gal."

Her voice wilted and weakened on the last words until *gal* was almost the breath of a whisper.

"Yes, ma'am," said Cain. "I will. I promise."

Ginger still clasped his hand as she stood up, leaning down to kiss her grandmother's sleeping face before letting him lead her from the room. As soon as they were in the hallway, Cain's strong arms wound around her, pulling her against his chest. Her forehead landed just below his shoulder as silent sobs racked her body.

He held her tightly and rubbed her back. He said, "Go on and cry, darlin'" and "It's okay, baby" and "Cain's got you, Gin," until her tears were spent and she took a deep, sobbing breath, looking up into his face.

"You will never know—I will never be able to express—what it means to me that you came here tonight, Cain," she said, shaking her head as she reached up to cradle his face, "I love you. I never stopped. I never will."

He gasped lightly, furrowing his brows together as he had yesterday, when he told her he loved her. And then he exhaled, letting the words "You love me" catch a ride on the long release of breath.

She nodded. "I do. I always have."

He pulled her closer, his lips near her ear, his voice strangled with emotion. "Thank God. You love me."

"I don't know how to live without lovin' you, Cain Wolfram. Promise me . . . promise me you'll never break my heart again."

"I promise," he said. "Your heart's been broken enough for two lifetimes, princess. From now on, we keep it whole. *I'll* keep it whole, 'cause it's mine now."

She rested her weary head against his chest, amazed that such a beautiful, long-awaited moment between them would happen in the corridor of a hospital, with her gran's days dwindling down so quickly nearby.

But then, she thought, this is a moment that matters, *really* matters: a moment when life has served up a platter of cold awful, and the man who loves you takes a seat beside you at the table to eat his share of your sorrow.

This is the moment you know that you can trust him, that

you can trust his love, and that your heart will be safe within his keeping, Ginger. This—right here, right now—is the first moment of your forever with Cain Wolfram.

"Gin," he said, pressing a gentle kiss to her hair, "if you can't make Friday . . . if you need to be here . . ."

"No, Cain," she whispered. "Friday's ours."

"I'd understand, princess," he said, his voice strained but level.

"I know you would," she said, leaning away from his chest to smile at him through her tears. "But she still has a little time left. And I *want* to be with you." She leaned up on tiptoe and pulled his face down to hers. "I *need* to be with you."

***

Cain was *buzzing* on Friday.

He'd woken up at the crack of dawn and gone for a five-mile run before heading home for an hour of free weights. The Navy had been an opportunity to get his ass in tip-top shape, and he wasn't about to let himself go now that he'd embarked on civilian life. But the whole time he was running and lifting, one thought buzzed in his head: *She's all mine as of seven o'clock tonight. All mine.*

Ginger arrived on time at noon, her cheeks flushing pink when they made eye contact in the garage bay as she walked into the showroom, and it was so fucking cute, he had to keep himself from reaching for her in front of the customers who'd arrived early. *You're thinking the same thing I am, princess, and I hope you want it just as bad.*

The couple of times he saw her throughout the day, however, he noticed that her eyes didn't connect with his, and her lower-lip biting was at an all-time high. She was nervous and getting progressively more so as the clock ticked toward seven.

At this rate, she was going to be a wreck, and he didn't want that, so when he realized no one was in the office waiting, he slipped in and locked the door, standing against it as he stared at her from across the room.

She looked up and gulped, her eyes wide. "H-hi."

"Hi," he said, cutting to the chase. "Why are you so nervous?"

"I'm not," she said quickly, looking down at the desk, two bright red splotches of color appearing in her cheeks.

He couldn't help smiling at her. "Princess? This is one of those times you're goin' to hate me for knowin' you since you were in diapers. There are few people's faces I read as well as yours. You're nervous. And bad. Why?"

"Are you kiddin' me, Cain?" she asked, her voice filling with sass.

He put his hands on his hips and shook his head. "Nope."

"We're havin' *sex* tonight!"

"Fuck," he said, totally straight-faced. "We *are*?"

Her mouth dropped open. "Well, yeah . . . I mean . . . I thought . . . *aren't we*?"

"Huh. Well, I mean, we *can*," he said, "if you really want to."

She nailed him with a look, cocking her head to the side, her lips finally tilting up. "You're teasin' me."

He laughed. "Maybe."

"We're havin' sex tonight," she grumbled.

"Lord, I hope so. I been waitin' to feel you under me for years, darlin'."

She sucked in a hiss of breath, pressing her palms to her cheeks. "How can you say things like that out loud?"

He took a step toward her. "Like what? Like 'I want to see

what your face looks like when I slide into you'?"

Her eyes darkened and her breath became audible.

He took another step forward. "Like 'I want to hear what sounds you make when you come'?"

Her breasts rose and fell rapidly as she stared up at him.

He took another step forward, placing his fisted hands on the desk and leaning toward her. "Like 'I want to know how it feels to fall asleep with your naked body pressed up against mine'?"

"Cain," she whispered, licking her lips and pursing them together.

"What, baby?" he purred. "What?"

"What if I'm no good at it?" she burst out, her voice a desperate whimper.

He straightened up, staring at her in confusion. "Wait, *what*?"

She gulped, standing up and putting her knuckles on the desktop as he had a moment ago. "What if it's not good? What if . . ." She lowered her voice. "What if *I'm* not good?"

"At sex?" he clarified.

She nodded. "You've been with so many women. I mean, they all knew what they were doin', and I'm just . . . I'm . . ."

"Oh, baby," he sighed, moving quickly around the desk and pulling her into his arms. "You've been worryin' about this? About . . . disappointin' me?"

"I love you," she whispered, her eyes wide and uncertain. "I want . . . I want it to be good for you. For us."

He put his hand on the back of her head and guided it to his shoulder, then clenched his jaw, his eyes, trying to calm the raging feelings that the cage of his chest didn't feel large enough to contain. She was worried she wouldn't please him. Fuck. He didn't deserve her.

"Princess, you know why tonight is goin' to be good?"

"Why?" she asked, her voice small.

"Because you're not the only one in uncharted territory." He opened his eyes, looking at the blonde strands of her hair under his hand. "I've been with a lot of women, that's true. But I've never *made love* to anyone." She didn't say anything. "And as far as I can tell, neither have you." His heart pounded as if it belonged to some teenage kid following a girl down to her basement to make out for the first time. "Whatever happens tonight, it's goin' to be good because I love you. And because you love me. And it won't just be havin' sex. It'll be a lot more'n that."

She took a deep breath, her chest expanding, her breasts pushing into him, and he felt his blood race south to his cock.

"You know why else it's goin' to be good?" he growled.

"Why?" She was breathless now but more confident. His words were making sense to her, and it made him happy.

"Because you're wet right now. And I'm hard."

She gasped, turning her face toward his neck, her lips dragging against his skin. He swallowed, blinking his eyes, trying not to be pulled under by the sweetness of her touch.

"I'm right, aren't I?" he asked.

"Yes, y-you're right," she panted softly.

He slid his hand from her hair down her back to her hips, changing course to the waistband of her jeans and slipping one hand inside the front, under her panties, until he felt the soft, trimmed hair that covered her cunt. His palm lay flush against the hair, firmly covering her sex.

"And if I touched you . . . right there . . . right now . . . you'd come for me quick, darlin'."

Her breath was shallow and ragged as she arched into him. "Y-yes. Yes, I would."

He slipped his hand out of her jeans and took a step back, placing his other hand on her shoulder to steady her from lurching forward.

"Huh?" she whimpered, her eyes popping open, her mouth gaping.

"Tonight's goin' to be just fine," he said. "Stop worryin'."

Then he adjusted his pants, winked at her, and left the office.

***

Three hours later, sitting beside him in her car on the way to his place, Ginger couldn't help wanting a little revenge for the way he'd left her hot and aching, though she couldn't deny that he'd alleviated her worries. Or rather, he'd distracted her from them. Her body had been soaked and primed when he left her alone after teasing her, rotten bastard, and she'd had to go through the remainder of the workday so aroused, it almost hurt.

"I thought we could go to my place and order food," he said. "I'm not much of a cook."

She glanced at his profile. *Too handsome.* Gran was right. *But all hers.* Finally.

"That's fine."

In the backseat was her flowered duffel bag, packed with shorts and a T-shirt for sleeping, her sexiest underwear, two pairs of jeans, two blouses, a soft, off-the-shoulder sweater, and her favorite fuzzy socks. It had felt exciting, and a little naughty, packing a bag to stay at Cain's place all weekend. And *right.* Oh, so right.

"You mad at me?" he asked. "About earlier?"

She sighed, staring straight ahead out the window. "It was

a mean trick."

"You still worried?"

She gave him side eyes, feeling ornery. "No."

"Then, mission accomplished." He chuckled softly and turned on the radio to country music. "And you better get your fill of me this weekend, darlin', because I will not be around next weekend."

She turned to him. "What? Where're you goin'?"

Old insecurities about Cain leaving rose quickly to the surface, but she forced herself to stay calm. *He's not runnin'. He's not runnin'. He loves me. He doesn't do that anymore.*

"Reserves trainin'," he said. "NOSC in Louisville, to be exact. I'm leavin' on Wednesday. Back on Saturday night."

"Oh," she said, her shoulders relaxing. "I didn't . . . I didn't realize you were still . . ."

"In the service? Aw, I doubt they'll deploy me again for a while, princess. But yeah, I'm goin' to keep my foot in with the Reserves. I liked it."

"You did, didn't you?" she said, turning slightly to face him. "And it was good for you."

He nodded. "Made me grow up. Learn how to be a better man."

"You were never a bad man, Cain."

"You were the only one who saw the good in me, once upon a time." They stopped at a traffic light, and he turned to her. "You *always* saw the good in me, Gin."

"There was always good to see," she said.

He stepped on the gas when the light turned green. "Raisin' hell down at the distillery? Screwin' my way through high school? Drinkin' until my momma called Woodman to come and find me? Breakin' the heart of the sweetest girl I ever knew?" He shook his head. "I was no good. I was trouble, baby."

"You weren't a saint," she agreed. "But you weren't the devil either."

He turned left, drove by a fountain, waved at the guard who raised a gate for them, and continued straight ahead, by rows and rows of lovely, landscaped, manicured townhouses in a posh, private community.

"*This* . . . this is where you live?"

He didn't answer, but she watched his lips twitch as he suppressed a smile. They drove for a half mile or so, past a clubhouse, a pool, and tennis courts, before he turned right, down Nightingale Lane, stopping at number 12 and pulling into the driveway.

"Home, sweet home," he said, cutting the engine and turning to grin at her.

"Cain!" she said, smiling back at him. "This is beautiful!"

He nodded. "I need to be honest with you. When I bought this place? The only person I was thinkin' of was you. I wanted you to like it, to feel comfortable here. Somethin' about it—aw, I don't know—somethin' about it sort of reminded me of McHuid's, I guess."

Her heart grew wings, fluttering in her chest as she processed his words. He'd bought this place for her, for *them*, knowing how much she would love it. She thought about him showing up at Gran's two nights ago, about how he'd pulled her from the depths of despair when she'd been grieving Woodman, and suddenly she saw him through six-year-old eyes, remembering how his black hair shone in the sun when he was nine and he told her to jump into his arms.

And right now, part of her wanted to jump again—to

launch her body across the seat, straddle his lap, and kiss him like the world was ending, but that would only delay what she *truly* wanted. She wanted *all* of him.

"Take me inside," she said, her voice husky and low.

His eyes darkened. "My pleasure."

He took the keys out of the ignition, walked around the car, and opened her door. Again, she kept herself from reaching for him, raking her teeth across her bottom lip in anticipation, and clasping her hands together so they'd behave. *We're almost there.*

He preceded her up the front walkway, unlocking the front door, then stepping back so she could go inside. She looked up at him as she crossed the threshold, stopping just for a moment.

"I love it here. I love everythin' about it."

He grinned. "I'm glad. I wanted you to—"

"I want to see the rest later. Right now, I want to see your bedroom," she said, her eyes focused on his like lasers, her body dictating her words, her voice ragged and hot. "We've waited long enough, Cain. I want to be with you."

His grin disappeared.

She took a step back as he followed her into the vestibule and kicked the door shut with the back of his foot.

The keys hit the floor at the same time he jerked her into his arms, his mouth slamming down on hers with such force, their teeth clashed, their bodies writhing to get closer, their breath shallow and rough as they reached for each other mindlessly. Turning her around, he backed her against the door, his tongue sweeping into her mouth, frantically sliding against hers as he pushed against her, his thick, hard erection pressing against her sex. She moaned, letting her head fall back, and felt Cain's hands at the buttons of her shirt.

"I'm sorry, baby," he panted, then ripped the two halves of the shirt apart, letting the buttons scatter all over his hardwood floor. "I can't go slow."

She scrambled for the front clasp of her bra, desperate to free her breasts for him, but he was faster, pushing the cups up and over her flesh and exposing two pebbled nipples. Her hands plunged into his short hair as he lowered his head and took one between his lips, sucking strongly as he rolled the other between his thumb and forefinger.

Whimpering from the sharpness of the sensation, she clawed at his skull, and he groaned, his teeth razing her nipple and making her cry out. Growling with impatience, his hands were suddenly cupping her ass, and he lifted her easily. She locked her ankles around his waist, clawing at the hem of his T-shirt as he strode through the house, to the stairs, ducking his head so that she could push his shirt over his head to bare his chest. The hard planes of his abs pushed into the softness of her breasts as he climbed the stairs, still nipping at her lips.

With one foot, he pushed open a door, and suddenly she was surrounded by Cain's smell—man and motor oil, cut grass and fresh air. As her feet touched the floor, he reached for her shirt and bra, pulling them over her head, then doing the same with his shirt, which was caught on the back of his neck.

Both bare from the waist up now, he grabbed her again, pulling her on top of him as he fell back onto the bed.

Taking a moment to catch her breath, Ginger sat up, straddling Cain, and smiled down at him.

"You are . . . the most beautiful thing I've ever seen," said Cain, pillowing his hands behind his head, his dimples deep and delighted.

She arched her back, cupping her breasts and pressing

them together.

"Fuuuuck," he growled. "And you are definitely goin' to kill me tonight."

"Not even," she murmured, sliding experimentally over the swollen bulge in his jeans. She leaned toward him a little and placed her hands on his hips, tracing the V of muscle that disappeared into his pants. "You are beautiful too."

He leaned up on his elbows. "What now?"

"You were my first kiss," she said, dropping her fingers to the button of his jeans and twisting it open. "And my first love," she said, pulling down the zipper.

She slipped her fingers into the waistband of his underwear and pulled both down at the same time, watching intently as she revealed his erection. His hair was jet black in coiled springs. His cock was huge and hard, twitching lightly like a bull ready to break out of its pen, with light blue veins bulging and twisting down its sides. She yanked again, and the ruby head sprang free, knobbed and throbbing.

Her eyes flicked to his for a moment—and she drowned in them a little as her hand slid around the base of his sex, her fingers clasping him firmly as they stared at each other. His eyes were wide and black, his nostrils flaring, his chest rising and lowering with panted breaths.

"Princess," he groaned, his eyes pleading with her.

"So many firsts," she murmured, lowering her head and slowly taking his entire length into her mouth.

He made a strangled sound from the back of his throat, and his hips lifted from the bed as she raised her head, dragging her lips back up over the taut pipe of flesh. Licking her lips, she took him deep again, her panties flooding from the sounds he made— deep, guttural moans of pleasure that made her feel like a goddess. She raked her teeth lightly against him as she raised her head. Swirling her tongue over the red knob of his head, she licked the pre-cum from his tip, then, without warning, took him deep again. Pumping the base of him with her hand, she fucked him with her mouth, reveling in the way his hands fisted in the sheets and his hips stayed lifted off the bed and elevated.

"Gin," he panted, "Gin, you have to stop."

"Nuh-uh," she objected, licking him slowly from base to tip before tonguing his head again with long, slow laps and soft moans.

"Baby, I'm goin' to come," he grated out.

She raised her head, nailing him with her eyes. "Promise?"

"Fuuuuuck," he hissed as she wet her lips with her tongue and slipped them over him again, lowering her mouth slowly.

She felt him jerk and throb, felt the tightening, the imminence of his climax.

"God! Ginger!" he yelled, thrusting upward twice into her mouth before finding his release. She sucked him lightly, milking him until his body thudded back onto the mattress and he sighed long and low and deep with pleasure.

Finally she slid her lips up to his tip, kissing it gently before sitting up. His arm was thrown over his face, covering his eyes, as his cut, muscular chest rose and fell with his ragged breathing.

"Cain?" she said softly, cocking her head to the side, suddenly feeling a little bit insecure.

She watched his lips turn up into the hottest, happiest smile she'd ever seen, and she felt laughter bubble up, joyful and free. She'd made him happy.

He moved his arm and looked up at her, his eyes warm and sparkling. "That. Was. Epic."

Careful of his spent sex, she shimmied over his pelvis and sat on his washboard abs. "Is that right?"

"I don't even want to *think* about where you learned to do that."

Her cheeks felt hot suddenly, and she looked away from him.

"Princess," he said, reaching for her face and turning it to face him. "I didn't mean to bring up Woodman. I'm sorry, I—"

"I never did that with Woodman," she blurted out. "I never did *that* . . . until now."

***

It was ridiculous that her words should make a chord of pure, unadulterated happiness thrum through his body, but they did. They did because Ginger loving a man that way would belong to him and only to him. And he wished he had something to give to her and only to her . . . and then he realized suddenly, he did.

"Well, Miss Virginia Laire," he said, keeping his voice light though his heart pounded with emotion, "you were very good at it."

"Was I, Mr. Wolfram?" she asked in a thick Southern accent, rocking back and forth lightly on his chest.

She needed relief, and fuck, he wanted to give it to her.

Reaching forward, he unbuttoned her jeans and worked the fly down, but she was still sitting on him, so he couldn't get them off. Giggling, she unstraddled his stomach and knelt on the bed beside him, pulling down her pants and panties, then sitting on the edge of the bed so she could shuck them to the floor. Cain took a minute to do the same, pushing his jeans and boxers the rest of the way off and toeing his sneakers onto the floor.

But his mood went from playful to reverent as he turned to find her naked, her back to him, still sitting on the edge of the bed. She'd pulled her blonde hair over her shoulder so he could trace the line of her neck and back with his eyes, and he drank her in like a man dying of thirst. The way her waist curved in and her hips curved out. The slight swell of her breasts. The smooth lines of her shoulders. She was a goddess, and he was definitely not worthy of her, though he'd worked his whole life—*his whole life*—to find himself here, to deserve her. And even if it took the rest of his life to earn her, he'd never stop thanking God for the chance to love her, for the second chance to be loved *by* her.

"Thank you," he whispered. "Thank you for givin' me that part of you."

"It was always yours to take," she said, looking at him over her shoulder.

"Thank you for lovin' me."

"I never stopped."

"Thank you for lettin' me love you."

"You're welcome," she murmured.

Sitting behind her, he pulled her into the V of his open legs, pressing his lips to her back, skimming them up to her shoulders and kissing each wing, then lingering at the base of her neck, his hands slipping around her body to cup her breasts and pull her closer. His erection strained against her back, and she leaned her neck to the side, granting him access to her throat as he massaged her breasts, playing with her nipples, circling them with his index finger and pinching them gently between his fingers.

He took a deep breath.

"I've never . . ."

"You've never what?" she asked breathlessly.

"I've never been inside a woman . . . without protection,"

he admitted, biting on the lobe of her ear, which elicited a gasp from her. "Without a barrier."

He flattened his palm over her heart, feeling the slight groove of an old scar and, just beneath, its strong beat under his hand, knowing that it was fully mended—from her surgery, from the heartbreak he caused, from the loss of Woodman. It was whole and strong . . . and his.

"Never?" she asked breathlessly, letting her head fall back on his shoulder as his cock throbbed against her.

"Not once," he said, his lips dragging across her skin, wondering if he had the right to ask her for such a thing. "But I want that . . . with you."

She raised her head and stood up, turning around to face him. Reaching forward, she cupped his face, and Cain Holden Wolfram, notorious manwhore, was speechless, struck dumb with the force and fullness of his love for this one woman, for this beloved creature, whom he'd known forever, who had owned a piece of his heart since his earliest days and owned all of it now.

She leaned forward and pressed her lips to his forehead, skimmed them to the tip of his nose, then to his lips, which she kissed softly, nibbling at his bottom lip and then gently nipping the top. Kneeling down between his legs, she put her hands on his shoulders, and he dropped his hands to her hips to help her, to guide her.

"I want that too," she whispered, so close to him that her breasts were crushed between them. He reached down and cupped her ass, lifting her gently, helping her bent knees settle on either side of his hips. She arched into him, against him, reaching down to position the tip of his sex at the entrance of her body, then winding her arms around his neck to hold herself up.

"Lionhearted woman," he sighed. "I love you forever."

"I love you forever too," she said, lowering herself, inch by inch, onto his swollen, throbbing cock.

She was wet and warm, tight and soft, squeezing him like a glove, sucking him forward and up up up into the heaven of her sex. He held his breath, feeling her stretch to take him, amazed by the tiny ridges that massaged his cock, waiting until she was fully impaled on him before exhaling. Her eyes, which had been closed, opened, finding his, owning his, and he knew, for the first time in his entire life, what it was to feel his body fused to another human being's, what it was to feel his soul open to hers, and why having sex was a completely different thing from making love.

"Baby," he panted, "are you okay?"

"Mm-hm," she sighed, smiling this ridiculously beautiful, dreamy grin that made his balls tighten and his heart burst.

He thrust up, into her, and she moaned, leaning forward to press her forehead to his.

"Again," she gasped, moving her hips, dragging her breasts against his chest.

"Kiss me," he said, pumping into her, trying to restrain himself, but unable to resist the unbelievable paradise of her pussy.

His lips fell upon hers, his tongue sliding into her mouth as he quickened his thrusts. She broke off their kiss, her fingers curling into his shoulders as her whimpers became faster and louder, and the walls of her sex started squeezing.

"Cain," she moaned, her voice breaking as a tear rolled down her cheek. "I love you. I love you so much."

She was so beautiful, he could barely breathe.

"Come for me, baby. I'm right behind you."

"Cain!" she screamed as her pussy fisted, then released, convulsing in waves. She threw back her head, her throat taut, her pulse fluttering like a wild thing.

Cain held on to her hips, plunging into her once, twice, three ti—he cried out her name, roaring his love for her as her wrapped his arms around her body and fell over the edge of bliss, knowing with profound certainty that his life was changed forever: baptized in love, reborn in devotion, his heart bound to hers until death.

Chapter 33

He was right, of course. Ginger had never made love until tonight. And now she wanted nothing more—*nothing*, for the rest of her life—than to spend every night making love with Cain.

The second time, he'd stared into her eyes and moved slowly, entering her with aching and maddening deliberateness, hovering over her, his weight braced on his veined arms, his muscles bulging, his thick erection moving inside her, leaving no part of her untouched, untaken, unloved. They'd come softly together with moans of pleasure, locked on each other's faces, captive in each other's eyes, with no need for pledges or promises. Just a million thoughts that they'd never expressed poured into one shared expression of seamless love as their bodies trembled together with the intensity of perfect union, and then they fell asleep still intimately joined, wrapped tightly in each other's arms.

Hours later her eyes opened lazily to a pitch-black room. She stirred just a little from her warm and cozy nest, checking out the clock on Cain's bedside table: 10:43. She smiled and nestled back into his arms. They'd been sleeping for a couple of hours, and she definitely wasn't sure she wanted to wake up yet so she closed her eyes, took a deep breath, and sighed.

"You hungry, princess?" he asked, his breath warm and soft against the back of her neck.

"You're awake?" She turned around in his arms to face him. Her tender breasts, which he'd loved to aching just hours before, scraped against the springy hair on his chest, and she bit her tongue to keep from moaning.

"I don't . . .," he started, then grinned at her, the crevices of his dimples deep in his cheeks. He shook his head and fell onto his back, scrubbing his hands over his face before looking back over at her with a goofy, happy grin. "I don't want to miss anythin'. Does that make me the sappiest boyfriend in the whole fuckin' world?"

She was lying on her side, one elbow propping up her head as she watched him. "*Boyfriend*?"

He blinked, his eyes suddenly uncertain. "No?"

"Yes," she said softly, laying her palm flat on the ripple of muscles on his chest, her heart bursting with tenderness. "Definitely, yes."

"Can we be together in Apple Valley?" he asked, eyebrows raised.

She winced, taking a deep breath. "Not yet."

"But he *wanted*—" Cain stopped abruptly, biting down on his lower lip, his expression troubled.

But he wanted . . .

"What? Who? 'He' *Woodman*?" she asked, rubbing his chest gently, leaning over to try to read his eyes, which he kept downcast. "Cain? What were you goin' to say?"

He closed his eyes and dragged his thumb back and forth

across his lip before opening them again but stared straight up at
the ceiling, not at her. "Leave it."

"No," she said firmly, sliding her hand away. "I can't.
What were you about to say?"

He reached for her hand and grabbed it, gently threading
his fingers through hers and placing both over his heart. When
he looked over at her, his eyes were glistening.

"I loved him," he whispered.

"I know you did," she said, squeezing his fingers. "I did
too."

"He was like a brother to me, Gin. You and Josiah were
the only ones who . . . who saw something good in me." He
searched her eyes. "I would've done anythin' for him. Time was,
I pushed *you* away, even though *I* had feelings for you, because
he was in love with you."

She gasped lightly, nodding her head. "I know. I
remember."

It hurt to remember his words, but they were burned onto
her memory:

He wanted to fuckin' die*! The thought of you*—of comin'
home to you—*was the only thing that kept him hangin' on most
days. You think I'd take that away from him? You think there's
any way in hell I'd hurt him like that? You think I'd let* you *hurt
him like that?*

"Remember your twelfth birthday?"

She nodded. "The year I didn't jump."

"While you were poutin', Josiah told me he was goin' to
marry you someday. He asked if I had a problem with that . . .
and I . . . I only saw you as a kid, Ginger. I said you were all
his."

"Like a pact?"

Cain shook his head. "Naw. Like one brother layin' his claim to a girl and the other respectin' it."

"How long did this go on? This . . . claim?"

Cain sighed, looking away from her again. "Doesn't matter. What's important is that it gave me a good reason to stay away from you. You have to understand, Gin, for a long time I thought—no, I *knew*—he was better for you'n me. I didn't fight him for you because I didn't think I deserved you."

"Even though I loved you."

"And I loved you," he said, his forehead creasing. He sighed, his eyes troubled. "Come here, now."

He propped a pillow under his head and pulled her over to him so that she was lying across his chest with her head snug under his chin. He wrapped his arms around her, running his fingers up and down her back gently, soothingly.

"If I loved you less, Gin," he said, his voice rumbling under her ear, "I might have taken you in the old barn that afternoon you offered yourself to me. If I loved you or Woodman any less'n I did, I might have made the worst mistake of my life."

"A *mistake*? To *be* with me?" she asked, and she couldn't deny it: his words hurt. Bad.

"To ruin the chance of *this*," he said, raising his voice a touch. "Of *now*. Of you here with me, and all of forever out in front of us." He cupped the back of her head lovingly, clutching her to him. "I wasn't ready to be the man you needed. And I'm sorry for that, but I still had a little bit of growin' up to do. And if I had taken you like you wanted me to, I would've destroyed my relationship with him and killed anythin' good between you and me for good."

His words made sense, but anger rose up within her.

Anger at a dead man who'd stood between her and the boy she'd loved so desperately. "He knew how I felt . . . and he stood between us."

"He knew I wasn't good for you. Not then. Not yet."

Her eyes filled with tears of frustration. "It wasn't up to him to play God with my heart, Cain! I'm . . . I'm angry at him!"

"You shouldn't be," he said evenly. "Every choice, every roadblock, every day led to *this* day, and I wouldn't trade this day for anythin'. So I'll accept everythin' that came before and ask for seconds . . . just to be with you."

She sniffled softly, trying to recontextualize ten years of memories with this new information. But sifting through her memories, she couldn't remember many times that Woodman had spoken against Cain or warned her away from him. He'd been mostly loyal to his cousin, defending and protecting Cain, even while defending and protecting her. What a fine line he'd had to walk. And maybe Cain was right—if Woodman hadn't stood between them, laying an early claim to Ginger, they wouldn't be wrapped in each other's arms now. Maybe it had, in fact, all worked out the way it was supposed to.

But still, flaunting her newfound happiness with Cain? She couldn't deny that it felt wrong somehow. Woodman had loved her, and she had made promises to him. She didn't care so much what other people thought, but Woodman had worked so hard to keep her and Cain apart, it felt like dishonoring his memory for them to be together. It made her feel guilty.

"What were you goin' to say before?" she asked. "What did Woodman want?"

Cain took a deep breath and released it slowly.

"He died in my arms, Gin."

"Woodman? But I thought he died in that barn where the

fir—"

"No," said Cain, his voice low and strained. "When I pulled him out, he was still alive. He died in my arms."

"No." She leaned up on his chest, looking into his eyes. "Oh God, I didn't know. I'm so sorry."

One of Cain's hands left her back, and he braced it on his forehead, over his eyes, staring up at her, pain coming off him in waves.

"He didn't die right away," said Cain, still watching her.

Her stomach fisted and she whimpered.

"No, darlin'. He wasn't in any pain. I don't think he felt much of anythin', but . . ." Cain's face was shuttered in sorrow. "He said a few words."

"He did? What did . . . Why didn't you tell me? What did he say?" she asked, ignoring the tear that rolled down her cheek.

Cain reached up and caught it with his thumb, pushing it away, into her hair. He searched her eyes gravely. "You know I love you?"

She nodded, but her insides were in knots.

"I need to hear you say it."

"You love me," she said softly. "I know you do. And I love you."

Cain nodded. "You know that I've *always* loved you? Even when I was pushin' you away? Even when it seemed like I hated you? You believe that?"

She nodded again, blinking as more tears joined the first. "I don't doubt your love for me, Cain."

"That's good, baby, because what I'm goin' to tell you might be hard to hear."

"Please just say it," she whispered.

Cain nodded. "Before Josiah died, he told me you loved

me."

She gasped, holding her breath as she stared at Cain.

"There's more. He . . . he asked me to be good to you, and care for you, and . . ." His voice broke, and he cleared his throat before speaking again. "To love you."

"Caaaain," she sobbed, covering her mouth with her hand as the terrible tragedy of Woodman's love for her came full circle.

"He made me promise," said Cain.

She shook her head, trying to hold back the sobs but losing the battle.

"That's why you started comin' around," she said.

He tensed, his whole body clenching. "You *know* I love you. Don't let Josiah's final wishes make you doubt that, baby."

"But you were so angry with me the night of the BBQ," she said, taking a gasping, sobbing breath. "You started comin' around because of your promise to Woodman. Admit that's true."

"Only partly," he said, furrowing his brows, his eyes searching hers desperately, willing her to know the truth of his words. "My promise to him forced me to forgive you for sleepin' with him after you told me you loved me. So yes, I started comin' around for him at first . . . but I *kept* comin' for *you*. It was so easy to fall in love with you all over again. Don't you see, Gin? The one thing that had always kept me from you was Woodman. His dyin' gift to me . . . was his blessing."

Her head fell forward with the power of her sadness, with the sheer magnitude of the devotion of Cain Wolfram to someone he loved, with the poignancy of Josiah Woodman's last request. Cain had stayed away from her out of love for Woodman, and Woodman had given his permission to love her out of love for her and Cain, and it just about broke her to know it. They'd always referred to each other as brothers, but never had Ginger seen it more clearly than now, and it filled her with joy and sorrow, comfort and gratitude, to know that Woodman had stayed alive long enough to say the words that would ensure her happiness.

"We were two cousins in love with the same girl," said Cain, lifting her chin and searching her face. "It doesn't make one of us a villain and one of us a hero. You can't help who you love. But someone's heart was goin' to break. In the end, he made sure it wasn't one of ours."

"He died talkin' about us," said Ginger, swiping at her tears.

Cain nodded. "He *always* wanted you to be happy, Gin."

Why's the sky blue, Ginger? Because it don't know no other way to be.

"Is it wrong for us to be happy? Is it bad that we're together, partly because he's gone?"

"We both loved him," said Cain tenderly. "It's terrible what happened to him. In a million years, we didn't want that." He paused. "But it happened, and he wouldn't have wanted us to grieve him forever. Not at all. His final words prove that he wanted us to be happy, princess."

Exhausted, but strangely comforted, she lay her head back down and let Cain wrap his arms around her, pulling her close. She rested her ear over his strong, beating heart, and that's how she fell asleep for the second time: bound to him in sorrow but united in peace.

***

Cain waited until her breathing was deep and easy before shifting to his side and pulling her close so they were spooned together as she slept. He had known all along that he couldn't share Woodman's last words with her until she was convinced of his love, but after sharing their bodies with each other tonight, he didn't want to keep the secret anymore. He didn't want any secrets between them. Ever.

Besides, he couldn't bear for her to feel guilty being together, when Woodman's final words on this earth had been about Cain and Ginger loving each other. Woodman wouldn't have wanted her to be unhappy. Not for a moment. He'd lived his life for her happiness. And now she knew that finding their way to each other wasn't a betrayal of Woodman, but a fulfillment of his wishes, and Cain hoped she would find the same peace that he'd been able to find in honoring his cousin's last request.

He closed his eyes and pictured Josiah's face as a freckled little kid—as Cain's first playmate, his best friend in kindergarten, at family birthdays and summer picnics. Josiah's blond hair shining in the sun and moss-green eyes crinkled with laughter, and there was Ginger in his memories too—pudgy little Ginger wearing a daisy crown on her white-blonde hair, holding tightly to the cousins' hands as they ran through meadows together.

For as long as he lived, Cain would miss Woodman.

For as long as he lived, Cain would be good to, and care for, and love Ginger.

Not because he'd promised Woodman, but because loving Ginger was so deeply ingrained into the fiber of Cain. If he concentrated hard, he could still feel those chubby fingers holding fast to his.

But he would be forever grateful to Woodman for finally letting him know that *his* time to love her had finally come—that he was worthy of her.

Tightening his arm underneath her breasts and bending his knees into hers, he matched their breathing, closed his eyes, and fell asleep.

Chapter 34

Ginger had been in love with Cain for a long time, but there was a precious, inconceivable dreaminess to knowing that her love was wholly and utterly reciprocated. They'd spent Saturday morning in bed, making love, before Cain took her out for a giant breakfast at a local diner, and then to Bed Bath & Beyond, where he asked for her advice in choosing curtains for his living room and a new comforter for his bed.

These were mundane activities—sitting across from one another in a diner booth and shopping for home goods—that millions of couples around the world were engaged in, but for Ginger, who'd waited her whole life to belong to Cain, and whose terrible guilt over loving Cain had finally been lifted, she could barely contain her happiness.

He reached for her easily, holding her hand, placing his palm in the small of her back or dropping a tender kiss to her temple as she held up a chocolate-brown blanket that matched the new tan comforter perfectly. There was an easiness between them, born of a lifelong friendship, and a heat, born of their newfound love, and the combination made her giddy.

Saturday afternoon he showed her around his townhouse complex, and she watched the proud expression on his face, in his eyes, as he pointed out the pond and the pool and asked if she was any good at tennis. She wasn't, but that didn't matter. What mattered was realizing that he'd grown into a responsible and self-reliant man who wasn't just giving her a tour of his community but—in every glance, in the subtext of every word— offering it to her, to share it with her when and if she was ever ready to give him that chance.

And the thing is? For all that she hadn't been ready, ever, to marry Woodman, thoughts of marrying Cain flooded her mind with anticipation and excitement. She couldn't wait to hold his hand and leap into forever.

On Sunday he offered to drive her to church, but she declined. She imagined the pain in Miz Sophie's eyes to see her nephew slipping into the shoes of her son, and she knew that compassion and discretion was the right path for them, no matter how impatient Cain felt about declaring their status to the world.

They both felt the quiet melancholy of Sunday afternoon as the sun set and evening approached, knowing that their perfect weekend was almost over. After kissing good-bye for almost an hour by the driver's side of her car, their hands reaching for each other, their bodies aching for more, Ginger finally wrenched herself away and cried the whole way back to Apple Valley, bereft at leaving Cain behind for even a day.

Which made her drive back down to Versailles on Tuesday morning all the sweeter. Unable to bear their separation any longer, she'd left McHuid's at ten thirty, texting Cain that she was on her way. When she arrived, he was waiting in the garage bay, his jeans slung low, his long-sleeved T-shirt hugging his muscular chest, his eyes—dusky blue and clear—fixed on her through the windshield of her car as she parked, cut the engine, sprang from the car, and ran to his arms.

He lifted her easily, and she locked her ankles around his waist, their lips fusing into a desperate kiss as he carried her inside.

"I need you," he growled, kicking the office door closed with his foot. "Christ, I missed you, princess."

She pressed kisses to his smooth jaw, to his cheeks, to his eyelids and lips.

"Me too," she gasped, her panties soaked, her body clenched with readiness.

"I can't go slow," said Cain, setting her down in front of the desk. He used his arm to swipe everything—including their laptops and the phone console—to the side, then turned her around, facing the desk. "Lean over."

She pulled her maxi dress up to her waist, yanked her panties down to her knees, and bent over the desk with her forearms flat and her forehead down. Behind her, she heard his zipper open with a quick *fffft* and the sound of his jeans being pushed down. She gasped as his erection pressed against the wet, sensitive folds of her sex and cried out when he grabbed her hips and thrust into her completely with one smooth stroke.

"Ahhh," he panted, buried deeply inside her, leaning over her back, his shirt pressed against the bunched-up jersey of her dress.

Ginger lay her cheek against the cool, slick wood of the desk and closed her eyes in gratitude and relief.

He pushed her hair aside and pressed his lips to her neck, still motionless within her, though he throbbed like a heartbeat. Her sensitive flesh felt every pulse as he swelled inside her, stretching her to fit him.

"I'm sorry," he sighed breathlessly.

"Don't be," she murmured. "I needed this too."

"What do you need, baby?" he asked, his tongue darting out to lick her neck as his hands slid between the desk and her dress to massage her breasts.

She whimpered, pressing her ass back against him. "More."

Withdrawing slowly, Cain thrust forward again, and Ginger moaned loudly. "More."

Winding her hair in his hand, Cain pulled, firmly but gently, as he withdrew from her, then slammed forward again.

"Oh my God," she moaned. "Again."

His other arm looped around her waist, and he pulled her up off the desk a fraction of an inch. "Hold on, Gin."

She flattened her palms on the desk, and he pumped into her again, but his arm skated lower until he could slip his hand into the slick, vibrating folds of her clit. His middle finger, coarse and hot, found the sensitive bud of flesh and circled it as he pulled on her hair and thrust greedily inside her again.

"I want you to scream my name," he growled. "I want you to scream my name when you come, princess."

She nodded, barely able to make words, her body so tight, aching so terribly with her need for release. She only managed a weak, "Okay."

"You ready for me?"

"*Please*," she begged him.

The pad of his finger pressed directly on her clit, rubbing as he thrust into her, faster and faster, her orgasm building to such a massive, almost excruciating pitch, she stopped breathing and her forehead hit the desk just as her body buckled with convulsions and she heard "Cain!" ripped from her throat.

"Ah! Princess!" he groaned, sliding his hands to her hips and holding her in place as he withdrew all the way from her body, then thrust into her with such force, she felt his cock touch her womb and explode with the power of his climax, hot and wet, pumping into her rhythmically until she realized that she was lying on the desk and he was lying on her back.

She was boneless.

She was barely alive.

She was satisfied.

"Mmm," she murmured, feeling her heartbeat in her temples and ears, and his against her back in strong, rapid beats.

"Are you okay?" he panted close to her ear.

"Oh my God," she said. "I had no idea . . ."

"That it could be like this?"

"That I could want it so bad," she confessed as her breathing finally started returning to normal. "That I could love it so much."

He chuckled, gently withdrawing from her body. Placing an arm under her waist, he pulled her back against him as he sank into a guest chair, holding her on his lap. Her head was on his shoulder, her feet were draped over the arm, and Cain looked down at her, his blue eyes shining with love.

"Hello, girlfriend."

"Hello, lover," she said, grinning up at him, loving the softness in his chiseled face, knowing that she was the one who put it there.

"Happy Tuesday."

"So far, so good," she said.

He leaned down and kissed her lips tenderly. "I love you."

"I love you too."

"Move in with me," he said, searching her eyes.

She chortled, then sobered when she realized he wasn't kidding. "Cain. We've been dating for five minutes."

"We've known each other for over two decades and been in love for at least one."

"Woodman died in the fall. It's only winter."

"He wanted us to be together."

She dropped his hopeful eyes, adjusting her dress over her lap.

"Ginger?" he prompted.

She took a deep breath before meeting his gaze. "I'm not ready yet."

His lip twitched to the side with disappointment, and his grin faded, but he nodded in acceptance.

"But I will be," she said. "Soon."

He shrugged, giving her a small smile. "Can't blame me for tryin'."

"Don't stop," she said, adjusting her legs on his lap and feeling the evidence of their lovemaking between her thighs. "I need to get cleaned up."

He held her tighter. "Not yet. Tell me about your gran."

She sighed, laying her head back on his shoulder. "Same. Fadin'."

"You saw her yesterday?"

Ginger nodded, sorrow filling her heart. "She doesn't know me anymore. She called me Amy the whole time."

"Your aunt."

"I didn't know her. She died before I was born."

"Maybe it's not such a bad thing," said Cain gently, his hand stroking her bare arm.

"How do you mean?"

"I imagine losin' a child is the worst thing that can happen to someone . . . but now? Her Amy's back. She can see her and talk to her, and . . ." He shrugged, looking sad. ". . . maybe it doesn't hurt as much anymore."

This hadn't really occurred to Ginger, but she felt an odd comfort in it, that her Gran was passing, little by little, from this world to a place where she could be together with her baby girl forever.

"You believe in heaven, Cain?"

"Do you?"

She nodded. "I do. Yes."

"Then I do too," he said. "Because if you're goin' there, I'm goin' to go there too."

She leaned up, cupped his cheeks, and looked into his eyes. "You always goin' to be this sweet to me?"

He reached for her hair, gently tucking the loose strands behind her ears. "As long as you let me, darlin'."

"How 'bout forever?"

He grinned. "You stakin' a claim, Miss Virginia Laire?"

"On you?" she grinned, nodding her head. "You better believe it."

His smile got wider and wider, until it turned into a laugh—a truly joyful sound that filled the room and filled her heart and filled her soul so full of Cain Wolfram that she knew for certain that whatever had ever been broken was whole, and that, as long as he was beside her, it would never break again.

***

Leaving for Navy Reserve training on Wednesday morning was the last thing Cain felt like doing, especially because Ginger had stayed overnight and he woke up with their feet tangled together, staring at her lovely face fast asleep. Groaning with self-pity, he rolled his naked body to the edge of the bed and left her as quietly as possible to get in the shower.

After this month, he'd need to attend Reserves training only one night a month, but he had deferred his December service because of Woodman's passing, which meant that he needed to make up two more days in January. He hadn't seen any reason not to make them up now, but as he came out of the bathroom with a towel wrapped around his waist, he stared at the beautiful girl asleep in his bed and had a pang of regret. He didn't want to leave her. Especially not for three nights.

Squatting by the bed, he blew softly on her cheek. Reflexively, she swiped at her face with the back of her hand, and Cain did it again, watching her eyes flutter open.

"Cain?" she said, rolling onto her back and sighing. "What time is it?"

"I gotta go soon."

She opened one eye. "Wish you didn't have to."

"Me too."

She reached out her hand as her eyes closed and her voice got dreamy. "Get back in bed with me for a few more minutes."

And fuck, he was tempted, but he shook his head, stood up, then bent over to press a kiss to her forehead.

"I'm goin' to get dressed and leave as quietly as possible. Stay as long as you want, okay?"

She nodded, curling onto her side and falling back to sleep.

He did PT upon arrival, at 0700, followed by a shower. And now he was hanging out until formation at 1100, doing nothing but missing her. And since the afternoon would be busy with classes and other busywork, he took his phone out of his hip pocket.

CW: Sure was hard to leave you this morning,

baby.

He stared at the message for a moment before slipping the phone back into his pocket, surprised when it buzzed almost immediately. He whipped it back out, looking down at the screen.

The Princess: I barely remember saying good-bye. Glad you got there okay. Saturday seems like a long way away.

He grinned at the phone.

CW: I'll come to you on Saturday night and stay at your place.

The Princess: ☺ Okay. What time?

CW: Suppertime.

The Princess: I'll have frozen pizza waiting.

He chuckled at her sass, then typed.

CW: Miss me?

The Princess: I do.

CW: Move in with me.

The Princess: Soon.

CW: I love you.

The Princess: I love you too.

He tucked his phone back into his pocket, then ate the shitty food and attended the remedial classes that felt a little silly after six years of active service. But on Thursday night, lying in his bunk, he pulled out his phone again.

CW: How was work today, baby?

It took a little longer for her to respond this time, and he was almost asleep when his phone buzzed.

The Princess: Still here. Just leaving.

CW: Late shift?

The Princess: Spent a little extra time with Gran.

CW: How's she doing?

The Princess: Not good. I wish you were here.

His heart twisted because he wished he was there too. For a moment he thought about calling her, but he knew that cell phone calls at Silver Springs were frowned upon.

CW: I'm halfway there. Day after tomorrow.

The Princess: I know. She's just . . . I don't know. She's so frail and weak. And the tube is bothering her. I can see it in her eyes. She's giving up.

Cain thought about Miz Kelleyanne—a woman he'd known his whole life. She'd been kind to him, an especially good friend since—

The Princess: How's training?

CW: Mostly bullshit. But at least I don't have to come back for four weeks.

The Princess: Hey, I've been meaning to ask, can we go away sometime? Together?

CW: Like on a vacation?

The Princess: Uh-huh. I've barely been anywhere.

Cain rolled onto his back, sighing with pleasure as he thought about all the wonderful places he'd seen on his travels—all the amazing places he'd like to take Ginger.

CW: Where do you want to go?

The Princess: Where would you take me?

He thought about her wearing a bikini on the white sand of Crete, or getting a tan poolside in Madrid. But when he thought of Ginger, really thought about who she was and what she loved, a different place sprang to mind, all the more perfect because it would be new to him.

CW: My pop always talks about the Lipizzaners. How do you feel about Vienna, baby?

The Princess: I wish you could see my face right now.

CW: Tell me how it looks.

The Princess: It looks happy because you are so right for me. It looks sad because it wishes you were here. It doesn't know how to love someone this much, this hard, quite yet. My face doesn't know what to do when you say the perfect thing. Yes, I want to go to Vienna with you.

CW: Then we'll go to Vienna.

The Princess: Just like that?

CW: Just like that. We'll go to the Spanish Riding School and see my pop's horses, and then we'll ride my bike all over Austria, all over Germany, wherever you want.

The Princess: And I'll hold on to you.

CW: Fuck, yeah.

The Princess: And you'll speak German.

CW: Scheisse, ja.

The Princess: I'm home now. And I'm not as sad. Thanks for cheering me up.

CW: I'd do anything for you, princess.

The Princess: Then come home to me on Saturday safe and sound. That's all I want.

CW: See you then.

The Princess: I love you.

CW: I love you too.

Cain sighed as he placed his phone on the bedside table, dreaming of Ginger and motorcycles and white stallions and making love all over Europe.

When his alarm sounded, at 0600, the little red text icon was red and waiting, and he swiped it urgently, wondering if he'd missed one last sweet PS to last night's conversation. He grinned at the screen, scrubbing a hand over his sleepy face, but his heart sank like a stone when he read the words that popped up on the screen:

The Princess: She's with Amy, Cain. Gran's gone.

Chapter 35

There is nothing good about a phone ringing at 4:43 in the morning. Your mind acknowledges, even before your fingers can move, that something terrible has probably happened.

It's not that she wasn't expecting it. She was. Just not yet.

"Ginger, baby? It's your daddy."

That's all it took. And she knew.

"When?" she asked.

"An hour ago. Or so. One of the night nurses stopped in to check on her and realized that she wasn't breathin'."

Ginger swung her legs over her bedside. "Are you there?"

"I am."

"Momma?"

"I let her sleep," he said. "But you . . . you had such a special bond with her."

Yes, I did.

"Wright's is comin' soon." He paused. "Virginia Laire?"

"I'll be there in a few minutes."

"You don't have to—"

"I want to say good-bye," she said, "before they take her.

Don't . . . don't let them take her yet, Daddy."

"I'll be waitin', baby."

"I'm sorry," she said, her eyes starting to burn as her brain processed the finality of Gran's death.

"Me too, Ginger. But, all things considered, she had a good life. And she was loved."

Yes, she was.

"I'll be there soon, Daddy."

She hung up her phone and clutched it in her hands for a moment, the quiet of Gran's cottage surrounding her with the sort of peace she wasn't expecting.

Her Amy's back. She can see her and talk to her, and maybe it doesn't hurt as much anymore.

Tears tumbled down her cheeks as his words gave her the strength to send him a quick text before getting up to get dressed.

It was still dark as she walked down the stairs to the kitchen, grabbed her keys, and headed out to her car. The tack room was dark as she passed the barn; the world was still fast asleep. She didn't know why she insisted on saying good-bye at Silver Springs—Gran's soul had departed for heaven hours before—but her body, as Ginger had always known it, would be poked and prodded into final prettiness once the Wrights took her. While it was still night, she wanted to say her final good-bye.

She pulled into the parking lot and used her employee pass to open the side door and take the service elevator to her gran's floor. Her father sat in a chair by his mother's body, holding her bony hand, his head bent, his shoulder shaking.

"Daddy?"

"Hey, baby," he said, looking up her, his eyes red-rimmed

and shiny.

She put her hand on his shoulder, and he reached up with his free hand to hold it. "She passed quietly, they said."

"She's with Amy now," said Ginger.

Her father nodded. "That's right."

"Dr. Sheridan?"

"Came by with his condolences."

She sat down on the bed bedside Gran's lifeless body. "Why don't you go splash your face with water and get us a couple of coffees? I'll stay with her."

It was the exact same line she'd used a thousand times to family members who'd lost an elderly loved one, and her father, like all the rest, nodded his ascent and stood up.

As he got to the door, he turned. "She, uh, she wanted you to have this." He held out an envelope with her name on it.

"She wrote it?"

"Her words. I just wrote them down."

Ginger took the envelope and stared at it, slightly dumbstruck.

"Cream? Sugar?"

"Both." She turned the envelope over and opened it. Before she took the letter out, she took Gran's hand and kissed it. "Thank you for this. Whatever it is, thank you for one last conversation."

***

January 2016

Doll baby,

I am fading fast now.

So fast that I don't always know you for the first few

minutes you walk into my room, though your smile fills me with joy. And when I realize, "That's your beautiful granddaughter," I am filled with pride.

A long time ago, a beautiful little girl who knew two cousins asked me, "What do I do if I love them both?" and I answered, "Someday you'll have to choose." What I didn't know was that your heart had already chosen. That day, so long ago, you'd already decided on Cain. Maybe you'd been born loving Cain. It doesn't matter why or how you started loving him. He was your heart's desire from the beginning, and I was frightened for you, and I wondered if the compass in your heart was broken.

A few years later, you came to see me, so excited that he'd asked you to a dance and desperate for me to love him as you did. But I couldn't. I couldn't give you my blessing because I didn't trust him. I believe my exact words went something like this: "I'm not saying he's *bad*. But I am saying if there's a good man hiding in there, I'd surely *like* to see him before I tell my only granddaughter that she's betting on the right horse."

Not long after that, he broke your heart.

It was a confirmation that everyone was right about him—Cain Wolfram wasn't a good man. And I was glad when he went away and you seemed to switch your affections to Josiah.

Except that you didn't.

Your heart—that little lion heart that had always roared with love for Cain—still loved him, and—I confess, doll baby—I hated him for his hold over you because I still couldn't see any good in him.

And yet the longer he stayed away, the more I lost my strong, brave girl. You became a shell of yourself, Ginger.

Without Cain to love, I think you forgot who you were. And over time, I became desperate for his return. I wanted him to come back and breathe life into you like Adam did for Eve. I thought to myself, Yes, Cain might break her again, but at least she'll be alive to feel the pain.

Except that Josiah died.

And part of you seemed to die with him.

Cain will be angry with me for telling you that he came to see me a month after Woodman's passing. I knew who he was right away—his unusual blue eyes were singular in Apple Valley parish—but I couldn't imagine why he was visiting me, and to my everlasting shame, I was cold to him and asked him to leave.

But he was persistent. At first he came with flowers— hothouse bouquets from the grocer—until I told him that wildflowers were my favorite, and after that, he always brought me wildflowers. Sometimes he'd bring a hammer and nails and fix something in my room. Once he brought a long fluorescent light bulb and fixed one of my ceiling lights. Another time he patched a broken tile in my shower. He worked quietly, silently, saying nothing, asking for nothing, letting his actions show me that he wasn't the person I thought he was.

After a week or two, I finally asked him why he kept coming around. He stopped working and fixed those blue eyes on mine. "Ginger," he said, simply. "I want to know her, to understand her, to love her the way she needs me to. I want you to tell me everything I need to know to make her happy because Woodman's gone and someday you'll be gone, and when y'all are gone, it'll be up to me to make her happy. And I was hoping you could help get me up to speed."

I thought long and hard about his request, doll baby, but in the end I didn't give him any advice at all. I just told him to be himself. What he didn't know, and I did, was that you'd loved him since you were small. He didn't need to do anything different. He didn't need any advice. He asked me over and over again, "What do I need to do to make Ginger happy, Miz Kelleyanne?" And every time I said, "Be yourself, Cain Wolfram."

Cain was being himself when he decorated my room for Christmas, as he continued to do little things to make my room more comfortable, as he read to me from *The Christmas Box*, and built the bookcase that held it. He was himself when he told me all about his new business, when he bought a townhouse he hoped you'd love, and when he hired you to come work for him. He was himself, giddy with hopefulness, when he told me that you were falling in love with him again. He was himself tonight—the night before they're putting that damned tube in my throat—showing up here with flowers in his hand because this is where your heart was hurting, so this is where he needed to be.

Here is what I know:

You were right, doll baby.

The compass in your heart was never broken.

Somehow you must have known that there *was* a good man hiding inside Cain Wolfram. I didn't realize it at the time, but you were always betting on the right horse. Seeing my beloved granddaughter come alive again over the past few months has been the greatest blessing of my long, happy life. It has given me, and this old, tired body, permission to say good-bye.

Josiah and I are gone, and I know you will miss us.

But Cain is left standing, and I promise you, doll baby, he is the man you always loved, the man you always knew him to be. Trust your heart. It was never broken. It was always whole, and it was always right.

Hold on to each other, and know that I am standing beside Amy and Josiah, celebrating your happiness from heaven.

Your devoted,

Gran

***

Tears wet the precious paper, so Ginger folded it carefully and slipped it back into the envelope, then laid it gently on the bed so she could hold Gran's hand with both of hers.

"Thank you, Gran. Thank you."

"She couldn't write anymore," said her father from behind her, holding out a steaming cup of coffee, "but she was lucid. They were her true thoughts, Virginia Laire."

"On Thanksgivin'," she said, searching her father's face, "when you sent me down to Klaus's place with the pie, you knew. You knew he was visitin' Gran."

Her father nodded. "More importantly, I knew he was bringin' you back from the dead."

She held the warm paper cup in her hands. "I guess he did."

"I was never fond of Cain. Didn't trust his wild ways. But he grew up into a fine man, Ginger. I'd be, well, that is, someday I'd be proud to call him my son."

"Daddy," she whispered, chiding him gently. "We're not there yet."

"Furthermore, I was wrong to let your momma shelter you

so much. Woodman was a good man, but Cain is strong. He changed the whole course of his life to be worthy of you, daughter. He loves you somethin' fierce. Always has, I reckon. Always will."

"I know," she said, managing a small smile. "I know he does, Daddy."

Her father sat down at his mother's feet and looked at her face, which looked peaceful, like she was sleeping soundly. "She was somethin', huh? Always had to get the last word."

I am celebrating your happiness from heaven.

"Yes, sir," said Ginger, turning to look at Gran's lovely face for the last time. "She was somethin'."

Thank you.

***

After the Wrights took Gran's body away, her father headed to the Apple Valley Diner to get some breakfast before heading home. She joined him there, pushing her eggs around her plate and thinking about Gran and Woodman and Cain. Once upon a time, they had been the three most important people in her life, and now two out of the three were gone. And although that notion should have made her feel terrifyingly lonesome, she found that the person she missed the most was not Woodman or Gran, but Cain. She longed for him with a desperate pang of self-pity, wishing he would suddenly appear and wrap her in his arms so she'd feel strong and whole.

She looked out the window at the cold, rainy day, part of her expecting him to suddenly appear on the sidewalk, but he wasn't there, of course. He was in Louisville until tomorrow night, which meant that she would have to bear her sorrow alone for a little longer.

"You want anythin' else?" asked her father, and she shook

her head no. "Want to meet me at Wright's later on today? They said the wake'll be on Monday night and the fun'ral on Tuesday mornin'. Not too much to arrange, really."

"I'll be there, Daddy."

"Your momma never much liked your gran."

Ginger shrugged. "Her loss."

"She felt threatened, I think. My momma was a force to be reckoned with."

"And mine isn't?" asked Ginger.

Her father chuckled softly. "I think she's mellowin' with age."

"As long as she understands that Colin Greenvale and I aren't happenin'."

"I'll have a word, let her know that Cain might be comin' around more often."

"You don't have to do that," she said. "Cain and I are still very . . . new."

"And here I thought the whole point of your gran's letter was that, actually, you aren't."

Her father took twenty dollars from his billfold and laid it on the table, then stood up and slid from the booth. "Three o'clock at Wright's, daughter. See you there."

As she drove home, the rain started falling harder, until her windshield wipers were slamming back and forth and the windshield still wasn't clear.

Which was why she didn't see Cain waiting on her front porch until she was running into the house.

She stopped in her tracks, the cold rain pelting her as she stared up at him.

He was wearing blue camouflage fatigues with thick black boots. In his hand he held his blue cap, and he worried it between his hands, searching her eyes gravely as she approached.

When she stopped, he rushed down the steps and grabbed her hand, pulling her under the awning and into his arms.

"Are you AWOL?" she asked.

"No, baby," he said, "I got permission to leave as soon as I got your text."

Her eyes closed, and she let all her sadness, all her weariness, rush forth, making her body sag against him. He swooped her into his arms. "Where's your key?"

She nestled into his neck, sighing with relief. "Extra one's always over the door."

Holding her with one arm, he reached up and felt for the key, then opened the door and stepped into her kitchen. He used his elbow to close the door, then stepped from the kitchen into her small sitting room and sat down on the couch, still holding her in his arms.

"How are you?"

"Better now," she said.

"I'm sorry I wasn't here."

"You *are* here."

"How's your daddy?"

"Sad. But he knew it was comin'." She lifted her head to look up at him. "I missed you."

Cain dropped his lips to hers, dots of rainwater caught between them as he kissed her gently. "I missed you too."

"Gran told me . . . about how you visited her."

His eyebrows furrowed. "She did?"

"A letter."

"She shouldn't have said anythin'," he said. "It was supposed to be a secret."

"Why?"

He shrugged. "I'd never want you to think I was butterin' up your gran just to get to you."

"Cain," she said, "when will you learn?"

"Learn what?"

"You skipped the most stones. You saved my doll. You knew I wasn't breakable. You brought me back to life. You visited my Gran. Do you know what a good man you are? Because *I* do. I've always known. And I love you."

"I'll miss her," said Cain. "Never had a grandmother of my own. Sort of got used to visitin' her."

"She liked you very much."

He grinned. "I liked her too."

She closed her eyes, burrowing her face into his neck. "I'm so tired. How do you feel about takin' me upstairs and holdin' me while I fall asleep?"

He pressed his lips to her hair, then stood up with her still in his arms and started for the stairs. "That's why I'm here, sweet girl."

"And come to Wright's at three."

"If you want me there. You could Tell Mr. Wright I'm a friend of the family. And I'll, uh . . ." He cleared his throat as he started up the stairs. "I'll go to the funeral on my own, so no one knows we're together."

She waited until he'd laid her gently on her bed, taken off his boots, and gotten under the covers with her, facing her.

"Cain," she said softly, reaching for his cheek and caressing it tenderly, "will you sit beside me at my grandmother's wake on Monday night, and will you escort me to her funeral on Tuesday? Will you come back here to McHuid's and receive guests with me on Tuesday afternoon, and when they leave, will you come back here to my cottage and stay the night in my bed? And when people ask who you are to me, will you tell them that you're my boyfriend and I'm your girlfriend, and will you hold my hand for the whole town to see?"

"Princess, are you—"

"Sure? Yes," she said, pressing her lips to his before leaning away to look into his eyes. "I love you. I've always loved you. I'll love you on the day I die. That's all that matters anymore. You and me." Through her tears she managed to smile at him. "And the two people who loved us most will be smilin' down, happy to finally see us together."

He blinked his eyes and clenched his jaw, and Ginger knew that there was a lump in his throat so she didn't force him to speak. Besides, the tenderness in his eyes told her everything she needed to know. She pressed her chest to his and tucked her head under his chin, closing her eyes and sighing as he wrapped his arms around her and pulled her even closer.

"I love you too," he whispered, his voice thick with emotion.

Jump to the one you love the most, darlin'.

Cain's heart, which had been hers all along, beat out its eternal rhythm against Ginger's heart, which was his until the last day of forever.

Epilogue

Eight months later

". . . happy birthday to you!"

Ginger looked around the table, smiling at her mother, father, Klaus, and, finally, at Cain, who sat beside her, holding her hand under the table.

"Happy birthday, princess," mouthed Cain, grinning at her.

It was the first time he could remember being invited to a birthday party at the McHuids' manor, and originally he'd told Ginger to go alone and they'd celebrate later.

"Hmm," she'd hummed, sitting up in bed and sighing before swinging her legs over the bed and padding naked into his bathroom.

Hmm. "Hmm" meant that she had something on her mind.

"What, 'hmm'?"

She peeked out of his bathroom, grinning. "*Hmm*, I guess I'll have to move myself then."

"Move what? What does *that* mean?"

"It means, *hmm*, I was plannin' to move in here with you on my birthday. Heck, I've got most of the cottage packed up, but if you're not interested in helpin' me . . ."

She ducked back into the bathroom, and Cain sprang out of bed, crossing his bedroom in three strides. He stood buck naked in the bathroom doorway, staring at her sitting on the counter, legs crossed, trying not to smile.

"Are you movin' in with me?" he demanded.

"Well, I stay here four nights a week anyway. I figure . . ."

He'd stayed rigidly still, arms splayed, hands clutching the doorframe, eyes trained on hers like lasers.

"Yes," she said. "I'm movin' in here with you . . . if I'm still invited."

He hadn't realized he'd been holding his breath, but as he released it in a whoosh, he stalked into the bathroom, placed his hands on her knees, and spread them gently so he could stand between them.

"Are you serious, or are you teasin' me?"

He'd asked her at least once a week since January. Eight months. Thirty-two weeks. And she'd always said "Not yet" or "Someday" or "Soon."

She straightened up, pressing her naked breasts to his chest and looking up into his eyes. "I'm serious. I'm ready. I want to move in with you."

His lips dropped to hers at the same time his arms encircled her, lifting her and carrying her back to bed to show her how much it meant to him that she was ready to take this next step.

That had been a few weeks ago, and she was mostly moved in at this point. Today they would pick up the last of her things and turn the cottage keys back to her parents, and she'd move in with Cain for good.

Which made today one of the best days of his life for many reasons—some still to come.

"Make a wish, Ginger," said her mother. "The candles are meltin'."

"They already came true," she said, smiling up at Cain, a million promises in her deep brown eyes.

"Make a wish anyway," said Ranger, gesturing to the cake and grinning at his daughter.

She took a deep breath and blew them out, and her parents, Cain, and Klaus clapped merrily.

"*Herzlichen Glückwunsch zum Geburtstag!*" exclaimed Klaus, who'd given Ginger a horse that he'd carved from a bright white piece of balsa. It was a prancing Lipizzan, of course, and it sat proudly at Ginger's place now, waiting for a bite of her cake.

"*Danke*, Klaus," she said, smiling across the table at Cain's father.

It had taken some convincing for Miz Magnolia to break down the high social barrier she'd built between the McHuids and the Wolframs, but Ranger's full support of Ginger and Cain's relationship had helped. And little by little, Ginger's mother seemed to accept that the Wolframs, for better or worse, were a part of her life, and it would be best to accept them, on behalf of her husband and daughter, than fight them all.

For his part, Cain still wasn't Miz Magnolia's biggest fan, but she was gentler now than she'd ever been, sobered by the recent losses of Woodman and her mother-in-law, and he could even imagine a day when there was a true and lasting peace between them. Someday.

An hour later, after cake and Champagne, Ginger and Cain bid good-bye to their parents, and Cain promised to drop off his father's truck tomorrow. The three parents waved from the front porch as they pulled away, headed down the driveway. But just before leaving McHuid's, Cain turned left, trundling down the gravel road and parking in front of the barn.

He cut the engine and faced Ginger, who looked at him with surprise.

"It's your birthday," he said, gesturing to the barn with his chin. "Don't you want to jump?"

She laughed. "I think I'm a little old for that, don't you?"

"Don't trust me to catch you, huh?" He got out of the car, his hands sweating as he neared the barn, where he waited for her to join him.

A moment later he heard her door open and her feet hit the ground. "You're not serious, are you? I'm liable to break more than my arm."

"Suit yourself," he said, turning back, uncertain if the wave of emotion he felt was relief or disappointment.

"Aw, wait!" she said, grinning at him. "But if you don't catch me, you're in big trouble!" she yelled, sprinting into the barn and up the ladder to the loft.

His heart started racing and his mouth went dry.

Oh, fuck. This is happening.

He reached into his back pocket for the small black velvet box that held a simple platinum ring capped with a 1.25-karat diamond. Princess-cut, of course.

Taking a deep breath, he dropped to one knee, his eyes fixed on the hayloft door, remembering all the times he'd caught her, remembering their first kiss, remembering Woodman and birthdays and happy times and Ginger's smile. And then . . .

She was there.

"Are you ready? Now, don't you drop— Cain!"

Her mouth opened, and she covered it with her hands, her eyes filling with tears.

"I got a question to ask you, princess," he said, grinning up at her, holding up the open box.

"Oh my God!" she cried, the words muffled under her hands.

"You want to come back down here, or you want me to come up there?"

"I can't move," she said, blinking her eyes furiously.

"Then I'm comin' up." He snapped the box shut, jumped up, and ran into the barn. Up the ladder, into the loft, he didn't stop until he was about a foot from her. "Different kind of jump this year," he said, bending down on one knee and opening up the box again.

She took a step toward him, and he could see she was crying, tears streaming down her face, her hands still covering her mouth.

"Come here, princess."

"Cain," she whimpered.

"Come on, now," he said, smiling up at her.

She took a step toward him, then another, sobbing once before dropping her hands. And she was smiling. Crying, yes. But smiling. And any worry left in his heart quickly lifted as he stared up into the eyes of the woman he'd loved since he was fifteen years old.

"Give me your hand," he said, reaching out with his.

Her fingers trembled as she placed them in his.

"I love you," he said. "You're my childhood friend and my best friend and my girlfriend and my lover. And I'm thrilled that you're movin' in with me today, but it's just not enough. Because I want to make love to you every day for the rest of my life. I want your name to be Virginia Laire McHuid Wolfram. I want my kids to have your blonde hair and my blue eyes. I want you to be my wife." She raked her teeth over her bottom lip and reached up with her free hand to wipe her tears. "Will you marry me, princess?" Cain asked.

He'd seen Ginger McHuid smile a million times.

But this one was new. And it belonged to him.

"Cain!" she cried, her shoulders trembling with sobs, her smile blinding. "Oh my God, yes! Yes!"

He pulled the ring from its soft velvet bed and slipped it over her third finger, then he stood up, pulled her into his arms, and kissed his fiancée as they agreed to hold hands and jump together into forever.

***

Four years later

"Remember, it's Momma's birthday today," said Cain, ruffling the blond hair of his two and a half-year-old son, Josiah.

"Momma," he answered, his moss-green eyes the spitting image of the uncle he'd been named for. "She get baba for Keyee-anne."

"That's right, little man, because Miz Kelleyanne here sure does get mad if she wakes up without a bottle, doesn't she?"

Josiah and Kelleyanne.

The two people who had been the guiding lights on the path that led Cain to Ginger and Ginger to Cain. Two strong spirits who would always, God willing, be with them.

He looked down at the sleeping baby girl in his arms—at the jet-black fuzz that covered her two-month-old head—and felt his heart swell, as it always did, with so much joy, he didn't know how his chest contained it all.

"Uh-huh," said Josiah, staring at his baby sister with a sour expression. "*Mad* Keyee-anne."

Cain chuckled. "You remember the song we're gonna sing to Momma, right?"

"The happy birfday song."

"That's right."

"We all sing. Oma and Opa. Grampa Jim. Gramp and Gramma," said Josiah. "And Auntie."

Oma and Opa were Cain's parents, Grampa Jim was his mother's husband. Gramp and Gramma were Ranger and Magnolia, and Auntie was Cain's Aunt Sophie.

Despite being invited, Aunt Sophie had refused to attend Cain and Ginger's wedding, but when little Josiah was born, ten months later, for reasons unknown to all but Sophie, she'd accompanied her sister, Sarah, to the hospital to meet her grandnephew. Maybe it was curiosity. Maybe it was that she couldn't resist the chance to see her twin sister's grandson.

Likely, she'd never expected for baby Josiah, named for her son, with his blond hair and green eyes, to snare her heart on sight. With tears of gratitude flooding her eyes, she thanked Cain and Ginger for honoring Woodman's memory, and from that day she'd worked to mend her relationships with the McHuids and with Cain. Through her love for little Josiah, and now for Kelleyanne too, she'd found a way to be part of her family again, and Cain was grateful for it.

"That's right," said Cain. "We're *all* gonna sing to Momma."

"I wuv her, Dada."

"Me too," said Cain, smiling at his son with soft eyes, full of love. "She sure is easy to love, little man."

The bathroom door opened.

"Lord, we're gonna be late!" said Ginger, bursting into the

sitting room of the tack room, holding out a pumped bottle of breast milk for Cain. She reached into her shirt to reclasp her bra, then smoothed her blouse, grinning at Cain. "Do I look all right?"

Cain nodded, blown away, as he always was, by his wife's natural beauty. "You look stunnin'."

"Byooteeful Momma."

Ginger smiled at their son and leaned down to press a kiss to the top of his head just as someone knocked at the door to the tack room, where they always stayed as a family whenever they visited McHuid Farm overnight. Klaus, at Ranger's insistence, had moved up to Kelleyanne McHuid's old cottage a couple of years ago, and joined Ranger and Magnolia regularly for dinner at the manor house.

"I guess it makes sense," Magnolia had said, finally welcoming Klaus into their social lives and inner sanctum, "since we're family now."

Ginger opened the door to find Magnolia, Sarah, and Sophie standing outside, three mother hens champing at the bit to spoil their grandbabies.

"Happy birthday, Ginger," said her mother, pressing a quick kiss to her cheek before marching inside and beelining for Cain. "You give me that child, Cain. I'll take her up to the main house so you and Ginger have a moment to breathe before the festivities begin."

Carefully Cain handed over his daughter and gave her bottle to his mother. "Make sure she gets this when she wakes up, okay, Mom?"

Sarah smiled and nodded as her sister, Sophie, called, "Josiah Woodman Wolfram, you come on over here to your Auntie Sophie now."

Josiah looked up at his mother for a second, waiting for her to nod before racing to his Oma and Auntie and taking their hands.

"We sing to Momma!"

"That's right!" said his oma. "How about you and me and Auntie practice as we walk up to the manor house?"

"Happy birf-day to youuuu . . ."

The sound of three happy voices singing faded away as Cain's mother, aunt, and son left the barn hand in hand, singing the "birfday" song.

Cain closed the door and locked it, then turned to his wife with a wolfish gleam in his eyes, and Ginger grinned back at him, her sweet lips tilting up in a smile.

"How long do you think we have?" he asked, stalking her a step at a time.

"Cain . . ."

Her voice held a warning, but her feet were already backing up toward the bedroom, her brown eyes sparkling.

"I mean, at least a few minutes, right?" he asked, following her lead. "And it *is* your birthday, princess. Anythin' special I can do for you?"

"We'll miss the cake," she said, giggling as she fell back onto the bed, her eyes beckoning him to join her.

"You're sweeter'n cake," he said, straddling her hips as he cradled her face in his hands, leaning closer and closer to kiss her, "my lionhearted woman."

THE END

Dear Reader,

Thank you so much for reading *Ginger's Heart*. I hope you enjoyed reading about Ginger McHuid's journey to true and everlasting love!

I had always intended that Woodman and Cain enter the military, and the choice to make them damage controlmen came from the belief that it was one of the many Navy careers that could segue organically into small-town employment at a local fire department. Every small town has a local fire department, right? Right. Stay with me here.

One day in December 2015, as I was researching the DC rating on the Internet, I came across the story of Nathan Bruckenthal. Bruckenthal, who served as a DC in the U.S. Coast Guard, died in the Persian Gulf in 2004, and was the first Coast Guardsman killed in action since the Vietnam War. At the time of his death, Bruckenthal was finishing his second tour in Iraq, looking forward to returning home to his pregnant wife and meeting his first child. Tragically he was deprived of that homecoming.

As I opened up another web page on Bruckenthal, I was shocked to learn that he actually (cue wide eyes and loud gasp) grew up in my hometown of Ridgefield, Connecticut and served for two years in our volunteer fire department. It was a breath-catching surprise to learn that the man I was researching had served not only in our U.S. military, but had *also* served as a firefighter in the town that I love and call home.

In honor of Nathan Bruckenthal's sacrifice, and in profound thanks for his service, both at home and abroad, I am proud to announce that 25% of the net profits of e-book sales of *Ginger's Heart* will be donated to the Ridgefield, Connecticut, Volunteer Fire Department for all sales in March and April 2016.

From the bottom of my heart, I thank you, dear reader, for

your purchase.

Love,
    Katy

ALSO AVAILABLE

from Katy Regnery

a m o d e r n   f a i r y t a l e

The Vixen and the Vet
(inspired by "Beauty & the Beast")

Never Let You Go
(inspired by "Hansel & Gretel")

Ginger's Heart
(inspired by "Little Red Riding Hood")
Thank you for reading!

Don't Speak
(inspired by "The Little Mermaid")
Coming 2017

Swan Song
(inspired by "The Ugly Duckling")
Coming 2018

ENCHANTED PLACES

Playing for Love at Deep Haven

Restoring Love at Bolton Castle
Coming June 2016

Risking Love at Moonstone Manor
Coming 2017

A Season of Love at Summerhaven
Coming 2018

The Blueberry Lane Series

The English Brothers

Breaking Up with Barrett
Falling for Fitz
Anyone but Alex
Seduced by Stratton
Wild about Weston
Kiss Me Kate
Marrying Mr. English

The Winslow Brothers

Bidding on Brooks
Proposing to Preston
Crazy about Cameron
Campaigning for Christopher

ACKNOWLEDGMENTS

A special shout-out to Katy's Ladies, my street team and a truly awesome group of friends. I honestly don't know what I'd do without all of you. You support and encourage me, keep me laughing with your funny comments and make me cry with your touching messages. I am the luckiest author in the world to have a group in my life that includes all of you.

To Selma and Sejla, thank you for being my German proofreaders for this project and for all of your many kindnesses to me. Your enthusiasm for my books makes my heart spill over with gratitude. #WonderTwinsOfWien

To the Sampsons – Teresa and Jeff – thank you for answering so many questions about life in the navy. I am so thankful for your "inside" knowledge and for your generosity in sharing it with me.

To Lauren, Toni and Kirby, thank you for kind eyes and boundless support. I knew my book was in safe hands when it was being read by you. I am so incredibly *blessed* with your camaraderie, kindness and friendship. #ReadLaurenS #TimesTwo #HotPants

To Amy and Mia. I love you two. I mean, I seriously, trulymadlydeeply *love* you two wickedly talented, hilarious, kind, smart, beautiful people. Thank you for letting me celebrate this release with yours and thank you for your one-of-a-kind fabulous friendship.
#m • a • kAttack #SideEyesForever #TheBestKind

To Cassie Mae, who has come through for me a million and one times. My books look good because of you, baby. Thank you for being my formatting guru.

To Marianne Nowicki for my gorgeous cover. (For *all* of my gorgeous covers!) You are the best at what you do and the easiest to work with. I am grateful to have you beside me on every step of this awesome writing journey.

To Tessa Shapcott, my developmental editor. I burst into tears when I read your report because your opinion and advice mean the world to me. To know that you love this book makes me confident enough to share it with the world. Thank you.

To Chris Belden and Melissa DeMeo, my editors, who don't let me get away with anything. That's the way I want it. That's the way I need it. Your insight, notes, and advice make my writing the best it can be. I am so thankful to work with a team like you.

To my parents, George and Diane, for being the guiding lights of my life. You encourage and inspire, support and celebrate. Thank you from the bottom of my heart for your unconditional love. I am the luckiest daughter in the whole world.

And finally, to George, Henry, and Callie. You are my dearly beloved, my heart, my soul, my whole life. The most important thing is kindness, and I love you all the much.

ABOUT THE AUTHOR

USA Today **bestselling author Katy Regnery** started her writing career by enrolling in a short story class in January 2012. One year later, she signed her first contract for a winter romance entitled *By Proxy*.

Now exclusively self-published, Katy claims authorship of the multi-titled Blueberry Lane Series which follows the English, Winslow, Rousseau, Story and Ambler families of Philadelphia, the five-book, bestselling ~a modern fairytale~ series, the Enchanted Places series, and a standalone novella, Frosted.

Katy's first modern fairytale romance, *The Vixen and the Vet*, was nominated for a RITA® in 2015 and won the 2015 Kindle Book Award for romance. Four of her books: *The Vixen and the Vet* (a modern fairytale), *Never Let You Go* (a modern fairytale), *Falling for Fitz* (The English Brothers #2) and *By Proxy* (Heart of Montana #1) have been #1 genre bestsellers on Amazon. Katy's boxed set, *The English Brothers Boxed Set, Books #1-4*, hit the USA Today bestseller list in 2015 and her Christmas story, *Marrying Mr. English*, appeared on the list a week later.

Katy lives in the relative wilds of northern Fairfield County, Connecticut, where her writing room looks out at the woods, and her husband, two young children, two dogs and one Blue Tonkinese kitten create just enough cheerful chaos to remind her that the very best love stories begin at home.

Sign up for Katy's newsletter today:
http://www.katyregnery.com!

Made in the USA
Middletown, DE
23 March 2016